CLOUDS ACROSS THE SUN

A Novel

Ellen Brazer

TCJ PUBLISHING
Miami Beach, Florida

Clouds Across the Sun

All Rights Reserved 2009 by Ellen R. Brazer

Cover Art Designed by Mario Chiaradia and Henri Almanzar
Cover and interior layout by Bookcovers.com

For information go to:
www.ellenbrazer.com
or write the author at
ellenb9815@bellsouth.net

ISBN: 978-0-615-31140-1

Printed in the United States of America

For my husband and best friend, Mel;
For my mother, Esther Glicken, who is watching from above; and
for my father, Irving Glicken, who brings sunshine into my life

Some people like the Jews, and some do not. But no thoughtful man can deny the fact that they are, beyond any question, the most formidable and most remarkable race which has appeared in the world.
—*Winston Churchill*

CLOUDS
ACROSS
THE SUN

1

1951
Naples, Florida

Jotto folded back the bedspread and slipped beneath the covers. She closed her eyes and waited, alert to every sound in the house. There would be no bedtime kisses on the forehead, no endearing words wishing her pleasant dreams, and no prayers said on bended knees—not on this night nor on any other night. Jotto heard footsteps coming down the hallway. The door handle turned and the light switched on. Her eyes flew open. She did not need to see a clock to know it was precisely nine-fifteen, and that her father, Hans Wells, had entered the room.

"Good evening, Father," Jotto said, her tone measured, her demeanor disciplined.

"I hope your eleventh birthday was pleasant," Hans said as he pulled the over-stuffed chintz chair beside her bed.

"Yes, Father." Jotto hid her disappointment in a smile. "Thank you for the encyclopedia." She could not tell him her real wishes, that she had wanted a Monopoly game and a record player. Her father did not believe in self-indulgent activities.

Hans shifted in the chair and frowned. He did not like the way his daughter had been acting lately: unpredictable moods, picking at her food, sulking. "Have you completed your day's assignments?"

"Yes, sir."

"Good. Then, we shall begin." Hans opened the German version of Mein Kampf. He reached into his suit pocket, removed a

1

silver music box, and flipped it open. The haunting refrain from Beethoven's *Fur Elise* drifted out.

Jotto blocked out the music, determined to say what she had been contemplating for weeks. "Father, I don't..." She swallowed hard, the demons of doubt screaming at her to remain silent. "I don't like that book." She sucked in her breath. "And, I don't want you to read to me anymore." The fury in her father's eyes told her she had gone too far. Jotto's hand flew to her mouth and her heart plummeted.

Her father slammed the music box closed and rubbed his forehead with the heel of his hand. The silence was pervasive.

"I will not tolerate your insolence."

The tone of his voice dripped ice, and Jotto cringed. "I'm sorry, Father," Jotto said, hoping he would not hear the insincerity in her voice.

Hans drilled his eyes at her. "We will begin now." He opened the music box again. "You will close your eyes and take deep breaths." The timbre of his voice was gentle and mesmerizing. "You will listen. Feel yourself growing sleepy. Feel yourself relaxing. You are a feather drifting to the ground. Floating, falling, floating, falling." He repeated the words over and over and over again.

Jotto slowed her breathing, fluttered her eyes open and closed a few times, pretending to settle into a trance-like sleep.

Hans began to read the book. *In mingling of Aryan blood with that of lower peoples, the result was the end of the cultured people.*

Hans took his time, lovingly translating every word. *North America, whose population consists by far with the largest part of Germanic elements, who mixed but little with the lower colored peoples, shows a different humanity and culture from Central and South America, where the predominantly Latin immigrants often mixed with the Aborigines on a large scale.*

By this one example, we can clearly and distinctly recognize the effect of racial mixture. He will remain the master as long as he does not fall a victim to defilement of the blood.

Jotto was disappointed and exasperated at the words her father read. It felt wrong to her—all the poison.

She took refuge by reciting the multiplication tables, as she always did when trying to block out his words. Only then could she drift out of harm's way.

* * *

The morning sun reflected off the windowpane, bathing the room in white and gold. A cardinal perched on the windowsill, pecking on the glass. Jotto awakened with a start.

The door opened without warning. Her father stood on the threshold, dressed in a navy blue pinstriped suit, his tie securely in place. His squinted eyes shot a look of disapproval her way. "Do you know what time it is?"

Jotto glanced at the clock on her night table. "I'm sorry, Father," she stammered. "I didn't realize it was so late."

"Get dressed. The newspapers have arrived, and we have many issues to discuss before you go to school."

Every day it's the same dumb things—up at dawn, read the papers, have my schoolwork checked, and be able to discuss the stupid books he makes me read. Who cares about German history anyway?

She slipped into a khaki skirt and a white blouse. *I shouldn't have to take etiquette lessons from what's-that-stuck-up-your-nose Miss Cheavers, and I shouldn't have to wear dumb dresses to dinner.*

Using her fingers as a comb, Jotto pulled at the tangles in her hair as she stared at herself in the mirror. Her hair was the color of freshly harvested wheat, blond and curly. She had almond-shaped sapphire eyes, magnolia-white skin, high cheekbones and a heart-shaped mouth, all suggestions of the great beauty she would become. That is not what Jotto saw as she stuck out her tongue at her reflection. *My legs look like beanpoles and my feet are huge. No wonder my mother disapproves of me. Who could blame her? It's not because she's sick, it's because I look just like Olive Oyl.*

She sneered at herself one last time, slipped into sandals, and took off down the circular staircase.

Jotto slid across the marble floor and jumped over the Persian rug in the hallway. Her breath came in short gasps as she tucked in her blouse and squared her shoulders, before tiptoeing onto the porch.

His mustache seeded with toast crumbs, Hans slowly wiped his face with the linen napkin and rang the bell beside him on the table.

Jenny, their cook, walked out, clicking her tongue. "I ain't no cow need calling," she said, under her breath.

"Miss Wells is ready for her breakfast," Hans said, ignoring Jenny's remarks.

Jotto stifled a giggle. "Good morning, Jenny."

"Good morning, Sunshine."

The affection hung between them, a transparent web strong and viable as a spider's lair, despite Hans's directive that there was to be no emotional relationships between Jotto and any of the staff.

"No dilly-dawdling, Missy." Jenny put the plate of eggs and bacon on the table. "You eat up before it gets cold."

"That will be all," Hans said, his scowl dismissive.

Jenny puffed out her chest, made a face, and walked into the house, slamming the door.

She is incorrigible," Hans hissed. "Good help is impossible to find." He spread the newspapers out so the front page of the *New York Times* and *The Washington Post* were clearly legible. "Look at this," Hans said, pointing to the headline. Hans shoved the paper across the table. "Read."

Jotto nodded. *It's going to be a bad morning.*

* * *

After dropping Jotto off at school, Hans climbed the stairs to his wife Ilya's bedroom and pushed open the door. It was dark and smelled of stale cigarettes and strong perfume. He pulled open the heavy brocade drapes, immersing the room in sunlight. He glanced around and for the hundredth time he berated himself for spending such a fortune on furnishings: Italian Venetian Murano etched glass wall mirrors, a five-piece salon set of French Art Nouveau furniture, carpets imported from Turkey, a nineteenth century Austrian Biedermier desk. Ilya groaned from under the covers.

Hans placed the newspapers on the bed beside her. "Are you planning on sleeping all day?" His voice dripped disgust.

"What else is there for me to do in this God forsaken shit hole?"

Ilya hissed in German. She propped another pillow under her head and stared at Hans. Looking much older than her forty-two years, the once beautiful Ilya was like a dehydrated persimmon. Her huge green eyes were lackluster, the blond curls dulled by strands of gray, and her skin was blotched a sickly, sallow shade of ash. She scratched at the festering mosquito bites dotting her bruised arms.

"Why should I get up? You're never here." Ilya poked her finger at his face. "You're too busy with your dinner parties, fancy luncheons, and golf."

Hans watched her with cold, uncaring eyes, infuriated by her whining, his face a dangerous shade of red. "You could make a life for yourself if you wanted."

Ilya spat out a laugh and gave him a half-grin, half-grimace. She raised both eyebrows. "I find it so interesting that you always find the time for that spoiled little brat."

"That's enough!" Hans smashed his fist on the night table. "You will not speak that way about our daughter!"

"Think about it, Hans. If you let me go to Bolivia to be with my brother, you and your precious little daughter could be together with no interruptions." She held her breath, waiting for his reaction.

He pulled at his mustache and stared off into the distance—remembering the war and why his brother-in-law was in Bolivia.

Hans and his family were hiding in a bombed-out house in Paris trying to decide what their next move would be, when the political situation took an unforeseen shift. America had identified a new and dangerous enemy—Russia.

Hans and his comrades recognized an unequaled opportunity, and wasted no time establishing a clandestine Nazi network throughout Europe. Soon, they were passing top-secret information to the CIA and the Army Counterintelligence Corps about Russia's plans to expand communism into all of Eastern Europe. As a reward for their loyalty, and despite laws passed by the United States Congress, selected Nazi scientists were allowed entrance into the United States. Unfortunately, his wife's twin, Otto, had interrogated thousands of prisoners during the war, and because of Otto's high profile, the Americans had refused him entrance into the country.

Ilya dug her nails into Hans's arm, bringing his attention back to the present. "Why keep me here, when we both know you hate me?"

Hans snapped his head toward her. "I don't hate you. I feel sorry for you."

"I want my brother." Tears streamed down Ilya's face. "Please. Don't do this to me. Let me go."

Hans took her hand. His eyes and face softened. "I know what you need," he said gently. "I'll give you something to make you feel better.

He moved into the bathroom, took a key from his pocket, and opened the locked cabinet. He inserted the syringe into the vial of morphine and pulled back the plunger. He smiled as he replaced the vial.

South River, New Jersey

A month later Hans Wells pulled into the parking lot of the Diakos Greek diner to meet with two of his German comrades. He stepped out of the rental car, straightened his tie, took a deep breath, and pulled back his shoulders as he pushed open the finger-smudged glass door. The midday crowd was animated with businessmen in suits smoking cigars and talking loudly, and students wearing Rutgers University sweatshirts drinking Pabst Blue Ribbon beer and scoffing down lamb gyros. Hans weaved between the tables.

"We were beginning to worry," said Alexander Lippisch, the renowned German aerodynamicist and full professor at Rutgers. He glanced at his watch and readjusted the gold cigarette holder clenched between his teeth.

"Sorry. My plane landed on time but I got caught in traffic." Wells slid into the booth. He was always uncomfortable around Lippisch. He was uncomfortable around all the elitists with their greater-than-thou attitudes.

Their other comrade, Kurt Blome, a research scientist with a background in biological warfare, smiled, showing crooked, cigarette-stained teeth. He pulled at the sleeve of his wrinkled, plaid corduroy shirt. "It's good to see you again."

"You too," Hans said, meaning it. "How have you been?"

"Ach!" Bloom said. "There are not enough hours in the day." Deep creases crinkled between his eyebrows, as if he was in perpetual contemplation. He scratched the two-day growth of stubble on his face. "How's Florida?"

"Naples is paradise," Hans said, unbuttoning the jacket of his hand-tailored suit.

"Yah, but it's in the middle of the Everglades." Blome's eyes twinkled.

Hans thought about the boulevards lined with swaying coconut palms, the sweet-smelling warm salt air, expensive stores, and charming restaurants. Aloud he said, "the city is small, but it's populated by the giants of American industry, people like the Smuckers and the Evinrudes, who come in the winter to play golf and languish in the pools of their sprawling mansions." He smiled. "And best of all, the appointment book of my psychiatry practice is filled with the wives of these men—women who accept infidelity, drug abuse, alcoholism, and physical abuse as a way of life. If the city of Naples is a reflection of America…"

"Not a bad life, living in a mansion on the ocean." Anger and jealousy poured from Lippisch's piercing blue eyes.

"It's not the ocean. It's on the Gulf of Mexico and the expense was necessary." Hans kept his tone neutral to hide his displeasure at the unspoken accusation. He had chosen Naples because it was only ninety miles from Miami and had no psychiatry practice. More important than that, no Jews lived there. Its isolated location gave him a safe place where he could indoctrinate his daughter without the distractions living in a big city would bring.

"Are you gentlemen ready?" The waitress asked. She wrote down their orders and poured coffee.

Lippisch grunted, his lips pinched in a scowl. "Let's get down to business."

"Always in such a hurry. You should learn to relax. " Blome took a sip of coffee.

Hans turned his eyes toward Blome. "How are things going here?"

"Couldn't be better. My wife is content, and my three-year-old son speaks perfect English. As for me, I have started to talk just like an American—telling people my son will grow up to be president, and who knows," he winked, "maybe he will." Blome laughed. "Alex, tell him about your new girlfriend."

Lippisch lifted one eyebrow. "She's an adjunct professor of physics at the university, who just happens to be the very ugly daughter of New York Senator Albert Willick." He stared at Hans. "I'm doing my part for the Reich," he whispered. "Now, tell us what's going on with our other comrades?"

Hans leaned on his elbows. "The papers were signed last week. We are now officially capitalists—owners of an oil company in Longview, Texas."

Blome smiled. "Interesting and brilliant decision. Oil dependency is growing exponentially."

"This is only the beginning," Lippisch said, a sinister scowl coloring his face. "To accomplish our mission we will need to build a network of people who share our ideology."

Hans smiled. "Take my word. That is going to be easier than we ever imagined."

2

Two months later
Bolivia

Hans arrived in La Paz, Bolivia in the early afternoon. At twelve thousand feet above sea level, the rarefied air gave him an instant headache. His brother-in-law's chauffeur, Eduardo, met him.

In the distance were the Andes Mountains and the peaks of Mount Illimani. Hans rolled down the window as they bounced along the pitted, poorly paved streets. He was struck by the horrendous stench coming from the raw sewage running in the gutters alongside the road. He gagged and closed the window.

The limousine took a hard right, circumventing the ramshackle huts perched on ledges and tucked into crevices along the mountainside.

Hans grew agitated as the car climbed the steep, narrowed, muddied streets. The thought of seeing his brother-in-law brought back unwanted memories of their final days together in Paris after the war.

Hans remembered them walking together on the rue St. Denis when he was forced to break the news to Otto, telling him that the Americans were not going to issue him a visa because of the Jews he had unmercifully interrogated during the war. All these years later, Hans could still see Otto's bulging eyes and the fury that they held, as Hans explained why Otto would be going to Bolivia, a country sympathetic to the Nazis, rather than to the United States.

Otto, in a fit of uncontrolled anger, had punched a brick wall and smashed his hand. He had spent the next six weeks with a cast, moping about, refusing to talk, making everyone miserable.

Hans' attention came back to the present as the limousine turned right down a dirt road. In front of the car was a ten-foot high wall and an iron gate, manned by a guard who allowed them entrance. Otto hasn't done too badly, Hans thought as the mansion came into view.

The twenty-six thousand square foot home was a hodgepodge of design afterthoughts and additions. He may have money, but he certainly has no taste, Hans thought as they pulled to a stop.

Otto bounded down the steps. "Welcome." He embraced Hans. "How was the flight?"

"Long and bumpy."

A servant appeared and took Hans's luggage.

"It's nice having you visit me for a change," Otto said as they entered the house.

The twenty-foot ceilings were painted in frescos of saints floating on clouds, looking down as they passed. They entered a cavernous living room with ornate, handcrafted Bolivian cherry furniture.

Otto snapped his fingers. A tiny woman, only inches over four feet entered. *"Vamos a almorzar ahora,* we'll have lunch now, Maria."

"Sí, señor. ¿En la veranda?"

"Perfecto."

"You've mastered Spanish," Hans said.

"I had no choice. The only one who speaks English is my chauffeur, Eduardo. Now tell me, why the sudden trip?"

"I need to talk to you about Jotto. She has suddenly started to question my authority. I am not sure how to approach the problem."

Otto sighed. "This was bound to happen. She is growing up. When I visited last summer, I had the impression she was beginning to resist."

"You need to tell me what to do." Hans hated himself for sounding so desperate.

"And I will. But, first you must have a decent meal, and a good night's sleep."

* * *

It was midnight. Otto kicked off the covers, propped himself up on two pillows and stared into the darkness. The only regret he had about those glorious years of service to the Reich were the nightmares that came every night—monstrous visions; beseeching eyes, screams, fingers reaching out to claw out at him, burning fires, smells that defied description, playing out over and over again in his brain like a broken record stuck in its groove.

Now, with his brother-in-law's arrival, other memories lurked in the shadows of Otto's mind. He thought back to those final moments in Paris. He and his twin sister, Ilya were standing in the foyer. Ilya was wearing a flowered dress bought for their trip to America. Otto's two-year-old niece, Jotto, was snuggled in her father's arms. Two cabs sat at the curb outside.

"Why two cabs?" Ilya had asked, clutching Otto's hand.

Otto remembered looking at Hans and then his twin. They had known Ilya would not take this well and had decided not to tell her until the very last moment. "Sweetheart, I'm not going with you," Otto had said. "I have to go to South America."

"You can't leave me! I am going with you!" Ilya had cried, stamping her feet, terror spitting from her eyes. "Hans can take Jotto with him to America," Ilya had sobbed. "Then it will be just you and me. Like it used to be."

A dog howled in the distance, bringing Otto back to the present. He shook his head to dispel the thoughts because, even after all this time, Otto still could not understand how his sister could be so disconnected from her own child, her flesh and blood.

Eventually Otto drifted off to sleep. Then it happened, just as it did every night: a thousand Jewish women stared at him, their eyes pleading, accusing, damning—their hands clawing to hold on as their children were ripped from their arms. Otto moaned, and his head moved from side to side. In his dream Jotto was lying on the ground, snuggled in her winter coat, her eyes saucers peeking from the fur. She reached her chubby little arms out for him. "Me go, me go." Steam rose from the ground. Otto couldn't see Jotto. There were gunshots, screams, fire, and smoke. He jolted awake, his heart racing.

A dream. It's just a dream.

Otto reached for the glass of water beside his bed and waited for his heart to stop racing. When he finally calmed down, his mind turned to short clips from his past: graduation from high school at sixteen, acceptance into medical school at the age of twenty, and his decision to specialize in psychiatry.

Traumatized as a child by a violent father and a mother who never found the courage to protect herself or her two children from that violence, Otto decided to commit his life to the treatment of mental and behavioral disorders.

In his final year of medical school, Otto became a research assistant to his favorite teacher, Professor Blundt. Blundt was involved in research to access the subconscious mind through the use of hypnosis. Otto was tantalized by the idea and read everything ever written on the subject. By the time he graduated from medical school, he was able to put people into trances deeper than any of his colleagues deemed possible.

Otto remembered the night he and his lover, Oberleutnant Edmund Heines, were invited to a party at the estate of Werner Gott— a personal friend of Adolf Hitler and Heinrich Himmler.

Dressed in the brown uniform of a Nazi Stormtrooper, Otto remembered how powerful, confident and proud he felt standing in that room with its thirty-foot ceilings, surrounded by Gobelins tapestries from France, and paintings by the 15th century Dutch Mannerist painter, Joachim Wtewael.

The crowd grew silent, and people moved aside as Himmler, the newly appointed head of the SS Schutzstaffels, and his friend, SA Chief Roehm approached.

"Oberleutnant Heines, it's good to see you again," Himmler said in a high-pitched shrill voice, an ingratiating smile on his face as introductions were made.

SA Chief Roehm stared at Edmund, his beetle-like eyes filled with desire. It was obvious to Otto that Roehm, an avowed homosexual, had never gotten over his affair with Edmund.

"It is nice to meet you Doctor Wells," Roehm said, turning away from Edmund. "We are hearing good things about you. As I am sure you must know, highly educated men with leadership qualities are hard to find. So, we are ecstatic that Edmund brought you to the attention of the Reich."

Otto remembered standing a little taller.

"Chief Roehm informs me that we have an opening in our exclusive Death's Head Unit of the SS at the Dachau concentration camp," Himmler interjected. "Thanks to your friend Edmund's recommendation," Himmler winked at Roehm, "I've decided to give you that assignment."

It was the opportunity Otto had been waiting for—the reason he had endured the suffocating relationship with Edmund.

"That bastard, Roehm," Edmund hissed, once they were alone, a dumbstruck look of horror on his face. "He promised me you'd be assigned to Berlin so we could be together."

That was the night Otto decided he would never see Edmund again. The relationship had been contrived from the beginning, nothing more that a vehicle for Hans to move into the inner-circle of the Reich. Now that he was there, he no longer wanted or needed Edmund.

Otto grinned, remembering the invitation he had received months after breaking it off with Edmund. He was working fourteen-hour days at Dachau when he was invited to a dinner party in Himmler's honor in Munich. He was standing in the mansion's main salon, transfixed by the fabulous work of the Russian expressionist artist Alexej von Jawlensky, a member of the New Munich Artist's Association and by the work of the German expressionist Wassily Kandinsky. When he turned, he found himself face to face with Edmund.

Edmund sneered, pulling back his lips like a rabid dog. "Why haven't you returned my calls or answered my notes?"

"I've been busy," Otto said, thankful Edmund's comments were muffled by the seven-piece orchestra playing in the background. The thought of a scene was so repulsive to Otto he could barely breathe. He leaned into Edmund. "Let's go outside where we can talk in private."

They moved through the double doors, across the crowded patio and into the night. The massive lawn was lit by torches and trees swayed in the moonlight. The scent of iris, herbs, and roses drifted on the warm breeze. Otto quickened his pace, holding firmly to Edmund's arm until they were far enough from the house to not be seen or heard.

Edmund turned to Otto, his eyes filled with tears. "Why are you doing this to me? You said you loved me."

Otto snickered and shrugged his shoulders.

"You used me. You lying, cheating bitch!" Edmund tore his nails across Otto's face.

Otto seized his arm, twisted it behind his back, and forced him to his knees. "Why did you come here tonight?"

Edmund scrambled to stand. "Why?" he spat. "I belong here, that's why." His eyes smoked. He panted. "It's you who doesn't belong here. And I intend to make sure they all know it!"

"You're a fool," Otto hissed.

"You didn't think that when I was screwing you and you were screaming for more."

"Shut the fuck up!" Otto slapped Edmund hard across the mouth. "I never gave a shit about you. You're a nobody."

Edmund pummeled Otto with his fists. "Liar. You loved me."

"You? Never."

"I know you did." Edmund stomped his feet and struck out with his fists.

Otto deflected the blows easily. He moved in and grabbed Edmund's wrists. "Look at me, Edmund." His voice was deep and precisely measured—his sudden calmness threatening. Edmund grew deathly still, his breath labored. Otto released him and reached into his breast pocket. He removed a slim, silver box and flipped it open. He had hypnotized Edmund dozens of times and knew he would be under in seconds.

"No!" Edmund shook his head back and forth, trying to draw his attention away from the music box that Otto was holding in his hand. His mind ached for the music—an addict needing an opiate fix.

The tune was only a few bars long—the kind of melody that

seemed immediately familiar—the kind of melody that remained in your ears long after the music stopped. Edmund's eyes grew heavy as he lost himself in the tin-like sounds.

"Take a deep breath, my love," Otto's voice purred. "You know you can trust me. Go deep inside your mind. You know you can trust the peacefulness that will come. Breathe deeply. Relax. Relax. Relax."

His inflections were monotonous, beckoning. Otto spoke ever softer, the words drifting around Edmund. "It could be over. You could have peace. Do you want peace, Edmund?" Otto caressed every word.

"Peace…I want peace…to end the misery." Edmund's voice was devoid of emotion.

A vicious smile contorted Otto's handsome face. "I am going to go inside now. You will stay here. When you are ready—this will bring the peace you seek." He removed Edmund's gun from its holster and placed it in his hand. "This will take you to a place with no more pain. Peace. Peace forever."

Otto walked back into the house. He took a glass of champagne from a passing waiter, and then heard what sounded like a car backfiring in the distance. He had known then that Edmund was out of his life.

Otto rubbed his eyes as he pushed the memories from the past aside, pulled up the covers, and fell back to sleep.

The next day

By noon, Hans was bored after spending the morning writing to his comrades in Uruguay. Otto had gone out on what he said was urgent business. Hans didn't expect him back for hours.

To break the monotony, Hans donned a heavy sweater and went out to explore the grounds of the estate. Heading west, he followed a path through the rolling hills. Twenty minutes later, Hans stood in front of a small cottage a quarter of a mile from the main house. He tried to peer through the grime-covered windows. He used a leaf to rub at the dirt, but it did little good. He could hear the sound of muffled voices as he moved to the front door. Hans turned the handle. It was unlocked and opened easily.

Otto stood with his back to the door. He held a black leather whip in his right hand. A naked boy, just sprouting pubic hair, hung suspended from the ceiling by chains. Otto laughed as blood from the child's slashed chest dripped onto the floor.

"Yo te bajaré pronto, mi amor," Otto said. "I'll take you down soon, my beloved, and then I'll teach you—"

"Are you crazy?" Hans yelled, finding it hard to believe Otto would risk everything to feed his sexual perversion. He grabbed the whip, fighting an urge to tear his brother-in-law to pieces. "Do you want to ruin everything? Take him down now!"

"How dare you spy on me?" Otto screamed, trembling as he released the boy from his shackles and he crumbled to the floor.

Hans could see from the expression on Otto's face that he felt no remorse, only shame from being caught. Hans assisted the boy to the king-sized bed. He placed his head on a pillow, as the white velvet comforter turned red.

"Hans, you're ruining my things." Otto's eyes blazed. "Do you have any idea how hard it is to find—"

"Do you think you would have any of this if not for me?" Hans kneeled in order to have better access to the unconscious boy. He smashed his hand against iron stirrups welded to the bed. "Get me some clean water and towels, you sick bastard."

Otto grunted and swore as he filled a basin with water and dropped a stack of towels on the floor.

"Go back to the house, and send your driver to me," Hans ordered. "And tell him to hurry!"

Hans washed the boy's torn flesh. The child moaned but did not open his eyes.

A short time later Eduardo, the chauffeur, charged into the cottage. He was a burly man in his early thirties, with small eyes, a round face, and a neatly trimmed beard.

"I found the boy when I was out walking. I have no idea who could have done this to him, but I don't want any problems." Hans reached into his pocket and handed the driver three twenty-dollar bills, a month's pay for the man.

"With boys like this one, señor," Eduardo winked as he stuffed the bills into his pocket, "these things happen all the time. I will take care of it. I can assure you there won't be any problems."

"Thank you, Eduardo. I'm sure my brother-in-law, Dr. Milch will be very generous with you for your efforts."

* * *

"What the fuck am I going to do with you?" Hans picked up a vase from the table and hurled it across the living room.

"This is Bolivia, for Christ's sake," Otto hissed. "He is nothing more than a poor street urchin. What are you so worried about?"

"Jotto's future. That's what I'm worried about." Hans sighed. "I can't let you put us all at risk. It's time for us to make a change. It's been ten years since the war. The Americans are not as vigilant as they once were. I will call in some favors and make arrangements for you to come to the States—permanently."

Otto scowled and shook his head. "I like it here."

"Listen to me." Hans closed the gap between them, and stood inches from his brother-in-law. "I made a vow to our Fuhrer—we all did. Would you put that in jeopardy?"

Otto hung his head.

"I know you love Jotto as much as I do. So, you must do as I say. You've indulged yourself long enough. We need you to find a wife and settle down."

Otto stared at Hans. They had collaborated throughout the war. Their relationship was complicated—Otto had been the teacher, helping Hans to perfect his hypnosis techniques. In the end, Hans had wrestled control away from him.

"I don't know about a wife. But, I want to be with my sister and if Jotto …." He shrugged. "I'll come. Just don't push me, Hans. I don't like it. It would serve you well to remember that."

3

Six months later
Naples, Florida

Otto and Hans carried their drinks from the open veranda into the main house. The late summer sky over Naples turned from turquoise to gray as thunder cracked and the clouds burst, the rain evaporating as it hit the burning, sun-scorched ground.

"You have made great progress with Jotto," Hans said.

Otto smiled, basking in the flattery. "Thank you. She resisted in the beginning but now she is definitely responding to the hypnosis."

"Now we must think about the future." Hans handed Otto a brochure. "I have decided to enroll Jotto in boarding school."

Otto's face paled. He shook his head. "This is a mistake. The child needs further indoctrinating."

"I know you don't want her to go. I don't either. But, she is almost twelve." Hans stood and began to pace. "She must start making the right friends. We both know that can't happen here. And, we will still have the summers with her." Hans could already imagine the loneliness he would feel with Jotto away.

Otto's face turned crimson. "Is this why you brought me here? I could have stayed in Bolivia, where at least I had a life!"

"Let's not digress, Otto. You aren't here just for Jotto, and you know that. Ilya needs you too."

"Ilya." He shrugged, disgusted at how his twin sister had slipped

18

into despondency and addiction. And, while his presence had helped some, his sister was far from being well. He snipped the end of his cigar and lit it, studying the burning tip. "I'm still not convinced Ilya wouldn't be better off in a hospital."

"We've gotten her sober a dozen times," Hans said. "What good did it do? Each time she was back drinking within a week. If you can't help her, what makes you think strangers can?"

Sadness darkened Otto's face. "It's just so frustrating. She is better than when I got here, isn't she?"

"Of course she is. And for that, I thank you."

* * *

The Mercedes pulled through the gate and came to a stop at the end of the driveway. Otto stood on the front porch waiting for Jotto and Hans.

"How was school, sweetheart?" Otto asked. His enormous blue eyes sparkled as he kissed his niece on the cheek.

"It was fine, Uncle Otto," Jotto said, following them inside.

The formal living room had two love seats, positioned in front of a ten-foot long glass-topped coffee table, its stone pedestals salvaged from the ruins of a church in Germany. Arranged around the space were six armchairs, all covered in identical Italian ivory silk. Jotto took her seat in the chair nearest the door. Her hands in her lap, she straightened her posture and waited.

"We have something very important to discuss with you," Hans said, smoothing his mustache.

Jotto tensed. "Have I done something wrong?"

"No. Of course not. It's about your future. It's about what's best for you."

Jotto tilted her head and scrunched her eyes. *It's always the future. Why can't they just let me be a kid?*

Hans cleared his throat. "You will be going to boarding school next term."

Jotto's eyes filled with tears. She stood, her arms crossed over her chest, her eyes defiant. "You want to send me away? Why? I'm getting all A's. And whatever I don't learn in school, you teach me." She scowled. "It's because of mother, isn't it? She is the one who doesn't want me here!"

Hans's face was set, belying his emotions. "Your mother has nothing to do with this."

Jotto looked to her uncle.

"You're mother is very sick." Otto ran his hand through his hair—ashamed for his sister. "But, I promise you, that it is not the reason why you're going away to school."

"Then why?" She stamped her foot. "It's not fair. This is my home. I won't go." Jotto stared into her father's eyes.

Hans's mouth turned down and his face paled. "You will not be disrespectful."

Otto placed himself between the two of them. "That's enough. Let's all calm down." He took Jotto's arm and led her to the love-seat. "You've had a charmed life, princess. Your father and I will always do what is right for you. You have to know that."

Jotto's face softened.

"The people you will meet in your life will pave the way for you in the future," Hans said. He lit a cigarette. "You will be an important person some day, and for that to happen, you must befriend the powerful children whose families run this country. That won't be accomplished by you going to school in Naples, Florida."

* * *

Jotto stood in the hallway outside her mother's closed bedroom door. Her heart pounded and she shivered. This was her only hope, a last ditch effort for someone to intervene. She knocked lightly and entered.

Ilya was laying in bed, propped up on pillows, half-eaten food on a tray beside her. The drapes were drawn and the musty smell of cigarettes clung to the air like mud on a shoe.

Ilya shook her head, the pain building as she focused her blood-shot eyes on Jotto. She could see no resemblance of herself in this child. Jotto's hair was curly, Ilya's straight. Jotto's eyes were almond, Ilya's round. There was nothing about Jotto, her looks or her personality that evoked even an inkling of love in Ilya. What she did see was the reason for all her misery. Ilya clucked her tongue in disgust. In her twisted mind, it was Jotto's fault she needed drugs and booze to make it through the day.

Jotto saw the look of disgust pass over her mother's face. This is going to be a waste of time. She never loved me, Jotto thought, taking a deep breath as she drew closer. "Can I talk with you for a moment?"

Ilya said nothing, just pointed to the chair in front of her dressing table.

Jotto sat with her knees primly together, her hands in her lap.

"I have a headache. What do you want?"

"Father wants to send me away to boarding school. I don't want to go. Will you talk to him for me?"

Her eyes lit up. She had prayed for this moment. With Jotto gone, she would have Hans all to herself. "What a foolish child. Why would I do that?"

"Please, Mother." Jotto moved to the side of the bed and reached for her mother's hand. "I don't want to go away."

"Stop your whimpering," Ilya said, slapping Jotto's hand away. "Get out. You're making my headache worse."

The tears stung Jotto's eyes as she ran down the hall. She did not understand what she had ever done to elicit such hatred from her own mother. The coldness she felt sifted into the very center of Jotto's being. She switched on the light in her walk-in closet and sat on the floor hugging her knees. There would be no reprieve.

She thought about her two best friends, Missy Lulejian and Nancy Downing. They had formed a secret club and taken a blood oath, cutting their fingers and pressing them together, promising to remain friends forever. At their slumber parties, Jotto had experimented with make-up, tried her first cigarettes, and learned how to dance. Leaving them felt like dying.

Jotto pushed aside her shoe rack and pulled out a box hidden away from prying eyes. She lifted Betsy, her favorite doll. She was dusty and one of her eyes had fallen out. Jotto clutched the doll to her chest. "They want to send me away and forget about me, just like I forgot about you when I stuffed you in this box. Well, I won't leave you again, I promise."

1952 Groton, Massachusetts

Jotto arrived at Wellsberry, an exclusive all-girl college preparatory school near Boston, with two Louis Vuitton steamer trunks and her father, and uncle in tow. After listening to orientation, which included all the rules and regulations and academic expectations, Jotto, her father and uncle walked around the one-hundred and fifty acre campus.

At the stables, a girl around Jotto's age was riding an Arabian mare, urging her over low jumps, the girl's body moving forward in the saddle each time the horse left the ground. Jotto could feel her heart beating faster and decided this was something she would master.

At the indoor Olympic-sized swimming pool, three girls were doing laps, their streamlined bodies cutting through the water effortlessly. Jotto's passion for the water, and her endless hours swimming in the Gulf of Mexico, would find a new outlet. She smiled as the smell of chlorine wafted around her. She knew she was going to be happy here.

After saying goodbye to her father and uncle, Jotto went to her room on the third floor of the Mayflower dormitory, a moss-covered brick building nestled amongst the ancient elms and oaks. The room had hardwood floors, two desks, twin beds and a window that overlooked the campus. Her roommate, Melinda Butler was from New York City. She was a curly-haired redhead with freckles, and a quick smile.

"Jotto. That's an interesting name," Melinda said as they lay in their beds that night. "But, Jo sounds so much more mysterious. How about we shorten it?"

Jotto let the name roll around in her head. She liked it. She liked it a lot. My first secret, Jo thought, knowing her father would object to the less formal use of her name.

"And you can call me Sweeny."

"Why Sweeny?" Jo giggled.

"No reason. I just like the name and figure I can be whoever I want now that I am on my own."

The notion of being on her own at twelve-years-old was so completely outrageous to Jotto she had difficulty with the concept. Yet, hadn't her new friend changed both their names in an instant?

"You and I are going to be great friends," Sweeny said. "I knew it the minute I laid eyes on you. Sleep tight and don't let the bed bugs bite."

September 1956

On the first day of their junior year in high school, Sweeny ran into the dorm room and threw her arms around Jo. "I missed you. How was your summer? Mine was fabulous. I met the cutest guy in Italy." Sweeny shook her newly straightened and streaked hair. "What do you think?"

"I love it. The blond looks fabulous." Jo laughed. It was great to be back at school—great to be back with Sweeny, her roommate for the past four years. Jo was overcome by a sudden feeling of sadness as she thought about the past summer. She knew how perfect her world looked from the outside: her father was a respected psychiatrist; she lived in a mansion: she had beautiful clothes, maids, and fancy cars sat in the driveway. For Jo, living in that house was like living in a bombed-out building—the walls were still standing but the inside was gutted and scarred.

Jo's thoughts turned to her father and Uncle Otto. She shivered. She was their puppet. They owned her. No matter how hard Jo tried, she could not comprehend that which was incomprehensible. Just a few words from her uncle and Jo would sink into the abyss, where time became nonexistent. She wished she could tell Sweeny everything, but the very thought made the muscles in her neck ache and her jaw lock. Otto's hypnosis had assured she would never be able to tell anyone anything.

"Are you alright?" Sweeny asked.

"Just thinking about getting back into shape."

Sweeny swatted Jo's rear. "Miss Iron Butt, tell your tale of woe to someone else."

Jo glanced at the trophies on her dresser and the ribbons tacked to the corkboard. She picked up the framed picture of Derby Day, an Arabian with strong, legs and a noble heart. Each time they left the ground and successfully cleared a gate, Jo felt triumphant and powerful, an athlete controlling her own destiny.

Jo pulled on her boots and shrugged into her parka. "See you later. My steed calls."

* * *

The alarm clock buzzed, piercing the quiet. Sweeny swore and put the pillow over her head as Jo mashed the button and got out of bed, the familiar pull present, just as it always was.

Jo needed to see what was happening in the world. She jogged to the headmaster's office in order to read the Boston Globe and the Washington Post, berating herself the entire way for her ridiculous obsession, an obsession she was unable to resist.

Jo was sitting on a chair in the outer office, a cup of coffee in one hand, the Globe spread out on the wooden table in front of her when Judge Walker, a retired federal judge who volunteered as the debate coach for Wellsberry, sat down beside her.

"Miss Wells, may I have a word with you?" he asked, his eyes twinkling behind a pair of thick glasses. He had a bulbous nose, large ears, a scraggly mustache, and silver hair. Jo liked him on sight. "Certainly."

"I have been told by your instructors that you have great analytical prowess and an inquisitive nature. Would you say that is a fairly accurate assessment of you?"

Jo blushed. "Yes, sir."

"Good. Then it is settled. You will join the debate team."

"I am flattered but I have too much…"

"Young lady, I know you have many extracurricular activities. That is one of the reasons I want you. Find the time to do this. It will assure your acceptance into the very best university."

Jo nodded and smiled. She would make the time.

Debate became her catharsis. She learned to expound her thoughts without restraint, taking apart issues bit by bit and then expanding her views. Her political knowledge and persuasive reasoning, along with her passion, brought her to the state finals in her senior year.

"I've been thinking a lot about you," Judge Walker said as they were strolling to the gym for a practice session. "I know it's an unlikely profession for a girl, but I think you should consider pursuing a career in law. Radcliffe would give you access to my alma mater, Harvard. I would be pleased to recommend you if you choose to apply."

Jo and Sweeny had already made the decision to practice law, but to hear the judge, a man Jo had come to admire, advise her to take such a path. It was a glorious moment. "Thank you, sir. I am honored you think so highly of me."

December 1957

Jo spent Christmas vacation of her senior year with Sweeny's family in Gstadt, Switzerland. Sweeny's parents, Thomas and Janet Butler, were easy-going liberals who left the girls alone while they went off hobnobbing with their jet-set friends. Surrounded by majestic alpine mountains, the girls skied from morning till night. Tempted by the excitement, Jo talked Sweeny into a mountain climbing trip.

Four hours into the adventure, Jo slammed her ankle against a rock as she was traversing the mountain and broke her ankle. She had to be taken out by helicopter and between the pain and the shame, Jo was miserable. She spent the rest of her vacation in a cast sitting by the fireplace, trying not to mope as Sweeny brought her chocolates and recounted stories from her adventures each day.

When they returned to school, Jo continued her recuperation. She had kept the news from her father and uncle, fearful they would make her come home.

She was sitting with her foot on a stool, the cast having just been removed when Sweeny swept into the room.

"Feeling any better?" Sweeny asked.

"I'm fine. Just glad to have the cast off."

"Good timing, my dear friend. Because we're having a mixer next weekend with Groton."

Jo made a face.

"Come on. It'll be fun," Sweeny said.

"You can't really believe that? They're a bunch of boring, up-tight snobs with attitudes. I'd rather stay home and read," Jo said.

"Well you don't have a choice. It's mandatory that you attend."

January, 1958

Jo sat on a wooden chair in a dance hall decorated with streamers and balloons. At seventeen, she was five feet eight inches tall with blond-white hair that fell in soft curls down her back. Porcelain-skinned, her sapphire eyes slanted with a hint of Asia. Jo didn't see herself as beautiful, and she hated dances. She was always the tallest girl, and she felt gawky and awkward. Besides, the thought of flirting—what could be more ridiculous?

She listened with half an ear as her friends gossiped about the boys standing in tight little groups on the other side of the dance floor, trying to get up the courage to bridge the distance and ask one of them to dance.

"Oh my God, there's Andy Taxton. He spends his summers at the Kennedy compound in Hyannis Port. I think he's headed this way," Kate Wilson said. She made a fanning motion with her hand. "He's so fabulous looking. I think I'm gonna faint. Oh please, God, let him ask me to dance," she squealed, straightening her skirt and throwing back her shoulders.

Despite herself, even Jo felt a quiver of anticipation as she watched Andy approach. He was, after all, quarterback of the Groton football team, and he was handsome in a rugged, outdoors sort of way. His hair was blue-black and he had aquamarine eyes. His nose was a little wide and his ears stuck out a bit, but the imperfections worked, somehow making him even more alluring. Jo's breath caught in her throat.

"How about dancing with me, beautiful?" Andy said to Jo with a toothy grin.

"No thank you," Jo said. "I don't dance."

"Because your ankle still hurts?"

"My ankle is fine." Why would he know about my ankle? Jo waited for him to turn away.

"Look," he paused and glanced across the room. "I've just made a five dollar bet with my friends that you'd dance with me at least once." Andy flashed an impish grin. "You won't be sorry. I happen to be a really nice guy."

Jo smiled. Her pulse quickened.

"You can't turn me down. My life would be ruined. I'd never regain my self-confidence, and all my dreams of being famous would bite the dust! Do you really want that on your conscience?" he said.

Jo laughed. Andy took her hand. He was a good six inches taller and for that alone, Jo was thankful. On the dance floor, they moved to the Everly Brothers' *Bye Bye Love*.

"My name's Anderson Reginald Taxton but my friends call me Andy."

"Nice to meet you, Andy. I'm Jotto Wells, and my friends call me Jo." Jo was fascinated by Andy's self-confidence and by the way his eyes sparkled when he smiled. His suit was expertly tailored and his dress shirt starched to perfection. It was clear to see why half the girls in her school had a crush on him.

"I hear you're quite the adventurer," Andy said, laughing as he spun her under his arm.

"Clumsy would be more accurate." Jo looked into his eyes. Pat Boone's, Love Letters in the Sand began. Jo had butterflies in her stomach as he held her for the slow dance. "How do you know so much about me?"

"Are you kidding?" Andy's eyes settled on her. "How could I not know about you? You're captain of the debate team, a fabulous horsewoman, a great swimmer and . . ."

"Enough!" She flushed red and smiled demurely. He held her a little tighter. She rested her head on his shoulder, her heart hammering, and her mouth went dry.

When the last dance played and the lights were turned up, Jo couldn't believe that the evening was over and that they had danced all night.

Andy took Jo's hand, moving with her to the doorway. "Thank you."

"For letting you win your bet?"

"No. For letting me get to know you," Andy said, kissing Jo on the cheek before he turned and walked away.

Jo tossed and turned all night. She had never met anyone like Andy. He made her laugh, and he made her feel beautiful. *He didn't even ask for my number. If he doesn't call, I'll just die. I will. I really will.*

As the sun peeked through the venetian blinds, she got out of bed and stood in front of her mirror. *You're just a small town girl who doesn't know the first thing about how to act with a boy. He won his stupid five dollars! That's all he wanted.* A tear slipped down her cheek. She wiped it away.

Sweeny walked into the room wrapped in a towel. "Honey, are you okay?"

"I'm fine."

"No you're not. You're standing in front of the mirror crying."

"I liked him. I really did. And he didn't even ask for my number."

"He was crazy about you." Sweeny's gaze skimmed over Jo. "Anyone with eyes could see that. He'll call. You'll see."

* * *

That evening Jo sat at her desk, rereading the same page over and over again, unable to concentrate. There was a knock on the door.

"Miss Wells, you have a phone call," the hall monitor said.

She padded into the hall in her bare feet, not at all in the mood to talk with her father. She picked up the dangling phone.

"Hello, Father."

"Hello beautiful."

"Who is this?" Jo's knees wobbled.

"An admirer who'll drop dead if he doesn't see those fabulous blue eyes of yours before the sun rises on another day." Andy said, sounding more confident than he really felt.

Jo laughed. "Andy Taxton, you're outrageous."

"I'm also serious. I'm going crazy, Jo. I've got to see you. We have to talk."

"That's impossible. There's a curfew," Jo said.

"Nothing's impossible. Just ask one of your friends how they manage it. I'll meet you at the soda fountain on Main Street at ten-thirty. Please be there, Jo. Please."

The phone went dead.

Jo knew her schoolmates had ingenious plans of escape from campus after lights out. Even Sweeny had snuck out a few times. Jo had never had the desire to join them, but tonight she did.

* * *

The Wagman's Drug store on Main Street had red vinyl booths, black and white Formica tables and a soda fountain. It was filled with students from Groton and Wellsberry, all breaking curfew. Jo and Andy sat in a booth and shared a banana split.

Jo's eyes darted around the room every few seconds.

"What's wrong?" Andy asked.

"If I get caught, and my father finds out, I'm dead."

"Come on. He can't be that bad."

"You mean your father wouldn't be angry?"

Andy shook his head.

"You're lucky. My father doesn't believe in breaking the rules. It probably has something to do with his German background," Jo said.

Andy made a face. "Right. Like the Germans didn't break any rules."

Jo fixed him with a hard glare. "What's that suppose to mean?"

"Nothing. I'm sorry. It didn't come out right."

Jo put her hands in her lap and looked down. She knew the perception people had about Germans. Who could blame them? Look what they did in the war.

"Come on," Andy said. "We can't be having our first fight so soon."

Jo found herself smiling. "Okay. If you don't want me to be mad at you, then tell me all about yourself, and be sure to add something that nobody else in the whole world knows."

Andy stiffened. "I'm a private kind of guy. I don't like to talk about myself very much."

"Good. Then telling me will be even more special."

"Okay. Here's the condensed version of my life. I grew up in a privileged and happy home. I'm the only child of an oil baron millionaire father, who dreamed of his son—now don't you dare laugh—becoming president, and a socially prominent mother who can trace her genealogy back to the Mayflower."

"Wow!" Jo leaned forward. "President?"

"I know how it sounds. I still have trouble saying it out loud. But, you said you wanted to hear something no one else knows."

"This is fantastic. Go on." Jo was actually flirting and she liked the effect it was having on Andy.

"They started grooming me from the time I could talk. My mother, Sarah Eaton Taxton, is a straight-laced lady who can be a real pain in the ass. But, she's the one with all the connections, and I'm crazy about her."

Jo was happy that Andy had a mother he loved so much. She only wished she had something nice to say about her own mother.

"My father, Anderson," Andy continued, "was born and raised in Texas—the son of poor dirt farmers. He has a really thick Texas drawl and when people first meet him, they think he's some dumb Southerner. I can assure you, that's the farthest thing from the truth. He attended Harvard on a full scholarship and graduated first in his class."

"He sounds like an extraordinary man," Jo said.

"He is. The people who know him revere him. He could have been president. But, he had just too good a time growing up, and my mother was mortified at the thought of anyone snooping into his past."

Jo dabbed her lips with the napkin, wondering what it would be like to confide in Andy about her family.

Andy continued, "I guess that's why my father is so intent on me having a political career. He always said, and I quote, 'I just couldn't hurt your momma. You, my son, are a different matter. You'll go to the best schools, you'll keep your nose clean, and then when the time is right, you'll enter politics. You got your momma's blood, and it runs blue, my boy. Blue enough for you to be president one day." Andy said, his impression of a Southern accent flawless.

Jo couldn't stop smiling. First Lady. Mrs. Reginald Anderson Taxton. *Wouldn't my father and uncle be pleased?*

* * *

Life changed for Jo after that evening at the soda fountain. She still studied hard and kept up with all her activities, but her thoughts always came back to Andy. She could be in the middle of a debate, and his face would flash in her head, all perfect teeth and impish smile. Or, looking down as she held Derby Day's reins, she would see his hands, the way his pinky finger swelled at the knuckle from a football injury. Doing laps in the pool, his voice would taunt her, her body aching to be with him.

They talked for hours about everything: their pasts, their futures, their likes, and dislikes. Jo portrayed her family as if she was reading from a script. She knew the picture she painted was a lie, but she could not stop herself from repeating what was programmed in her brain.

If Andy knew the truth, she thought, that her uncle and father hypnotize her and fill her head with God knows what, and that she had a mother who hates her, takes too many pills, and spends most of her days in bed, he would never see her again. *Perhaps this way is better.*

In mid-March, Andy managed to borrow a friend's car and they drove to the bluff overlooking the city. In the backseat with the windows steamed and their breath coming in short hungry gasps, Jo let Andy touch her body in places no one had ever touched before. It excited her: the feeling, the danger, the being naughty.

As they sat in the car, rain battering the roof, Jo glanced at her watch. "Yikes! It's 2:00 a.m. We have to go!"

"A few more minutes." Andy kissed her neck, her cheek, her mouth.

Jo loved the feel of his breath against her face, the smell of his hunger.

"God, I want you." He slid his hand up her leg. "Please…don't stop me."

Jo wiggled and pushed his hand away.

"I can't stand it," Andy said. "At least help me."

Before Jo realized what was happening, he had taken her hand and was rubbing it over his erection. Jo gasped and yanked her hand away. She was no longer having fun. "What are you doing?" Her voice was tense and angry.

"You're a tease." Andy fixed her with a hard glare. "I have blue balls, for Christ sake!"

Jo cringed at the anger beneath the words. "Anderson Taxton. How dare you talk to me like that? I'm not that kind of girl."

Andy bit on the knuckle of his thumb. "I know that, damn it! If all I wanted was sex, there are plenty of takers." His eyes flashed.

"Then maybe you should find one. Because I'm saving myself for my husband on my wedding night."

Andy raised his hands in surrender. "Enough. I don't want to fight." He opened the car door and moved to the front seat. Jo followed.

He put his hands on the wheel to stop them from shaking and stared into the night. Then he turned to Jo with a thoughtful, sober expression. "I love you and being without you over spring break is going to be horrible."

"You what?" Jo's mouth felt parched and she could hardly swallow.

Andy held her eyes. "I love you, Jotto Wells."

"Oh, my God. You do?" Jo started to cry. "I love you too." She closed her eyes and rested her head on his chest. *He loves me.*

5

Spring Break, 1957
Naples, Florida

"Welcome home, Miss Wells," the butler said, opening the car door for Jo.

Maybelle and Jenny, the cook and the housekeeper, bounded down the front steps.

"Look at this child, will you? She gets prettier every day." Jenny planted a kiss on Jo's cheek.

"I do declare, for once in your life you speak the absolute truth. Give me some sugar," Maybelle said, throwing her arms around Jo.

Jo laughed. If there was anything worth leaving Andy for, it was these ladies. They had fed her, cared for her, and always loved her. "I missed you both so much."

Maybelle held Jo away from her and clicked her tongue. "What's that sparkle in your eye? You find yourself some nice young man?"

"Oh, how you do go on. Leave the child alone. She not even in the front door yet," Jenny scolded. "She tell us in good time. Won't you child?"

Jo laughed. "What would I do without the two of you? Are my parents home?"

"They went to Ft. Myers early this morning with your uncle. Your momma has some new doctor that seems to be fixing her up real good. They should be home soon."

"Then I think I'll take a quick swim. I'll see you in a little while."

"And then we'll talk?"

"Yes, Maybelle. And then we'll talk."

* * *

Jo looked around her bedroom. Everything was exactly as she had left it—the stuffed animals on the bed, the books on her desk, the record player, the records, the Elvis Presley, Nat King Cole and Ricky Nelson posters, and yet it seemed diminished, less important, as if she had grown larger and everything else had shrunk—as if she were a stranger to all that she had grown up with. She took her doll, Betsy out of the suitcase and put her on the bed. The time for dolls and make-believe were past. Jo was ready to be an adult.

* * *

With a faint smile on her face, Jo walked passed the pool with her raft in one hand and sunglasses in the other. She followed the sandy path, her eyes crinkling against the sun. It was a dazzling, cloudless day. Sandspurs clung to her ankles, their needled barbs biting her skin. She tugged them off and kept walking. When she reached the line of sea grape trees that guarded the Gulf, she paused on the snow-white sand and looked over the shimmering Gulf. A seagull swooped into the water and came up with a fish dangling from its mouth.

I'm home.

She ran into the sea, paddling past the breakers—floating on the current until the shore became a smooth line on the horizon. The sea was her refuge, her strength, a place she had always retreated when she was confused and frightened, or when she needed to escape the scrutiny of her father and uncle.

As always, with the stillness came the questions. *Why have they always tried to fill my heart with hate? What will become of me?* A new thought emerged, one she had never had before. *They can't hurt me, not any more.*

Jo closed her eyes and drifted. She felt empowered and secure that the sea would protect her. As she floated, she reflected on the conversation she had with Andy the night before she left for home.

"I know you're waiting to hear from Smith and Radcliffe. But, what are we going to do if you don't get into Radcliffe? We'll never get to see each other," Andy had said, intertwining his fingers with hers. They had been sitting under an elm in the commons at Groton.

Jo wanted to go to Radcliffe more than anything in the world, but her chances, while good, were not assured. "We'll just have to find a way to see each other on weekends."

"We don't have to settle for that." Andy's eyes had turned determined. "Wesleyan is a great school and it's close to Harvard. They'd take you in a heartbeat."

Jo felt her stomach lurch. "Andy, it's way past application time. Besides, Wesleyan is not as good a school as Smith or Radcliffe." Jo felt insulted. "I've worked my entire life to get into the best university. You wouldn't settle for second best and neither will I." Jo knew she was being stubborn but if they were going to have a relationship, he needed to understand she was not like other girls. Her life wasn't just about getting married and having babies. She wanted more.

"I'm sorry." His face had scrunched up as if he was about to cry. "It's just that I can't stand the thought of being without you."

Now, as she lay drifting, with Andy far away, she was frightened. *What if he really didn't understand her need for a career? What if she didn't get into Radcliffe? Would he find someone else—a girl that would go all the way and steal him from her?* She squeezed her eyes shut and pushed away all the negative thoughts. Andy loved her and things would work out, as they should.

* * *

Jo cut around to the side of the house where the limousine was parked. She slipped into the side door, cut through the pantry and took the back stairs to the second floor. Dressed in shorts and a T-shirt, hair still wet from her swim, she knocked on her mother's door.

"Who is it?"

Jo pushed open the door. The shades were drawn and the room had the familiar smell of stale cigarette smoke. Ilya lay propped on a lounger, a glass of tea in her hand, a magazine on her lap.

"Hello Mother." Jo approached. She bent down and kissed Ilya on the cheek, surprised at how fragile her forty-seven year-old mother appeared. Her skin seemed translucent, with broken blood vessels dotting her drooping cheeks. Her eyelids had tired folds and feathered lines framed her mouth. "How are you feeling?"

"As good as can be expected." Ilya squinted her eyes and studied Jo. "You've turned into a very beautiful young woman," she said, her inflection more accusatory than complimentary. "How long will you be home?"

"Just a couple of weeks."

"Then we'll have time to talk later. I need to rest now."

Jo wanted to scream, not at her mother, but at herself. Had she really expected a warm reception? Why would it be different than it always was? Why couldn't she accept that? She was simply not important to her mother.

* * *

Hans and Otto were sitting on the veranda when Jo approached. They stood, the joy evident on their smiling faces. Jo noticed a few more wrinkles around her father's green eyes, and his hair had thinned a little, but compared to her mother, he looked like the model of good health. Her uncle, with his longish blond hair and his mischievous blue-eyed grin always reminded her of an aging rock star. He laughed and twirled her around.

"You're gorgeous. How do I make it through even a day when you are away?"

"Sorry we weren't home when you got here," Hans said, kissing his daughter on both cheeks. "You look well. Have you seen your mother yet?"

Jo nodded. "Just now."

"Good," her father said. "Here, sit under the umbrella. It's hotter than hell today." Hans took the bell from the table and shook it several times.

Jenny poked her head out the sliding glass door of the kitchen. "I don't need no calling. I knows what you want. I'll be out real soon with some lemonade, Miss Jotto," she said, slamming the door.

"That woman is incorrigible," Hans sneered.

Jo smiled. No one else could talk to her father that way. "How's married life, Uncle Otto?"

His mouth curled in a lazy smile. Otto had married Elaine Swift, a small-time actress who was willing to put up with his bi-sexuality as long as she had unlimited money to spend and the freedom to have a voice in their threesomes. As a reward for her silence and obedience, Otto spoiled her with expensive jewelry and a mansion in Port Royal, the exclusive enclave where the Gulf of Mexico sat to the west, Gordon Pass to the south, and Naples Bay to the east.

"Better than I ever imagined. Elaine went to Miami for a few days of shopping. I'm afraid I'll be a poor man by the time she returns," Otto said, not sorry he had given up his lifestyle for Jotto's future—for the plan.

Jo laughed. "You've never looked better. Uncle Otto, please don't think me rude, but I need to speak with Father alone."

Otto's face flushed, and he dropped her hand. "I have a phone call to make anyway." Otto balled his fists as he walked away, angry at being dismissed.

Jo took a deep breath and looked at her father. She needed to be calm, to sound confident. "I've met someone at school—someone very special. I've made some decisions I need to discuss with you." She lifted her head and continued, "His name is Anderson Taxton. He's going to Harvard in the fall. I'm hoping to get accepted to Radcliffe so we can be together." *There, I said it.* Jo blinked back her fear and waited for his reaction.

Hans scowled, an act to remind his daughter that he could still turn her dreams away. In truth, he was ecstatic. He knew all about Jotto and her boyfriend, Anderson Taxton. A private investigator followed Jotto everywhere, and had from the moment she first left home. Hans knew about her evening trysts with the young man. What he hadn't known, but had certainly hoped for, was that they were in love. He smiled. "I am not pleased that you are making such momentous decisions without my approval . . . and I will certainly not acquiesce until I've met this young man of yours."

Jo blinked several times. *Did I just hear that? He's willing to meet Andy?*

"We'll finish our conversation over lunch, then you can tell your Uncle Otto and me all about Anderson Taxton."

Jo jumped up and threw her arms around her father. She kissed his cheek and ran from the porch. Her mind was racing as she charged up the stairs to her room. She grabbed the phone and dialed Andy's private home number.

"Andy it's me. I told him about us and he wants to meet you."

There was silence. Jo feared he had changed his mind and didn't want her anymore. Tears burned her eyes and then she heard him laugh.

"Get that guest room ready because I'm going to be on the next plane out!"

Beaumont, Texas

The Taxton ranch sat on twenty-five hundred acres of prime real estate. The south end of the property jutted up to the Neches River, just thirty miles upstream from the Gulf of Mexico.

The property had a skeet shooting range, bowling alley, private movie theater, tennis courts, three swimming pools, and a private airstrip.

Andy's quarters were in the east wing of the twenty-thousand square foot mansion. He had a private kitchen with his own chef and a full gymnasium. His room was filled with football memorabilia, family photos, and books. He pressed the intercom on his desk, and his father answered immediately. "Have you a moment to see me, father?"

"I always have time for you, son," Anderson said, his voice booming. "You just hightail it right over here and we'll have ourselves some nice sweet tea."

His father rose from the desk, an original Duncan Phyfe. The room was decorated in early-American furniture, over-stuffed and comfortable. Like the man himself, it looked lived-in and inviting, but anyone who received an invitation to visit Anderson's home knew that it was all an illusion—there was nothing casual about him. Anderson was six feet tall but appeared larger. He had wide shoulders, a massive chest, and legs like tree trunks. Perpetually tanned, his face was deeply lined and he always looked in need of a shave. His blue-black hair was streaked with white and heavy eyebrows accentuated his inquisitive turquoise eyes.

Anderson hugged his son, greeting him as if they hadn't seen each other in days instead of hours. "The place isn't the same when you're away. Now, what can I do for you?" Anderson moved back to his desk. Andy sat in the leather armchair across from him.

"I have something important to discuss with you, Dad."

"You in some kinda trouble, boy? You go and knock-up some pretty young thing?"

"No. It's nothing like that. I've met a girl. Her name is Jotto Wells."

Anderson raised his eyebrows. "We have a goal, son, and that goal does not include you getting involved with anyone. It will only distract you."

"I love her, Father."

"For Christ's sake, you're still a kid," Anderson said, his southern drawl intensifying his intended sarcasm. "You'll be in love a hundred times before you find the right one."

"That may have been true for you, Father, but it isn't for me. You'll change your mind when you meet her. She's smart, beautiful, athletic, and strong-willed, which should fit right in with this family."

"And her family?" Anderson asked, his eyes angry and challenging. "Just what do you know about them?"

"She's from a small town in Florida. Her father's a psychiatrist, and she's an only child." Andy could see the darkness in his father's eyes. It terrified him.

"Do you know what makes a great first lady? Do you know what it means to come from a good family? I love you son, but sometimes you're a God-damned fool!" His father's voice had risen with every word until he was shouting.

"What are you talking about?" Andy yelled back. "You don't even know her!"

"I know what I need to know." Anderson shot back, suddenly very angry. "I've spent eighteen years of my life making it my business to know what my boy does. You don't wipe your ass without me knowing."

"You spy on me? How dare you?" Andy hissed, feeling betrayed and furious. He stood, his eyes blazing. "I am not listening to another word you have to say."

"You put your ass back in that chair," Anderson commanded, "and stop acting like a fool."

"It's my life. You can't tell me what to do," Andy shouted, staring at his father.

"She will ruin your career," Anderson said, drawing out every syllable.

"What are you talking about?"

Anderson took a deep breath. "Your sweet little lady is the daughter of a Nazi. That's what I'm talking about."

"That's ridiculous. Her father is a doctor." Andy felt his life spinning out of control.

"He's a Nazi!" Anderson let his words hang in the air as he lit a cigar. "If you're serious about becoming president, you can't have a Nazi father-in-law. It's up to you boy. Consider this your first real test. Do you have what it takes? It's time to find out before we waste anymore time."

* * *

Andy sat in his room for an hour, pondering his next move. He needed to talk with his mother, Sarah. She would help him make sense of all of this. He found her in the greenhouse tending the prized orchids she so adored. Andy leaned against the table and watched her. She was wearing a flowered shirtwaist, a wide-brimmed straw hat, sunglasses and gardening gloves. Her once slim body had thickened with age; she had lines around her eyes and her skin crinkled where once it was smooth. She was like the flowers she tended, her petals withered, her color faded.

She gave her son a tender look. "I talked with your father and I know you're hurting. That just breaks my heart. And I know you think you'll never be happy again but, in this life, we have to be willing to make compromises. You're handsome, brilliant, and moneyed. The right woman will come along."

"You married Father and he wasn't . . ."

"He was a good American." She bore her eyes into his. "Just tell the young lady it's over. Believe me, that's the most humane way to do it. Just call and end it."

* * *

Andy sat on a lawn chair overlooking the stables, a bottle of gin beside him, a glass in his hand. Tears of anger, disillusionment, and grief burned his eyes as he watched the horses graze in the ankle-high grass. His mind gyrated like a windmill, his thoughts rushing out of control. He had known about Jo's family emigrating from Germany, and had never given it a second thought. He swigged the gin, waiting for it to do its work—then he would be able to think.

Jo's father a Nazi? Andy knew his father would never level that type of accusation without proof. *Did Jo know? Had she lied to him? Of course she lied. That's why she so rarely spoke about her family.* Andy was growing angry—needed to be angry. How else would he find the courage to break it off? How else could he survive without her?

By the time Andy stumbled into his room, the sun had set and his mind was numb. His only emotion was a tiny ache in the pit of his belly. He had trouble focusing his eyes as he dialed Jo's number and dropped the phone twice.

"Andy, what happened? I've been waiting for your call all day."

"I"…he faltered; the sound of her voice was like a knife twisting in his gut. *I have no choice.* The room was spinning and he felt sick. "I don't know how to tell you this but—"

"But what?" Jo's voice cracked. "Andy, what's going on?"

"It's not going to work." Andy said, his mouth dry as cotton. *Don't think. Just get it said.* "We are too young. We need to see other people. I'm really sorry. Really I am."

Jo's head pounded, and she felt dizzy. "You said you loved me."

"People say a lot of things they shouldn't say. And sometimes they don't say the things they should say." Andy knew he was talking in circles. "Next time you have a boyfriend, try being more truthful."

"What are you talking about?" Jo's teeth began to chatter as tears stung the corners of her eyes.

"It doesn't matter anymore. Good-bye Jo."

Jo slipped to the floor, her legs splayed before her. She buried her face in her hands and wept.

Part 2

6

October 1958
Northampton, Massachusetts

Jo lugged her always-too-heavy book bag as she strolled the crisscrossed pebble paths that led to her dorm at Smith College. The leaves had reached their zenith—golden yellow, cherry red, and burnt purple.

She watched in sullen jealousy as couples strolled arm in arm, chatting and laughing. It had been months and Jo knew it was time to forget, but the pain refused to subside, residing in the pit of her belly and burning like an ulcer.

It's the beauty of fall, Jo thought. *It brings back the memories of Andy, his eyes, his voice, the broken dreams and promises.* Jo took a deep breath and quickened her pace, pushing aside her melancholy mood.

She had enrolled in comparative religion, politics, and international business and would soon declare an economics major; a move her advisor said was the best pathway into law school. For now, she was enjoying the eclectic nature of her studies. She smiled despite the looming deadline three term papers posed.

Jo thought about the school's open academic philosophy, one that espoused a woman's entitlement to enter fields traditionally held by men. She knew it was the reason her intellect had soared. Being surrounded by other young women with aspirations as high as hers gave her strength. The possibilities burned in her belly.

* * *

Jo found time to join the equestrian and swimming teams, and on the weekends, she took long aimless walks under the cauliflower clouds. In her last year she met Ron Studdard, a medical student from the University of Massachusetts. She liked him, and thought they might have a future. When he began insisting they have sex, Jo became cynical. When he professed his love for her, she broke it off. Jo was too afraid to be in love again.

1962, New York City

After graduating magna cum laude from Smith, Jo was admitted to New York University Law School. Her father bought her a town home in Greenwich Village on Commerce Street, in a federal–style brick building, complete with a hip roof and fanlight entrance.

Jo convinced her boarding school roommate, Sweeny, to share her three story, two bedroom home. Sweeny had graduated from Cornell and enrolled in law school at Columbia, her father's alma mater.

Jo was sitting at her desk in the book-lined study when Sweeny barged in, waving something in her hand. "I have tickets for Edward Albee's play, *Who's Afraid of Virginia Woolf.*" She placed the tickets on the desk. "Sixth row center, compliments of my father."

"I'd really love to go, but I have too much. . ."

"You're really pitiful." Sweeny picked up the tickets and waved them under Jo's nose. "It's one thing to refuse every man who asks you out, but being in New York City for months and never seeing a Broadway play. That's obscene."

Jo sighed. "That's not fair. First of all, I date, and you know it."

"Yeah. Right. That's why you are the only virgin graduate student left in the city." Sweeny pulled Jo out of the chair. "Go. Get dressed. I'm not taking no for an answer."

* * *

The curtain rose and the French actor, Robert Osborne, stood center stage, still handsome at fifty-one. He was slim and fit, with broad shoulders, blond hair streaked silver, and a face that reflected his years. His blue-green eyes twinkled and his smile still radiated a sexiness and a danger that women of all ages found irresistible. Applause broke out the moment he spoke.

Robert played the part of the aging professor, George. Jo was fascinated by the way his eyes flashed when he delivered his lines, the way his hand gestures seemed so intimate. She felt a profound connection—as if he were performing just for her.

"My God, he's the most beautiful man I've ever seen." She fanned herself with the program.

Sweeny leaned in. "So, you do like men after all."

Jo laughed. "I like that man."

When the play ended, Jo clapped until her hands stung. "Oh my God!" She hugged Sweeny. "Thank you so much. This has been the most fabulous night of my life."

Sweeny put her arm around Jo as they made their way up the isle. "Sweetie, if that's true, then we have to get you out a lot more."

* * *

Jo sprawled on the couch in the den. *The Kingston Trio* played on the hi-fi as she read through a chapter on tort law. Her mind kept wandering, and she found it impossible to concentrate. Jo had fallen in love with the theater. In the two weeks since seeing the Albee play, she had seen, *A Funny Thing Happened on the Way to the Forum, Stop the World I Want to Get Off* and *Little Me.*

It wasn't just Broadway that beckoned and turned her brain to mush. Jo was obsessed by Robert Osborne. She had seen his play three times. At night, when the moon rose to its apex and the stars filled the sky, Robert Osborne became Jotto Wells's fantasy lover. As she touched herself, she could imagine his kisses and his hands exploring her body.

* * *

Sweeny walked into the room, threw her coat over the back of the chair, and collapsed on the sofa next to Jo. "It's friggin' freezing outside," she said, her lips chapped, her cheeks purple-red. "Here's your early birthday present." Sweeny handed Jo an envelope.

Jo's eyes lit up as she slipped her finger under the flap. Her eyes grew wide. "Are these what I think they are?"

"You betcha. Backstage passes to meet Monsieur Robert Osborne, in person, in the flesh, up close."

Jo jumped up, knocked her books to the floor, and hugged Sweeny. "How did you ever pull this off?"

"Daddy. I told him you were madly in love, and that's all he had to hear. One phone call and poof—passes to meet the man!" Sweeny winked at her friend. "Anything to get you laid, girl."

* * *

Who's Afraid of Virgina Wolf?
December 1962

Jo and Sweeny made their way down the isle of the Billy Rose Theater. Sweeny wore a black velvet dress, sassy spiked heels, her red hair pulled into a twist. Jo wore a slinky black Missoni knit dress and black pumps. Her hair, which had always curled down the center of her back, had been cut earlier in the day to shoulder length. The shorter hair accentuated her sapphire eyes and the dimples in her cheeks. People turned their heads and stared as the girls moved into the third row.

The moment the performance began Jo was transported into Robert Osborne's character George. She had memorized the lines and knew what his expressions would be, how he would shift his eyes, walk, smile.

As the play neared its end, she found herself in a state of awe, her stomach churning as she worried what clever thing she might say to make the great actor notice and remember her when they met. She tugged at the bodice of her dress to let a bit more cleavage show.

When the final lines were spoken, the curtain fell to a round of thunderous applause. Robert stood center stage, surrounded by the cast as the curtain opened again. He smiled at the cheers and bowed.

He closed his eyes for a moment, reaching out for the vision of his wife, and leading lady, Morgan. Although she had been dead for more than a quarter of a century, for that instant the pain of her loss was reborn. He greeted the grief as one might greet a lover— with open arms. For the audience he appeared to be reaching out to them, in truth he was reaching out for Morgan—the need to remember and hurt as important to Robert as breathing. He took another bow and left the stage.

Robert pushed open the dressing room door. William Belmont, his manager and best friend for over thirty-five years, stood at the portable bar putting ice in a glass.

He smiled, thinking what an unlikely pair they were. William kept his grey hair unfashionably short, accentuating a large nose, chubby cheeks, and narrow lips. He wore thick horn-rimmed glasses that magnified his cloudy gray eyes. He was dressed in a pinstriped navy-blue suit, white shirt, and his ever-present bow tie.

William smiled at Robert and his face turned cherubic, all teeth and creases. "You have a crowd waiting to meet you," William said, handing him a scotch and a wet towel.

Robert scrubbed the make-up from his face and then changed into a pair of navy slacks and an alpaca sweater. He was tired and would have gladly gone home. He didn't understand why people were so fascinated with actors or why they were so anxious to meet him. He was no different from anyone else, just a man doing his job—a man just trying to live life the best way he could. "Let's get it over with. It's been a really long day."

Robert stood in the middle of the room as people jockeyed to get closer. He signed autographs and smiled until his mouth hurt. He was half-listening to the banter of a buxom woman with too much make-up when his eyes found Jo. His head snapped in her direction. It happened too often. He would be walking down the street and see a walk like Morgan's, or hair like hers. His senses would heighten and for a millisecond, he would think it was Morgan. This time it was different. He stared in disbelief. His ears buzzed and his pulse quickened, and the room suddenly turned hazy, as if the lights had been dimmed. He felt an excruciating pain in his right arm and jaw. The wine glass slipped from his hand and crashed to the floor.

"Good God!" William put his arm around Robert for support. "What's wrong?"

Robert couldn't speak. He shook his head as tears filled his eyes.

"Call an ambulance!" William yelled. He half carried his friend to a chair. Robert tugged at William's arm. He had to find his voice—to tell his friend Morgan was alive!

"Shh. It's okay. Help is on the way."

Robert tugged harder. William took Robert's trembling hand.

"Look at her!" Robert said in a strangled whisper. His eyes stared over William's shoulder.

William turned. "Holy shit," he said under his breath. His eyes burned through Jo. "She could be Morgan's twin."

The security people were moving the visitors out of the area. Robert squeezed William's hand, staving off the urge to slip away from the pain. "Don't . . . let . . . her . . . get . . .away."

William touched Robert's ashen face. "You just take it easy. I'll be right back."

Jo and Sweeny held hands as they moved towards the stage door. "That was so awful." Jo kept looking back. "He's so pale. I hope he's not having a heart attack."

"Excuse me, Mademoiselle."

Jo turned.

William's breath caught. Her face, her eyes, the way she carried herself. It took monumental concentration for him to find his voice. "Mr. Osborne would like a word with you before you go."

"Are you talking to me, sir?" Jo asked, her eyes wide.

William could not believe that even the cadence and timbre of her voice sounded like Morgan. "Please come with me." He touched Jo's arm and turned.

Sweeny gave her a nudge.

The sight of Jo approaching thrust Robert back in time. *Please God, don't let me die. Not now. Not without knowing.* "Your name. What's your name?" Robert's breath came in short, uneven bursts.

Jo knelt beside him. "Jotto Wells, sir."

That voice. Robert's eyes rolled in his head. He was losing consciousness. *No! Not yet. Not yet.*

"Robert." William took his hand. "Hold on. An ambulance is on the way."

"Your number . . .give William . . .your number. I must see you again, Jotto Wells." Robert's vision began to blur.

"Let us through. Out of the way!" The medic slipped a blood pressure cuff around Robert's arm while another one tore open his shirt and put a stethoscope to his chest.

Jo took a scrap of paper from her purse and scribbled her phone number with a trembling hand. She handed it to William. "I'll pray for him."

"Pray hard, Jotto Wells."

7

Two weeks later
New York City

Robert and William sat in the back seat of the limousine on a horrid winter morning, when the cold feels like needles piercing your skin, and every breath is visible. They skirted Central Park and headed toward Sands Point.

"How are you feeling?" William asked, adjusting the blanket thrown across Robert's legs.

"Like a man who just got out of the hospital after having a heart attack." Robert laughed. "And found out it wasn't his time to go."

"Thank God." William smiled.

"Any news from that private investigator?"

William shook his head. "It's only been a couple of weeks."

Robert shifted in the seat. "Not knowing is driving me crazy."

"Be patient."

An hour later, they pulled through the gate of Robert's fifteen bedroom, shingle-styled mansion that sat on fourteen manicured acres with fifteen hundred feet of waterfront on Long Island Sound. It boasted a sandy beach, pool, pool house, tennis courts, a seven-car garage, and a guest cottage. The trees were bare, but in spring-time the grounds exploded in a chaos of dune grasses, Shasta daisies, black-eyed Susan's, and splashing fountains.

"It's so good to be home."

* * *

Robert had been home for seven weeks when the private investigator, Clyde Turner, a retired army officer with gray-hair, a tight face, and the eyes of a fox, arrived. They sat in the library. The room had maple bookcases, a 19th–century architect's desk, and two sofas covered in bright red cotton. The walls were British-club green, and a brass-trimmed Zanzibar chest sat against the wall.

Robert offered a cigarette.

Turner accepted a light and inhaled deeply. He puffed out his chest in a self-important way. "I found records that listed Jotto Wells' father, Doctor Hans Wells, among the resistance forces during the war." Turner flipped open the fifty-page dossier with his beefy hands. "That would make him appear to be one of the good guys."

Robert crinkled his eyes and stared at the investigator in disbelief. "One of the good guys?" *This is bullshit.* Robert's head pounded. He rubbed his temples.

"Sir, are you alright?"

"I'm fine. Go on."

"Since Doctor Wells and his wife didn't arrive in the United States until 1945, it is obvious Jotto Wells was not born here. Yet, when I tried to get hold of the immigration records, things started to get dicey. I was told, by no other than an esteemed member of the CIA, to back off. When I refused, I was threatened and told my P.I. license could be in jeopardy if I insisted on pursuing the matter any further." He pulled air through his teeth. "I don't take well to being threatened." He flicked an ash and took a drag.

"My investigation then led me to Naples, Florida, where the family now lives." Turner flipped a few pages. "Jotto's mother, Ilya Milch Wells, has battled a drug and alcohol problem for years and rarely leaves the family compound. The doctor, on the other hand, is quite the philanderer."

"I don't see what. . ."

Turner held up his hand. "Ilya Milch Wells has a twin brother, Otto Milch. He relocated to Bolivia after the war, and according to our connections there, often bragged about his involvement with the Schutzstaffel SS. Of course, now that he lives in the States, he's a model citizen. If Milch was in the SS, then there's reason to believe Wells may also have been involved." The investigator shrugged in a sign of helplessness. "The problem is, it's impossible to prove any of this. Still, I'd say we are pretty safe in assuming Doctor Wells was not one of the good guys."

Robert leaned forward. "If they are being protected, it can mean only one thing—this government allowed Nazis to . . ."

"People in government don't like to talk about it, but it's a well-known fact that the United States helped relocate hundreds of Nazis in return for information about the Russians."

"Where does that leave us?" Robert's face was grave.

"With no way to get proof of Miss Wells' parentage. I am sorry, sir."

* * *

Robert and William sat side by side on a leather sofa in the cozy mahogany paneled den. Flames sputtered in the fireplace, and the setting sun, filtering through ceiling to floor windows, turned the room into soft beige hues.

"You know that she's Morgan's child," Robert said as he stared into the fire.

"And?" William waited.

"When I got that telegram, telling me she was dead…it was bullshit. Morgan didn't die when those Nazi bastards said she did." Robert held the report to his chest. His eyes were manic. "She could even still be alive!"

William shook his head. "If Morgan were still alive, she would have contacted you."

"Maybe she's sick. Maybe she's too ashamed." Robert flinched, as if he'd been slapped. His face darkened. "Morgan had a child with another man." Saying the words aloud cut so deeply he expected to see blood ooze from his broken heart.

"Morgan loved you." William folded his hands and studied Robert. "Terrible things happened during the war. You know that."

Robert fought back tears as he thought about his beloved wife in another man's arms, or even worse, the thought of her being forced. Adrift in his agony, he buried his face in his hands.

"If you keep this up you're going to find yourself right back in the hospital." William poured tea from a carafe. He handed the cup to Robert. "You have to accept what you can't change."

Robert was certain of only one thing at that moment: the child of the woman he loved was alive and living in New York City. "I have to see Jotto—to have her in my life—to know her."

January 1963

Books sat on the dresser, the floor, and the bed. Used glasses and old newspapers littered the room. Jo did not even notice. She was too busy studying for mid-term exams. The phone rang. She underlined the passage she was reading before picking up the call.

"Hello. Is Jotto Wells there?"

She recognized the voice and gasped, holding the phone so tight her hand hurt. "Mr. Osborne? How are you? Are you feeling better?"

"I'm fine now. Did I get you at a bad time?"

"I was studying," Jo stammered.

"Sorry. I can call back."

"No. Please." Jo tugged at her hair.

Robert was trembling and glad she couldn't see him. "I was wondering if you'd have dinner with me tomorrow night?"

Jo squeezed her eyes shut, unable to believe what she was about to say. "I have exams all week."

"I see," Robert said, understanding her need to refuse but feeling rejected anyway.

"I can do it next week," she blurted.

Relief washed over Robert like water over river stones. "Terrific." He laughed. "Next Sunday, around eight?"

"Perfect. My address is . . ."

"I know your address, Miss Wells. Good luck with your exams."

The phone clicked.

Oh, my God! I just made a date with Robert Osborne. "Sweeny," she screamed, charging from the room. "You're never going to believe who I'm having dinner with."

* * *

Robert stood in the foyer, coat in hand, ready to leave for his date with Jo when William approached.

"We need to talk before you go," William said, his face scrunched and troubled. "I've never interfered in your life. But, what you're about to do has me really worried."

"Relax. You have nothing to…."

William lifted his hand. "You've been hanging around the house for weeks, now you're going to see this girl. You're placing yourself under the very strain that brought about the heart attack in the first place."

"Bullshit," Robert said. "You heard the doctors. It was going to happen. Sure, the shock might have brought it about a little sooner, but that wasn't what caused it."

"Let me come with you."

Robert shook his head. "If I remember correctly, you weren't much help that night. You almost had a heart attack yourself."

"Very funny." William walked Robert to the door. "Don't scare her, Robert. Don't say too much."

* * *

Robert took Jo's arm as they entered his favorite restaurant, L'Ami Louis. The elegant French bistro catered to celebrities and was located on the Upper West Side.

Jo slipped off her coat. She wore a knee-length black Balenciaga chemise, stiletto heels and a Hermes scarf draped around her neck. Her blond hair was tied back in a red velvet ribbon.

"You're beautiful," Robert said, as the waiter pulled back her chair.

Jo turned her face away so he wouldn't see her blush.

Robert had called ahead and ordered a bottle of *Romanee Conti 1957*, considered by many to be the best red wine in the world. The sommelier presented the bottle and poured. Robert savored the glorious taste and nodded. He lifted his glass. "To new friendships."

"To friendship." Jo hoped the wine would settle her nerves.

"May I order for you?" Robert asked, scanning the menu.

"Please."

"We'll start with escargot and pumpkin soup with gruyere. For the main course, wild duck with Reinette apples. How does that sound?"

"Perfect." Jo smiled.

"How did you do with your exams?"

Jo shrugged. "I hope I did okay. I won't know until the scores are posted. Law school is harder than I ever imagined. Lucky for me, once I read something it stays in my head forever—and that includes a lot of junk I would rather forget." Her eyes danced.

Robert wished he could tell her she had her mother's gift. Morgan could memorize an entire script in an evening.

Jo allowed the sommelier to pour her another glass. She was feeling the affects of the wine. "May I ask you something?"

Robert nodded.

"The way you talked to me that night at the theater—like I was so important to you. I don't understand why."

Robert looked into Jo's eyes. He wanted to tell her everything; how she had Morgan's eyes, her nose, her neck, and maybe even her courage, spirit, and curiosity. Instead, he gave Jo a soft, burdened smile.

"You remind me of someone, someone I loved very much."

Jo knew it was none of her business but she couldn't stop herself. "What happened to her?"

"She was killed during the war."

"Oh, God." Jo's hand flew to her mouth. "I'm so sorry."

"So am I." Robert grew pensive as he tried to decide how much he wanted Jo to know. "She was my leading lady, my wife, and the love of my life."

"I didn't mean to make you sad."

"It's something I've learned to live with." Robert smiled at Jo. "Tell me about yourself."

I might as well get the lies out of the way, Jo thought. "Let me see. . . my family lives in Naples, Florida. My father's a psychiatrist and my mother's a housewife. I'm their only child."

"Do you go home often?"

"No. I'm too busy trying to prove myself to a bunch of professors who still think a woman's place is home having babies."

Robert's eyes twinkled. "You don't want babies?"

"Of course I do. But, I want more than that. I want to make a difference." Jo tugged on her hair.

Robert's breath caught. Morgan always pulled on her hair when she was nervous. "You sound like an amazing young woman," he said, trying not to betray the emotions swirling in his head. "Will you share your dreams with me, Jo Wells?"

Jo fell into his eyes, her heart pounding like a drum. She couldn't believe Robert Osborne was asking about her dreams. She thought about being demure, but it would have been an act, and she wanted him to like her for who she was.

"Women need a voice in government, and I intend to be one of those voices," Jo said.

Robert smiled. "You want to run for office? That's certainly a lofty goal."

"I know. It's all I ever wanted." Jo knew more lies would follow. "Even as a little girl, my father encouraged me to learn about politics and world affairs."

"It doesn't sound like you had much time to be a child," Robert said, hating the bastard that had raised Jo in such an environment. "And what are your aspirations, Jo Wells—senator…president?"

Jo stiffened. "Are you making fun of me?"

"Making fun? Absolutely not. I applaud you. It's important that idealistic, bright young people go into government. And, I'd very much like to help when you're ready."

This can't be happening to me! "Are you serious?" Jo asked.

Robert grinned. "We're going to be great friends, Jo Wells. And I'm going to do everything I can to help you fulfill your dreams."

8

December 1963
New York City
Jo's town home

Jo checked herself in the foyer mirror and wiped a smudge of liner from under her eye while the delivery boy from Kim's Chinese counted her money. The grandfather clock chimed. It was seven-thirty in the evening. Robert would be here any moment.

Jo giggled as she put the food containers on the coffee table in front of the sofa. It was their ritual every Sunday night, sharing their food, shoes off and chopsticks ready. Tonight would be special. They were celebrating Jo's graduation at the top of her class.

* * *

Robert held his chopsticks in one hand and pointed at Jo with the other. "Why the sad face? Mark Twain said, 'A man, or in your case a woman, cannot be comfortable without his own approval.' And, after your great accomplishments, don't you think it's time you gave yourself your own approval?"

Jo blinked her eyes to fight back the tears. "My father and uncle were here all week."

"Oh, sweetheart. I'm so sorry. I didn't know. I would have saved the lecture for another time."

Jo smirked and shook her head. "No you wouldn't have."

"Was it awful?"

"Just the same endless conversations about what I should and shouldn't do and who I should befriend." Jo frowned.

"Are they giving you a hard time about our friendship?" Robert asked.

"I wouldn't care if they did," Jo said, proud of herself for standing up to her father and uncle, threatening not to see them if they tried to interfere in her relationship with Robert. Jo's eyes smoldered. "I hope you know how I feel about you?" She hadn't intended to say that, but now that she had, she was not sorry. *Someone has to take the next step.*

Robert had been afraid of this. He did not want to hurt Jo, but the time had come. "You and I . . . it can never be anything more than friendship."

Jo's face dropped. "I don't understand."

Robert took her hand, his eyes tender. "Because I am old enough to be your father." He saw the anger flash in her eyes, and the pain. He understood she needed time. Needed silence.

Jo's mind danced over the past months. *How could I have been so wrong? There had been so many intimate moments, so many times when Robert revealed his thoughts and feelings to me. Sure, we talked a lot about politics, how could we not when things like the Berlin Wall, the failed Bay of Pigs invasion, the Cuban missile crisis, the escalating conflict in Vietnam, were happening? But, if he thought of me as just a friend, then why had he tried so hard to change me?*

Jo slipped back to the time when Robert first told her about his friend Dr. Martin Luther King and the civil rights movement.

"You must see both sides of the situation, to open your mind, to see beyond the written words of strangers, to form your own opinions," Robert said. "This is about equality, fairness, and opportunity, regardless of race or religion."

Jo had spent her entire life being fed anti-Semitic and racist ideologies. Robert's words were like finding glittering diamonds in a muddied stream.

Passion had burned in his eyes when he talked to me. I know it!

Jo let her mind turn to November 22, 1963, when the thirty-fourth president of the United States, John Fitzgerald Kennedy was assassinated. The country virtually fell to its knees in sorrow. Jo and Sweeny cried day and night. Robert had rearranged his schedule and moved into the third bedroom. He was their rock, forcing them to eat, shower, and sleep.

If he didn't care, why did he come?

I got it all wrong.

He doesn't love me—not the same way I love him.

A tear slipped from Jo's eye.

Robert reached for her hand. "You have to trust me, Jo. One day the right man will come into your life, I promise you. And when he does, you will thank me."

* * *

Jo interviewed with the New York law firm of Stubengoord, Wurth and Brandt. Hans and his comrades were Stubengoord's largest clients, and that association brought a huge retainer into the firm's coffers each month. The interview had been a mere formality—Jo's employment settled on long before she walked through the door. Still, they were thrilled to have the top graduate from New York University joining their firm.

Jo's days became a blur. She would eat a rushed breakfast at five o'clock in the morning, hail a cab to her windowless office, and lose herself in briefs, files, and phone calls. She viewed the seventy-hour work week as a challenge. While the other junior associates complained about the hours, Jo was happier than she had ever been except, at the end of each day when she came home to an empty house.

Sweeny fell in love with her constitutional law professor Dr. William Bennett Steele and they moved in together a week after Sweeny graduated from Columbia Law School. Sweeny was the sunlight in Jo's world, the friend who pushed her to the edge, daring her to try new things and not be afraid. Even though they talked almost every day, they were both so busy with their new careers; they rarely had time to see each other. Jo really missed her.

Happiest when she was working, Jo was the first to volunteer for a new case. That brought her to the attention of the partners, and at the conclusion of her two-year review, they appointed her the political liaison for the firm.

"Where are you going?" her boss asked as Jo stood at the elevator on the thirty-fifth floor of the Empire State building. Jack Wurth was a kindly man with bushy white eyebrows, and a mane of silver hair.

"A Young Republican's meeting. Nelson Rockefeller is going to be there."

"I spoke to Nelson just yesterday. He's very impressed with you," Wurth said.

"Thank you, sir. I find his liberal domestic policies in keeping with my own beliefs."

Wurth put his hands across his massive chest and smiled. "I got another call. Do you remember meeting Aaron Blumenthal?"

"Yes. He's a political power broker."

"Who happens to work for David Rockefeller, the Chairman of Chase Manhattan." Wurth winked. "He's going to be calling you."

Jo felt a shiver go up her spine. "Do you know why?"

"Some very important people," Wurth said, "think you may have the potential to be a viable candidate for state office one day. What do you think, Miss Wells?"

The elevator came and went. "I'm flattered." *This is not the time to be reticent. I've been waiting my whole life for this.* "I believe I would be an excellent choice, sir."

* * *

Five days later the phone call came from Aaron Blumenthal, power broker extraordinaire.

"My own political beliefs tend to be a bit more conservative than the governor's," Blumenthal was saying, his European accent coloring each word. "You seem to be in agreement with his thinking."

"That's true. I do agree with the governor." Jo found Aaron's honesty disarming. She smiled, wishing they were having this conversation in person, rather than on the telephone. "I believe we need stringent laws in place to safeguard the citizens of our state against the sale and use of illegal drugs. And I think we must do everything we can to help secure the passage of those laws.

"As to the governor's collaboration with the labor unions," Jo continued, "his desire to expand the state's infrastructure, the highway system and the universities, and his stand on environmental issues and the arts—he would have my sincere support."

"Wow. That was a mouthful. You already sound like a politician." Aaron smiled into the telephone.

"Sorry. I get carried away," Jo said.

"On the contrary, this has been a pleasure. I look forward to having you work with us to further the governor's goals. I will be in touch. Have a wonderful day."

1969 Naples, Florida

Jo had been making excuses about being too busy to come home for months, but even underlings get vacation time. She was sitting on the veranda with her father and uncle, paying halfhearted attention to her lunch and the gulls swooping into the aquamarine Gulf.

"With Richard Nixon as president and the end of the Vietnam war in sight, the mood in the country is beginning to change," Hans said, sipping a martini. "I think the time could finally be right. I have some pull with the Republican leadership . . ."

"Father, I have made my own contacts." Jo held her breath, waiting for an explosion that never came. Instead, her father smiled. Jo continued, "In fact, I've already been approached." Her eyes sparkled. "I'm going to be the first woman to run for the New York State Senate."

Hans made a fist and pounded the air. "I knew you could do it! I will personally raise the funds for you." Hans would tap the coffers he had set aside for just such an opportunity.

Jo blanched. She couldn't bear the thought of having her father involved. She slid her eyes toward her uncle. He sat with his hands on his ample belly, his eyes gleaming like a fox. Jo knew this was not the time for her to make her thoughts known. She turned to her father and smiled sweetly. "I have other good news. Robert Osborne has offered to campaign for me."

Hans pulled inside himself, fighting for control. On one hand, he knew Osborne's support would help Jotto get elected. On the other hand, the danger Osborne posed was extraordinary—after all, he had been married to Jotto's birth mother, Morgan.

Hans knew that no matter how much Jotto looked like Morgan, Osborne would never have any definitive proof about Jotto's lineage—the Americans had made sure of that. Still, he hated the influence Osborne held over his daughter and had contemplated using hypnosis on Jotto to end her relationship with Osborne, but then decided it was too dangerous. Osborne might fight back by saying things to Jotto that could put her political and emotional future at risk.

He glanced over at his brother-in-law. Hans never doubted that Otto and Ilya knew the truth. The resemblance between Morgan and Jotto was impossible to miss. Yet, the twins had remained silent all these years.

Hans knew why.

They feared him.

As well they should.

Fourteen years earlier

Otto sat by the pool sipping vodka and orange juice with Ilya, watching fourteen year-old Jotto as she dried off from a swim. Jotto waved and walked into the house.

"She has really become a beautiful young woman," Otto said in a pained sigh, despairing how quickly the years had passed.

"She is beautiful," Ilya agreed, devoid of all emotion, as one might comment on a lovely flower.

"I guess I'll always be partial to women who look like Morgan." Otto's hand flew to his mouth, the other hand gripped his belly, and he gasped. Morgan was the only woman he had ever loved.

Ilya's lip stretched in a sneer, and her eyelids flattened. "I wondered how long it would take you to notice."

"You knew?" Otto's nostrils flared. "Morgan was mine," he hissed, his mouth going dry as he slipped back in time.

The celebrated actress Morgan made the dangerous decision to leave France and enter Poland after the German occupation. Her husband and fellow actor Robert Osborne had held a press conference, begging the German government for Morgan's safe return.

Morgan was captured while boarding a train in Warsaw for Vilnius. Otto was given the high-level assignment to safeguard the actress while the Reich made its decision. In the ensuing days, Otto became captivated by Morgan's charm and beauty.

Otto closed his eyes, remembering the joy he felt when Himmler called personally to tell him that Morgan was a Jew and that she was to be sent to Dachau without delay.

He had defied those orders, keeping Morgan locked in his room for almost a week. He pushed away the memories—her fighting off his advances, her attempted suicide. *I tried to tell her that I loved her. That she would be safe. That I would take care of her.*

He wrenched himself back to the present and shot a killing look at his sister. "I trusted you! When I sent Morgan to Dachau you swore you would take care of her for me."

"Do you think I knew Hans was fucking your precious little actress?" Ilya hissed, her face crimson. "What about me? I was pregnant! What happened to my baby?" Tears pooled her eyes.

"I'm going to find out! Then I will kill that lying, no good, son of a bitch!" Otto stood.

Ilya reached out and touched his arm, shaking her head. "If our comrades ever find out Jotto had a Jew for a mother, they will kill all of us. No, my dear brother, we will wait." Hate seethed from her eyes. "You have remained in the background long enough. Our comrades must know you are not expendable." Ilya waved the mosquitoes from her sweaty face. "I am a very patient woman but the day will come, and when it does, I will kill that bastard."

Otto stared at his sister, his twin—they shared the same black soul.

9

November 1970
New York

Jo was the first woman to ever campaign for the New York State Senate. She ran in a district that included Manhattan's Upper West Side, SoHo, Greenwich Village, TriBeCa, Downtown, and parts of Brooklyn.

With Robert Osborne by her side, she campaigned for racial and ethnic diversity, fair treatment, and conditions for prisoners, and a woman's right to have an abortion. In her predominantly Jewish district, she was known as a tough liberal with impeccable credentials, who could convince a crowd with her great passion.

She spent months walking the streets, surrounded by the towers of brick, steel, and glass shaking hands and talking to anyone who was willing. With each passing day, she grew more and more in love with the kaleidoscope that was New York City: the sounds of church bells pealing, jackhammers, beeping horns, ambulances screeching, and construction workers whistling, crowds on corners, children with runny noses, students with backpacks, mother's pushing their babies, and people talking to themselves.

* * *

"You did it." Robert lifted his glass. They were sitting at their favorite table at L'Ami Louis. "To Senator Jo Wells."

"I still can't believe it." Jo giggled. "I'm a senator. And it would have never happened without your help."

"All I did was hand you the microphone."

"Come on. Modesty doesn't suit you. We both know most of the women who came to hear me really came hoping to meet you."

Robert winked. "And then they got to know you instead."

The owner of the restaurant, Paul Henri, approached. "Congratulations, Senator Wells. It is an honor to have you dining in my establishment, and in celebration of your overwhelming victory, dinner is on the house."

Jo blushed. "That's very kind of you, Paul."

He bowed and walked away.

Jo turned to Robert. "Do you think it's appropriate to accept?"

"I think it's just fine." Robert looked at Jo over the menu. "Your father kept a pretty low profile through all of this." Robert placed a napkin on his lap. "It kind of surprised me."

"It didn't surprise me. He's the consummate schemer, and he knows a German accent in my district would be a great distraction."

"Do you think I'm ever going to meet him?"

Jo sipped her drink, a faraway look on her face. "I thought you would be meeting him tonight. But he and my uncle went back to Naples on a chartered plane early this morning. My mother is not well."

"I hope it's nothing serious." Robert rarely discussed Jo's mother—it was a subject that always upset her.

"It's not nice to think of your own mother as a hypochondriac. But I have never known her to be well, and she has never been diagnosed with anything that a few drinks wouldn't cure." That had slipped out, a truth. It felt good. Tonight she was not going to dwell on her always-absent mother. "I don't want to talk about any of them." Jo reached for Robert's hand. "Leaving you is going to be so hard. What am I going to do on Sunday night?" A tear slipped down her face. "I'm going to miss you so much."

Robert dreaded the thought of Jo moving away; it would be like losing a part of himself. He patted her hand. "We'll see each other. That's what family does. And you are my family."

1972 Albany, New York

A year and a half later, thirty-one year old Senator Jotto Wells stood in front of the State Capitol building on Empire Plaza. The five story, gray granite building was four hundred feet long and three hundred feet wide. Built in the nineteenth century, it was a hodgepodge of Italian Renaissance, Romanesque, and French Renaissance.

She climbed the steps, repositioned her briefcase to her left hand, and shifted her purse to her right shoulder.

She stood at the doorway of the senate chamber. The ceiling was carved golden oak, designed with deep paneled recesses, creating an acoustically perfect debate arena for the senators. The walls were covered with gold leaf. Siena marble arched above the visitor's gallery, and red granite pillars, and onyx panels covered the north and south walls. Red leather and carved mahogany paneling covered the walls below the galleries.

Her executive assistant Michelle Kabat, a fifty-year-old with silver hair, huge black eyes, and an extensive knowledge of government, intercepted Jo as she headed for her seat.

"Mr. Blumenthal is here, Senator Wells. He's waiting for you in the Caucus coffee shop across the street."

Jo handed Michele her briefcase. "Please take notes."

"I will. There are no votes scheduled until this afternoon. And by the way, Senator..."

"Yes," Jo studied her.

"Mr. Blumenthal is a very handsome man."

"Michele!"

"Just wondered if you'd noticed."

Jo straightened the jacket of her pink wool Chanel suit as she entered the crowded coffee shop, a favorite haunt for congressional members. Aaron Blumenthal was already sitting at the mica-covered table. He waved and stood. He was broad-shouldered and solidly built. Only thirty-eight, his black hair was streaked with silver and his eyes were dark. He had a cleft chin and a square-shaped face. His nose was a bit too sharp, but it all went together—giving him an air of easy sexuality and confidence. When he smiled, which he did often, his eyes twinkled and his face took on the look of a mischievous bad boy.

"Aaron, how nice to see you*." Michelle's right. He really is handsome.* She had been so busy with the campaign, she had never noticed before. Jo extended her hand.

"It's so good to see you again, Senator, and not just because you are the most beautiful woman I know." Aaron winked.

Jo blushed as he held a chair for her.

"I am very serious. You also happen to be the smartest woman, maybe even the smartest person I know. That still bothers the hell out of me."

Jo shot him a look. "Aaron, you're absolutely hopeless. Being a male chauvinist in 1972 is not exactly in vogue. In fact, your limited flexibility towards women underscores why change is so desperately needed and so hard to come by."

Aaron feigned hurt as he took a seat opposite Jo. "See, all you women are the same. You throw the insults around, and then men of good breeding, like me, have to smile and continue to act like gentlemen."

"I would expect nothing less." Jo batted her eyes and laughed.

"I've ordered us coffee. I have to catch a plane in two hours."

"Too bad." She masked her disappointment with a shrug. "I had hoped you were staying a couple of days." She wanted to get to know him better.

Aaron was caught off guard by her words, and his stomach knotted. He didn't think she even knew he existed. "When I return we'll find time for a quiet dinner together." He beamed. "Now, if you'll excuse me for being somewhat abrupt, today I'm here to do some recruiting on behalf of the United Jewish Appeal."

Jo tilted her head to one side, put her fingers in a vee, and pretended to be smoking a cigar. "To quote Groucho Marx," she quipped, "'I don't want to belong to any club that would have me as a member.'" Her eyes twinkled.

"Funny, very funny. Maybe you should give up politics and go on the stage."

Jo gave him a sheepish grin. "I'm sorry, I just couldn't resist. Go on, please. I'll behave."

"I've come here to extend an invitation for you to join me and a group of business people and politicians for a seven day trip to Israel. We need you to see the country firsthand, so you can form your own ideas and reach your own conclusions. The truth is, Jo, we need friends if Israel is to survive in the years ahead."

Jo's mind swirled. She could barely breathe. Her mind flew over her life—the years she was bombarded by her father's anti-Semitic rhetoric—the nights she had spent hiding under the covers with a flashlight, reading Leon Uris's *Exodus*. It was the first book she ever read about the Holocaust and Israel and it had ignited feelings deep within Jo. It was not just curiosity but something more—a pull, as if she were somehow connected to this persecuted, trampled people who never gave in or gave up.

At Smith, Jo took religion courses. It was always the tenets of Judaism, their practices and customs, that intrigued her most.

She thought about the time she went with some Jewish friends to the Hillel house on the NYU campus to hear the opening prayers of Yom Kippur, the highest holy day for Jews. The Kol Nidrei music, the haunting chants and melodies pulled at Jo, like gentle hands caressing her soul. For that hour, Jo had never felt closer to God. Now Aaron was sitting here, inviting her to go to the land of these people. She could hardly believe it.

Aaron watched Jo. He noted the distance in her eyes and the way she seemed to move away from her surroundings. The waitress approached with their coffee. It brought Jo out of her reverie.

Jo added sugar and cream and took a sip. She looked at Aaron. "When are you leaving?"

"The nineteenth of April. Israel is its most beautiful then, and it's also our holiday season."

"We are all paying our own way?"

Aaron nodded. "Once you get to Israel, you will be hosted by the government."

"That's perfect. It's the Easter break. I'll have my assistant, Michele block the time off and I'll take it as a vacation. "

Aaron smiled. "Thank you, Jo."

"Thank you for asking me."

Aaron looked at his watch. He took a few bills from his pocket and laid them on the table. "I have to go."

On the steps of the Capital, Jo reached to shake Aaron's hand. He ignored her hand and brushed his lips across Jo's cheek. "Next time, try kissing me hello and goodbye. You might learn to like it. Handshakes are a man's business." He winked at her as he turned away.

10

Albany, New York

Aaron opened the taxi door against a sudden gust of wind. The sky darkened and the air smelled of coming rain. He took a deep breath, relieved that his mission to recruit Jo had been a success. The prospect of spending seven days with her was an added bonus. He leaned his head against the back of the seat and closed his eyes. Images flashed. Israel—its birth, its fight for the right to exist, its need for friends. Aaron's commitment was his life.

His mind pulled him back to when he was six years old. It was a cold November night in 1939. His mother, Esther, a tiny woman with black hair and green eyes, and his father, Seymour, a studious man with a receding hairline and kind eyes, had each held one of his hands as they walked from their house through the town of Tournai, Belgium. Aaron remembered being so confused by his parents tears and their silence.

An hour later, they moved up the path to a tiny cottage that sat atop a hill overlooking a pasture where two dozen cows grazed. His father pulled the string on a bell that hung from the doorframe. The sound, a tinkling cry, still haunted Aaron.

"Aaron, say hello to Mr. and Mrs. Grunwald," His mother said, her voice a whisper as they moved inside. The house was cozy, its furniture lived-in, rugs faded, and walls scrubbed so often the paint had worn thin.

Aaron was bewildered. "I want to go home," he had cried, burying his head in his mother's skirt.

His mother kissed the top of his head. Her entire body shook. "You must stay here, my precious child. They will keep you safe."

"Someday you will understand. But, for now, my son, you must trust our decision," his father said, his eyes brimming.

Aaron shook his head and opened his eyes. Those last minutes, when they parted had vanished from his memory. Had he told them he loved them? Did they tell him? He didn't know.

He could still remember that very first night, sleeping in a strange home, in a bed not his own. Mother Adele, what she insisted he call her, came into the room with warm milk and cookies. She sat on the bed, took his hand, kissed his cheek, and whispered, "You must never forget who you are *now*, my son. You are Aaron Grunwald, a good Christian boy. All of our lives depend on you never forgetting."

The terror in her eyes had said it all.

Aaron's mind moved back to that first year, living with strangers, trembling every time he went to school, terrified that Hitler was personally going to come into his classroom and take him away.

In retrospect, Aaron understood that his parents gave him to Adele and Daryl Grunwald so that he would be protected from Hitler's grasp. He also understood the enormous risk the childless Grunwald's had taken. But the agony of being abandoned, even now after all these years, was so painful it sucked his breath away.

Aaron tried to picture his birth parents. Their faces had vanished.

His head pounded.

He thought back over those twelve years of his life. Everyone who knew him saw a good-looking, friendly, very intelligent kid with a great sense of humor. No one saw the truth. No one saw the pain. He lived the lie, kept his secrets.

When the war ended, his parents were dead.

At eighteen, Aaron traveled to America with money in his pockets given to him by the Grunwalds. When he passed through customs on Ellis Island, he gave his name as Blumenthal, a decision he had made with his adoptive parents' blessings. He then elbowed his way through the crowds, exhausted but exhilarated, ready to begin his life.

Representatives from the Jewish Agency were there, waiting to help. The Agency was funded by contributions from other Jews, and its goal was to rescue, and give aid and hope to survivors.

They moved Aaron into a tenement on the Lower East Side of New York, where other Eastern European Jews lived. He could still remember how he felt that first time he walked down Second Avenue between Houston and 14th Street. There were kosher Jewish butchers, Jewish newspapers and shops, people speaking German, Yiddish, Polish—his people, alive, vibrant, hopeful.

Aaron's memories turned to the day he walked into the Beth El synagogue on Fifth Avenue and East Sixty-Fifth Street. The twenty-five hundred seat main sanctuary had a quiet dignity, its vastness softened by the light refracted through the clerestory windows.

In the empty chapel, he had picked up a prayer book and said a prayer for his dead parents, reading aloud and stumbling over the transliterated Hebrew words. Then he closed the book and his eyes. He had come here out of respect for his parents and to talk to this God he had grown to hate.

My people lived on the brink of hell, begging for your mercy. You didn't hear. You destroyed everything I ever loved, but you haven't destroyed me. I will become someone, someone who would have made my parents proud.

He had stood up then, with tears running down his cheeks, crying for the past, for his dead mother and father and for the millions who had no one left to cry for them. When he left the synagogue, it was twilight.

He could still picture the gray sky tinged with dark cherry and pink. He saw it as an omen of clear days to come. He moved from the shadows of the taller buildings, and with each step, his intentions cleared. He would do what Jews always did—get an education, become a success, and never again let others decide his fate.

He remembered watching two drivers standing beside their cabs, speaking a language he couldn't understand. *That's it! I'll drive a cab. What better way to learn the language?*

Aaron sighed. The year that followed had been so difficult. He studied English at night and drove a cab during the day. When he perfected the language, he applied to City College and was accepted.

The next four years flew by. He was an excellent student and whether in class, at a Yankees game, or at a reception at the College for guest lecturers, Aaron seemed to draw a crowd of admirers—women and men.

Women saw a well-groomed young man with a European accent and the build of a football player who could charm them with his worldliness—a man with whom they would be safe, but not too safe. His male friends saw a man on the way up, a hard-driving force who could drink with the best of them, a man destined to succeed.

At his graduation in 1956, Aaron Blumenthal stood at the podium as president of his senior class. Finance degree in hand, he fielded dozens of offers. J.P. Morgan offered him a brand new Lincoln and a four-week vacation his first year.

But it was a dinner at the Plaza Hotel with David Rockefeller, the Chairman of Chase Manhattan Bank, that turned his head. Rockefeller offered no perks, only a small office with a window and the opportunity to become an international financier, surrounded by the best minds in the banking world.

Aaron had used his first paycheck as a down payment on a tailor-made, three-button gray flannel suit with a vest. He fully intended to portray himself as a successful banker, even though he lived on the Lower East Side.

Over the next fifteen years, with David Rockefeller as his mentor, Aaron established a network of wealthy, well-connected friends. He had a feel for the market and made a fortune for his clients and the bank.

Then in 1970, when Wal-Mart made an offering, Aaron took all his savings and invested in the company. A year later, there was a hundred percent stock split, and Aaron became a wealthy man.

As he sat in the back of a taxi headed for the Albany airport, Aaron Blumenthal thought about his great success. At the age of thirty-nine, he was now president of Overland Mutual, one of the most prestigious banks in the country.

Never forgetting the assistance he received as an immigrant to America, Aaron gave large sums of money to the United Jewish Appeal. He also contributed to political campaigns of candidates that shared in the ideology of Israel's right to exist.

* * *

On the plane ride to Washington a plan had formed in Aaron's mind. He found a pay phone and dialed Jo's office.

"I would like you to invite your friend Robert Osborne to join us," Aaron said, crossing his fingers, knowing that if the actor agreed to go they would not have to fight for media coverage.

"Aaron Blumenthal, you are shameless." Jo smiled into the phone.

"Guilty as charged," Aaron said.

"I'll ask. I'll even beg him if you'd like."

"Beg, Jo. Israel needs some good press for a change."

* * *

The following weekend Robert met Jo at her New York apartment. He handed her his coat. "You look wonderful." Robert kissed her hand. "Being important obviously agrees with you."

"What agrees with me is seeing you." Jo hugged him.

They walked arm in arm into the study. Law books were tucked into the bookshelves, and every nook and cranny bulged with magazines, old newspapers, photographs, and memorabilia from Jo's political campaign. The room smelled of old leather and furniture polish. Jo looked around, her embarrassment obvious.

"I guess I need to get this place organized," she said. "I kind of moved out in haste. Would you like a drink?"

"If you'll join me," Robert said. He walked over to the side table. "Allow me." He poured the Scotch into two glasses. "How are things going in the Senate?" Robert handed Jo a glass. "Is it what you had hoped it would be?"

"Yes and no. Being the only woman, every time I open my mouth I'm expected to say something either brilliant or stupid. I think stupid is winning out."

"That's not what I hear."

They sat next to each other on the sofa. Jo switched on the Tiffany lamp. "What did you hear?"

"That you are exceeding everyone's expectations. Everyone but me, that is."

"Thanks. I needed to hear that. I've been feeling a little fragile," Jo said.

"Is that why you decided to come home for the weekend?"

Jo snuggled against Robert. "Not really." She gave him her innocent, little-girl look.

"What are you up to, young lady?"

"I'm going to Israel as a guest of the United Jewish Appeal. Aaron Blumenthal extended the invitation. And, he's invited you to go as well." She smiled, all teeth and dimples.

The color rose in Robert's face. "I can understand why they invited you. They need political friends." Robert could imagine the total horror Doctor Hans Wells would feel when he found out his daughter was going to Israel. "Why do they want me?"

"Aaron needs media attention," Jo said. "And you can help get him that attention."

Robert shook his head. "Taking a trip together would put our faces on every gossip tabloid in the country. It wouldn't be good for your career."

Jo shrugged. "Like they haven't been speculating for years. Have you read the latest story in the Mirror? They say we're secretly married, and that I'm going to have a baby. But, let's stay with the issues."

Jo was on fragile ground. Morgan's best friend, Claire, and her husband Saul, lived in Israel. They were pioneers for the State, and a link to Robert's past. They had been begging him to make the trip for years.

"You should go, Robert. It would be good for you."

Robert stood and turned his back to Jo. Her words had catapulted him into the past. The year was 1938, and he was standing on the train platform in Paris. Morgan and Claire were holding on to each other, tears streaming down their faces. They had become so close, like sisters—Claire filling the void for the family Morgan had left behind in Poland.

Robert knew that Morgan put her own feelings aside and encouraged her friend to go to Israel. But, watching them that day, seeing the agony on their faces, knowing they might never see each other again, it had been a memory Robert tried to forget.

Robert understood Saul. He was a Zionist—determined to build a Jewish homeland. Claire—she wasn't even Jewish. Still, she had followed Saul, determined to make a life with the man she loved.

It had been a difficult life.

Claire suffered and survived malaria, their kibbutz had been attacked numerous times by the Arabs, and worst of all, their second child had died. Robert touched the wedding ring he still wore.

I kept in touch, hundreds of letters over the years. Letters aren't enough. I should have gone to see them years ago.

"I'll go with you," he said quietly.

Jo smiled. "That makes me so happy. By the way, I got a call this morning from my good friend Senator Bill Stanton. He just came back from a finance and funding mission in Israel." Jo winked at Robert. "You are going to love this. The lead negotiator for the Israelis was your friend Saul Lapinsky."

"And the senator called to tell you this because…"

"He knows we are friends." Jo laughed. "Saul shook hands with the senator and said, and I'll quote: 'I have a friend in your America—a big star. His name is Robert Osborne.' The moment he said your name, he got all emotional and excused himself from the room. Senator Stanton was overjoyed by the show of sensitivity, convinced that Saul was going to be a pushover."

"That does not sound like the Saul I remember," Robert said.

"I can assure you, it was a momentary show of weakness. Saul spent the next several hours convincing the Senator that Jews could and would stand strong and take care of themselves, never again being fodder for an uncaring world. Saul pointed out that the government of the United States should loan money to Israel because in the years to come, she would be their only ally in the Middle East. He was adamant that while Israel would gladly accept a loan, they would not allow anyone to dictate policy to them. The Senator said Saul was the most exacting, exasperating negotiator he has ever dealt with. And, the most convincing patriot he has ever met."

"That's the man I knew." Robert's face softened. "They have

been through so much. In 1947, they fought for independence, in 1956, it was the Suez Campaign, and in 1967, the Six Day War. Imagine a country filled with armed survivors of the Holocaust. Would you want to fight them?" Robert studied his hands. "Sorry. I got a little carried away."

"No, you didn't."

Robert smiled. "By the way, I forgot to tell you. When Claire moved to Israel and converted to Judaism, she changed her name to Rebecca."

"Rebecca." Jo repeated the name slowly. "Rebecca was the wife of Abraham's son, Isaac—a maiden of great beauty, modesty, and kindness. What a perfect name."

* * *

Later that night Robert lay in his bed having a conversation in his mind with Morgan. *She charmed me into going, just the way you always were able to charm me into doing your bidding.* Robert pictured Morgan smiling at him, her eyes catching the light, her hand slipping into his. *I will find the answers, my beloved. Your daughter has a right to know who her mother was.* Robert closed his eyes and drifted into a deep, dreamless sleep.

11

1972
Moscow, Russia

Vladimir Vloriscoff sat at his desk, staring out the window of his study. The sweeping curve of the Moskva River was off in the distance, sparkling between the hand-painted cupolas, gilt domes, and spires of the great Russian Orthodox cathedrals dotting the skyline.

It had been twenty-seven years since the war's end and in that time, Vladimir had successfully managed to live his life as an imposter. The man he once was, David Kandel the Jew, was buried in the farthest recesses of his mind. In David's place a new man was created, Vladimir Vloriscoff, the Russian.

During those years he had won an Olympic gold medal in wrestling at the Games of 1948. He also held the Kandidat Nauk Degree from Moscow State University, and was one of his country's premier scientists.

He had been hiding in the belly of a ship bound for Palestine with hundreds of other people. He was young, barely out of his teens, dressed in the heavy garb of an orthodox Jew. A man approached, his clothing clean, his skin healthy, pink, and plump. How strange that vision had remained so strong.

"Why are all of you down here?" The man had blinked back tears as he sat.

"We are Jews running for our lives." David could still remember every word of the ensuing conversation. "I'm from Vienna. The others," David had looked around, "I don't know. Everywhere, I guess."

The man had put his hand on David's arm. It had been like a caress—reminding him he still lived. "What happened?"

"It was a day much like any other day—cold and clear—March 15, 1938. I was a student at the University of Vienna when Hitler's army marched into our city and claimed all of Austria. Overnight they rounded up one-hundred and eighty thousand of us." David had pounded his chest with his fists. "We'd been warned, but we refused to listen. All that changed when our own countrymen turned against us. "Jews were beaten and tortured."

David did not tell the stranger what happened to his parents. He had been certain at the time, if he mentioned it, he would curl up in a corner and die. "Do you see these clothes?" He had pulled at the coat. "The Nazis forced an old Rabbi to strip in the middle of the street, for the fun of humiliating him. Then they made me put on his clothes. The old man's heart gave out. As he lay dying, I promised him I would bury his clothes in the earth of Palestine. I swore I would go there for him and pray at the Wailing Wall. And, I will! I will do it for that old man. I will keep the promise, or die in the process."

The stranger had cried then—loud, gasping sounds that were lost in the chaos of the moment.

"Tell me your name," the man had asked.

"David. My name is David Kandel. But, there is no one left to call me that...no one to remember my name. Please just go away. I can't talk anymore."

The man stood up. "My name is Saul Lapinsky. I'll be back to help you, David Kandel."

Saul had not come back. However, David had managed to send a note. He could see it clearly, every word, every tear that had fallen as he wrote it.

Dear Saul,

I can only pray that this letter and package finds its way to you. I have sent the old man's clothing. I promised to bury them in the soil of aretz Israel. Please help me keep my promise. Find a spot that feels right, and say Kaddish. His name was Morris ben Abraham.

As for me, just think of me once in a while, and add me to your prayers. I intend to survive. I will marry and make babies in the land of our people. One day I will tap you on the shoulder. Watch for me. Our future is in your hands. Build a place for us to come.

May G-d protect you until we meet again,
David Kandel

Vladimir pulled back from his reverie.

He held a gold embossed note in his hand inviting him to speak at a conference in Sweden. His heart beat wildly. It was what he had been praying for—the opportunity to defect. Now, all he had to do was convince Doctor Anna Gurevich to go with him.

Anna had been one of his students, and even though she was twelve years younger then he, Vladimir had been smitten by her determination and brilliant mind. He envisioned Anna's soft brown eyes, and the silky chestnut hair that she wore in a braid down the center of her slender back.

He knew a relationship was dangerous for both of them—Anna was a Jew, Russia was an anti-Semitic society, and Vladimir was one of the country's premier scientists, under constant surveillance by the KGB. To keep Anna close, Vladimir had convinced her to become one of his research assistants after she graduated.

Vladimir picked up a picture of Anna with the Ural Mountains in the background, remembering the day in December 1968, when he received notification he was being sent to monitor a Soviet nuclear research facility in Omsk, in the southern corner of western Siberia.

He and Anna had traveled on the Trans-Siberian Railway. Each car had ten compartments and two Provodniks, conductors. In the front of each car there were toilets and a hot water boiler. The sleeping berths were four to a compartment, and Vladimir smiled when he thought how loudly Anna had complained about men snoring and farting in their sleep.

The trip from Moscow to Omsk was seventeen hundred miles, and took eight days. They passed Samara, the secondary capital of the Soviet Union during the War. From there they traveled east through the vast, flat and barren landscape to Chelyabinsk. The industrial city of Omsk, their final destination, stood on the banks of two rivers, the gentle Om and the powerful Irtysh.

They arrived at noon. Dressed in heavy parkas, earmuffs, fur boots, and gloves, they walked along Lyubinskiy Prodpedkt, past chapels built in the eighteen hundreds and down little side streets lined with stately mansions once owned by insurance companies and banks.

Escorted by a soldier named Vasily, they drove to the top-secret facility, Stasov, five miles outside the city. The complex was nothing more than a row of metal buildings surrounded by barbed wire.

Vladimir closed his eyes. He remembered Anna's reaction to their surroundings.

"You take me from my home. You talk me into coming with you. And you bring me here?" She had trudged ahead of him, her hair whipping in the howling wind.

By the next day, the weather had turned nightmarishly frigid. The mid-morning reading was thirty-two degrees below Celsius. Anna's response to the weather was to become equally frigid toward Vladimir.

Sitting alone one evening in his laboratory, surrounded by flasks, beakers, chemicals, vacuum air pumps, and scales, Anna had wandered in. Her face was chapped and she was bundled up against the freezing Arctic temperatures.

"Vladimir Vloriscoff, I'm never going to forgive you for bringing me to this horrible place," Anna had said, her eyes shooting darts. "And I want you to stop your stupid flirting because I only go out with Jewish men." She pointed her finger at his face. "And besides all that, you have a terrible reputation as a womanizer."

Vladimir had stood up, knocking over the stool he was sitting on. He grabbed Anna roughly by the shoulders, his face only inches from hers. Darkness filled his eyes, and he could feel Anna tremble. "What do you know about my reputation? Is it such a crime I like women? Have you ever asked yourself why I never married?" he shouted, his fingers biting into her shoulders.

Anna froze at his touch.

"You don't know me because you've never bothered trying to get to know me."

"Why would I want to know a man who thinks he can make a woman love him by dragging her to some Godforsaken place in the middle of nowhere?" Anna said.

"Make you love me? If only I could," Vladimir had said. "Do you know about love, Anna? Do you know about desire? Do you know what it's like to want something so badly that the wanting of it only brings you pain?"

"I know, Vladimir," her voice a whisper. "And I wish to God things could be different between us. But, they are what they are." Anna's eyes had filled with tears. "This thing between us is wrong. You must send me back to Moscow."

I must tell her. It's the only way. "Come and sit for a moment," he had said, pulling over a stool. "I have a story to tell you." He let time sit between them as he gathered his courage. "I'm not...I'm not a Russian," he had said. "I'm from Vienna."

Anna's eyes grew wide. "I don't understand."

"My family lived in Vienna before the War. My father was a doctor, my mother . . ."

Anna touched his face with her fingers, her eyes moist.

"The Nazis shot my mother and took my father." He had bowed his head to hide the rage and his tears. "I wanted revenge. But, my father's brother insisted I be sent away—to get the word out, to tell the world what was happening. I was smuggled onto a boat with hundreds of other Jews. Our destination was Palestine. When the boat arrived, the English wouldn't allow us entry. We were sent back to Germany—to the camps. The ship's captain allowed me to escape. To this day, I don't know why he picked me."

"Vladimir," Anna said, her lips quivered.

"I grew up speaking Russian to my grandfather, so it was easy to disguise myself as a Soviet soldier. They wanted me to survive, and that's exactly what I've done," he had said. "So you see, my darling

Anna, I too am a Jew—a damaged, angry, disenchanted Jew, but still a Jew."

"If only I'd known," Anna caressed his face with her eyes. "So much time wasted." Anna moved into his arms. "I love you, Vladimir. I've loved you from the very first moment I saw you," Anna said. She had kissed him then. It was their beginning.

* * *

Anna walked into the study, pulling Vladimir back from his wandering memories.

She switched on the lamp. "What are you doing sitting here in the dark?" Anna kissed him gently on the forehead. "Is something wrong?"

"No, my love, nothing's wrong. I was just thinking."

"About what?" Anna asked.

"I was thinking it's time for us to go."

"Not again," Anna said, showing him her palms. "We've talked and talked about this."

Vladimir folded his arms over his enormous chest. "I want to tell you about my day," he said, a dark look crossing his face. "There was an accident at the plant. Nikolay Edorov was mortally burned."

Anna's face paled. She collapsed in the chair.

"With his last breath he said to me, 'You must get out before you become the angel of death.'" Vladimir was quiet a minute. "Anna, you know what I'm talking about. The things we're working on, in the right hands, could change the world for the better. But it has the potential for destruction that could be more devastating than anything the world has ever seen before."

"I'm sorry about Nikolay. I really am. But we have our work to do."

Vladimir handed a letter to Anna. "I received this last week."

"An invitation to Sweden. That's nice." Anna shook her head just slightly. "I don't see how this changes anything."

"It changes everything." Vladimir smiled. "Finally, after all these years, I've been given permission for you to travel with me."

Anna handed the invitation back to Vladimir. Her eyes never left his face.

He lowered his voice. "We're going to defect."

Anna gave a quick shake of her head. "Are you crazy? The KGB would kill us before they would ever let us go."

"If we stay here, you can never become my wife," he said, eyebrows raised, his face a mingling of longing and regret.

"I'm happy this way." Anna kissed Vladimir's hands. "It's all I need." She extended her arms. "Look at me, Vladimir. I'm almost forty years old. It's too late to have children, so what difference does it make if we marry or not?"

"It is not good enough!" he roared. "You deserve to be more than a mistress."

"I know this isn't just about you and me. It's that stupid promise you made to the man on the ship that's driving you so crazy. Do you think he remembers you? Do you think he ever expects to see you again?"

Vladimir touched Anna's hair, pushing it away from her eyes. He thought of Saul—they had met for only an instant, but the memory and the promise tugged.

"I want to go to Israel. I must go."

"We can't always have what we want, my beloved." she held his gaze.

"Perhaps that's true. But we must try." Vladimir began to pace, his face intent, as if he were looking at something Anna could not see. "I know the hotel in Stockholm well. It has a half dozen exits."

He told her his plan.

"Even if we make it to the American Embassy, what then?" Anna stood in front of him, her face inches from his.

"We request asylum."

Anna smiled. "And that's going to get us to Israel?"

"I will trade information in exchange for safe passage to Israel."

"My poor, sweet, naive Vladimir. With all that you know, do you really think the Americans are going to just let you walk away?"

"They will have no choice. It's that, or I tell them nothing."

"What about Boris Blanchack? He trained you for the Olympics, treated you like a son? Will you just leave? Is that how you'll thank him for loving you?"

"With you as my wife, living freely in the land of our people—what greater gift could I ever give him?" He leaned in and kissed her for a long, sweet minute.

12

The plane touched down at the Stockholm-Arlanda airport in the early afternoon. Vladimir and Anna, escorted by three KGB agents, were whisked through customs with their diplomatic passports. One agent rode in their Mercedes limousine, while the other two followed in a black Volvo.

"What a beautiful city," Anna said as her eyes danced off the waters of Lake Malaren.

"The city of Stockholm is made up of fourteen islands, all part of the archipelago," Vladimir said. "Our hotel is on the water's edge in the Bay of Riddarfjarden."

"My own tour guide." Anna laughed. She opened the window and the warm summer breezes drifted in, bringing the smell of the sea. Anna stuck her hand out and waved to a group of teenagers passing by on bicycles.

Anna never had a childhood. She was identified as a prodigy at four years old and by the age of twelve, she could extract the root to the seventh degree of numbers with as many as twenty digits. Her mind belonged to the State and she was expected to study harder and be more accomplished than everyone else. Learning was all she ever knew until she fell in love with Vladimir.

She reached for his hand. "How many people live here?"

"Close to a million, I should think," Vladimir said.

They turned down Giorwellsgaran Street and drove through the gates of the Russian Embassy.

Ambassador Uury Ushakovit, a slight man with silver hair, a bulbous nose, and thick eyebrows that transversed his forehead, greeted them in the embassy library. The room had heavy red velvet drapes, an expansive rug in red, with a yellow sickle and star woven into the design depicting the Russian flag, and ceiling-to-floor bookshelves.

The ambassador embraced Vladimir. "It is my great honor to meet you, Doctor. I have followed your career since you the won Olympic Gold for wrestling." He looked Anna up and down. "And who is this lovely lady?"

Vladimir tipped his head toward Anna. "My research assistant, Miss Gurvich."

"The pleasure is all mine." The ambassador kissed Anna's hand. "Please have a seat. This will only take a moment, and then you can go to your hotel and rest before the conference begins."

Sitting on uncomfortable wooden chairs, their knees almost touching, Ambassador Ushakovit began his debriefing. "As you know, scientists from around the world have gathered here to share information. You," his eyes bored into Vladimir's, "one of the Soviet Union's greatest minds will be a target for the capitalistic opportunists who have come here hoping to steal information from you. Your job," he punctuated the air with his forefinger, "is to give your paper, as approved by our esteemed leaders, and gather information when the other scientists give their papers. You will offer nothing. Is that understood?"

"Absolutely," Vladimir said, swallowing his rage, a rage he felt every time free choice was withheld from him.

The ambassador stood. "I'm glad we understand each other. Don't hesitate to call if I can be of further assistance. Now, if you will please excuse me, I have some pressing issues."

Anna and Vladimir followed the ambassador down the hallway. He turned left and they continued straight.

"How dare he tell us we can't talk to the other scientists?" Anna asked, swearing under her breath.

"Because they can," Vladimir replied. "Because they can."

* * *

Anna and Vladimir arrived at the Hotel Diplomat, an Edwardian mansion located on Strandvagen Street in the Embassy Row district. As they made their way toward the hotel, they were jostled by crowds of businessmen rushing to their offices. Anna stopped to watch a group of children marching in line with their teachers.

The lead KGB officer elbowed his way next to Vladimir. "This way. We must hurry," Fyoder said. He was a giant of a man with huge biceps, and a constant scowl.

He led them past the reception desk and into the lift, keeping his finger on the stop button until his two comrades entered carrying the luggage.

On the third floor, situated at the very end of the hallway were rooms 327 and 328. Fyoder opened the doors and pocketed the keys.

"Have a good sleep, comrades. One of us will be right outside if you need anything."

Anna kicked off her heels and tapped softly on the adjoining door. She walked into Vladimir's room.

"They have us locked in like prisoners."

Vladimir put his finger to his lips. "Shh."

He took Anna's hand and led her into the bathroom. The room was white marble, had a glass-enclosed shower, an over-sized bathtub and floor-to-ceiling mirrors. Vladimir closed the door and turned on the faucets to block the sound of their voices.

He held his fingers to his lips. "You must be careful what you say. They will be listening."

The pressure was more that Anna could handle. Tears streamed down her face. "They know we're up to something. I can see it on their faces."

"This is how they always act."

"Please, Vladimir, let's just do what they say and then go back home."

"No, Anna. It's not about us anymore, or about going to Israel. It's about being free. It's about being able to collaborate with other scientists."

"I don't want to let you down, but I'm so terrified," Anna said, blinking away her tears.

Vladimir lifted Anna's face and kissed the tip of her nose. "You can do this. I know you can."

* * *

The Stockholm convention facility, a massive structure of steel and glass, was located on Drotlninggatan, only a six-minute drive from the Hotel Diplomat. Arriving at ten in the morning, Vladimir and Anna made their way down the aisle of the five-hundred-seat auditorium. Anna wore a simple black dress. Vladimir had on a fifteen-year-old navy-blue suit, red tie and a starched white shirt.

The third speaker of the morning was the 1970 Nobel Laureate in physics, Alfven Hannes of Sweden. Fifteen minutes into Hannes's speech, Vladimir nudged Anna.

"Magneto hydrodynamics, the dynamics of electrically conducting fluids to create forces and change the magnetic field. My God, this man is working on theories we couldn't even imagine five years ago," Vladimir said, pulling at the too-tight collar of his shirt.

"Compared to you, my darling, he's an ignoramus."

Thirty minutes later Enrich VonLouster, the Chairman of the conference stood at the dais and said, "It is my distinct honor to welcome our next speaker, Doctor Vladimir Vloriscoff. He will discuss the shell-correction approach to nuclear shell effects and its applications to the fission process. Doctor Vloriscoff, if you please."

Vladimir straightened his tie, squeezed Anna's hand, and moved into the aisle.

The applause was polite as Vladimir placed his speech on the podium. "Thank you, Doctor VonLouster, it is indeed an honor to be speaking in front of such an esteemed audience," Vladimir said, his huge chest leaning into the podium.

"This morning I will discuss the single-particle structure in spherical and deformed nuclei, from the viewpoint of the so-called shell-correction method. This method stresses the importance of large-scale non-uniformities in the energy distribution of the individual particles especially near the Fermi energy." Vladimir spoke from memory, his eyes darting from one face in the crowd to the next.

A half hour later, his voice growing hoarse, Vladimir said, "In conclusion, this paper is a review in the narrowest sense of the word. Comparison with other approaches, as well as historic references, is given mainly to clarify specific points, because to give you a complete review would be a monumental undertaking and would take days."

He moved back from the podium, took a deep breath, and smiled.

The aura of self-confidence the great athlete and scholar had shown while delivering his topic captivated the audience. They rose to their feet, the applause enthusiastic as VonLouster banged the gavel, ending the morning session.

Vladimir and Anna were standing in the lobby surrounded by well-wishers when KGB agent Fyoder grasped Vladimir's shoulder.

"We will go now."

"I wish to speak with my colleagues," Vladimir said, pushing the man's hand away.

"I'm sorry, sir. My orders are specific. You will have no contact. Now, please come with me. We have lunch reservations."

* * *

Vladimir and Anna arrived at the Operakallaren on Karl XII:s Torg—a turn of the century restaurant situated on the ground floor of the world famous 1890's opera house. Mozart's *Ave Verum Corpus* played in the background as they entered the main dining room with its twenty-foot ceilings and magnificent view of the King of Sweden's palace. Mythical paintings by Oscar Bjorck adorned the oak-paneled walls.

They were shown to a cordoned off area, where a waiter in a white button-up jacket with epaulettes pulled back the crimson velvet armchair for Anna. A crystal vase full of red roses was the table's single centerpiece.

"Compliments of the house," the sommelier said, making a great show of opening and pouring from a bottle of *Chateau d'Yquem*, 1967.

As a lover of fine wine, Vladimir appreciated the quality of the offering. He held the glass by its stem, swirled the wine to bring out the full bouquet, sniffed deeply and then took a sip. He nodded to the sommelier and smiled. "It is superb. Please thank management for their kindness."

"I was so proud of you today," Anna said. She lifted the glass to her lips. Her hands trembled.

"Please, Anna. You must relax," Vladimir said, glancing at the KGB agents sitting at the next table

After ordering scallops with sorrel sauce, foie gras mousse, quail breast, and sweetbreads from the hovering waiter, Vladimir unbuttoned his suit jacket.

It was their signal.

"Please excuse me," Anna said as she placed her napkin on the table. Fyoder was by her side before she took the first step.

The walk through the restaurant seemed interminable to Anna.

Once inside the bathroom, she stood against the wall and waited. A few minutes later Anna heard a man yell, "Hurry! The Russian is having some kind of attack."

Fyoder glanced at the closed bathroom door and then turned on his heels.

Anna opened the door a crack. The hallway was deserted, the only sound her heels clicking on the marble as she ran to the pay phone on the wall near the stairway. She fumbled with the coins and dialed the number she had memorized from the telephone book in their room.

"American Embassy. How may I direct your call?"

"My name is Dr. Anna Stein. I am here in Stockholm with Dr. Vladimir Vloriscoff." Anna spoke in Russian, so nervous she was sure her words were unintelligible, but Vladimir had assured her the call would be recorded. "Tonight we will defect from the Soviet Union and come to you." She slammed the phone down. It had taken less then twenty seconds.

Anna moved into the dining room. She saw Vladimir sprawled on the floor. People were standing, pointing, whispering. She ran to his side. Seeing Vladimir's ghostly-pale face, Anna knew this was no act. The stress had brought on a full-blown angina attack.

"Get out of my way," Anna hissed as Fyoder reached to take Vladimir's pulse. She dropped to her knees and dumped the contents of her purse on the floor. She found her pillbox, took out the nitroglycerin tablet, and placed it under Vladimir's tongue.

"A bad attack," he moaned.

"Take slow, easy breaths, my darling. You are going to be fine," Anna said, placing two fingers alongside the outer edge of Vladimir's windpipe to feel the pulse of his carotid artery. Whatever else was going on around her, Anna was in control again—the doctor doing what she did best. "Your pulse is one-hundred and twenty." She looked at her watch and counted for two more minutes. "Much better. It is already down to ninety and there is no irregularity in the rhythm."

"We will go to the hospital," Fyoder ordered, his eyes darting toward the door.

"I don't need a hospital. Just get me back to the hotel," Vladimir said, the agony in his chest diminishing. He smiled at Anna. "I'm better," he said, his mind already focused on the next phase of their plan.

* * *

Back in the hotel room, Anna closed the blackout curtains. Then she handed Vladimir a cold glass of water, and turned down the bed.

"You must rest for a little while," she said.

Vladimir sighed. The pain was gone, but not the overwhelming emotions he had experienced at the restaurant. It was not fear. Dying had never been his enemy. It was fury at the prospect of failing. He had been through too much in his life not to win when it mattered most. He believed with all his heart that he had earned the right to marry his beloved Anna, to wander the streets of Jerusalem, and to camp under the stars in the Negev. I will have to be more careful, take better care of myself, he thought as he stretched out on the bed.

"Just for a few minutes."

He closed his eyes.

13

Hotel Diplomat

Anna stared into the bathroom mirror. She could see the fire of fear smoldering in her eyes, knowing the slightest doubt would whip that fear out of control.

I can do this. I will do this! Anna thought as she slathered Vladimir's shaving cream on her legs and shaved them for the first time in her life. She then cut six inches off her skirt with a practiced hand making a perfect hem.

Anna stepped into the skimpy skirt, and unfastened the first three buttons of her blouse, exposing the tops of her breasts.

Her face inches from the mirror; she smeared gold eye shadow on her lid and brow. Wetting a black make-up pencil, she drew a heavy line around her eyes, applied mascara in several layers until her lashes were thick and caked, dabbed her face with powder, and used a heavy hand with the rouge before adding apple red lipstick. She shook her hair loose from the braid. It fell in wild curls around her face and down her back.

Anna leaned over the bed and kissed the sleeping Vladimir's forehead.

He opened his eyes and stared, pursing his lips in a silent whistle. "Unrecognizable but magnificent," he whispered.

Anna blushed. "How do you feel?"

"Perfect. All I needed was a little nap. Now, just give me five minutes."

Vladimir zipped up a black leather jacket, pulled on a pair of jeans, slicked back his hair, and added a pair of thick, black-rimmed glasses.

"Ready?" he whispered.

Anna held up both hands with her fingers crossed. "As ready as I'll ever be." She took a deep breath.

Vladimir nodded.

"Help! I need help!" Anna screamed, pounding her fists against the locked door.

The door flew open. Fyoder stepped into the room.

"What the . . .?" He reached for the gun holstered at his shoulder when he saw how Anna was dressed.

Vladimir lifted his arms, and with all his might smashed the lead crystal ice bucket over Fyoder's head. There was a sickening thump as the agent crumpled to the floor. Vladimir kicked the door closed.

"Oh my God," Anna cried, her breath coming in strangled gasps. "I think we've killed him!"

Vladimir reached down and placed his fingers on Fyoder's carotid artery. "He's alive. Let's go."

* * *

The night clerk looked up from his desk as the lift opened. A man, apparently one of his guests, was in a passionate embrace, his hands cupping the behind of a hooker he had never seen before. The clerk memorized her every curve.

The KGB agent sat in the chair reading his newspaper. He glanced up as the couple passed. The magnificent legs of the hooker caught his attention. He stared as she moved through the lobby and out the doorway, never lifting his eyes above her swaying hips.

A taxi was parked in front of the hotel.

"Take us to the American Embassy on Dag Hammarskuolds Vag 31," Vladimir ordered as he and Anna jumped in. "If you hurry there's extra kronas for you."

Six minutes later the taxi squealed to a halt in front of the embassy, a modern brick and steel building perched on a hill. Floodlights switched on and the taxi followed the driveway up. The gates opened.

"Pull in," Vladimir ordered.

The taxi slid to a halt.

"Please step out of the car," a soldier ordered, his hand resting on the gun at his hip.

The ambassador stood next to the soldier. He had relayed Anna's message to Washington and been instructed to protect them at all costs.

"Hurry! We must get you inside," the ambassador ordered in Russian.

Anna and Vladimir were surrounded as they moved into the embassy. The massive foyer was fashioned in concrete with stone floors and exposed steel beams.

"I'm Rodney Kennedy-Minott." The ambassador extended his hand first to Vladimir and then to Anna. "My first duty is to ascertain exactly why you have come."

"We are requesting political asylum," Vladimir said.

"Then I welcome you," the ambassador said, all teeth and crinkled eyes. "For your protection we'd like to get you out of Sweden tonight."

"We go now!" Vladimir said, switching to English.

The ambassador nodded his head. "You'll be taken to a private landing strip, a three hour drive from here. A United States transport plane will be sitting on the runway waiting to take you to England. It's in transit as we speak."

"That is good," Vladimir said, taking Anna's hand.

The ambassador led them out to the armored Volvo, deciding he would call ahead and forewarn his associates in England that the Russian scientists were much more than colleagues.

London, England

Nine hours later a limousine pulled up in front of the nine-story American Embassy at One Grosvenor Square. As Vladimir and Anna got out of the car, his eyes grew wide at the sight of the gilded eagle, with its thirty-five foot wingspan, sitting atop the Chancery building. He squeezed Anna's hand.

"We are finally free."

"Let's hope you are right," Anna said.

* * *

Three floors below ground, Vladimir and Anna sat at an ebony conference table in a room with concrete floors, florescent lights and a dozen black leather armchairs. Ambassador Walter Annenberg, a serious man with thick black brows, a straight nose and a cleft chin, stared at the pair. At his side sat a man in his early thirties with a crew cut and cobalt colored eyes that never blinked.

"You came to us for help, and now you won't talk unless the Israelis are present. It doesn't make any sense; it doesn't work that way. You answer my questions, and then we'll arrange a meeting," Annenberg said, his voice edged with impatience after twenty minutes of trying to get Vladimir to cooperate.

Vladimir shook his head, his face a scowl. "I have information invaluable to your government. I'll give you that information only when a representative of the Israeli government is present." He puffed out his massive chest. "We wait."

The men moved out into the hallway. "Son of a bitch! What do we do now?" Andrew Madison, the CIA agent asked.

"I'll have to make a call to Washington," Annenberg replied.

"Listen, I've dealt with the fucking Israelis before, and I'm telling you, Mr. Ambassador, it's a mistake to bring them in. You just give me a few hours alone with these Russians, and I'll have them singing like canaries."

"We can't do that," Annenberg said. "Take them to the penthouse and let them get some rest."

Jerusalem, Israel

Golda Meir, the fourth Prime Minister of Israel, picked up the phone in her office. She closed her eyes and listened.

"Mr. President," she said moments later, "I must be certain I understand this correctly. You have two top Russian scientists that have defected from a conference in Sweden. They have information invaluable to your country, but they will only give you that information when a representative of the Israeli government is present— is that correct?"

She listened.

"Very good, sir. I will need twenty-four hours to deliver our people. Thank you for calling, Mr. President." Golda hung up the phone and smiled. She rang the buzzer on her desk. "Get me General Zwi Zamir."

A few hours later, Golda and Zwi, head of Mossad, sifted through a stack of personnel files.

"We need two men who speak Russian and have strong scientific backgrounds. Nixon says it can't be anyone directly representing the Israeli government. So tell me, Zwi, who do we have?" Golda placed her arthritic hands on the table and lifted her smoky eyes.

Zwi pushed two files towards Golda.

She flipped them open, read for less then three minutes, and passed the files back.

"Yuval Ne'eman is perfect."

"I think so too," Zwi said. "As the director of the School of Physics and Astronomy at Tel-Aviv University, he is not directly associated with our government. Also, he's an expert in particle physics, astrophysics, cosmology, and the philosophy of science."

"And this next one..." Golda's eyes twinkled. "He's a friend. I will call him. You call the professor."

* * *

The phone rang in Saul's apartment office. He lifted the receiver and after identifying himself, he listened without speaking.

"They are Russian scientists," Golda said, "and we have no idea why they are insisting on speaking with us. We must tread lightly. Nixon is not happy about being blackmailed and we cannot afford to do anything that might anger one of the few allies we have in the world. It's a big responsibility, Saul. I can't think of anyone I would rather have as the front man on this."

"Thank you," Saul said.

"A car will pick you up in fifteen minutes."

"I'll be ready."

"May God protect you," Golda said.

Saul's wife, Rebecca walked into the room as he put down the phone. "What's going on?"

"That was Golda. She needs me in England to debrief two Russian scientists who have defected to the Americans. The interesting thing is the Russians are refusing to cooperate unless representatives from Israel are present."

"Maybe they are Jews," Rebecca offered.

Saul opened the closet and pulled out a packed suitcase.

"Top Russian scientists being Jews? Not very likely."

American Embassy
London, England.

Vladimir and Anna sat on one side of the ebony conference table, Ambassador Annenberg sat at the head, and the Israeli team consisting of Saul and Professor Ne'eman were seated across from the Russians. Four visiting American scientists teaching at Oxford and a stenographer occupied the other seats.

Vladimir stood. "I will debrief all of you now, as promised," Vladimir said in English, without waiting to be introduced. "I will answer all your questions, no matter how long that takes." Vladimir turned his eyes on Ambassador Annenberg. "As long as I have your assurance, when our work here is completed, you will give us passage to Israel."

Saul's muscles tensed. He squinted, staring into Vladimir's eyes. Saul never forgot a face, or a voice. He pushed himself back in time as he listened to the cadence of Vladimir's speech patterns. He was positive he knew this man from somewhere.

Like a flash flood, he was back in the bowels of a ship heading towards Israel. He was staring into the eyes of an emaciated, terrified young man dressed like an Orthodox rabbi. Saul blinked, seeing no resemblance to that man-child. But, the voice…he would never forget the voice!

Saul pushed back his chair, his knees threatening to buckle. Every eye was on him as he rounded the table.

Vladimir watched Saul approaching, confused by the lack of protocol. Suddenly a kaleidoscope of images flashed. Vladimir could hear the desperate screams of starving babies, smell the unwashed, putrid bodies of adults forced to sit in their own waste, see the vacant, hopeless stares.

Saul stood in front of Vladimir, his mouth quivering, his eyes filled with tears. He put his hand on Vladimir's shoulder.

The two men looked at each other.

"Hello, David," Saul said, his voice cracking. "I have been waiting all these years for you, my friend. I promised you a homeland and now I will take you there."

Part 3

14

1972
Kibbutz Ayelet Haba-ah
Israel.

Doctor Rebecca Lapinsky was finished for the day. Her last patient was a five year-old boy suffering from nightmares and bedwetting. She put her final comments on the child's chart and tucked it into the filing cabinet. Her eyes lighted on the whiskey bottle tucked into the bottom of the drawer. *Why not?* She took a tiny swig. It burned going down. Seconds later a bit of the edge came off the day.

Robert's letter! She pushed the cabinet shut with her foot. *I've been so busy I forgot about it.* She rummaged through the stacks of correspondence on her desk. She tore open the envelope and read slowly, her eyes wide. She held it to her heart.

I can't believe it! Robert is finally coming to Israel.

Rebecca looked around her office, trying to see it as Robert would. The sun filtered through the lace curtains, bathing the cluttered room in a gentle yellow hue. The walls were painted mint green, pink, powder blue, and white. An artist from the kibbutz had drawn rainbows, stars glittering in silver, pink and white, and her favorite, a cow jumping over the moon.

In the far corner was a child-size table and chairs, where Rebecca's patients sat to draw pictures that gave her insights into the workings of their young minds. A dollhouse, large enough for the children to crawl into, faced the courtyard window, and dolls of every description lined an entire wall. Stacks of coloring books were haphazardly piled on a rickety old table.

Overflowing file cabinets occupied every available nook and cranny, and on the floor next to her desk sat years of reference books and medical journals. It was all the product of years of begging, hoarding, and bargaining—what it took to obtain possessions on a kibbutz, a place where personal possessions were discouraged.

He'll think I'm a slob. She laughed. *He'll be right.*

Rebecca closed her eyes. Robert's imminent arrival flooded her brain with memories, slashing away the years, pushing her back to another life—thirty-five years before, when she lived in Paris, the obedient daughter of devout Catholic parents, and her name was Claire Sornet.

Morgan's face materialized in Rebecca's mind.

They had met in France on the set of *The Death of Dr. Faust.* Claire was working as a seamstress and had been instructed to do a fitting for Morgan—the young actress whose beauty and talent was all anyone talked about.

Claire had walked into the dressing room, a gown over one arm, her sewing pouch tucked under the other arm.

Morgan reached for the gown, staring at Claire. "You know, you really are very beautiful."

"Thank you," Claire had said. She didn't see herself as beautiful. She liked her teal-green eyes and strawberry-blond hair but would have preferred curls instead of stick-straight hair, hated her freckles, wished her nose was not so tilted, and would have liked the dimples in her cheeks to be a little less pronounced.

Claire helped Morgan into the dress.

"Do you like being a seamstress?" Morgan had asked as Claire pinned the hem.

"I like it for now. I attend the university, and it helps pay my tuition."

"I have never met a woman who went to college before," Morgan said, her eyes huge. "What are you studying?"

"Psychology."

"Wow. Where I come from," Morgan said, "a Jewish woman is expected to marry young and have lots of babies."

"You're Jewish?" Claire had asked, enchanted by Morgan's honesty, considering that no one in the cast knew she was a Jew.

Morgan flinched and her eyes turned cold.

"No, no, please, don't take offense," Claire said. "My boyfriend Saul is Jewish."

Morgan's eyes drifted from the floor to Claire's face. At the time, Claire thought the silence interminable.

"I left my family, and my friends in Vilna to become an actress," Morgan finally said, a tear sliding down her cheek. "I'm not sorry but...I haven't had a real friend since I left home. I know this is a lot to ask but, would you consider being my friend?"

Tears flooded Rebecca's eyes as she recalled the look of sweet innocence and trust on Morgan's face. *It must have taken so much courage to reveal yourself so completely to a stranger.*

That beguiling question had changed everything. Their alliance was instantaneous and so special that Rebecca never found another friend that could even begin to take Morgan's place. *I still miss you so much.*

Thunder cracked, bringing Rebecca back to the present. She blinked several times trying to acclimate herself.

She turned her eyes toward the photograph on her desk of her eight children and her heart swelled. *Maybe not a best friend, but I had my babies.* They ranged in age from nineteen to twenty-nine. All had served their time in the army, and when needed, they had fought to defend their country.

Her children were her glory—Sabras, Israeli-born. She named her fi rst child after her best friend Morgan, despite pressure that such a name was not Hebrew and thus inappropriate. When her other daughters were born, Rebecca followed the tradition of her newly adopted religion by naming them after the prophetesses: Devora, Chanah, and Esther. Her four boys were named after great men in Jewish history: Yaakov, Abraham, Moshe, and Hillel.

Rebecca's head pounded, and her hands shook as she remembered Miriam. *Yes, my little one—my sweetest. I'm not leaving you out of the count, nor do I ever forget you.* Their second child had been a daughter—so happy, and so very sick. Rebecca and Saul watched her die from leukemia, moment by agonizing moment. To this day, Rebecca didn't know how she and Saul survived. Perhaps it was living in a country where there was so much courage, where so many had lost so much—perhaps that is what kept them sane.

Life went on, and the children continued to be born. Now their little kibbutzniks were all grown and had begun their own lives, and it was just the two of them once again.

Rebecca looked at the diplomas and plaques that adorned her walls. Her professional accomplishments were a source of great pride. She was a nationally recognized, many-times published doctor of psychology specializing in adolescent behavior.

In the past few years, her practice had taken a new course. Holocaust survivors began turning to her for help. Their nightmares, submerged for so many years as they built new lives and raised families, had returned to the surface. Rebecca committed herself to finding ways to help them cope, never letting the doubled caseload dissuade her.

Being an expert in a modality few people could claim put Rebecca in great demand. She was often absent from the kibbutz, traveling to Europe, lecturing on the psychological effects the Holocaust had on the survivors, especially those who had been in the camps as children.

Rebecca let her mind drift back to the conference held two weeks earlier in Jerusalem at the King David Hotel. She had spent three days teaching seminars, making speeches, and attending dinners with visiting dignitaries.

On the last day, Saul had arrived to take her home. When he entered the lobby, people turned to stare, his energy and strength always magnetic. He was her aged warrior with his bald head, fire-filled eyes and contagious smile.

He loaded her papers and luggage into the trunk of their five-year-old Mercedes. "We're going to Eilat for the weekend. You need some rest," Saul had said, kissing her cheek.

"That sounds fabulous." It had been so long since they visited the seaside city at the southernmost tip of Israel.

Rebecca had rested her head against the back of the seat, her eyes suddenly so heavy she could barely keep them open. She didn't know how long she slept, but when she awakened, they were driving through an area of the Negev Desert with barren valley floors and soaring stone mountains.

"We have to talk," Saul had said, his eyes leaving the road and settling on her. "You can't continue to take on the entire Holocaust problem all by yourself. I see the effect it's having on you and I can't stand by and watch while you work yourself to death." He pulled the car to the side of the road. When he faced Rebecca, his eyes were filled with tears. "I brought you here. I'm responsible for what you're doing to yourself. I'm begging you to stop."

Rebecca shook her head. "When the survivors come to me and speak about the murders of their grandparents, parents, and children, or tell me the horrors of being starved and beaten," Rebecca said, placing her hand on Saul's arm, "they unburden themselves. I see the light come back into their eyes. If I drop dead from exhaustion, so be it. Know if that happens, I died doing what Hashem, blessed be his name, intended me to do. One day I will face our God, and I will tell Him I tried to right the wrongs.

"Then, I will ask Him *why*? Why did he let this happen?"

Saul said nothing for almost a full minute. "I insist on a compromise."

Rebecca crossed her arms over her chest. "What would you have me do?"

"Learn to say no once in a while."

"Okay. No."

"Not funny," Saul said. "Please, all I'm asking is that you slow down."

"Okay. I will try." She touched Saul's face. "We have had a good life."

"It has certainly been challenging," Saul said, his eyes crinkling.

"I would do it all again, just to be near you, to share my life with you." She had begun to cry then.

He held her.

"I am so tired," Rebecca said. She took out a hanky and wiped her eyes.

"Then stop for a while."

"Could you?"

"That's not fair," Saul had said.

"I know. So, let's just accept the facts. I have my work, and you have yours. You live for today, keeping our country safe. I live in the past, reaching out my hand to people who are trying to keep from falling into the abyss. We both must keep doing what we do if our people are going to survive."

Rebecca pulled herself back to the present, pushing the memories aside. She stood and stretched. Her body ached. The long days were becoming harder and harder. She glanced down at her watch. *I've been sitting here for an entire hour, and now I'm going to be late for dinner. I must really be getting old. Young people don't sit and meander through time when they're supposed to be eating. Maybe I should straighten all of this up before Robert comes?* Then she said aloud, "Ack! I'm a mess. My office is a mess. Who cares?"

"Who cares indeed?" Saul said as he entered the room.

"You scared me to death! I thought I was alone," Rebecca said.

"Darling, if you're going to talk to yourself, you really should say kinder things. And, you're not a mess. As a matter of fact, I think you're the most beautiful woman in all of Israel," Saul said, kissing Rebecca's cheek.

"And you, sir, are as blind as a bat. But I do thank you for the compliment. Now, what are you doing here? Why aren't you at dinner?"

Saul looked at her with concern. "I was at dinner, but when you didn't show up, I became concerned. So here I am. Now tell me, what happened? It's not like you to miss a meal."

"This came today." She handed him Robert's letter to read.

Saul smiled. "He's coming. It's about time!"

The day of Robert and Jo's arrival

Saul sat in a makeshift office in a spare room off the main lobby of the kibbutz. He contemplated one of a dozen problems that needed his immediate attention, and was about to pick up the phone when there was a knock on the door.

"This came this morning through diplomatic pouch, sir," a soldier said, his eyes so innocent, looking too young to be in uniform.

Saul took the envelope. "Thank you." Saul waited until the soldier left before opening the letter.

> *Dear Saul,*
>
> *I look forward with great anticipation to seeing you and Rebecca again, meeting your family and seeing your beloved country.*
>
> *I can't explain, but I must insist that you do not meet me at the airport in Tel Aviv. I have arranged for us to have a private reunion at the U. S. Embassy. I will meet you there at midnight. I am sorry for the imposition but I will explain everything when we meet.*
>
> *Until then,*
>
> *Robert*

Saul reread the letter, tapping his fingers on the desk. Intrigued, he tucked it into his pocket. The phone rang.

He would think about this later.

15

April 1972
New York City

Robert and Jo entered the concourse at John F. Kennedy International Airport and were immediately engulfed in a frenetic sea of humanity—hundreds of voices jabbering in a symphony of dialects—African, Arab, Oriental and Indian, all jockeying for place in the interminable lines to process tickets, check luggage, and obtain boarding passes.

"There they are!" a photographer yelled as they neared the El Al counter.

Bulbs flashed.

"Mr. Osborne, are you and Miss Wells secretly married?" a reporter asked, muscling his way closer.

Robert laughed. "Will you never tire of the rumor? We are just friends."

"Then why are you going on this trip, Mr. Osborne?" another reporter shouted.

Robert turned full-face to the reporters. "I have good friends in Israel and I have been promising to visit them for years. Also, what better opportunity than to go with an incredible group such as the one assembled here today? Now, if you'll please excuse us."

Aaron pushed his way to Jo and Robert's side. "I'm sorry if it got a little out of hand."

"Don't worry about it," Robert said, shaking Aaron's hand. "I

114

saw you in action on Jo's senate campaign, so I kind of expected this."

A porter placed Jo and Robert's luggage on a makeshift steel table. Israeli security searched each suitcase while a gun-toting female member of the Israeli Defense Forces flipped through their passports. She then questioned them about their reasons for traveling to Israel, where they would be staying and with whom.

They were led through a cordoned off area and into the private El Al lounge reserved for visiting dignitaries. When they entered the room there was a sudden lull in conversation as two dozen sets of eyes turned to watch Robert and Jo.

"Go introduce your celebrity," Jo whispered to Aaron, walking away. Needing a moment to gather her thoughts, Jo moved past the group with aplomb, stopping only once to accept a kiss on the cheek from the chairman of the board of Revko.

She collapsed on a sofa and kicked off her heels. She was exhausted from work and emotionally drained from the phone call she had with her father just before leaving for the airport. She closed her eyes, reliving every dreadful word.

"How dare you make this kind of decision without consulting me first? You have no business going there. The Jews are occupying the country illegally, and your going will only give credence to their illegal trespassing. It will be the death of your career," he had screamed, his anger so intense Jo felt strangled by it.

"Have you forgotten that a very large portion of my electorate is Jewish?" Jo replied, intent that nothing he could say would ruin this trip for her.

"Let the Jews vote for you," Hans yelped, his voice quaking. "You don't have to visit. I forbid it!"

"I'm sorry you don't approve, Father." A lump had threatened to close her throat but Jo pushed aside her fear and said, "I am a grown woman, entirely capable of making my own decisions. Now, if you'll excuse me, I have a plane to catch."

There will be hell to pay, Jo thought.

"Hello, Jo."

That voice.

Her eyes flew open. Senator Andrew Taxton's aquamarine eyes were pointed at her. His black hair was silver streaked and longer than she remembered, but time had only served to improve the rugged, outdoorsman look Andy had in high school.

"May I sit down?" Andy asked.

Jo nodded, her heart thumping like a drum as she slipped her feet back into her shoes. *What is he doing here?* She had seen the list of participants going on the mission, and Andrew Taxton, the United States Senator from Texas's name had not been on it.

"Surprised to see me?" Andy asked as he settled on the sofa beside Jo. "I decided to come at the last minute."

Jo pasted a smile on her face, infuriated for being so unnerved by Andy's presence. *He means nothing to me.*

"I didn't mean to impose on your privacy. I just wanted to tell you how proud I am of you," Andy said, turning his dazzling smile on Jo.

Jo's mouth felt parched and her palms were sweating.

"The brilliant and beautiful Jotto Wells a state senator—blazing new roads—an icon for women everywhere."

"That's very kind of you to say. But I can assure you, I am no icon." Jo pushed some stray hairs from her face, her composure returning. "Congratulations on your marriage. Ashley Meriweather—very impressive." The announcement had been in all the newspapers and people were asking if *Camelot* would reappear. "I guess it's pretty safe to say your childhood dreams of living at 1600 Pennsylvania Avenue are right on target."

"It's not as idyllic as it seems," Andy said, a darkness shadowing his eyes. He had married Ashley because she would make a perfect first lady, as close to American royalty as any woman could ever be. Not loving her had seemed incidental, and during their courtship and engagement, their relationship had actually worked. But, after just a few months of marriage, he could barely stand to be in the same room with her.

"There are so many things I want to say to you."

Jo held up her hand. "Andy, please." *I don't want to hear it. Not now. Not after all this time.* "We were just two silly kids who thought we were in love."

"I never meant to hurt you."

Jo stood. Her eyes were cold.

"Can we at least be friends?" Andy pleaded.

After all the pain you caused me? Jo was seconds from losing her always-under-control temper. "Please excuse me."

Robert had been watching the animated exchange and was at Jo's side by the time she took ten steps. "What's going on?" he whispered, bewildered by the fury etched on her face.

"Nothing. Just some unfinished business," Jo said, tucking her hand in Robert's hand.

* * *

The El Al jet soared through the majestic clouds and leveled off at twenty-six thousand feet. Jo fell asleep. In her dream, she and Andy were sitting on a blanket by a sparkling lake. Andy's hands caressed her, his lips against hers. They were young, innocent, in love. Suddenly everything changed. Looming over Jo was a grotesque being, its face half Andy's likeness, the other half her father's. The image snarled something she couldn't understand and then struck her in the face with a closed fist.

A silent scream. Jo began to moan.

Robert shook her awake.

Jo touched her mouth, expecting to find blood.

Robert took Jo's hand. "Go back to sleep, child. I'm here with you. You're safe."

Jerusalem, Israel

Jo stood in the center of her room at the King David Hotel. Compared to American standards, the room was nothing special, an upholstered headboard, club chair, writing desk and a queen-sized bed. It was not the accommodations that thrilled Jo. It was the history of the place.

Built in the 1930's, the hotel had hosted such dignitaries as the dowager Empress of Persia, King Abdullah, Alfonso XIII of Spain, Emperor Haile Selassie, and King George II of Greece. During the British Mandate, the southern wing of the hotel was the administrative and military headquarters for the English. It had been blown up by the Israeli Irgun in July of 1946. Ninety-one people died in the explosion.

Jo moved to the window. The Old City of Jerusalem sparkled in the distance, white against the dark, and her heart filled. Suddenly bone weary, Jo let her clothes drop on the floor and she slipped into bed. She wished she could talk to Robert, but from the moment the plane touched down, he seemed to collapse into himself.

"Are Saul and Rebecca meeting us?" she had asked as they stood in line at customs.

"No. We won't be seeing them for a couple of days," he had replied, his demeanor leaving little room for further discourse.

Perhaps after he's had a good night's sleep he will tell me why they didn't come, Jo thought, trying to find a comfortable position on the too-firm mattress. The eight-hour time difference and the excitement of being in Israel, combined with her confrontation with Andy, made sleep impossible. She kicked off the blankets, turned on the light and stared at the wall.

The phone rang.

"Hi, beautiful. Did I wake you?"

"Aaron? Thank God you called. I can't sleep and I'm going crazy!"

"How would you like to throw on a pair of jeans, a heavy sweater, and meet me in the lobby?"

"Give me ten minutes."

When the elevator opened on the lobby level, Jo saw a dozen men and women sitting in tight little groups drinking coffee, smoking cigarettes, their conversations loud and animated. It was her first lesson in Israeli behavior—Israelis seldom sleep.

Aaron was leaning against the wall dressed in an alpaca sweater, jeans and cowboy boots, his hair messy, his eyes sparkling, looking much younger than his thirty-seven years.

Jo kissed his cheek. "I'm so glad you called."

"So, finally I get kisses," he said. "I am most definitely coming up in the world."

"You are a character, Mr. Blumenthal. Now, where are you taking me," she looked at her watch, "at three-forty-five in the morning?"

"To one of the most unique places on earth—the Wailing Wall,"

Aaron said as they moved into the chill Jerusalem night and turned right down King David Street.

"Don't you mean the Kotel?" Jo smirked.

"I'm impressed. How did you…?"

"As I recall, it's what remains of the western wall that once surrounded the ancient Temple—Jewry's holiest shrine. Your people have been coming here to pray for thousands of years." She winked, a self-satisfied look etching her face.

"You did your homework. But, we have not always been allowed to pray here. As a matter of fact, even after the creation of the State of Israel in 1948 the Arabs refused us access to the Wall. It wasn't until the Six-Day War in 1967, when Israeli parachutists broke through, that we reclaimed our right to pray at the Kotel."

Aaron took Jo's arm as they turned right onto Mamila. In the golden darkness, they meandered over the uneven stones and through the labyrinth of winding streets that comprised the Old City of Jerusalem. The scent of stone, grass, flowers, age, and wisdom swirled around Jo like pages being turned in an ancient book.

Once through the Jaffa Gate, a massive courtyard opened in front of them and Jo caught her first sight of the sixty-six foot high, one hundred and sixty-four foot long ancient stone wall, and the gleaming golden dome that sat atop it.

"Tell me about the Mosque," she said.

"I thought perhaps you'd tell me," Aaron teased.

"It's not my area of expertise." She nudged his arm. "Come on, tell me."

"It's called the El Aksa Mosque," Aaron said. "The Moslems believe the Prophet Mohammed ascended to heaven on a white stallion from that very spot."

Aaron took Jo's arm as they descended the long, irregular stone stairway that led to the massive courtyard. The moonlight reflected off the ancient Jerusalem stone, surrounding them in hues of taupe, pearl, bone, and dusty pink. Dozens of people, mostly men in uniform, milled about the square. Israeli soldiers, eyes darting from face to face, guarded the grounds.

"One side is for the men and the other for women," Aaron said.

Jo gave him a look.

"It's just how it is," said Aaron, as if that explained everything.

Jo watched as a young, machine-gun-toting Israeli soldier covered his head with a prayer shawl and walked toward the Wall. A stooped old man sat on a metal chair, swaying back and forth. Soon the soldier began to sway, as if the two men were connected by an unheard mystical rhythm. *Guns and prayers.* The incongruity sent chills down her spine.

"This is always the first place I visit when I come back to Israel. It reminds me of who I am and just how blessed I am to be able to come here," Aaron said, interrupting Jo's thoughts.

"Do you have to be a Jew to walk down?" Jo asked, a little intimidated but feeling a pull to go closer, to touch the stones, to connect with its history.

"No, as long as you follow protocol, which is really no big deal. You have to cover your head and be dressed modestly…which you are. Do you want to?"

Jo nodded.

"We Jews, who I must admit are somewhat superstitious, consider it good luck to write a prayer on a piece of paper and then place it in a crack in the Wall."

Jo dug out a scrap of paper from her purse. The words were written before she could give it a second thought: *Guide my heart toward truth.*

She folded it into a tiny square.

Aaron took a skullcap out of his pocket and placed it on his head. "I didn't have a Bar Mitzvah as a boy, but I did have one as an adult. This is the yarmulke I wore when I officially became a man. I wear it whenever I come to Israel." Aaron nodded and moved into the square.

Jo watched as Aaron accepted a *tallit* from a departing soldier, and then kissed the corners of the prayer shawl with great ceremony before placing it around his shoulders.

Seeing Aaron, a man so huge in stature, a man so self-assured and strong behaving with such reverence, brought tears to Jo's eyes as she moved to the women's side.

A wizened old lady with sad eyes sat in a makeshift little booth at the entrance. Jo took a scarf, and tied it under her chin.

A lone young woman sat on a wooden chair facing the Wall. She held a tattered prayer book in her hands, her body swayed and trembled, and she cried, a soft mournful sound that died in her throat, swallowed by the depth of her grief. Feeling like an intruder, Jo moved away.

Surrounded by silence, and the golden glow of the beckoning stones, Jo stood on tiptoe, found a tiny opening, and pushed her prayer into a crevice. She leaned her cheek against the frigid stone, overcome by a longing to connect with the energy. The glacial cold kissed her face like the warm caress from a summer sun.

She closed her eyes and soared, an eagle drifting across the universe. Ethereal music surrounded her. An angel, a beauty in gossamer white silk, suddenly appeared.

That's me, Jo thought. She looked again. *It's not me.*

The woman had Jo's face, but her hair was dark as midnight. Their bodies merged. It was the sweetest moment Jo had ever known. The woman's golden words poured over Jo, submerging her into a sea of light.

Too soon it was over. Jo's eyes flew open.

She was cold and confused.

Jo found Aaron standing on the steps at the back of the square waiting for her.

"What just happened to me?" Jo asked, expecting Aaron to have the answer to her unexplained question.

Aaron kissed her hand. "You're exhausted. When people are exhausted, their imaginations and their emotions can get the best of them. I shouldn't have brought you here at this hour."

They sat on the step. Jo leaned her head on his shoulder.

"When I put my cheek against the Wall I began to float." Jo did her best to recreate the magic. "When it was time to part, the woman kissed me on the mouth." Jo touched her lips. "Right here. I've never felt such love. When she spoke to me, her voice was so…I wish you could have heard her. She kept saying that she and I were one, and that she prayed for my life and my happiness every day.

"Right before she disappeared she said, 'We will meet again.'"
Jo watched Aaron's expression. She sensed no scorn, and continued, "Logically, I want to say it was my alter-ego trying to tell me something. My heart tells me it was something else."

"Perhaps if I tell you what happened to me the first time I came here you won't be so frightened," Aaron offered. "I was a very angry young man. I remember approaching the Wall in 1968, as if it were the enemy, thinking to myself what a joke it was that people came here to pray. Because of the Holocaust, I believed that God was deaf to a Jew's prayers. I hated him for giving us the Commandments. I had come to the Wall to tell him that. I didn't write a prayer. I didn't cover my head.

"As I was approaching the Wall, an old man walked over to me and put his hand on my arm. I pulled away. He stared at me, and then he removed his prayer shawl. Kissing the words written on the edge, he placed it over my head and shoulders. I was furious. I had no intention of giving in to his ways.

"'Your heart is cold as ice, my son,' he had said. I was mortified by the truth of his words. I didn't move. 'Is your life so tragic that you believe you have a right to close out the Almighty?' I remember the unexpected tears as I listened to his next words. 'Is this what your parents would have wanted? Will you give the Nazis the ultimate victory—your soul?'"

Aaron took a deep breath and looked at Jo, his eyes intense. "'Recite the Kaddish, the prayer for the dead, with me, Aaron, so that the God of Abraham, Isaac, and Jacob will know that you've learned to forgive.' When he said my name, I was sure I was going crazy. Then the old man whispered in my ear, 'Remember the words of Isaiah. When the soul is sick, we begin to believe that evil is good and good is evil, that darkness is light and light is darkness. We take bitter for sweet and sweet for bitter. You must not live your life like this, my son. Come now. Come and pray the words of our ancestors.'"

Aaron turned his face away so Jo would not see his tears. They sat that way for a long time. "And I did, Jo," Aaron said finally. "I walked to that Wall, and just like you, the generations reached out and touched my heart. I had no book, but I had the vision of my father and mother, and they helped me to remember the words."

Jo took his hand. "Thank you for trusting me."

"Walk with me," Aaron said, putting his arm around Jo.

Day was breaking, the sky turning a resplendent pink and gold. The trees, all shades of green and blue pointed their branches toward the sky. The sounds of everyday life echoed throughout the Old City, footsteps on the pavement, shutters opening, donkeys baying, children laughing, pots clanging.

"The old man gave me back my faith, and from that day on, everything became clearer to me." Aaron stopped and turned his eyes toward Jo.

The kiss lasted longer than he had intended, longer than it should have.

The voices began to scream in Aaron's head as tidal waves of guilt washed over him. He knew she was a *shiksa*, a gentile. He could never have her. Using every ounce of his willpower, he pulled away.

"You're my adorable little *shiksa*, and if things were different, I would throw my hat in the ring."

"I wouldn't put up much of a fight, Aaron Blumenthal...not much of a fight at all." Jo tucked her arm through his and they walked on in silence.

16

Midnight
Tel Aviv

Rebecca and Saul sat in Ambassador Walworth Barbour's private living room at the United States Embassy. It was tastefully furnished with upholstered furniture in broad navy blue stripes on a white background. There were fresh red roses in vases and a game table with a chess set, the match obviously left while in progress. Hanging on the walls were paintings by the American watercolorists Thomas Eakins and Winslow Homer. A portable bar sat against the wall.

"May I bring you something to drink?" asked Ben, the ambassador's assistant, a man with thick glasses and a brush cut. He switched on a lamp.

"Some coffee, please," Rebecca said, her knees bouncing up and down as she scanned the day-old newspaper.

"Nothing for me," Saul said, his gentle, sun-creased face worried. "Rebecca, are you all right?"

"I just don't want to fall apart when I see him." Rebecca folded the paper and walked to the window. "The plane landed two hours ago. What's taking him so long?"

Saul lit his fourth cigarette in less than half an hour. He was imagining himself as Robert's tour guide. Showing him Tel Aviv, Jerusalem, Haifa, cities where Jewish children lived and learned without the threat of being gassed—a Jewish homeland that would have been a safe haven for Morgan, and the millions of Jews who perished in the Holocaust.

The door pushed open.

Rebecca ran into Robert's arms. "My God, my dear God, how I've dreamt of this day," she wept, burying her face against his chest.

Saul hung back, fighting his own tears as a lifetime of memories rose to the surface, and a closed door into his heart cracked open.

Rebecca regained control and moved from Robert's embrace.

"It's so good to see you," Saul said, extending his hand. Robert laughed, ignored the hand, and embraced him.

"You must be exhausted," Rebecca said, pulling Robert to the sofa.

Robert pulled off his tie, and stuffed it in the pocket of his suit jacket. "Rebecca." He said softly, and smiled. "The name fits you so well." He took her hand. "The years have been good to you. You're still beautiful."

Rebecca smirked. "I guess the years haven't been so good for your eyesight."

"Don't waste your time with compliments," Saul said. "She won't believe a word."

"I'm well-acquainted with the mirror, and we are not on good terms these days. So, both of you can save your breath," she chided.

The men laughed.

"How was the flight?" Saul asked, pulling over a chair.

"Not bad. But, arriving in Tel Aviv, driving to Jerusalem, and then turning around and coming back to Tel Aviv—it's been a long day. I'll explain why in a little while. First, I could really use a cup of coffee." Robert's mind was churning, a thousand thoughts and feelings threatening to overtake him. He poured from the carafe on the coffee table, added three sugars and cream, stalling for time.

"When the proclamation came," Robert said, after taking a few sips, "and you finally had your own country, how I worried. Your letters—the fighting—I don't know how you found the courage to stay."

"Courage? Who had courage?" Rebecca said. "I was terrified. One day I'm safe and living in Paris," she kicked off her shoes and tucked her feet under her, "and the next thing I know, I'm aiming a gun at another human being and pulling the trigger."

"She's a great marksman, I might add." Saul winked at Rebecca.

"Did I have a choice? With two small children, it took all of us fighting to protect the kibbutz." Rebecca pulled in her shoulders and appeared to shrink with the memories.

"We had spent years turning the flooded, malaria-filled swamps into lush farmland, and then the Arabs came and set our crops on fire. It was the only time I considered leaving Israel and Saul. Not because of the burning fields—fields can be replanted." Rebecca's eyes turned dark. She turned her eyes toward Saul.

"Dozens of our friends were killed," Saul said. "They were people who managed to cheat death in the concentration camps, only to be cut down by the Arabs. Their loss was excruciating."

"In fairness, we had our glorious moments too," Rebecca interjected, "harvesting our first crops, sitting on the sweet-smelling grass at sunset watching a concert musicale. We even got to see Arturo Toscanini conduct the Israeli Philharmonic Orchestra."

"Unfortunately," Saul said, "peace never seems to last long. And I'm worried."

"Maybe you're just being overly pessimistic?" Robert said, easy in the conversation, as if a lifetime hadn't passed.

Saul shook his head. "The world now knows that Jews can fight. And that pisses off a lot of people."

"Let them be pissed," Rebecca said, "they'll never drive us out."

"See, she hasn't changed one bit. Still says exactly what she thinks." The adoration in Saul's eyes reflected like the sun against the sea.

"I hear you say exactly what you think as well," Robert added. "I was told you're one of the toughest negotiators the Americans ever dealt with." Robert crossed his arms over his chest and smiled.

"Ack," Saul said, waving his hand. "David Ben Gurion and Golda Meir are tough negotiators. Me, I'm just an idealist with a big mouth."

"Morgan would be so proud." Robert's voice caught.

Saul stood and began to pace. "I spent hundreds of nights wading into the Mediterranean Sea, helping new immigrants to shore. Each time I reached for a hand, I prayed it would be Morgan's hand."

Rebecca swallowed hard. "I still miss her."

"As do I," Robert said. After a brief silence, he continued, "I asked to meet you here tonight, instead of at the airport, because I have something to tell you. You'd better sit down, Saul." Robert took a deep breath. *God, give me the strength.* "Morgan had a child. She's come with me to Israel."

Rebecca shook her head, her eyes wild. "What are you talking about?"

Robert spent the next thirty minutes telling them about meeting Jo, hiring the detective, and what the detective had found. He finished by saying, "Do you remember the press conference I held, begging the Germans to release Morgan?

They both nodded.

"It was probably the biggest mistake I ever made. I brought her name to the attention of the Nazis. They must have discovered she was a Jew and—"

"You were trying to save her," Rebecca offered.

Robert shook his head. "When the Polish government sent that telex in 1939," Robert's heart ached at the memory, "saying that Morgan had died from complications of pneumonia, I had no reason to doubt it. Now I know it was bullshit. They must have captured her and God knows what happened after that. What I can tell you is that Jo was not even born until 1940."

"I always wondered why Morgan's name wasn't…"

"Saul!" Rebecca scolded.

"Wasn't what?" Robert's eyes blazed.

Saul took a deep breath. "The Germans kept impeccable records of the people they murdered. I've seen the lists. Morgan's name was not on any of them."

Robert stared at Saul. "Are you suggesting she could still be alive?"

"No. I'm not saying that. What I'm saying is the detective you hired might have had to pull some strings, but given the reasons, he would have been given access to those same lists." Saul's voice turned angry. "Unless someone paid him not to look?"

Robert's jaw clenched. "I don't understand. If the investigator was paid off, then why would he implicate both Hans and Otto? He went so far as to tell me Otto Milch bragged about being with the SS when he lived in Bolivia. Why would he do that?"

Saul shrugged. "He closed the door on you ever having proof of Jo's parentage. Still, he had to give you something, just enough to satisfy you and keep you from looking further."

Rebecca stood. "Morgan loved you, Robert. She would never be with another man. That can only mean one thing." Her lips quivered. "If Hans Wells is Jo's father, than he must have taken Morgan by force." She made a fist and shook it in the air. "He must be punished!"

"I want to get the bastard, too. But my number one priority is to protect Jo," Robert said. "I don't want her hurt."

"Let's all calm down," Saul said. "This is too complex for us to handle by ourselves." Saul stuffed his hands in his pockets. "I think I know someone who can help us. I will call him in the morning."

Part 4

17

1972
Miami Beach, Florida

Kurt Blome, Alexander Lippisch, Hans Wells, and Otto Milch huddled around a marble and glass dining table in their suite at the landmark Eden Roc Hotel at 45th Street and Collins Avenue. They sipped Stoli vodka from Waterford crystal glasses and munched on Beluga caviar.

"Gentleman, I have a theory I would like to extrapolate with you," Lippisch said. In his early sixties with barely a wrinkle on his face, he wore an expensive hand-sewn suit and alligator shoes. "Taxton has spent the past several months campaigning for the president. Now that Nixon has been reelected, we know Taxton is waiting for his reward—a seat on the powerful Appropriations Committee. Once that happens, he will have to begin strategizing and positioning himself for his own run at the presidency in four years.

"So, I asked myself, why at such a critical junction in his life, would he choose to go on a mission to Palestine?" Lippisch didn't recognize the state of Israel and wouldn't say the name. "It makes no sense unless…" he let the words dangle for a few moments, "the senator heard Jotto was going and decided to take this opportunity to try and rekindle the relationship." His eyes turned sinister.

Blome smiled, the crease between his eyes deepened. Dressed in a faded Lacoste shirt, khaki pants, and loafers without socks, his belly bulged and his jowls hung like a bulldog. "Wouldn't that be the answer to our dreams?"

Hans was territorial when it came to his daughter and he resented these men talking about her as if they had any influence on Jotto's life. He swallowed hard. "The relationship took place when they were children. It is ridiculous to assume they still have any feelings for each other."

Lippisch stared at Hans, his eyes fierce. "Otto's and your very unique talents are what brought you into the inner-circle of the Reich." He turned his face toward Otto. "If Jo has any reservations as to a renewal of their relationship, we expect you to use those talents to change her mind."

Hans's nostrils flared, and blood rushed to his head. He would not be told what to do. "This entire conversation is superfluous." He bored his eyes into Lippisch's. "Taxton is a married man!"

Lippisch curled his lips. "Not for long. He's about to become a widower."

Silence settled over the men. Hans and Otto looked at each other.

Lippisch studied his manicured nails. "Alex and I paid Anderson Taxton a little visit a few days ago. We showed him copies of a letter we have."

Blome stood, his eyes dancing. "A letter so damning, if it fell into the wrong hands, it would derail his son's march to the White House."

"What letter? What are you talking about?" Hans's eyes bulged. He was furious. How dare they not consult me first?

"Taxton was a very close friend of Henry Ford," Blome said.

"So what?" Hans snapped, his blue eyes glazed, curious but so furious he could hardly breathe.

"You're going to love this." Blome smiled at Hans. "Mr. Henry Ford and the Fuhrer were also very good friends. Such good friends that the Fuhrer kept a portrait of Ford on the wall next to his desk."

"Again, what does that have to do with Anderson Taxton?" Hans was growing impatient.

"Ford poured hundreds of thousands of dollars into the Reich's coffers. He also opened an automobile factory in Berlin for the Fuhrer. He produced four-wheel-drive vehicles that could travel over terrain no standard truck could even think about traversing. The letter we have is from Ford to the Fuhrer. It named Anderson Taxton as one of the investors in the plant," Blome said.

"And how did you happen to get this letter?" *Done behind my fucking back!* Hans wiped the perspiration from his face with a linen handkerchief and shifted in his seat.

"That's not important!" Lippisch snapped.

"I can control Jotto," Otto interjected, determined to assert himself, and come out from his brother-in-law's shadow. "But, how will you get to Taxton?"

"You don't need to worry about that. Senator Taxton listens to his father, and as of a few days ago, the father listens to us." Lippisch smirked.

"We have another problem you may not be aware of," Hans said, determined to reestablish his dominance in the meeting. "Osborne has been digging around, asking questions about Jotto and about my family. I paid off the detective he hired, but if he goes to the Israelis for help, we could…"

"Don't worry about Osborne." Lippisch smiled. "When we have a problem, we do what we always do—we eliminate it!"

Hans could not help but smile. He wanted Osborne out of Jotto's life. It was the only way he could maintain control of her, and be certain that his secret would remain safe.

Soon it will be over.

Then it can begin.

The Tamiami Trail towards Naples, Florida

Hans was behind the wheel of the Mercedes as it sped across the Everglades through the dark, moonless night. Otto was asleep in the passenger seat, his head bobbing on his chest. The silence and hum of the engine transported Hans back in time.

It was February, 1939. Hitler had summoned him to Berlin. He could still picture the room where they had met: an enormous rosewood table, at each seat a printed name card, a glass of water, a notepad, and pencils. The walls were covered in rosewood panels and a crystal chandelier hung from the fifteen-foot ceiling.

Standing in small groups were two dozen of Germany's most famous scientists—some Hans knew personally, others he only recognized.

The door opened. Hermann Goering and Heinrich Himmler walked in.

The silence was absolute as they all saluted.

Goering, the swashbuckling, blue-blooded Commander-in Chief of the Luftwaffe, the German Air Force, walked to the head of the table. He leaned forward and smiled, an intimate gesture—a human gesture—believed only by fools. "Gentlemen, if you will please be seated."

Himmler, head of the Gestapo, stood in the background, a sinister smirk on his face.

"I should not want to leave any doubt, gentleman, as to the aim of today's meeting," Goering had said. "We have not come together merely to talk, but to change the history of the world."

Himmler stepped forward then, his small stature looming, the intensity in his eyes ferocious as a mad dog. "Lebensborn, Fountain of Life." The word dangled in the air as recognition dawned. "Our goal is a Master Race. Young unmarried Aryan girls mate with our soldiers and are brought to maternity homes to gift Germany with their children—the future soldiers of the Reich." He smiled. "This is a great honor—the greatest gift of all!"

The door flew open. Hitler strutted into the room. His bloodshot eyes bulged—his magnetism a lightning bolt—a power supreme with his signature mustache, slicked back hair and beady eyes.

They stood. Arms outstretched.

Hans had wanted to savor the moment—the most glorious moment of his life.

"Gentleman," the Fuhrer said, "In the course of my life I have very often been a prophet, and have usually been ridiculed for it. During the time of my struggle for power, it was in the first instance, the Jewish race, which only received my prophecies with laughter when I said that I would one day take over the leadership of the State, and with it that of the whole nation, and that I would then among many other things settle the Jewish problem. Their laughter was uproarious, but I think that for some time now they have been laughing on the other side of their face." Hitler had placed his hands behind his back and leaned forward.

"Today I will once more be a prophet: if the international Jewish financiers in and outside Europe should succeed in plunging the nations once more into a world war, then the result will not be the Bolshevization of the earth, and thus the victory of Jewry, but the annihilation of the Jewish race in Europe!

"A new era has begun, comrades. You will be the architects of that future. It will be your duty to build a thousand-year Reich for the new German empire." He balled his fist and struck his chest, like an exclamation mark at the end of a sentence. "I have personally selected each of you." Hitler made eye contact with each man. As a recipient of that glance, Hans tasted immortality. He became the vision, the path for his life set, he was forever changed.

"Never doubt. We will reign supreme. With patience and foresight, Germany will rule the world!" Hitler smiled. "It begins now. It begins with you, the great minds of Germany. I am charging you with a sacred mission." Hitler paused. The only sounds in the room were the clicking of the wall clock.

"You will select women of superior breeding, intelligence, and talent. You will impregnate them. These children, the most outstanding, will be chosen and trained with one goal in mind—world domination and the continuation of our ideals." Hitler's face beamed.

"These children, your children, will be our future. The future of the world." He had closed his eyes. "We will infiltrate their countries. I can see it now—in the United States, in South America, in Africa, in the Middle East—we will rule—presidents, prime ministers, saviors all—the world will be ours." His eyes had flown open. His voice thundered. "We will take power! We will rule! And no one will know until it's too late!" Hitler laughed.

"As I declared in *Mein Kampf,* the political opinion of the masses represents nothing but the final result of an incredibly tenacious and thorough manipulation of the mind and soul." Hitler stood ramrod straight. His eyes glazed.

Hans was enthralled. If the scheme was pure madness, he could not see it. If the man standing in front of him was out of touch with reality, and a little mad, so be it. Every great man in history had been, at the very least, a little insane.

Hitler had posed with one hand on his hip and the other holding his lapel. "All of Germany is depending on you. Heil Hitler!" The Fuhrer raised his arm, turned, and walked from the room.

The city lights of Naples brought Hans back to the present. *I made a vow, to you, my Fuhrer. I will keep that vow. We will prevail!*

18

Jerusalem
The King David Hotel

The morning sky glowed aquamarine, pink, white, and red as breezes murmured through the open window of Jo's suite. She stirred, threw off the covers, and stretched. She had been dreaming about Aaron—dreaming about the kiss.

The phone rang. She fumbled for it.

"Did I wake you?"

Jo sat up. "Aaron?"

"I was expecting to see you at breakfast."

Jo pushed the hair from her eyes. "What time is it?"

"Almost nine."

"I'll be right down."

* * *

Jo took an apple from the basket on the front desk and stuffed it into her purse. Dressed in beige slacks, a white turtleneck and blue blazer, she laughed aloud when she realized she was the first person on the bus. She settled in a seat near the back.

"Good morning."

Andy was standing in the aisle, his hair disheveled, and his eyes mischievous. He took the seat beside her. "You look beautiful."

"Thank you." Jo could feel herself blush. *Don't you dare let his flattery get to you.*

People began to board the bus, jetlag written on their sleep-deprived faces. Jo watched as Robert approached, his face even more drawn than the others, as if he had not slept at all.

Jo smiled. Robert responded by crossing his arms across his chest and glaring at Andy. "Excuse me, Senator, but I believe you're in the wrong seat," Robert said, sounding more like a protective father than a friend.

Jo was surprised by the angered tone of Robert's voice. She cringed.

Andy stood, his embarrassment obvious. "I am so sorry, Mr. Osborne. I certainly did not mean to intrude. If you'll excuse me."

"Robert Osborne, that was so rude," Jo whispered as Robert tucked himself into the seat.

"Perhaps," Robert said, "but a married man shouldn't look at a woman the way he looks at you."

"If I wanted a chaperone, I would have brought my father," Jo snapped, sorry the minute the words left her mouth.

Robert's face fell. "I guess I deserved that."

Jo took his hand. "No, you didn't. I'm just tired."

"Perhaps one day you'll tell me what went on between you and the senator."

Jo shrugged. "It's not a big deal. He was my first boyfriend. I haven't seen him since high school. Now tell me, did you speak to Saul and Rebecca?"

"I did."

"And?"

"We'll be seeing them at their kibbutz. Rebecca wanted me to—"

"Good afternoon," Aaron said from a microphone at the front of the bus. "Welcome to Israel, the land of milk and honey."

The sound of Aaron's voice startled Jo. She craned her neck to see him and then fell back into the seat. Her heart pounded. It was all so disconcerting, seeing Andy after so many years, and the emotions she was feeling towards Aaron. She closed her eyes and listened.

"Over the next several days we're going to do our best to introduce you to this country and her people, so that when you return to the United States you'll have a fuller understanding of exactly who and what Israel stands for," Aaron said, his enthusiasm pouring into every word.

"You will be meeting with officials from the Israeli government, and we hope you will have open and honest discourse. It is not our intention to bombard you with political propaganda. We are simply going to show you the country: her heart and her soul. Then you can draw your own conclusions. Of course, in the end we hope you will have fallen in love with her."

Polite laughter followed.

"A hundred million Arabs surround this land, and they have vowed not to rest until every Jew has been pushed into the sea." Aaron's tone grew serious. "Those threats have turned the Israeli soldier into the fiercest fighter on earth. This country is small, no larger than Rhode Island, and Israel's soldiers, her sons and daughters, know how vulnerable their families are. The Israelis know if their front lines are ever breached the Arabs will be at their mothers' doorsteps within hours. So they fight, not to conquer, but to survive.

"Today," he continued, "we'll be traveling into the Judean Desert on our way to the ancient city of Beer Sheva. In Beer Sheva, we will be hosted by representatives from Ben Gurion University. From there, we will check into the Moriah Hotel and go for a swim in the Dead Sea, the lowest spot on earth at thirteen-hundred feet below sea level. People come from all over the world to float in its healing waters. I think you'll find it to be quite an experience."

As the bus pulled away from the curb, Aaron began walking up and down the aisles, shaking hands and making small talk. When he came to Jo and Robert, he nodded politely.

"I hope you both slept well," Aaron said.

Jo laughed. "Are we talking quality or quantity?"

Aaron's eyes lingered on Jo. "Quantity always works for me in the end." He winked and walked back to the front of the bus.

Aaron picked up the microphone. "May I have your attention, please?" He waited for silence. "It's my distinct honor to introduce Major General Menachem Perlman. He will be our guide, companion, and expert on both the Jewish and the Christian sides of Israel. Menachem, if you please?"

Moriah Dead Sea Hotel

Andy watched as Jo collected her room key. His mind reeled. Being so close to her brought back the memories, the innocence of a relationship that had held such promise.

He knew he was not the same man Jo had loved, and she too had changed. The feelings he once held for her were still there, dormant but hungry to be released. He wasn't sure what he expected or even hoped would happen—coming here to Israel, but Jo being on the trip was the catalyst that pushed him to accept the invitation from the United Jewish Appeal.

Andy understood on every level that coming to Israel was good for his career, but not because he cared in the least about its people or its policies. In fact, so far he felt like he was on a mind-bending, propaganda-spewing odyssey.

He had been raised to see the Jews as money grubbing, inferior human beings, who denied Christ's birth and were out to control the world. Regardless of his own personal abhorrence for the Jews, he could not ignore the significance of the only democracy in the Middle East. He needed the American Jewish press, their money, and votes if he was going to win the presidency in four years.

He followed Jo into the elevator. She nodded her head and smiled. Andy saw it as an opening.

"How about climbing Masada with me in the morning?"

Jo looked hard at Andy. "I'm going to take the cable car up."

"And miss all the fun of a climb at 3:00 am?" He put his hand on her arm. "Come on, it will be fun."

His touch burned. She pulled away. "No, thank you."

Galilee toward Nazareth
The next day

"This is where Jesus grew up," Major General Perlman said from the front of the moving bus as the lush green mountains of Tabor and Meron lay off in the distance.

"I can't believe I'm finally going to meet Saul and Rebecca," Jo whispered.

Robert smiled but said nothing.

Jo tugged on her hair. "Are you mad at me?" She was fearful that her cross words about Robert acting like her father had ruptured their friendship.

"No, silly girl. I am just preoccupied." Robert took her hand. "A lot of memories have surfaced. I am just trying to deal with them." Robert kissed her cheek.

* * *

It was late afternoon when the bus pulled into the parking lot of the kibbutz hotel, Ayelet Haba-ah. Dozens of kibbutzniks were gathered, all dressed in shorts and t-shirts. Rebecca and Saul concealed themselves in back so they could have a chance to see Jo before they actually met her.

"There she is. Oh my God!" Rebecca's hand flew to her mouth and her eyes flooded with tears. "It's like seeing a ghost." She grabbed Saul's hand. "I'm going to scare her to death if I'm crying like a blubbering idiot when we meet." Rebecca wiggled her fingers at Saul. "Please, your handkerchief."

Saul tightened his grip on Rebecca's arm. "Here they come. Smile."

Rebecca put her arms around Jo. She held her too long—battling the memories, holding back the tears.

"Let me look at you," Rebecca said, finally releasing Jo. "You are so beautiful. Now come along. My children haven't stopped talking about finally getting to meet the famous Robert Osborne."

* * *

The Lapinsky children gathered in the garden outside Rebecca and Saul's two-story communal apartment building. The fragrance of chrysanthemums, anemone, poppy, and mustard plants drifted in the air, and the sky twinkled. Noisy conversation, clinking glasses, and laughter filled the night.

Robert spent time with each of Saul and Rebecca's children, being charming, answering questions about his profession, and his fame, and what it was like living in America. He enjoyed every moment but was suddenly exhausted from the onslaught of too many emotions, melancholy seeping in like a rising tide.

"I'm tired. I'll see all of you tomorrow," Robert said, kissing and shaking hands.

His departure sparked the end of the evening.

* * *

Robert walked along the pebble path of the kibbutz, tucking his hands into his pockets against the cool mountain air. He ached for Morgan and his head throbbed as his thoughts drifted back to the first time he met her.

He had traveled from Paris to Eastern Europe, searching for his next leading lady. On a stop in Vilna, Poland, his friend Jacob Gold took him to the Reduta Theatre to see Morgan perform.

The stage set for Macbeth had been a simple garden-trellised latticework with climbing ivy, silken rosebuds, and potted trees. Jacob had leaned close to Robert's ear. "That's her. The one with the dark hair."

Morgan was the tallest woman on the stage, and Robert had thought she was thin enough to approach a scale smiling. He remembered succinctly how fascinated he was by the way the light captured Morgan's rich blue-black hair, all curls and confusion cascading to her shoulders, framing her face. Her lips were full; her complexion snow white, and her indigo eyes slanted exotically. Robert remembered how his cheeks had burned with desire. When the curtain fell after a standing ovation, he raised an eyebrow and looked at Jacob. "Take me to her."

Morgan stood in a corner, surrounded by a jubilant cast. Her face turned crimson as a path opened in front of her to allow Jacob and Robert to approach. Robert reached for Morgan's hand and brought it to his lips. He stared into her eyes, holding her hand for four or five heartbeats before he spoke.

"I've seen hundreds of young actresses perform, but I've never seen one better than you."

The color drained from Morgan's face. Robert caught her as she collapsed. A cast member passed smelling salts under her nose. Morgan gasped and her eyes jerked open. She pulled away from Robert.

"I'm so sorry. That's never happened to me before. I guess I should have eaten something before the performance."

"Rule number one, a star never goes on stage with an empty stomach." He smiled at the memory. He had seen her talent and foresaw that she would become a great star. What he had not seen that night was that her presence in his life would change everything. She would teach him to love another more than he loved himself. She would teach him to honor every moment of their journey together.

Saul moved from the shadows. "Are you all right?"

Pulled back to the present, Robert straightened his back, smoothed his hair, and nodded.

They walked in silence, over bridges and down a winding path until they reached Rebecca's office.

"I'm sorry we don't have a more appropriate place for this meeting," Saul said. "kibbutz living doesn't have many amenities. When I want to pretend I'm important I have to go to Jerusalem or Tel Aviv, because here I'm just another kibbutznik."

Strain was on both their faces as Saul flipped on the lights.

"You can never accuse my wife of orderliness, but rest assured if we moved even one thing, she'd know." Saul moved toward the door. "Make yourself at home. I'll be back in a few minutes."

Robert tried to imagine what would happen next. He paced. He sat. He stood. He tried closing his eyes and reciting poetry. Nothing worked. He was too nervous, too excited, and too frightened by what he might hear.

Saul walked into the room ten minutes later with Natan Savronesky, a scholarly looking man in his mid-thirties, with short hair, thick glasses, and a slouch.

He looks more like a literature professor than a Nazi hunter. Robert forced a smile.

After introductions, Natan said, "I've located the investigator assigned to your case here in Israel. His name is Irving Aronowitz. He found out some very interesting things—things omitted from the reports you received from the American investigative team."

"Jesus Christ!" Robert said.

Natan pursed his lips "Does the name Jacob Gold mean anything to you?"

Robert's pulse quickened. He hadn't thought about Jacob in years and now twice in one night. "I stayed at his home in Vilna when I first met Morgan. He went on to become a doctor. But what does Jacob have to do with this?"

"He was a prisoner at the Dachau death camp."

"And?" Robert needed the information hard and fast, his fear so strong it took everything in his power not to run from the room.

"Survivors interviewed said the doctor hid and cared for a very sick young woman that fit Morgan's description."

Robert began to tremble. Saul touched his arm. "You must remain calm. We don't want you. . ."

Robert drilled his eyes into Natan. "What was wrong with my wife?"

"Physical complications from childbirth." Natan fumbled with his notebook.

Robert tried to clear his head. *So many words. What is he saying?* Then it all came together like a lightning bolt striking steel. "Are you telling me you think my wife is alive?"

"Yes. I think she may be. Gold disappeared after the liberation. No records have been found on either one of them, and that could mean they are both still alive."

"Oh my God." Robert blinked several times. *Is this really happening?* He envisioned Morgan, vital, spirited, his lover and companion. "If she were still alive she would have contacted me!" Robert pulled out a cigarette with shaking fingers.

"We have to consider the possibility she's living in a place where she is unable to communicate with the outside world," Saul offered.

"Or that she is damaged and wants to spare you the agony of that," Natan said.

Robert snarled, stepping towards Natan.

"Don't shoot the messenger," Natan said softly.

"If Morgan is still alive, it's obvious that Doctor Wells and his comrades do not want you to find her," Saul said, handing Robert an ashtray. "That's why you were passed misinformation."

"And that means the Nazis know you have been snooping around," Natan said. "I'll arrange for a bodyguard."

"This is insane." Robert looked from one man to the other. "Do you actually think I'm afraid of those bastards?"

Natan stared at Robert. "If you're not, then you're a fool." His face went pale. "I was seven years-old on the day the Nazis came to our home. I hid behind a tree and watched them tear my baby brother, only three months old, from my mother's arms and smash his head against a brick wall. Then they raped and shot my blessed mother. I ran away and lived in the forest, surviving on garbage the Nazis left behind."

Robert felt the blood drain from his face. He had been a soldier, fought in the war, killed Germans—his motivation revenge. Afterwards, he had seen pictures of the atrocities, seen the newsreels of the liberation of the camps. This was somehow very different. It was the look on Natan's face. Beneath the ice-cold scorn that emanated from the man, Robert could see and feel that little boy's agony. He tried to imagine the strength it must have taken for a seven year-old boy to witness such a horror and then to go on living. "I don't know what to say. I'm so very sorry."

Natan nodded. "Today, I track Nazis. That's what I do. But, for you, Mr. Robert Osborne, I will make an exception. I will hunt for your wife. And you have my word, if she is alive, I will find her."

"Thank you," Robert said.

Natan's face softened. "This is going to take time. You go about your life and forget about everything for a while. When I find out anything, I will contact Saul. He'll keep you informed." Natan stood.

Robert shook his head. "I'm sorry, but that's not acceptable. This is my problem and my wife. I want you to contact me."

Natan scratched his face, his mouth set in a stubborn scowl. "That is not how I work."

Saul put his arm around Robert. "Natan is used to doing things his own way. It's time to let go, my friend. It's time to let other people help you."

19

Rutgers University

Professor Alexander Lippisch sat in his tiny office shuffling through papers when the phone on his desk rang. He picked it up, listened, and said, "Once I have definitive proof, the rest of the money will be delivered."

The Nazi hung up and dialed a number in Florida.

Doctor Hans Wells picked it up on the first ring.

"It's done," Lippisch said.

Hans smiled at his brother-in law.

Otto returned the smile with his arm outstretched. "Heil Hitler."

Kibbutz hotel, Ayelet Haba-ah
Israel

Aaron lay in a fetal position, the covers over his head, in a deep, dreamless sleep. A persistent knocking awakened him. The glowing clock on the night table read five o'clock in the morning. He switched on a light.

"I'm coming, I'm coming," Aaron shouted as he pulled on his robe and yanked open the door.

A young man with huge black eyes and a heavy beard stood on the threshold. "I'm sorry to awaken you, Mr. Blumenthal. There's an urgent call from the United States."

They jogged down a narrow path and up a small hill to the main office of the kibbutz. The lights were blazing and a young girl stood behind the counter holding the telephone. She handed it to Aaron.

"Aaron, is that you?"

Aaron recognized the voice of his administrative assistant. "Steve, do you know what time it is here? This better be damn important."

"I'm afraid it is, sir. Senator Taxton's wife was killed in an automobile accident about five hours ago."

"Holy shit. What happened?" Aaron held the receiver in one hand and motioned for a cigarette with the other. The girl lit one and handed it to him.

"She was returning home from her parent's estate when she apparently lost control of the car. It went off the side of a mountain."

"And I'm supposed to tell the senator?"

"I'm afraid so."

"Shit."

"President Nixon is friends with the Merewethers—Senator Taxton's in-laws. On his orders, an Air Force jet is on its way to you from England. It should arrive at the Lod airport in about three hours."

Aaron moved into the darkness, his head bent, his body tense. He had no idea of the senator's religious beliefs, but hoped the man had faith. It would make things easier. He put his hands in his pockets and walked a little faster.

Aaron thought about his own faith. It had come to him later in life and so perhaps that made it more special. Still, he continually had to battle the skeptical side of his personality, the side that was born the day his parents left him as a young boy in the home of strangers.

His adopted Christian family schooled him to believe that the soul survived past the loss of its physical body. He thanked God for that similarity in all the religions. It was what had kept him sane when his family perished in the Holocaust. As for the rest, the rules, the obligations that Judaism and all the other religions of the world required of their followers—too much had happened in Aaron's life for him to believe without reservation. Yet, there was one fundamental belief he lived by and it had served him well: it is not what happens to a person in their life, but how they handle what happens that matters.

Moments later Aaron found himself in front on the Senator's hotel room door. He shivered, put his fist to the door, and knocked.

"Who is it?" an annoyed voice called.

"It's Aaron Blumenthal. I'm sorry to disturb you, but…"

Andy stood in the doorway. The look on Aaron's face paralyzed him with fear. "What's wrong? What happened?" Andy backed away.

"I'm so sorry. There's been a terrible accident. Your wife is…" Aaron had to say the words. "She's dead."

"That's ridiculous." Andy slashed the air with his hand, "I talked to Ashley this afternoon. She was fine."

Aaron told Andy what he knew.

A tear slipped down the senator's face. "My God. Her parents. She was their only child. This is going to kill them." Andy dropped his head to his chest. "I have to get home."

"An Air Force jet is on its way."

Andy looked around the room. He needed to pack, to get dressed, and to move. But he felt as if his feet were nailed to the floor. He fumbled with the buttons on his pajamas.

"If you'd like, I could have someone come in to pack for you," Aaron offered.

"No. No. It's okay. I just need a few minutes."

"I'll wait outside."

* * *

Andy sat huddled against the window in the dimly lit car. It had been two hours since the horrific news of his wife's accident. In that time, he had called the States and spoken to his in-laws, his office, and his parents. His mother had been particularly distraught and had kept Andy on the phone for almost half an hour.

Now that he was alone the memories came, like a window into the past—Ashley, blond hair falling into her sparkling eyes, the dimple in her left cheek when she smiled, the way she slipped her hand in his whenever they walked into a crowded room. *I never really loved you enough. You knew that. I'm sorry. I will miss you.*

Aaron watched as the car pulled away and then he turned down the path on his left. It was only seven in the morning, but the kibbutz was in full swing. A young boy ran by chasing his dog, three teenaged girls, their hands full of books, chatted and giggled, a lawn mower sounded in the distance—all of it lost on Aaron as he looked for room number twelve. He found it at the end of the hallway. He knocked.

"What a nice surprise," Jo said. She was dressed in shorts and a t-shirt, her hair tied back in a ponytail. She wore no make-up.

Aaron's breath caught in his throat.

"Don't tell me," Jo said, pulling him into the room. "You've decided you can't live without me." The teasing fell away when Jo noted the expression on Aaron's face. "What's wrong?"

"I have some bad news. Senator Taxton's wife was killed in an automobile accident last night."

"Oh my God!" Jo collapsed on the bed. "That's horrible. Where is Andy?"

"On his way to Lod Airport. President Nixon arranged for his flight home."

"What are we going to do?" Jo pulled in her knees and stared at Aaron.

"Andy made me promise I wouldn't let this interfere with the mission."

"My God, Aaron, are you the one who had to tell him?"

He nodded. "It's been a horrendous night."

"I'm so sorry." Jo could see the strain etched on his face. She reached for his hand. "Come on. Let's go get a cup of coffee."

Four days later
Jerusalem

The bus with the delegation from the United States headed north on Hayim Hazaz Boulevard and took a sharp left into Ruppin Road. At the top of the hill sat the Israeli Parliament, the Knesset.

The Major General cleared his throat. "Many of you are politicians, and I would not think to give you a lecture on the politics of my country. What I would like to give you, in as few words as possible, is an overview of the legislative branch of the Israeli government. The Knesset enacts our laws, elects the prime minister, and supervises the work of the government. We have elections every four years, or less, if early elections are called, which is often the case. We have one hundred and twenty members who are elected by the Israeli citizenry. The Knesset has de jure parliamentary supremacy, can pass any laws by a simple majority, and has the right to remove the president.

"This building we are now pulling up to was donated by James de Rothschild as a gift to the State of Israel," the Major General said, moving to the front of the bus. "You will note the magnificent sixteen foot bronze Menorah, the seven-branched candlestick that sits near the entrance. It was a gift from the British Parliament. The interior is decorated with mosaics and tapestries by Marc Chagall."

The bus doors opened and its passengers walked into a garden filled with roses and robins, greenfinches, blackbirds and jays, their songs a concerto as they jumped from branch to branch.

Robert took Jo's arm, and they walked toward the building. It was modern and functional, a suggestion of Classical, yet it had pillars in the Greco-Roman style. They walked past the eternal flame, a monument in memory of Israel's fallen soldiers.

After passing through security, they were led into the Knesset Chamber. Jo waited with Aaron as the rest of their group was directed to the visitor's gallery.

"It's almost time." Aaron squeezed Jo's hand.

"I'm so nervous."

"You'll do just fine."

"I still don't know why they chose me," Jo said.

The Israeli President, Ephraim Katzir, stood in front of the Knesset. He had a long face, tanned and deeply lined, with small intelligent eyes, a curved nose, and a head of pure white hair. Born in Kiev, Ukraine, he studied at Harvard University, and received a Ph.D. from Hebrew University. Before becoming president, he was head of the Department of Biophysics at the Weizmann Institute. He smiled and a hundred eyes looked back. "It is my distinct honor to introduce the first female state senator from New York, Jotto Wells."

Jo, dressed in a black Chanel suit, walked to the platform, and placed her prepared statement on the lectern. She found Rebecca's eyes, beaming from the front row of the visitor's section. *I can do this.*

"To the State of Israel, to her people and her government, we salute you," Jo began. "Arriving here we thought we were well-educated and sophisticated, and that we understood the concerns and dynamics of your country. How foolish we were. How little we knew.

"We visited your universities and research centers, marveling at the advances you're making in the fields of medicine and agriculture.

"We traveled to the Negev Desert, where we tasted wonderfully delicious tomatoes grown miraculously from the once barren desert soil.

"We walked the ancient streets of Jerusalem, watching in awe as you lovingly excavated beneath her streets, reaching back into the mysteries of the past.

"From the ashes of Treblinka, Majdanek, and Auschwitz, a great nation has emerged. Although it's time for us to leave you now, I can assure you we are going back to the United States enriched and inspired.

"We came here strangers. We leave as family. We will never forget you."

Jo delighted in the sound of the applause as the assembly rose to its feet. Tears spilled down her face.

"She was brilliant," Rebecca said, looking at Robert and then Saul, her eyes glistening. "It wasn't just the words; it was the passion, the emotion. Divine providence brought Jo here. She's one of us."

Saul slid his eyes toward Robert. "By Jewish law, when a child is born to a Jewish mother, that child is a Jew. Even if Jo never knows—she feels it," Saul pointed to his heart. "In here."

Rebecca put her arm around Robert and placed her lips against his cheek. "One day, with God's help, we'll tell Jo who she really is. You must help us make that happen, Robert. We owe it to her and we owe it to Morgan."

Robert looked at Saul. "Have you heard anything more?"

"Yes. I wanted to wait until Jo's speech before telling you. Natan called today," Saul said. "Simon Wiesenthal is interested in Morgan's case."

"That's great news," Rebecca said.

"Thank Natan for me, will you?" Robert added as they all stood and moved toward the exit.

"You're going to have to be very careful who you trust," Saul said. "People may not be who they appear to be. Don't let your guard down. And don't ever forget how cunning and dangerous your adversaries can be."

"I know that now."

"May God protect you, my brother." Saul said, clasping Robert's hand. "Until we meet again."

20

Albany, New York

Jo unlocked the apartment door to her twenty-six hundred square foot penthouse. She flipped on the lights while Victor, the building doorman, brought in her luggage. Standing in the doorway, she looked around, feeling like a character out of Robert Heinlein's novel, *Stranger in a Strange Land.*

It's my own damn fault. I should have paid better attention to the selections Suzette showed me. Suzette was the designer recommended by the wife of one of her senatorial associates.

Jo glared at the bronze and granite table in the foyer. In its center was a two thousand dollar Frederick Carder Steuben Gold Aurene Vase from the 1920's, filled with beaded silk flowers.

Artificial flowers! Ugh. How could I have let this happen?

She walked into the living room. The carpet was a ridiculous shade of lavender, and the sectional sofa, window drapes, and armchairs were all covered in a matching floral pattern. A mahogany bookcase was lined with books purchased for the sake of filling the shelves. Having books in her home that she had never read insulted Jo's reverence for literature. Every time she looked at them, she promised herself she would bring books back from her townhouse in New York.

Albany will never feel like home but at least I'll be sleeping in my own bed.

She let her clothes fall in a heap on the bedroom floor. The room was all white, walls, carpet, spread. The furniture was cherry. If there was a room in the entire place she tolerated, it was this one. She tossed the decorative pillows in a corner and plopped the bedspread on top of them.

Having traveled for almost twenty-four hours, she was past exhausted, but she had one more thing to do. She cradled the phone in the crook of her neck and dialed.

The intercom buzzed in Andy's Washington office.

"Senator Wells is on the line sir," his secretary announced.

"Andy, I am so sorry. I tried to reach you from Israel several times. I hope you got my messages?"

"I did. Thank you." Ashley's face flashed in his mind. He had failed to make his wife happy because he had never stopped loving Jo. The guilt overwhelmed him.

Silence.

Jo pulled her knees into her chest and tugged on her hair. "Is there anything I can do?"

"Just talking to you helps. When did you get home?"

"Ten minutes ago."

"You must be exhausted," Andy said.

"You could say that."

"Look, I know I have no right to ask this. But, after you get caught up at the office, I would really like you to come to Washington."

His request surprised Jo. Her heart leapt.

"Please say yes. I really need to see you."

He needs to see me. Jo let the words hang for a few seconds as her brain screamed, *Say no. Stay away!* However, the thought that her dreams could get a second chance, that she might rekindle feelings she had never had for anyone but Andy. "I'll come," she said, her heart winning the battle.

One week later
Washington, DC

Jo stood on Constitution Avenue and C Street in front of the Dirksen Senate Office Building. Her plane had been delayed for over two hours and she hoped Andy had called to check on her arrival time. She climbed the steps of the seven-story marble-faced building and entered through the bronze doors at the north entrance. The central lobby was a sea of dark suits and briefcases. She stepped into the elevator. Her stomach knotted in cramps, and she took slow, even breaths as the elevator operator called out the floors. On six, she exited.

Andy's secretary, a silver-haired woman with piercing green eyes, smiled and said dryly, "The senator is expecting you."

Jo tried to envision Andy's office. It was a game she often played, and she was usually quite good at guessing. Not this time. Instead of what she expected—ultramodern décor—Andy had chosen the sleek lines of traditional American furniture. Floor to ceiling cherry wood bookcases filled with leather-bound books covered the west wall. Hanging behind Andy's enormous Georgian antique desk was a photograph of President Nixon with Andy and his wife. There were a dozen other photos, Henry Kissinger, House Minority Leader Gerald Ford, Vice President Spiro Agnew. In all the photos Andy looked relaxed and happy.

"It's good to see you, Jo." Andy kissed her cheek. "Please," he said, motioning her to the leather sofa. "I can't tell you how much I appreciate you coming."

A buffet lunch was set up on the coffee table that included an assortment of fruit platters, salads, and sandwiches.

"Heard you had some rough weather," Andy said.

"Not too bad."

Andy motioned to the platters. "Please, have something."

Jo stared at the food. "Maybe in a little while." She knew, as nervous as she was, eating would make her sick. "How are you doing?"

"Shitty." Andy's face flushed and his eyes filled with tears. He swiped at them with the back of his hand.

"Please don't be embarrassed. I understand," Jo said.

"I feel like I've been sucked into a tornado, and I don't know how to get out." His whole body tensed. "I'm so pissed off! Ashley never hurt anyone in her life. It's just not fair. This isn't fair either. I am not going to dump my miserable life in your lap!"

"Andy. I'm here to listen."

Andy looked off in the distance, as if he were waiting for something.

Jo heard the sound of a plane flying overhead. She remained silent.

Andy began to talk, slowly at first. Then, like the opening of floodgates, he opened up to Jo, rambling on about the funeral, the hundreds of people in attendance, the devastation for his in-laws losing their only child.

Jo nodded her head at the appropriate moments.

Eventually, Andy stood and began to pace.

"The press is in a feeding frenzy, and I'm the bait." He scowled, sucking in his cheeks, "Photographers and reporters follow me everywhere—when I come out of my home in the morning, when I leave the office, when I get a damn haircut. Ashley and I are on the cover of every two-bit tabloid in the country."

"It will pass," Jo said.

"God, I hope so. It is driving me mad."

Andy sat back down. "Thank you for letting me vent. I actually feel a little better."

Jo smiled. "I think you need to get away from all this for a while."

Andy looked around the office. "If only it were that easy. My life may be a wreck, but the pressure is on regardless of my personal needs." He looked at his watch, his expression hooded. "Oh my God. I don't know how it got to be so late. You are going to have to forgive me, but I have a very important meeting that I couldn't reschedule."

Jo masked her hurt feelings under a smile. "I understand."

Give the guy a break. He's been through hell. That was the good Jo talking to herself. *Never mind that I rearranged my entire schedule.* That was the bad Jo talking to herself and, that Jo was mad as hell.

"I've made arrangements for you to stay in my family suite at the Parker Hotel."

"That's very sweet but Aaron Blumenthal has invited me to stay with him."

A dark look crossed Andy's face. "Are you and Aaron—?

"We're just good friends," Jo said, thinking about the phone conversation she had with Aaron before coming. He had lectured her about the Washington rumor mill, reminding her, not just as a friend, but also as her political advisor, that it would be disastrous for her career, and Senator Taxton's, if the press found out about their earlier romantic relationship. That is when he had offered his home.

"I think I have Aaron's address," Andy said, thumbing through his address book. He smiled. "I do. There's a great little Italian restaurant in McLean. I'll have my driver pick you up at eight-thirty, and I'll meet you there if that's okay?"

Before Jo could respond, his secretary entered.

"Senator, your appointment has arrived."

"I'm so sorry, Jo. Believe me, I'd have gotten out of this if I could have. My driver, Bennett, will take you to Aaron's," he said, rising. "Give me five minutes," he instructed his secretary, "and then show the congressman in." He put his hand on Jo's elbow. "I promise I'll make this up to you. You do understand?"

"Don't give it another thought," Jo said, moving toward the door.

"Wait!" Andy said. "Use the side door. The elevator is just down the hall on your right. Bennett will meet you in the lobby. He's a tall black man with a mustache."

He doesn't want anyone to see me. Jo suddenly felt cheap.

She was sorry she had come.

21

McLean, Virginia

It was only twelve miles from Washington to Aaron's home in Virginia. With traffic, the ride took forty minutes. It was just enough time for Jo to put aside her hurt feelings and regain her composure.

Bennett pulled to a stop in front of huge iron gates at the entranceway to the driveway. He announced Jo, and the doors swung open. As the limousine pulled to a stop in front of a mansion complete with antebellum verandas, stained-glass windows, Japanese cherry trees, and crawling ivy vines, Jo couldn't help giggling. It's perfect, she thought. The front door opened and Aaron came bounding down the steps.

Aaron helped her out of the car. He kissed her gently on the cheek, his mind flashing to Israel and a kiss that had meant so much more. "Well, what do you think of my humble abode?" He smiled his bad boy smile. "Pretty good for a once penniless immigrant." Taking her by the hand, Aaron led Jo up the steps. "My butler will see to your luggage," he said, winking.

They moved from room to room, past priceless paintings by Rico Lebrun, Morris Louis, Marcel Janco, and Hans Richter. There were sculptures, works on paper, photographs, archaeological artifacts, and Jewish ceremonial objects.

"It's like a museum," Jo said. "And yet, you've created a warmth that permeates every room. It's fabulous. I could move in here and never leave."

Aaron's smile faded, but only for an instant. "Come with me. I've saved the best for last."

They entered a room with wood floors, a skylight, and a wall of glass overlooking a resplendent garden. Old photographs, hundreds of them, hung from the walls and sat on ten-foot long mahogany tables. They were photographs, not of famous people, but of people doing what people do: Bar Mitzvahs, high school graduations, marriages, family gatherings, birthday parties.

"Through these pictures I've tried to tell the story of the survival of the Jewish people."

Jo moved from photograph to photograph, losing herself in the faces, the expressions, the frozen moments in time. "Where did they all come from?"

Aaron stood a little straighter. "From collectors, from my travels, from friends who heard what I was doing. Many of these photographs are copies from pictures people buried in their backyards, or gave to neighbors for safekeeping during the war."

"I'm honored to be your friend." Jo slid her arm through his.

In the garden, they sat in old-fashioned rockers surrounded by the explosion of color from azaleas trees, daffodils, forsythia, and daylilies.

Aaron laughed. "Just wait until you see what happens next." With that, the butler appeared, carrying a silver tray of pink lemonade and home-baked cookies.

"I feel like I'm on the set of *Gone with the Wind*."

"Genteel Southern hospitality, that was my goal. But, enough already. Tell me, how was your first week back at work?"

"My staff did a great job without me. I guess I'd kind of hoped they'd have missed me more," Jo said. "How about you?"

"About the same. I think we make ourselves more important than we really are," Aaron said, noting the troubled look that crossed Jo's face. "What's the matter?"

"I don't know. I guess I'm just being silly, but I don't like the way Andy treated me. He asked me to come. I rearranged my entire schedule, and yet he didn't do the same. And then to top it off, he had me sneak out of his office through a back door." Jo scowled.

"Here I am trying to be his friend, and he makes me feel like some kind of sleazy tramp."

Aaron's skin prickled with anger. He saw Andy as the stereotypical politician, self-indulgent, narcissistic, and priggish. Since Ashley's death, Washington was wild with stories about Taxton's extramarital indiscretions. A part of Aaron wanted to tell Jo what he had heard, but because his own motivations were suspect, he bit his tongue and decided instead to be charitable. "In all fairness, the senator has been under an enormous amount of pressure. You should also consider the fact that people do change. So, give yourself some time to see if you even like the person he's become."

"You're right, of course. We were only kids when I knew him." Jo glanced at her watch. "Jesus, it's almost seven. I better get ready."

Aaron watched as Jo moved inside. Just as he was about to sit down, Jo came back outside and hugged him. Then, without saying a word, she was gone.

Aaron stood on the veranda. The billowed grey and blue clouds danced overhead, painting illusions of mountain ranges perched in the heavens. The elms and poplars were majestic shades of green, beige, and blond.

Aaron poured himself a scotch and soda from the portable bar and settled into the lounge chair. He kicked off his shoes. *Admit it. You're jealous she's going off with that blue-blooded WASP.* Aaron ran his finger around the rim of the glass.

He forced his thoughts inward. Aaron had spent his adult life striving for things out of reach. That's what motivated and challenged him. If it came easy, he didn't find it worthy of his efforts. He accepted and even embraced that quirk in his personality. It had served him well in his career.

When it came to women, he took an opposite tactic. He dated accomplished women who were self-confident and did not need coddling; he didn't have the time or the desire for complicated relationships. While his affairs were mostly passionate and intense, the moment expectations were attached—and dating Jewish women meant there would always be expectations—Aaron would find a way to break it off.

His feelings for Jo were different. He wanted her.

Aaron took a deep swallow of his scotch. *I have to stop kidding myself. She doesn't care about me. Even if she did, I could never have her, not even if she was willing to convert to Judaism.*

It was about the vow.

In memory of his parents, Aaron swore that the woman who birthed his children would be of Jewish heritage.

He would never break that vow.

* * *

Jo looked around the guest room. A Louis XV rosewood bed and a 19th century armoire in hand-carved walnut dominated the room. The armoire stood open—her clothing unpacked, ironed, and hung. *I could get used to this.*

Ten minutes later, she stepped from the shower, dried herself, and slipped into a hand-embroidered silk bathrobe that had been left in a ribboned box with her name on it. She applied a touch of eye shadow and dusted her face with powder. The intercom buzzed as she fastened the last gold button on her Yves Saint-Laurent black evening suit.

"Senator Wells, your driver is here."

Escopazzo Restaurant
McLean, Virginia

The décor was quaint: red checkered tablecloths, Chianti bottles with candles melting, and a crowded, noisy bar. Jo sat across from Andy at a table towards the back.

"I've been waiting here nervous as a school boy. I hope you're not mad at me for the way I acted today?" Andy poured Chianti into her glass.

Jo shrugged.

"You are mad."

She placed the napkin on her lap. "I understand you not being able to get out of the appointment." She looked hard into his eyes, her mouth tight. "But, making me sneak out—."

"—I swear I didn't mean to upset you. I keep doing things I wouldn't normally do. It's very disconcerting. I really am so sorry."

God, I am being such a prig. "I shouldn't have said anything. With all the pain and pressure you have in your life right now, I had no right—"

"—You had every right. How about this," Andy said, "we both stop apologizing, and start this evening all over again."

Jo smiled. "Deal." She stuck out her arm.

"Deal." Andy shook her hand.

They sipped wine, talked about their youth, about people they knew in common, skirting issues of substance. During the meal, they discussed politics, her job, and his.

Coffee was served.

"I know this may not be the ideal time or the place but, I have something I need to tell you." Andy bored his eyes into Jo's. "Ashley and I—we cared about each other but we were never in love."

The words dangled in silence.

"I don't understand. If you weren't in love then why—"

Andy held up his hand. "Please. Just hear me out. What I am about to say is going to sound cold and calculating to you. But, it was a decision Ashley and I made with our eyes wide open. We were good together. We enjoyed the same people, traveled in the same circles, and our families were life-long friends. It seemed like the right thing to do for both of us. But we were wrong, and both of us were miserable."

The pain and the longing in his eyes sent shivers down Jo's spine.

"I tried to convince myself otherwise, but you are the only woman I ever loved."

"You walked away from me," the tears welled in Jo's eyes, "without an explanation. Do you have any idea what you put me through? I spent years trying to figure out what I did wrong—what I might have said, or didn't say—what I could have done to change the outcome."

Andy reached for her hand. "I was young and restless and terrified of making a commitment when we were so young." He couldn't tell Jo the truth, that her father's questionable background was deemed toxic for his career, and that defying his own father had not been an option for a young man wanting to be president. But the world had changed. What was a problem then would not be a problem now. "I know I don't deserve it, but I'm begging you to give me another chance. I swear to God, if you do, I will never hurt you again."

Jo was pulled into the past. Visions flashed—the affair she had the year before—mostly because being a virgin was a stigma she hated. There was no love, just lust—Andy always in her fantasies. *Did she still love him?* Jo made a tent with her fingers and pressed them to her mouth. Her eyes held Andy's. "You're going to have to be patient and give me time."

Andy's eyes danced. "Take as much time as you need. Just as long as you're willing to give me another chance."

* * *

Surrounded by narrowed darkness, the trees stood like soldiers, a line of defense against her decision. Jo breathed a long tired sigh and climbed the steps to Aaron's home. Before she could knock, Aaron opened the door. He was sulking, his hands stuffed into the pockets of his pants.

"How was your date?" His speech was thick and slurred.

"Aaron Blumenthal, are you inebriated?"

"That's entirely possible."

"Have you been waiting up for me?" Jo teased.

"Guilty as charged. Did you have a good time?"

"Yes."

"Too bad."

"That's not nice."

"So, you still care about him, huh?"

"I'm not sure how I feel."

"He's in love with you, isn't he?"

Jo nodded.

"I knew it." Aaron winced.

Jo stood on tiptoes and kissed his cheek. "I've decided to go back to Albany in the morning. I need time to work all this out in my head."

"You don't have to leave. You could stay here with me. I'm harmless, and I promise we'll have fun."

"Thanks. But no thanks." *I need to get away from both of you.*

22

The next day
Albany, New York

Every light in Jo's apartment was turned on, and the television was blaring. Her father Hans tapped ashes from his pipe into the ashtray, and added more tobacco. He lit it, blowing smoke rings into the air.

Otto ignored him, lost in his favorite television show, *The Virginian.*

Hans looked at his watch. He had checked the airlines and knew Jotto's flight would be arriving from Washington within the hour. "We need to talk," Hans said, leaning forward, and switching off the television.

Otto shot him a furious look. "We have been talking for days. What more is there to say?"

"Do you fully understand the implications of what has happened? My daughter defied me! She went to Israel without my approval. She has been back for a week and has not called. It was your job to keep her in line. You have failed!"

Otto pointed his chin at Hans. "No, I have not failed. A few hours of reinforcement from me, and I will have Jotto doing exactly what we want her to do. But, that's not going to solve our other problem—Osborne. I'm telling you, let me use my influence on Jo to end that friendship." Otto snickered.

"Believe me, I would like nothing better," Hans said. "But, if she suddenly didn't want to see him, it could push Osborne into going public with whatever he *thinks* he knows."

"Then let our comrades eliminate him."

"It's not that easy. My own wishes aside, and looking at this from a psychiatrist's point of view, if something happens to Osborne, Jotto will be inconsolable. That would push back any hopes we have for a wedding to Taxton within the year." Hans removed a monogrammed handkerchief from his pocket and dabbed his face. "Now that Senator Taxton's wife is no longer part of the equation, we will just have to find a way to work around the Osborne problem."

Otto kept his expression neutral. He hated Robert Osborne. The man was Jotto's confidant, a role *he* had always held in his niece's life. To make matters worse, Osborne had been married to his beloved Morgan. In Otto's demented mind, if not for Osborne, the actress might have loved him.

Otto thought about the relationship between his duplicitous brother-in-law and Morgan. It made him feel crazy and out of control. He didn't blame Morgan. The dire circumstances of being in Dachau was reason enough for her to turn to Doctor Hans Wells for protection. He balled his fists.

Hans did not notice the hate in Otto's eyes. He was too busy refilling his pipe again, lost in his own thoughts as he pictured the child he had fathered with Ilya. The infant came from the damaged gene pool of Otto and Ilya Milch. He shrugged, feeling no remorse for destroying an inferior infant that could never be a reflection of his superior intelligence.

The child he had fathered with Morgan was another matter. Everyone knew Morgan was beautiful, an exceptional talent and very intelligent. But there was something else about the woman, something that set her apart, even under the adverse conditions of Dachau. She had a presence, a way of making everything around her seem insignificant, as though she were above her circumstances. That spirit was what he wanted in his progeny, and he knew Morgan would produce such a child.

The Fuhrer wanted perfection.

Jotto was perfection.

Hans cradled the pipe in his hand and lifted his eyes. "Osborne thinks that hiring the fucking Israelis will scare us. He's a fool. Nothing can stop us! Think about it, Otto. We've spent a lifetime preparing Jotto for this role. Now, it is in your power to take us to the next step. She will be first lady of the United States of America. When that happens, we will have unrestricted access to the President of the United States." Hans's eyes glazed over and his arm shot forward in the Nazi salute. "We will have fulfilled our destiny."

* * *

Jo tipped the taxi driver and waited while Victor, the doorman, took her suitcase out of the trunk. "I'll bring this up in a few minutes. By the way, your father and uncle arrived yesterday," Victor said, holding back the elevator door as Jo entered.

Jo knew there would be hell to pay. Her belly clenched. *Shit! I knew I should have called when I got back from Israel.*

Standing in front of her apartment door, Jo took a deep breath and turned the key in the lock.

"What a nice surprise," Jo said, pasting a smile on her face. "Sorry I haven't called. I was intending to come to Naples in a couple weeks," she said, hoping to avoid the coming storm.

Her Uncle Otto smiled and came forward for a hug. Her father held back, his face a mask of fury.

"Look, Father, before we get into a fight you need to understand that I did what I believed to be the right thing for my career, and for me. It is done. I really think we should move past it."

Hans knew he had little choice but to relent. A fight would only keep Jotto on her guard, and he needed that guard down. He rose and kissed her cheek.

"You were in Washington?"

Jo nodded. *They always know where I am.*

"We heard about Senator Taxton's wife. What a tragedy," her uncle said.

"We were surprised to hear he was with you in Israel," Hans added. "Did you know he was going?"

"It is tragic and no, I had no idea." *Why would they care?*

"Come and tell us about the trip," her father said, moving toward the sofa.

Jo felt her skin prickle. *He's making this too easy. What's going on?*

There was a knock on the door.

"That will be my luggage," Jo said.

"Sit with your uncle. I'll see to it," Hans said.

Jo sat next to her uncle. He put his arm around her. "Tell me everything. I want all the details."

Jo laughed. This was the man she had always loved. He was her pal and would really listen. Jo began to recount the trip. When her father returned, he pulled up a chair and remained silent.

At some point in Jo's nonstop narration, she saw her uncle pull out the music box, a memory from her youth, a memory that made her heart pound. He flipped it open. The refrain from Beethoven's *Fur Elise* overtook Jo, capturing her mind as if she were sitting in the front row of the New York Philharmonic.

So, this is what the visit is about. Well it won't work.

"Close your eyes my little butterblume...just relax...you're safe. . ."

Go ahead. Say what you want. I won't give in. I won't listen! Jo rested her head against the back of the coach. She blocked out her uncle's voice, pushing the sound away, constructing a wall of will between herself and his words. She felt strong and capable. Then her mind began to wander, and that's when it happened. He pulled her into a trance so deep that she lost her will and her way.

* * *

Jo awoke the next morning with a memory lapse, and an ache in the pit of her stomach. While standing in the shower, the tears suddenly came, her chest heaved. *It was Uncle Otto. He's too powerful. That's why I couldn't fight. What did he say to me? What did he plant in my mind? Why don't they just leave me alone?*

She dressed, thankful that they were going back to Naples today. She wrote a note wishing them a good trip, and slipped from the apartment.

Alone in her office, Jo drank coffee and began to read the new bill coming up in the Senate. As hard as she tried, she was unable to concentrate, the words blocked by a manic compulsion to hear Andy's voice. Driven mad by racing thoughts, she dialed his private number.

"I'm so glad you called," Andy said. "I tried all last night to reach you, but the phone was busy."

"My father and uncle paid me an unexpected visit. I guess the phone must have been left off the hook."

"Listen, I know I'm moving too quickly. and I don't want to frighten you. But we've lost so much time. I can't stand the thought of not being with you." He took a deep breath. "I love you, Jo Wells. I don't want to lose you again."

The center of Jo's universe shifted, and suddenly all she cared about was seeing Andy. "I love you too. I always have." *What am I saying? Do I even mean that?*

Andy had anticipated a long wait. Jo's declaration of love caught him off guard, and his heart soared like a teenager after a first kiss. "When can I see you?" Andy held his breath, the loveless, wasted years lifting from his shoulders.

The need to be with Andy was so strong that Jo felt it from the top of her head to her toes. "I'll check my schedule and call you right back."

23

November 1972
Seven Months later
Senator Andrew Taxton's Washington DC office

Andy loosened his tie and propped his feet on the desk. It had been a busy morning of meetings and phone calls. He closed his eyes, took a deep breath, and contemplated the events of the past months.

Andy's political advisors, his father included, had thought it was too soon for Andy to be seen in public with Jo. So the last six months had been a time of arranging weekend getaways, flying to the Bahamas, sailing on the Hudson, staying in the family lodge in Maine.

Then last month, he took Jo to a political fundraiser for the president. Their picture found its way into the Washington Post. The public was enchanted by the stories that followed, Senator Andrew Taxton dating his high school sweetheart.

Andy was ecstatic. He was in love and desperate to keep Jo happy. That was not always easy. Jo was altruistic. She wanted to revolutionize life for the blacks and the downtrodden. She believed women deserved equal pay and was openly behind abortion rights. When Andy tried to explain that presidential politics were different from state politics and that he had to think of the entire country, and how they stood, Jo would become furious and accuse him of being shortsighted, egocentric, and narcissistic.

She will learn.

He picked up the picture of Jo that sat on the corner of his desk. He smiled. *Soon you will be mine.*

The door to his office opened.

"Doctor Hans Wells and Mr. Milch have arrived."

"Oh, Jesus! I lost track of time," Andy said, taking his feet off the desk. He slipped into his suit jacket. "Show them in, and bring coffee."

Hans entered first. Andy, as always, was struck by his future father-in-law's good looks. His neatly trimmed beard and hair were pure white, accentuating dark-green eyes that rarely blinked and seemed to see right through him. He wore a white dress shirt, impeccably starched and pressed, a light blue silk tie, and a black cashmere suit.

Otto followed. In contrast, he was dressed in a gray silk shirt, left casually open at the collar, black wool slacks, and black Gucci loafers. He had high cheekbones, meticulously cut silver hair. Andy thought Otto was prettier than he was handsome.

"It's nice to see you both," Andy said as they shook hands.

"We thought it was time to come by and have a private little chat," Hans said.

Andy led them to the leather sofa. He sat in an armchair across from them and watched as Otto took out cigars.

"Have one." Otto winked. "They're Havana's finest."

"No thank you," Andy said. "I don't smoke."

Otto held the cigar just outside the flame and rotated it slowly, just charring the tip. He took gentle puffs, a look of ecstasy on his face. "You don't know what you're missing."

"We understand," Hans said, flicking his lighter without the obvious joy of his brother-in-law, "that before her death, your late wife's family was using their enormous political influence in Washington to insure your eventual nomination for the presidency. It's most unfortunate, now that you and my daughter are together, that they've withdrawn their support."

Andy shrugged. "We all make choices in this life, and I've made mine." Andy knew his decision to marry Jo would alienate his exin-laws. His father had assured him it would be a very small bump in a very long road, and that other arrangements had already been made.

"My brother-in-law and I are in the position to hand you the presidency," Hans said, intertwining his fingers, the cigar dangling from his mouth.

Fascinated, Andy sat a little straighter. "And how are you going to do that?"

"The way it's always done." Hans blew a smoke ring and watched it rise. "We're going to buy it for you."

"And in return, gentleman?" Andy asked, noting the sinister smirk on Otto's face.

"We want to be more involved with the decisions being made now, and in the future."

Andy tensed. "I really appreciate your offer, but I believe I'll secure the nomination of my party on my own merits. Now perhaps we could discuss something—"

"—I don't think you understand." Hans brushed a piece of thread from his jacket before looking up. His eyes burned dark. "We are not asking you. We are telling you."

"With all due respect," Andy said, his heart racing, his temper threatening to explode, "I think you are out of line, sir."

"Pick up the phone, and call your father."

"I don't know what this is all about but I take great exception to—"

"Call him," Otto growled. The nerves jumped in his left eye.

Anderson Taxton was at his Texas ranch, sitting with his hand on the receiver, waiting for the phone to ring. His blood pressure had spiked, causing an excruciating headache. He rubbed his temples as he contemplated the reality of the horrendous dilemma he had gotten himself into.

All he had ever wanted was to insure that his son would have enough money to win the highest office of the land. Befriending Ford during the war, and giving money to Hitler had seemed so innocuous, just a wealthy man hedging his bets. It had backfired, and now he was being blackmailed—held captive by the fucking

Nazis. All he could do was submit himself to their demands. If his involvement ever came out, it would ruin his son's life, and his life. The realization was almost more than he could bear.

The phone rang. His hands trembled as he lifted the receiver.

"Jo's father and uncle are here. They're insisting—"

"Do you want to be president, son?" Anderson asked, the fear in his voice foreign to Andy.

"Yes, sir."

"Then, you need to listen to what they say." Anderson waited a couple of heartbeats. "Call me after they've gone. I'll explain everything then." Anderson could hardly breathe. "I love you, son," he said, breaking the connection.

Andy's throat went dry. He buzzed his secretary. "Hold my calls, and cancel all my appointments for the rest of the day."

Hans smiled. "That's much better. Now, I have a question for you. I want you to think long and hard before answering."

Andy nodded.

"How do you feel about the Jews running this country?" Hans's voice was testing, cold.

"Excuse me?"

"We think the time has come to stop them. We need to know where you stand on this issue." Hans stubbed out his cigar and stared at him.

Andy's eyes moved from Hans to Otto. *Jesus Christ. Is this really happening?* He took a deep breath and said, "Okay. You want the truth. The Jews have their hands in every newspaper, bank, and business in the country. Their liberal views are ruining this country. But this is America," Andy trembled with anger, "and, I am going to be a Republican candidate. Without the Jews, I will not be able to win the presidency."

"We quite agree." Hans undid the buttons on his jacket and stretched his legs. "We want you to take the stance of a Jew-loving politician." Hans made a tent with his hands and smiled. "It is not what you say to get elected that matters to us. What matters is what you do and say after you are elected."

Friday, November 10, 1972
New York City

The taxi pulled to a stop in front of Jo's favorite New York restaurant, Luminaire. She was in New York for the weekend because of a disturbing phone call from her best friend, Sweeny. Jo had no details, only an urgent request that they meet on Saturday. She would face that problem tomorrow. Tonight she was excited about spending the evening with Robert and Aaron, who happened to be in New York on business.

I have butterflies in my stomach, Jo thought. She knew it was the anticipation of being with Aaron. It was that night at the Kotel in Jerusalem—that kiss. It wouldn't go away. *Stop acting like an idiot. It was one dumb kiss.*

Jo stepped from the car and shivered. No matter how long she lived in the North East, she would never grow accustomed to the cold. Albany may have more snow, and the temperatures might be lower, but to her, no place was colder than the City with its cavern-like streets, where the frigid air got trapped between the massive buildings and assaulted ones body with unprecedented malice.

Robert and Aaron were standing at the bar when Jo entered. A wave and a smile, kisses and hugs ensued. Jo handed the full-length ermine fur, a gift from Andy, to the coat check.

Robert's 6'2", two-hundred and fifty pound bodyguard, Manny, who never talked or smiled, led the way to their table.

Jo ignored Manny, convinced he was responsible for turning her beloved Robert into a neurotic eccentric who drove around in an armored limousine, and installed bulletproof glass in his home along with movement sensors and alarm systems. She believed Robert's newfound need for security was disconnected from reality.

Then again, Jo too felt disconnected. She had spent months hiding from the press, sneaking around the country like a paramour, feeling more like a fascinated observer than a participant. She had promised herself that she would try to evaluate things on a deeper level, and stop allowing Andy's family to dictate their every move. She intended to do that. Instead, she did nothing.

Robert took Jo's arm as they moved into the main dining room with its crystal chandeliers, Wedgwood china, and moneyed patrons. Conversations tilted, and people stared and whispered as the foursome moved past.

Manny's eyes traveled over the room before he sat at a nearby table.

The waiter pulled out the chair for Jo. She sat between Aaron and Robert. The two men had become close friends ever since their trip to Israel—the bond nourished by their mutual relationship with Jo.

"So, last weekend in Texas, and this weekend in the Big Apple. My, my, aren't you the jet-setter?" Aaron teased. His eyes widened. "What's that on your finger?" Aaron reached for Jo's hand. "Are you kidding me?" He stared at the emerald-cut seven-karat diamond ring surrounded by round cabochon emeralds.

"I wanted it to be a surprise." Jo wiggled her finger. "It's official. We're engaged." Jo smiled. "What can I say? The man is crazy about me."

"He's not the only one." Robert leaned over and kissed Jo's cheek. "You make sure you tell that young man of yours that he better take good care of you, or he will have to answer to me."

"Correction," Aaron said. "He will have to answer to both of us."

Jo's eyes moved from Robert's face to Aaron's. "You are both so special to me," she said.

Aaron forced a smile. "Have you set a date?"

"You know how it is. We have to check with a hundred people before we can make a decision. But it will be soon."

"Then we will consider this our private little engagement party celebration." Robert nodded to the waiter. "A bottle of Cristal, if you please."

* * *

Later that evening the wind howled and naked trees huddled against the cold, their branches scraping against the frozen windows of Robert's Sands Point home as he and Aaron stood by the smoldering fireplace, each holding a glass of cognac.

"She's infatuated. She doesn't love him; she couldn't. They have absolutely nothing in common," Aaron said, pointing his eyes at Robert.

"I'm not sure you're right. Whenever I talk to her about him, she seems absolutely smitten. Think about it, Aaron. We all know that Jo could win a second term in the senate without even a fight, and yet, she is willing to give that up to marry Taxton. That sounds like love to me." Robert put his drink on the Georgian mahogany sideboard and picked up the poker to stoke the fire.

Aaron moved the screen aside. "He cheated on his first wife, and when he grows tired of Jo, he'll cheat on her too. I know the type. How can she not see that he's a schmuck?"

"You may not like him but he treats her well, and people do change." Robert rearranged the sparking logs and gazed into the fire. "Besides, there isn't much we can do about it now that she's engaged."

"Maybe not. But I'm telling you, Jo is acting weird. You know how she feels about her family, and yet she is spending weekends with her father and uncle at the Taxton ranch." Aaron sat down heavily on the leather couch. "Does that sound like something Jo would do?"

Robert tensed. "What are you talking about?" His hands trembled.

"You didn't know? They've become one big family."

Robert's heart pounded. "She never said a word."

Aaron waved his hand and scowled. "See what I mean? Can you even imagine Jo not telling you something as important as that?"

What Aaron says is true. Jo has changed. She still calls me every few days, but the conversations are more forced, less open. Suddenly it all began to make sense as his thoughts expanded exponentially. *Oh, my God! There is something else going on here.* "Aaron, please excuse me for a few moments. I need to call Saul in Israel."

The next morning

Jo was dressed and waiting by the front door twenty minutes before Sweeny was expected to arrive. She sat on a chair next to the umbrella stand in the foyer of her townhouse fiddling with the umbrellas, humming a senseless tune. The doorbell rang. She pushed open the door and pulled her friend inside.

"God, have I missed you!" Jo threw her arms around Sweeny.

"It feels like it's been ages. You look fabulous," Jo said. She helped Sweeny out of her coat, and tossed it across the chair.

"Okay, show me the rock." Sweeny grabbed Jo's hand. She whistled. "Looks just like what a first lady should be wearing."

The girls giggled their way into the den.

"It feels so good to be back here," Sweeny said as she sprawled on the sofa, and pulled out her cigarettes. "Come on. Let's be naughty. Pour us a couple Gin and tonics."

They were on their second drink when Sweeny's eyes filled with tears.

"What's that about?" Jo asked, putting her arm around her friend. "You aren't from the criers."

"I need a place to crash for a few days. Can I stay here?"

"You still have your key, and you are always welcome. But why?"

"Here it is in a nutshell. Mr. Professor said he wanted to get married, have stability. But, every time I broached the subject, he had another excuse. Then I thought I was pregnant. He didn't take it well—started staying out late, being distant. When I finally got my period, two months late, I realized that I really didn't love the prick anymore.

"So, I am bidding farewell to my budding law practice, shedding the shackles that bind, and becoming a trust-fund baby for a while. And, may I add, with Daddy's approval. Seems he never liked my professor very much. So, I'm off to Nepal. I'm going to climb a few mountains, meditate, and find myself."

"I don't know what to say." Jo could see the sadness in Sweeny's eyes.

"Not to worry. I will come back for your wedding. Other than that, I am outa here baby! Now, tell me about your Mr. Wonderful. How's the sex?"

"Sweeny!"

"Don't Sweeny me. I have waited years to hear about my virginal friend doing it."

"I was not a virgin."

"I know. Save it. Doing it once with someone you barely even liked does not count. Now, tell me."

Jo grew pensive. "It's okay."

Sweeny's eyes became huge as saucers. "What does that mean? I hope your not faking it with him?"

Jo nodded slowly.

"Shit. I expected he would be a great lover."

"I think it's me. He tries. I just can't seem to let myself go."

"Does he do cunnilingus on you?"

Jo cringed. "Come on, do we have to get so graphic?"

"Yes. This is important."

"He does but, it takes me too long, and he kind of gives up. So, I pretend to climax."

"This isn't good," Sweeny said. "I'm telling you, honey. Even with great sex, you eventually can get bored. Without it, you don't have a chance."

"Thanks for your encouragement. Can we talk about something else, like you dropping out and moving half way around the world?"

"We sure can. After I give you some priceless advice on your sex life. "

Jo ran her hands through her hair. "I think part of my problem is Aaron."

"You're kidding, right?" Sweeny said. She had met Aaron during the campaign and thought he was magnificent. She had also sensed that he adored Jo. When she had asked Jo about him, the response had been cryptic.

"On the trip to Israel, Aaron and I spent some time together. We kissed. I know it sounds ridiculous, one stupid moment. But, I can't stop thinking about that kiss."

"Honey, are you in love with Andy?"

Whatever Jo might be feeling, the words were out before she could stop them. "I adore him. I want to be his wife."

"Okay, then. Forget the kiss. It's called unfulfilled sexual desire. You probably should have slept with Aaron, then we would not be having this conversation. But, you didn't. So, chalk it up to one of those dumb decisions we all make in our lives and move on. Now on to my priceless advice on your sex life."

The girls talked all night, and into the next day.

24

One month later
Washington, D.C.

The Mercedes limousine sped along the George Washington Parkway heading toward Aaron's home in McLean. Aaron reached over, removed the crystal decanter from the car's sideboard, and poured Chivas into two glasses. He handed one to Robert.

"Thank you. You heard Jo and Andy set a date?" Robert said, his eyes hooded as he sipped his drink.

"Yeah. Jo called me yesterday. She said they were getting married at the Taxton ranch on February fourth. For Christ's sake, what's the big rush?"

"I think that is exactly the point—the big rush." Robert's shoulders sagged.

Aaron watched his friend. "You okay?"

Robert shook his head. He dug into his pocket and pulled out a crumpled paper. "This is why I made the sudden trip to Washington." He smoothed out the creases and handed the telegram to Aaron. "I got this yesterday."

URGENT! INFORMATION YOU REQUESTED AVAILABLE. MEET AARON BLUMENTHAL'S AFTER 8 P.M. 12-6-72
SAUL

"Has this got anything to do with that call you made to Saul when you found out about Jo's father and uncle spending weekends

178

with Andy's family?" Aaron asked.

"Yes. And, I need you to understand that this could potentially expose you to a dangerous situation." Robert felt as if the air in the car had grown stale and he was suddenly claustrophobic. He opened the window a crack. The wind whistled, the outside sounds from the swishing cars too much of a distraction. He forced himself to focus as he pushed the button and raised the window.

"Robert, you know I'm your friend. I'll do whatever you need."

"Then there are things I must tell you."

* * *

Golden rays of moonlight sent shimmering slivers of light through the window, shadowing the book-lined study where Robert and Aaron had been talking for over an hour.

Aaron ran his hands through his hair, his mind churning. "I'm trying to understand. I swear I am. But, first you said your wife Morgan died in Poland, and that you were notified of her death while on active duty during the war. Then you said she was in a concentration camp where she gave birth to a child, after she was supposed to be dead. And, you believe that baby was Jo. Now you are telling me that you think Morgan could still be alive." Aaron squinted, his head pounding in disbelief and frustration at the confusing, almost surreal story.

"I know I sound crazy, and this information must seem more convoluted than it needs to be. I am sorry. There was no simple way to explain this to you. So much of this is speculation. What I do know for certain—Morgan is Jo's mother." Robert bore his eyes into Aaron. "And Hans Wells is her father."

"And you believe all this because Jo looks like your deceased wife?" Aaron bit his tongue. He had not meant to sound so accusatory and disbelieving, and he wished he had thought more carefully before speaking because his words had hurt Robert. He could see it in his eyes.

Robert stood, reached into his pocket and hesitated a moment before taking out an envelope. He carefully slid out its contents, a photograph, and handed it to Aaron.

Aaron looked at the photo, then up at Robert, blinked a few

times, and looked at the photo again. "I've never seen anything like it. Except for the color of their hair, they're identical. I think it's my turn to tell you a story," Aaron said. "That first night in Israel, when everyone in the group had gone to their rooms, I invited Jo to go with me to the Wall."

Robert smiled. "She never said a word."

"She had some type of epiphany and may have been too embarrassed to tell you. Jo said she saw a woman who looked exactly like her—a woman who spoke of love, and of protecting her. At the time, I thought she was just over-tired and over-stimulated. Do you think—?"

"—that it's possible she may have seen her mother?" Robert asked. "When you've lived as long as I have, and have seen as much as I've seen—" Robert smiled. "Yes, Aaron. I think anything is possible."

"Does Jo suspect?"

Robert shook his head. "I can't tell her until I have answers to the questions I know she's going to ask."

Aaron could only imagine the hell his friend had been through, the suspicions, the deceit, the not knowing. Aaron felt a tingling in his mind, a need to grasp something just out of reach. It hit him like a gigantic wave, knocking his breath away. *Jo is the child of a Jewish mother. That makes her a Jew! I could tell her how I feel!* Then the cold hard truth struck and his joy turned to deep abiding sorrow. *She loves Andy. She said so herself.*

A door slammed somewhere in the house. Aaron shivered and finished his drink.

December 6, 1972

It was early evening when Saul and Natan's taxi passed through the security gate at the Blumenthal mansion. Saul turned in his seat and watched as the tail lights of the car that had been following them from the airport faded from view. "The son of a bitch doesn't even have enough sense to stay out of sight." Saul said.

"He isn't trying to. When he got on in London—aviator glasses, crew cut, holding a newspaper—he was being obvious," Natan, the Nazi hunter, said, groggy from too little sleep, his ulcerous stomach acting up. "They want us to know they're on to us. We should have been expecting it. You can't disturb a beehive without getting stung."

"Shit," Saul said. "I don't want to put Aaron and Robert in unnecessary danger. Perhaps we should call off the meeting."

The front door opened.

"It's a little late for that," Natan said getting out of the car.

Aaron, Robert, Natan and Saul shook hands, and exchanged greetings.

"I need all of you to keep away from the windows." Natan hit the three switches by the front door as they entered. The room went dark.

Robert laughed. "That seems a bit melodramatic."

"We were followed from London," Natan said. "We need to go to the basement. Now!"

They followed Aaron down hallways and through the kitchen. He pushed open a door and they all moved single file down the wooden steps that led to the climate-controlled basement where Aaron kept remnants of his collections. The men sat in a semi-circle on folding chairs.

Robert crossed and uncrossed his arms, his eyes blazed and his legs bounced up and down as Natan arranged his notes.

"What we are about to reveal," Natan said, "could put your lives in danger." He looked from Robert to Aaron.

Robert held up his hand. "Not another word! Aaron, I appreciate all that you have done for me, but it ends here."

"Robert, we've already had this discussion. I appreciate your concern for my well-being. You told me about Morgan and Jo, so let's not pretend I'm not involved. Besides, there are bigger issues at work here. I lost my family in the holocaust." Aaron exchanged a glance with Natan. "That is reason enough for me to be here." He paused, took a shallow breath and said again, "It's reason enough."

Saul shifted in his seat and looked at Robert. "I think the man has a viable argument."

Robert pulled at his collar, sweat dripped down his neck, and his skin tingled. He looked from Saul to Aaron and then to Natan. "Fine. Now, please tell me what you've found."

Saul stood and faced the group. He shifted from one leg to the other, seeking equal footing, a balance for his mind and his body. He looked at Robert and lifted an eyebrow."I need to give you a little background information. It may not seem pertinent, but it is. So, please just try and be patient a little while longer." Saul crossed his arms over his chest.

"We've known for a long time, and when I say we, I mean the Israeli government, that the Nazis have secret vaults all over Europe. In those vaults, among other things, are priceless paintings stolen during the war—Crecos, Cézannes, Monets. The Nazis have been quietly selling them off to investors willing to keep them hidden, then depositing the money into numbered accounts in Switzerland. They have amassed a virtual fortune—more money than some small countries have in their treasuries. The Americans know about all of this as well." Saul intertwined his fingers. "The strangest thing about this fortune is that it has remained intact and untouched since the war. Now suddenly there is activity. A lot of activity. Money is being transferred into numbered accounts all over the world. We haven't figured out exactly what they're doing with this money, but we think it has something to do with Hans and Otto." He nodded to Natan.

Natan flipped closed his notebook. "My goal was to substantiate Otto and Hans's Nazi past. Working with colleagues from the Wiesenthal Center in Vienna, we decided on a two-pronged approach. First, we sifted through testimonies given by survivors. Then we came to Washington and studied transcripts the Allies had on displaced persons after the liberation. We focused primarily on refugees given passage into the United States."

"They gave you access to the transcripts?" Aaron asked, an astonished look on his face.

"Believe it or not, Israel has friends in Washington," Saul said.

"We located a dossier on Hans Wells," Natan continued, "that listed him as a prisoner of war, part of the Free Polish Forces. He was processed, along with his wife, Ilya Milch Wells, and their infant daughter. Shortly thereafter, he was given a position within the United Nations Relief and Rehabilitation Agency in France. At the back of his file, inside an envelope marked confidential, we found a picture of Wells as he looked when the Allies interrogated him. That in itself seemed highly unusual. We found other interviews and coded entries."

"We know the OSS established a Nazi spy network in France after the war," Saul interjected. His face darkened. "Its primary goal was to gather information about the Soviet Union's development of an atomic bomb."

"And according to the codes we broke," Natan interjected, "Hans Wells and Otto Milch were collaborators, passing information to the United States. As a reward, even though it violated laws passed by the U.S. Congress, an elite group of Nazis were allowed to immigrate to America. Others, who were deemed too dangerous, like Otto Milch, were relocated to South America."

Robert's investigator had intimated the same thing. It had infuriated him then, and it infuriated him now. "How the hell could America be so duplicitous when their own sons and daughters died fighting the Nazis? It disgusts me!" Robert's head pounded. What little patience he had left evaporated. "All this is all very enlightening, but what about my wife? What did you find out?"

Natan showed his palms. "When we got back to Israel, we showed Hans's picture to survivors. Within a month, we had ten positive identifications." Natan paused. All eyes were on him. "Hans Wells worked as a doctor at the Dachau concentration camp during the war."

Robert made a fist and pounded his thigh. His face turned crimson. Saul moved his chair closer and draped an arm over Robert's shoulder.

"One of the survivors we interviewed said Wells performed hypothermia experiments, using hypnosis, watching to see if inmates experienced pain as they froze to death. He was also involved in experiments with low-pressure chambers to determine how long people could survive at maximum altitudes. These people were starved of air, suffocated, but not before Wells performed his ritual hypnosis. I'll spare you the rest of the details.

Hypnosis! If he is using it to control Jo, it would explain so much. Aaron was going to interrupt Natan until he saw the look of agony on Robert's face. He decided to wait.

"We asked questions about Morgan, hoping someone would know what happened to her." Natan took out a handkerchief and wiped his forehead. The silence was pervasive, except for Robert's labored breaths. "Morgan—" Natan made a tent with his hands and then paused at the sight of Robert's ashen face.

Robert leaned forward on his elbows. "Tell me."

"Morgan was first brought into the hospital at Dachau after an apparent suicide attempt," Natan said, his voice a whisper.

Robert stared into the past—lines of sorrow etched his face. In the flash of a second he visualized his beloved Morgan as she must have been, starved, abused, humiliated. He wanted to cry out, fight off the demon-like images, to dissuade himself from believing any of it. His Morgan was a woman who loved life, and only total desperation would precipitate her trying to end her own life.

Natan continued, "According to the scrupulous records kept by the Germans, Otto Milch interrogated Morgan. Such a high-level assignment gives us insight into Milch's standing within the SS. We don't know what transpired between the time of her capture and her being sent to Dachau. It appears that Otto had a special interest in Morgan and that she was sent to the camp under the protection of Otto's twin sister, Ilya and her then fiancé, Dr. Hans Wells.

"Wells did much more than protect Morgan. According to the gossip, he impregnated her and Ilya at the same time." Natan blinked several times, deliberately not looking at Robert. "In the camps, as you may know, all Jewish babies were destroyed. It appears that Wells took Morgan's child as his own. We don't know why, and we don't know what happened to Ilya's baby."

The last time Robert had been debriefed by Natan, he was told there was a chance Morgan was still alive. Robert had been holding on to that hope, needing to believe in a miracle. "And Morgan?"

"We told you your friend from Vilna, Doctor Jacob Gold was at Dachau. After the baby was delivered and taken, he hid Morgan. After that, the trail goes cold. We couldn't find them or proof either of them had survived. That's all we know. I'm sorry. So very sorry."

Robert gasped. His world felt as if it were disintegrating. A sudden chill filled the room, a cold that had nothing to do with temperature or existence or even reality. He was suffocating within a vacuum where hope is removed, and the future appears as a void. They sat in silence.

Natan's words lingered over him like a hangman's noose.

Robert's life experiences had turned him into a pragmatic man. He expected even his most precious beliefs to disappear—beliefs held too long, held in abeyance like the dark spring of death is held, like awkward avowals and passionate compromises are held. It took a determined strength of resolve to voice his next question. "Is my wife still alive?"

Saul shook his head. "I'm sorry, my dear friend. We just don't know and probably never will."

"That's it? That's all you can say?" It started slowly, a dispersion of crushing pain that spread across Robert's chest, his body imploding upon itself. His first reaction was panic but that lasted only seconds as his mind shut down and darkness pulled him under. The next thing Robert knew he was on the floor, gasping for air, as if his brain had short-circuited and forgotten the internal secrets of breath.

"Robert, can you hear me?" Saul crouched beside him, his heart a hammer of terror. "Get me something to put under his head!"

"I'll call an ambulance," Natan yelled as he raced for the stairs.

The color seeped from Robert's face as his heart's electrical system malfunctioned. Signals that control the pumping became rapid and chaotic, and his chest rose and fell in sporadic bursts. His breathing became ragged and labored as the lower chamber of his heart quivered rather than contract—losing its ability to pump blood to the rest of his body.

Robert's eyes fluttered open.

He wanted to tell them that he was fine—he was drifting away—into forever. He wanted them to know there was nothing—nothing to be afraid of.

Aaron slipped a folded jacket under Robert's head. "Help is on the way. Just hold on!" Aaron demanded, as if his insistence could keep his friend alive.

Robert's eyes rolled back. Time became an enigma. He was young, waiting at the Vilna train station for Morgan. He could see the hope and fear on her face—was struck by her sweet innocence—how beautiful she was—the trust shining from her eyes. He could hear the random twitter of birds as she moved into his arms, touching his face with gentle hands. They talked and laughed—birthing their love, changing their destiny.

The kaleidoscope of his life shifted. They were on stage in Paris reciting lines from Romeo and Juliet, the world at their feet. The applause was thunderous. Morgan laughed, winked at him and bowed. The moment froze and was gone.

He lifted his hand, it held a rifle. He was ambushed, festering hatreds, discipline forgotten, heroics aside, shooting, killing. The noise from the bombs ached in his ears, and the heat blistered his skin. Surrounded by fallen comrades, he was now the observer and the judge, cool and detached, understanding finally that which has no words.

Another shift.

Morgan was sitting beside him on the beach, her head in his lap, half slumbering in a haze, the breath of wind against their skin, the gray night filled with stars.

She looked up at him. What he saw was Morgan's eyes and then Jo's eyes eclipsed all else. The child he never had, the unencumbered, uncomplicated love. So much more to say to her. He would miss her most.

The applause came again, growing louder, like the sound of trumpets calling the angels. Then it all began to fade, the sounds, the colors, the thoughts. Silence beckoned like a waiting lover.

"Fight, damn it. Don't give in. Don't let go!" Saul's body trembled and he wept. He needed his mind to prevail over his emotions, needed to be in control. He was a warrior, having done battle with the black angel of death. He had held his precious daughter, kissed her tears, bade her farewell, seen friends killed defending Israel.

Now again he was entering a vast empty land where fires seethed his heart and pain turned to daggers.

Too much time lapsed between Robert's next breath.

"Breathe," Aaron screamed, imposing, insisting, his hands in a fist.

A shallow breath. Another one—shallower still.

He's not breathing!" Saul cried.

Aaron placed his mouth on Robert's. Compression…breath…compression…breath. His head against Robert's chest—listening.

Silence.

It was over.

Part 5

25

Thursday, December 7, 1972
Washington, D.C.
Andy Taxton's manor house

The alarm clock's ring jolted Jo awake. She groaned and mashed the button. Andy rolled to his side and threw an arm over her. "Don't go yet."

Jo smiled. She liked him most when he was like this—groggy, without pretense. "I'd stay if I could. But I'll miss my flight back to Albany." She kissed his forehead. He was back to sleep before her feet hit the floor.

Jo padded barefoot into the kitchen of Andy's three-storied, 19th century manor house that he had purchased only four months before. It was located in the Capitol Hill neighborhood, where for over one-hundred and seventy-five years members of Congress, Supreme Court justices, and Cabinet Members had lived.

Every room was impeccably furnished, an eclectic mix of antiques and contemporary. The decorator had an eye for comfort, and each room was expertly planned for intimate gatherings. But, just like Jo's apartment in Albany, this house did not seem to reflect Andy. She doubted he had even bothered to approve the choices.

Jo made her way into the kitchen. The staff kept it fully stocked, and for that she was grateful. She plugged in the coffee pot and put two pieces of Wonder Bread in the toaster. Then she turned on the television, and twirled the dial until she found the morning news.

The drone of the newscaster's voice was company as she carried her breakfast to the table.

"Robert Osborne," Jo whirled around at the mention of his name. "Was airlifted to George Washington University Trauma Center where he was pronounced dead from an apparent heart attack. Mr. Osborne is best known for his . . . ."

The coffee cup dropped from her hands and shattered on the floor. The agony was so intense, the shock so insidious and pervasive, all she could do was scream. It began as a low wailing that rose and lengthened until she was hysterical.

Andy rolled over. He thought he was dreaming, caught in some weird nightmare. His eyes shot open. He heard the scream again. He ran toward the sound.

"My God. What happened? Are you okay? Did you get burned? Are you cut?" He was all over Jo, touching her arms, moving her away from the broken glass.

"It's Robert." She trembled from head to toe. "The news." She pointed to the television screen. "They said he's dead."

"Maybe you heard it wrong." Andy turned the dial, changing the station. "Mr. Osborne will be remembered . . .," the reporter said. "Jesus Christ. Oh, Jo. I'm so sorry." Andy put his arms around her.

Jo sobbed, deep wrenching tears, the pain transporting her, as if she was struck by a violent and sudden storm that tossed her into a lightening charged sea. She was drowning, and gulped for air. Andy held her by the shoulders. She could see his lips moving, the fear in his eyes. She was unable to hear his words. Then everything went black.

Andy caught Jo as she collapsed in his arms. He sunk to the floor.

"Jo. Can you hear me?"

She was lying across his lap on the kitchen floor, dizzy and disoriented. "What happened?"

"You fainted." Andy held a glass to her lips. "Take a sip. Slowly. Good girl. Better?"

"I'm okay," Jo said.

"Let me help you up." Andy put his arm firmly around Jo's waist.

He half carried her to the den and helped her to the sofa. He draped an afghan over her.

Jo stared ahead, paralyzed with fear. She shuddered, the echo of reality dawning, a hungry beast devouring her. She wept yet again.

Andy stroked her head, murmuring inconsequential words meant to soothe.

Jo knew she had to do something. She couldn't just sit here wailing like a fool. What should she do? The thoughts wouldn't stay in her head long enough for her to make any kind of decision. Andy handed her a box of tissues. She wiped her eyes and blew her nose.

The news. They said Robert was taken to GW. That had to mean that Robert was here in Washington with Aaron. Jo's arms felt like lead, and it took a Herculean effort to reach for the phone. *Why hadn't Robert called me? He always called me.* She dialed Aaron's number. His longtime housekeeper, Hattie, picked it up on the first ring.

"Oh, Miss Jo, It was so awful. Mr. Osborne collapsed right here in the house."

Hattie's words brought a vision Jo was not ready to see. She closed her eyes and pushed it away. "Please. . . I. . . need to speak with Aaron."

Hattie's voice broke. "He's on the other line with the. . .funeral home."

Funeral home. Jo separated from herself, feeling shapeless and inert. She put her hand to her mouth.

"Wait one minute. I see he's off. Hold on," Hattie said. The phone clicked.

"Jo?"

"Aaron . . ." Jo started to cry again. "Is it true . . .is Robert really gone?"

"I'm so sorry, Jo."

"How could he come to Washington and not call? And then, when it happened," Jo paused long enough to take a breath, "why didn't you call and tell me?" She was suddenly furious at Aaron and most of all at Robert for leaving her.

"I called half a dozen times last night. The line must have been out of order." Aaron needed her friendship now. He needed to talk. "Can I come and get you?"

"No. That's okay. I'll get a ride." She hung up and turned to Andy. "They couldn't get through. Did you take the phone off the hook?"

"I wanted us to have some private time. Had I known something like this would happen—I'm so sorry, sweetheart."

Jo couldn't think straight. "I have to get dressed. I have to go to Aaron's." She was furious at Andy, but recognized it as misplaced.

* * *

They sat side by side in Andy's black Mercedes cabriolet. The traffic was heavy as they headed toward Virginia. Andy tried to make conversation with Jo but she didn't respond. She was stuck in a time warp—suspended between shock and reality. When they pulled into Aaron's driveway Jo was so confused she had to remind herself where she was and why she had come.

Andy turned off the ignition. Jo shook her head and put her hand on his arm. She needed to be with people who knew and loved Robert. "Please. Go back home. I'll call you later."

"Don't do this, Jo. Don't shut me out. I love you, and I want to be with you—to help you through this."

"I appreciate that. But, right now, you can't help me. No one can. Please, Andy. Just go."

Jo watched until Andy's car was out of sight. She walked to the front steps, but in her mind, she was careening off the side of a mountain toward the abyss. She was so dizzy she had to stop twice.

The front door opened. Aaron stood there, his eyes a reflection of Jo's pain. He rushed down the steps and took Jo's arm.

"I didn't even get the chance to say goodbye." A tear slipped from the corner of her eye.

"I'm sorry. We have to be grateful that it was over quickly, and he didn't suffer."

Jo leaned into Aaron, her head on his chest. She didn't know how long they stood on the porch, and she would never remember what they said to each other, but his very presence seemed to reach out and soothe her aching soul.

Aaron kept his arm firmly around Jo as they entered the living room. The first thing Jo saw was Saul, standing beside a chair, surrounded by golden white sunlight that spilled into the room through the glass windows that framed the upper walls. His hair was disheveled and his face was grey. Seeing him dumfounded Jo. She blinked her eyes as he kissed her.

"I had an unexpected business trip," Saul said. "We were going to surprise you." He swallowed hard.

Jo just nodded. She wanted to tell him she was happy to see him, but the words just wouldn't come.

William Belmont, Robert's best friend and lifetime agent, sat in a high-backed chair near the fireplace. He had arrived only minutes before from New York, and he too seemed to be trying to comprehend the incomprehensible. He raised his head and looked at Jo with a frozen expression. His eyes were red-rimmed and vacant.

Jo knelt in front of the chair and took William's hand. She could sense his need, and knew she had to turn her thoughts to someone other than herself. As important as Robert was to her, he had still been an ancillary part of her daily existence. Not so for William— the two men had been together daily for the better part of their lives. "I'm so very sorry, William. I know this is going to be hardest on you."

William nodded. "That's very kind of you to say. I'm sure we are all going to miss him." William looked into the distance. "Robert knew he pushed too hard. I begged him to slow down, but he refused to compromise even one moment of his life. As a fatalist, he said we were all travelers riding the waves of time, lifted toward the shore, never knowing how many waves we would traverse or storms and tempests we would have to survive before our days would come to an end." William's eyes misted as he gazed at Jo. "And then you came into his life and everything changed. You gave him so much joy. He was so proud of you."

The phone rang.

All eyes turned to Aaron as he answered. He spoke for a few

minutes, writing on a pad, his voice strained. "The arrangements have been finalized," he said, hanging up the receiver. "The funeral will be this Monday at St. Patrick's."

"St Patrick's." William pictured the lavish cathedral, and a soft smile curled the corners of his mouth. "Robert would have liked that."

"Monday's good," Saul said. "It will give Rebecca time to get here. Please excuse me; I need to make some calls."

"Aaron, can we talk alone for a minute?" Jo asked.

Aaron walked her to the veranda. The freezing wind rustled the branches of the denuded trees. He slipped his jacket over Jo's shoulders.

Jo stared into the distance—every minute seemed days long, every breath an effort. The shock of Robert's death had unleashed something inside her brain—emotions, an audacity of mind that elevated her thinking, a sensation that both frightened and confused her. *How can sorrow bring such a feeling?* She could see the future standing before her, like an obscure horizon. Yet, something had shifted, the waves of truth beginning to surface from the inside, a fault, a tiny crack that threatened to become a full-blown earthquake. "Robert's death, it's changed everything." She rubbed her temples, and looked at Aaron. "I feel so alone."

Aaron smoothed the hair from her eyes and kissed her forehead. "You are not alone. I'm here for you, and I always will be."

Jo saw something in Aaron's eyes she had never noticed before—reflections of hope, like the fairytales she had loved as a child. She blinked and looked away. When she looked back, her thoughts flew to her father and uncle. *Is it possible that they have taken control of my emotions? Can they can make me think I love someone if I don't?* Terror ripped at her gut. She needed time to be alone. Time to think.

"Aaron, can you get me away from here?" She put her hand on his chest. "I want to go tonight, before the news media surrounds this place, and the craziness begins."

"I have a friend who owns an airline charter company. I'll make the call."

* * *

A little after eleven o'clock, a King Air carrying one passenger glided in for its landing at a private airfield hidden among the stone walls and horse farms a few miles north of Bridgeport, Connecticut. Waiting in the shadows of the hangar stood a black limousine with its engine idling. Ten minutes later, the car was on I-95 heading toward the Triborough Bridge where it melded with the southbound traffic on FDR Drive.

The limousine dropped Jo at her townhouse.

The door opened before Jo could put her key in the lock. Sweeny was standing there. She took Jo into her arms.

"He's dead, Sweeny. Robert's gone," Jo sobbed, reeling in her agony.

"I know, baby. I know. Cry, it's good to let it out," Sweeny said, holding Jo tighter.

"I didn't make time to see him," Jo bawled. "That's why he came to Washington and didn't even call me. It's all my fault. Now it's too late."

"Shh," Sweeny cooed. "Robert loved you and wouldn't want you berating yourself." Sweeny took Jo's hand. "Come on. I'll make you some hot chocolate and we'll talk for a little while. Then I am going to tuck you into bed. You need sleep or you're going to get sick."

26

Friday morning, December 7, 1972
Naples, Florida

Hans stood with the telephone cradled against his head. He was standing on the veranda, looking at the storm lying along the horizon, the dark clouds gathering. A single seagull glided on a current of cool air, and some pieces of debris tumbled with the rising wind.

"What do you mean, you haven't seen her?" Hans said, the timbre of his voice threatening.

"I've spoken with her a dozen times. She went back to New York last night. She wants to be alone," Andy replied, his own anger seething. He didn't like the way Hans was speaking to him and, he didn't like his judgment being questioned.

Hans realized he needed to calm down. Andy was not the kind of person to be bullied. "Listen son, this is important. The media will be expecting you to support your fiancé, to be with her. So, please, be on the next flight. Just go to her. I know my daughter and, I promise you, once she sees you, she will be glad you came."

"I have a dinner meeting with the president tonight. I can't go until morning," Andy said. "Are you coming to the funeral?"

"It's best that I don't," Hans said. "I didn't even know the man."

"This isn't good," Otto said, when Hans hung up the phone. "I don't like the way Jo is exerting her independence. The shock of

Osborne's death may have overwhelmed the hypnosis. We need to get Jo alone so I can reinforce our control."

"We will. But, first we have to get through the funeral," Hans said, a smile pasted on his face. He slapped Otto on the back. "This is a great day! Robert Osborne is finally out of Jo's life."

* * *

Jo awakened Friday morning aching in sorrow. Sweeny, lying beside Jo in the king-sized bed, cradled Jo in her arms, patting her back, and stroking her brow as she cried.

The two girls decided to stay in their pajamas and, in between phone calls from Jo's father, Andy and Aaron, they talked. Jo wept, bargained with God, and speculated on how her life would change. Sweeny just listened.

"How do you know if someone is right for you?" Jo blurted between bouts of tears. "What is love, anyway? You thought you loved the professor and look what happened. Maybe I should just cancel the damn wedding."

"Honey, you can't make life-changing decisions when you're in this state. Besides, are you so sure you don't love him?"

"I don't know! I love the idea of being first lady," Jo said, forcing herself to be honest. "Who wouldn't? But, something feels wrong. Take my trips to Texas: every time we go Andy, his father, my father and uncle, they all hide out in a room with the door closed, as if planning a major invasion."

"Maybe you should give them all a break. It's no easy feat, mounting a campaign for the presidency," Sweeny said, running her fingers through her hair.

"I get that," Jo said, the frustration spilling over into her voice. "That's what pisses me off the most! I'm a senator, for Christ's sake. I've mounted and run a successful campaign. Furthermore, I'm giving up my career to marry Andy. The way I see it, that gives me a right to be involved in the planning and implementation of his campaign."

"So, say something," Sweeny interjected.

"I have. All I get is promises that when the time is right, I will be included." Jo pursed her lips.

"I don't know what to tell you," Sweeny said.

"Oh, there's more. My future mother-in-law, Mrs. Taxton, has taken it upon herself to teach me how to dress when going to such and such an occasion, how I should wear my hair, when to keep it up, when to wear it down. How do I tell her I don't give a shit? The whole thing infuriates me!"

"Okay. You do have a point. But, still—"

The phone rang, pulling Jo back into the moment. Her stomach lurched, her conversation about Andy suddenly so meaningless.

"It's done," Aaron said, calling for the third time that day. "The Stevens Funeral Home is on twenty ninth and Madison Avenue." Aaron sighed. "Are you sure you want to do this?"

"Yes. I need to see him. I need to say goodbye."

Sweeny leaned against the kitchen counter, a coffee cup in her hand. "Do you want me to come with you?"

"No thanks. I need to do this alone."

* * *

A stooped-shouldered lanky man with sleepy eyes greeted Jo at the funeral home. "Please." He bowed his head. "This way, Senator."

Jo followed the man down a carpeted hallway with a dozen closed doors. He stopped, turned, and tilted his head and eyes to the left. "Would you like me to accompany you?"

"No. Thank you."

Jo moved through the door. The room was dimly lit, wooden chairs in rows, a podium, and the leftover smell of bygone flowers pervasive.

In the far corner stood a gurney where Robert lay. His body was covered by a white sheet—all that showed was his frozen profile. A deep abiding horror tugged Jo forward.

She stood over the inert body, her mind refusing to register what her eyes were seeing. Deep within her psyche emerged the need to touch Robert. She stood on tiptoes and pressed her lips against his too perfect, unlined, expressionless face.

You're so cold! I have to find a blanket.

Frantic, she searched the shelf under the gurney. The absurdity of her actions struck and she collapsed on the floor, hugging her knees into her chest, crying so hard she could not catch her breath.

Jo didn't know if five minutes or fifty minutes passed but at some point, the tears stopped. She was drained, convinced that she might never cry again. She stood on trembling legs, again face to face with Robert's body. She placed her hand lightly on his chest.

My God, Robert, where are you? How can I be touching you, and yet you're not here? It was then that Jo drifted back to the Wall, back to the time when reality had suspended and she had touched another reality. In that remembering, a peace descended over Jo. Now, as she looked at Robert's body, a new truth became apparent: his physical body was an empty vessel, but his soul was here in this room—she could feel his presence.

There would be no goodbye. He would never really leave her.

Rest in peace my beloved.

One day, I will join you.

Saturday morning

Sweeny heard the door chime and nudged Jo, sleeping curled in a fetal position on the other side of the bed.

"Are you expecting anyone?"

"No," Jo mumbled.

Sweeny swung her legs to the floor, slipped into a pair of jeans and a sweatshirt and ran down the stairs. She looked through the peephole.

"Oh shit!" She pulled open the door.

Andy's eyes widened in surprise.

Sweeny stuck out her hand. "Nice to meet you, Senator. I'm Jo's best friend, Sweeny."

Andy smiled. "I know. I've seen your picture and heard all about you. Nice to finally meet you."

"Please come in," Sweeny said. *What am I going to do now? Jo will throw a fit when she finds out he's here.*

"Hello, Andy," Jo said, descending the stairs.

Sweeny swung around and mouthed the words, "I'm sorry."

Andy set his suitcase down on the floor, and kissed Jo's cheek. "Forgive me for showing up unannounced. But, I had to see you."

Jo wanted to blink him away but knew it was a ridiculous thought. He was, after all, her fiancé and she knew he meant well. She forced a smile. "Thank you for coming."

Danzel, her new butler approached from the hallway. "Allow me to take your luggage, sir."

"Please take it to the master suite," Jo said. "Let's have some coffee." Jo reached one hand for Sweeny and the other for Andy. "It's high time the two of you got to know each other."

Monday, December 11, 1972
The day of the funeral
New York City

Aaron, William, Saul, and Rebecca were chauffeured in from Robert's home in Sands Point. Before going to the church, they picked up Sweeny, Andy, and Jo. Now they all sat in silence as the stretch Mercedes limousine drove past the hundreds of fans standing two and three deep along Forty-Ninth Street and Fifth Avenue.

"Robert would be telling all of them to go home," Jo said.

William smiled, a tear trickling down his face. "True. But, he would have loved that they cared enough to be here."

The limousine pulled to a stop in front of St. Patrick's Cathedral, a gothic gray marble building with soaring spires. Jo reached for Sweeny's hand.

"Hang on, sweetheart. It will be over soon," Sweeny whispered as the doors of the car opened.

Jo was wearing a simple black cashmere sheath, black stockings, and heels. As she stepped from the car she pulled the collar of her fur coat up around her ears, and slipped on dark glasses. She held Andy's arm as they climbed the steps of the great cathedral.

She had studied the architecture and history of St. Patrick's in undergraduate school, and she loved the building. At any other time, she would have lingered at the St. Michael and St. Louis altars designed by Tiffany and Company and said a prayer at the St. Elizabeth altar designed by Paolo Medici of Rome. The only thing Jo took notice of was the echoing refrains coming from the 1930 gallery organ.

As they walked down the center aisle, making their way to the front row, a hush fell over the church. The priest came to the podium and the funeral mass began. Jo sat with her head down, trying to recall the eulogy she had written and memorized. The words refused to stay in her head.

"And now," the priest said, "we will hear from Senator Jotto Wells."

Jo looked up and felt herself go stiff. Her legs would not move. Panic set in. *I'm in trouble!*

Aaron looked over at Jo and knew she needed help. He stood, took Jo's hand, and walked her to the podium. Jo sent him a look that said thank you.

"You can do this," Aaron whispered.

Hundreds of faces stared back at Jo. *I will do this!*

"Today is a very sad day for all of us who knew and loved Robert Osborne." Jo said, looking over at the closed coffin. "You were one of the finest actors of our time and it is my honor to stand up here today and thank you for all the great performances you gave to us, and for all the magical moments—moments when you helped us suspend our realities. You were my best friend, my mentor, and the most incredible man I ever met."

Jo turned her eyes back toward the people in the pews. "To quote Robert Louis Stevenson, a friend is a gift you give yourself. Robert Osborne was my gift."

Her eyes settled on William. His nod reassured her. "Robert lived in the limelight of fame and he was always grateful. He would be the first to say he lived a charmed life. But there was another side to Robert—the very private side. He loved to read, recite poetry, listen to music, and spend quiet times with his friends. I was lucky enough to be a small part of that life. But the only woman Robert ever loved died during the Second World War. She had his heart and his love for her transcended time.

"Robert was a decorated soldier, too. He fought for France when death and hunger and tears were Europe's shroud. I know those times changed him forever. Yet he remained an optimist, a believer in humanity, always looking for the good in people, always offering hope.

"After the war, Robert moved to America. He became a citizen, got involved in politics, and was an ambassador of peace, a quiet warrior, a generous philanthropist.

"Yes, the stage was his career path, but what drove him was his deep abiding commitment to a world free of hunger and war. A world where people were judged by merit, not by the color of their skin or their religious beliefs.

"George Eliot said, 'The golden moments in the stream of life rush past us and we see nothing but sand; the angels come to visit us, and we only know them when they are gone.'" Jo turned to the coffin. "You were my angel, Robert. I knew it then, I know it now," she paused, her voice breaking. "Thank you for the days you walked among us. Go with God, Robert Osborne. We will all miss you."

* * *

Eight New York City police officers, riding motorcycles, escorted the two-hundred-car funeral procession to the Woodlawn Cemetery in the Bronx. It took thirty minutes from the City, over the Bronx and the Major Deegan Expressways. The hearse entered the cemetery on Webster Avenue and 233rd Street.

In summertime the four hundred acres of rolling lawns would have been lush with shade trees and blooming flowers. On this winter day the trees stood bare, the ground hard and cold, the sky overcast, and the temperatures in the low thirties.

"At least Robert will be in good company," Aaron said as the car pulled to a stop in front of the gravesite. "Woolworth, Macy, Westinghouse, Whitney, Guggenheim, Duke Ellington, and Damon Runyan are all buried here."

"It's a fine place," William said. "Robert would have approved."

Standing in the cold, they watched as the bronze casket was taken from the hearse to the open grave and put in place for burial.

Sweeny took one of Jo's hands; Andy took the other as they walked toward the chairs set up for the mourners. It seemed an interminable time to Jo as she waited for everyone to assemble.

During the short service, Jo sat still as a statue, an observer, unwilling to allow the experience to penetrate the barrier she had set up around herself. It was the only way she could get through what happened next—the metallic grinding of the gear mechanism as Robert's casket was lowered into the ground.

The priest made the sign of the cross.

It was over.

27

Robert Osborne's Estate
Sands Point, New York

It was only twenty-five miles to Robert's fourteen-acre waterfront estate in Sands Point. But the traffic was heavy on the Cross Bronx and Long Island Expressways and it took over an hour.

"The caterers should have everything ready by the time we get there," Aaron said, looking at his watch. He had hired Nemade Stuart, the best caterer in Manhattan.

When they arrived, it was obvious Aaron had spared no costs. There were banquet tables and serving stations set up throughout the downstairs: in the den, living room, dining room, and the main ballroom. Bartenders, waiters, busboys, and chefs stood at each location ready to feed the three-hundred invited guests.

* * *

The marble floors echoed as Jo walked from room to room, accepting condolences, making small talk, listening to corners of disjointed conversations from people standing in tight little groups, balancing their food, laughing and talking.

It's not a party. It's a wake! Jo wanted to scream. *Why don't you all go away?*

Instead, more people kept arriving.

Jo looked at her watch. She couldn't believe it was after seven. She went searching for Andy and found him in the library sharing a bottle of Hennessy Cognac with Deborah Kerr, Peter Ustinov, Carol Channing, and Sweeny.

"You know my fiancé?" he said as Jo approached.

Jo stuck out her hand for Peter and kissed Carol and Deborah. "We've met. Thank you for coming. Andy, Sweeny, may I speak with you a moment?"

"Don't go away," Andy said to the actors, his speech slightly slurred. "I'll be back in a second."

"I'm going upstairs to lie down for a while. I just wanted you to know."

"Are you okay?" Andy said, kissing her cheek.

"Just very tired."

Sweeny slid next to Jo and took her hand. "I'm going back to the City. If you want company in the morning, I'll come back."

"Thanks. I'll call you," Jo said, giving her a hug.

* * *

Jo climbed the marble stairway, her hand sliding over the hand-tooled brass banister. At the top of the stairway was an eight-foot circular window. At the end of the hallway, past eight guest suites, Jo turned left and pushed open the double doors that led to Robert's study. She switched on the light and scanned the room, thinking about all the hours she had spent here, surrounded by the brimming bookcases, studying for the bar while sitting at Robert's desk, or lounging on the sofas as they talked about strategy for her election. She glanced at the photograph of her taken with Robert at her swearing in ceremony as a state senator. Her knees grew weak.

"Hello."

Jo spun around. Rebecca was sitting on the sofa in the dark, her stocking feet on the coffee table. She had taken down her hair, and removed her suit jacket.

"Sorry. I didn't mean to disturb you," Jo said.

"You're not, silly girl. I just needed a breather."

"I know what you mean." Jo collapsed on the sofa across from Rebecca. "So many people."

"Do you think they're ever going to leave?"

Jo laughed. "God, I hope so."

"It's all Aaron's fault, you know." Rebecca grinned. "Hiring one of the best chefs in the country."

Jo pulled off her shoes and rubbed her aching feet. "Let's kill him."

The two women looked at each other. The facades fell and the smiles turned to tears.

"I miss him."

"I know," Rebecca said.

Jo reached over and grabbed a rubber band from the desk.

"You were lucky to have known him," Rebecca said, slipping her wedding ring on and off her finger.

"I'm not sure I ever really did," Jo said, pulling her hair into a ponytail. "He would talk to me about his past, about Morgan, but I always felt he was holding back."

Goose bumps broke out on Rebecca's neck and arms. She yearned to tell Jo that Morgan Osborne was her biological mother.

"Tell me about them," Jo said, her voice childlike, as if she were asking for a bedtime story.

Morgan and Robert's lives were an integral part of Rebecca's history. She nodded, happy for the opportunity to share at least part of their story with Jo. "Robert was traveling through Europe, looking for his next leading lady when he stopped in Vilna, Poland and saw Morgan on stage.

"Robert said he always knew that Morgan was destined to be a great star and even though she was only seventeen, he pursued her as only Robert could do."

"What year was that?"

Rebecca put her finger to her lip as she counted back the time. "It was 1937."

"She would have been fifty-two this year."

"Yes. That's correct." Rebecca felt the stab of time. She had aged, but in Rebecca's mind, Morgan was forever young. "To this day, I don't know how Robert convinced Morgan to go with him to Paris," Rebecca said. "Things were so different then. Young women from prominent Jewish families did not run off, particularly when it meant breaking the contract on an arranged marriage."

"An arranged marriage?" Jo asked, a look of astonishment on her face.

"I know. It's easy to judge. But Morgan's family were Orthodox Jews. It was their custom," Rebecca said.

"Poor Morgan. No wonder she ran away."

"It's more complicated than that," Rebecca offered. "Morgan didn't run away because of the marriage contract. She would have gone through with that. It was meeting Robert and his promise to make her a star." Rebecca put her hands in a prayer position by her heart. "Still, had she known what it would do to her father—" Rebecca paused. "She would not have gone."

"What happened?" Jo asked.

"Doctor Samuel Rabinowiszch suffered a stroke when he found out his only child had run away. He almost died."

Jo's hand flew to her mouth. "That's horrible."

"It gets much worse," Rebecca said. "He could not find it in his heart to forgive Morgan. He declared her dead, and sat Shiva."

"Shiva?"

"Formal mourning," Rebecca said. "That's what a Jew does when there's a death in the family."

"I don't understand," Jo said, tucking her feet under her.

"Neither do I. At the time I knew Morgan, I was not a Jew and so, when she told me, I just listened, trying not to pass judgment on a religion I did not understand. Today I sit here as a Jew, and today I can tell you: I still do not understand how a father can mourn for a child that still lives. But, he did.

"The hardest part was that Morgan adored her father. They had been very close when she was growing up and she suffered terribly at his unwillingness to forgive her.

"The one good thing was that Morgan did have contact with her mother, Sara. They wrote to each other and when they could, spoke on the telephone. Still, Morgan never saw either parent again." Rebecca's eyes grew distant.

"How horrible it must have been for all of them."

Rebecca sighed. "People make decisions, sometimes right, sometimes wrong. You make your bed—you lie in it. Jewish parents hammer that into their children's heads, even in Israel."

"Was she happy anyway?"

Rebecca's expression changed. Her mouth set and her eyes twinkled. "Damn right she was. When Morgan stood on the stage, she captured it in a way I have never seen any other actress do. When she and Robert were on stage together, it was astonishing.

"Off stage, as corny as this is going to sound to you, they were like two halves fitting together to form one perfect person." Rebecca blinked back tears.

"And you, Rebecca? After everything Morgan went through, how did you ever find the courage to leave your family and go with Saul? And to Israel no less!"

"First of all, I had my family's blessings. And second," Rebecca laughed. "I was madly in love and a little mad. I had absolutely no idea what I was getting into. Not that I would change anything." A shadow fell across her face. "That's not entirely true. I would change a lot of things, but nothing about my relationship with Saul. I loved him then. I love him still."

"That's the kind of love I always thought I would have," Jo said, her voice a whisper. "The kind of love that transcends time."

Rebecca lifted her face toward Jo. "And you don't?"

Jo sighed and shook her head. "I love Andy, but I am not sure I love him enough to spend the rest of my life with him."

Rebecca had been debriefed by Saul when she arrived from Israel and she knew all about Natan's report on Otto Milch and Doctor Hans Wells. To add to that information, Aaron had posited the possibility that Jo was under some type of hypnotic suggestion perpetrated by her father.

Rebecca had studied hypnosis, knew the power of suggestion, and seeing the disconnect between the words Jo said and the lack of expression on her face convinced Rebecca that there was reason for concern.

"Would you like some advice?" Rebecca said, concentrating on keeping her voice neutral.

"Please."

"Postpone the wedding until you are sure."

"Oh, Rebecca, how I wish it were that easy."

Rebecca leaned forward on her elbows. "You ran for the Senate and then decided to give up your career to marry. I would say you are a very decisive young woman. Make your needs known and then do something about it."

Jo's skin prickled. She bit her finger. "I'm good at professional decisions. That's always been easy for me. On the personal front, I'm insecure as hell."

"Insecure?" The therapist in Rebecca was fascinated. "I would have never thought that about you."

"I'm sure it has something to do with having a mother who doesn't like me very much and never has. In fairness to her, she has serious problems; she drinks too much and takes pills. As a kid it was hard to reconcile that or to excuse her behavior toward me." Jo's face flushed.

"I kept trying to win her approval. I never could. You know the saddest thing of all? I can't remember a moment of intimacy or a kind word from my mother.

"Then, to top it off, and make my life even more confusing, my father and uncle hovered over me like two clucking roosters." Jo wanted to tell Rebecca the truth about her father and uncle but the words got scrambled in her brain, and then disappeared. "The incongruity of it all really screwed me up." Jo frowned. "I know what you're thinking. And you're right. I should have had therapy."

"It's never too late."

Jo laughed. "I guess not." She stared at Rebecca. "I wish I could go back to Israel with you. It was the only place I ever felt totally whole."

"You came as a tourist. Believe me when I tell you, Israel is not an easy place to live. Besides, right now you're just looking for an escape. Running away is not the answer," Rebecca said, sucking in her cheeks, hating herself for sounding like a doctor instead of a friend. "The pain will follow you. That is why you have to find the courage to make a decision."

"I just can't," Jo said, a stubborn scowl deepening her sapphire eyes. "I don't have the courage to face them."

"Them? Who are you talking about, Jo?"

"The people in my life who say they love me."

Rebecca leaned on her knees and stared at Jo. "I am going to give you my professional opinion. Talk to Andy. If he loves you, he will understand. You can do this, Jo. I know you can."

"And Israel?"

"She will be there waiting for you, and so will I," Rebecca said. "Now, let's go see if we can get those caterers to start cleaning up so that everyone will leave."

28

The next morning
Sands Point, New York

Jo slipped from the bed. Sleep had been elusive and the night interminable. She picked up the clock for a better look. It was five o'clock in the morning. Andy was still asleep, lying on his back, the covers tucked under his chin.

They had spent the night in the guesthouse. Robert always referred to the three-bedroom, two-storied place as his French country chic, couture bungalow. He furnished it himself and was the first to admit it was kitschy, sentimental, and totally tasteless. There were pillows embroidered with the French flag, fleur-de-lis tables in the shape of lilies, wooden cottage swans sitting on a distressed Illumination chest, a black Rhapsody credenza, and a Louis XVI sofa that was so uncomfortable no one ever sat on it.

Jo went into the kitchen, turned the tap on the antique farm sink, and made coffee. She was on her second cup when Andy came into the room. He was dressed in suit and tie, briefcase in hand.

"It's nice of you to get up this early," Andy said. "Unnecessary, but nice."

That's me. Always nice. Jo glanced at Andy from the corner of her eye. Rebecca's words reverberated in her head, *talk to Andy. If he loves you, he'll understand.*

Andy looked at her and smiled. "Sweetheart, if you need me to stay with you today, I can change my flight and go back to Washington tomorrow."

"Thanks. I'll be fine."

"If you're sure." Andy perched on the stool beside the counter. *Make your feelings known.* Jo handed him a coffee mug. "We have to talk."

"What is it, darling?"

The words Jo wanted to say began dissolving before they formed. She battled the barrier preset in her mind. Determination seemed to disable her. She steadied her breathing and took another tack. "Andy, you know that I love you," Jo said, relieved how easily those words came. "And, this has nothing to do with the way I feel about you but, I want us to postpone the wedding for a little while." *There, I said it!*

Andy placed the coffee cup on the counter; his hand was trembling discernibly—the look on his face incredulous. "Darling, I know you've had a terrible shock. But you have to trust me on this. The best thing for you, for both of us, for our future, is to go ahead with our wedding."

Jo felt herself weaken, his words having the power to dissuade. "Please, Andy. If you really love me, you will do this for me."

The wedding was scheduled to take place at Andy's home. His thoughts turned to the elaborate plans his mother already had in place, the orchestra, the caterers, the flowers scheduled to be flown in from tulip farms in Holland, the hand-written invitations, crafted by a renowned calligrapher. She would be furious. Of course, all of that was of little consequence when he thought about the reaction he would get from his future father-in-law. "You know I would do anything for you. But it's not like the wedding is tomorrow. You'll have plenty of time to grieve." Andy knew the moment he said those words it was a mistake.

Jo glared at him. Something inside her brain exploded, tearing away a barrier. "This is my grief. And, unlike yours, mine doesn't have a timetable. So tell your family that I'm sorry, but we are going to wait at least six months."

* * *

Rebecca sat alone in the living room. The sun had been up for an hour yet the windows were still frost-covered, prisms deflecting and distorting the view, casting a shadowed gloom throughout the room.

She could hear the house staff in the kitchen preparing breakfast. The noise of clanging pots and chattering women made her long for Israel, the kibbutz, and her children. She needed to get back to work. It was how she kept sane and kept the monsters in the closet. It had been like that ever since Rebecca lost her second child, Miriam, to leukemia. The vision of her dead little girl hovered. The depression struck like a bayonet. Rebecca closed her eyes and forced herself to push aside the image.

Jo. I have to think about Jo. What are we going to do? She is going to have to be deprogrammed. That will take time. Time I don't have.

* * *

The sideboard was set for breakfast with hot steamers, pancakes, fried potatoes, scrambled eggs, fruit platters, bagels, and an assortment of smoked fish. The sweet smell of brewing coffee filled the room, poured from a silver decanter by Robert's cook, a woman with silver grey hair, cherry red lips, and a belly that had seen too much of her own cooking.

Saul and Rebecca sat on one side of the twelve-foot table, Aaron and Natan, the man handling the investigation into Jo's past, sat on the other side.

Aaron looked at his watch. "I know William said he would not be down for breakfast, but where is Jo?" He turned to Rebecca.

She shrugged, her face drawn. "Andy left at dawn. Maybe she went back to sleep."

Saul could sense that his wife was upset. "Rebecca, what's on your mind?"

"Jo and I had a long talk last night, and I'm concerned about her. First and foremost, I think Aaron's supposition that Jo has been subjected to mind-control is correct. I found a disconnect or personality split; call it abject disassociation between Jo's words and her desires.

"In my opinion it appears that Jo has been a victim of repetitive behavior control techniques, stimulus-response, or feedback loops.

We know the human subconscious can be manipulated without upsetting other intellectual functions. Jo seems to be the perfect example of that."

Suddenly Aaron wished he had paid closer attention in psychology 101. "Can it be reversed?"

"Given enough time," Rebecca nodded. "I think so. There's something else." Rebecca looked hard at Natan. "Jo intends to postpone the wedding."

Forks froze in midair.

Natan placed his hands on the table and pushed himself up. "They aren't going to allow that to happen. These people, and who knows how many there are, have been grooming Jo and planning her future since she was born. Don't think for even a second they'll allow her to postpone. Not when Taxton can give them access to the front door of the White House."

"I've wanted to talk to you about that," Aaron said. "I've studied Taxton's voting record. He has sided with Israel on every occasion and has never done one thing in all his years in office that would identify him as an anti-Semite."

Saul leaned forward. "We've been doing some checking of our own. The senior Taxton seems to have ties to the Reich. He and Henry Ford, a known anti-Semite, were friends. Huge sums of money passed between the two men. We don't know the particulars, but it is not farfetched to think that Anderson Taxton is not the good American he would have the world think he is."

"That being said, we also know for a fact that Anderson is in total control of his son," Natan added.

"What are our options?" Aaron tensed, his elbows on the table, his hands in a prayer position. "How do we protect Jo?"

"We have to establish the upper hand and make them afraid of us—very afraid." Natan's eyes blazed. "I know exactly how to put the fear of God into those Nazi bastards.

"We know that Hans Wells is under the protection of the Americans. We can't touch him," he said, as if continuing a discussion that hadn't been interrupted by Robert's death. "But, Otto Milch is another story. We didn't get to this the other night and," he glanced at Saul, "I never even told you what I found."

Saul's stomach tightened. He wiped his mouth and waited.

"Wiesenthal was sure he had seen the name Otto Milch before. He just wasn't certain where. So we started digging through files we haven't touched in years.

"Call it the hand of God, but we found the file we were looking for—testimony from a survivor taken at a displaced persons camp in Cyprus just a few months after the liberation of Auschwitz.

"The survivor, let's call him Max, reported seeing a man he identified as the SS guard who had beaten him. The guard was masquerading as a survivor, living beside and sharing food with the very people he had starved and mutilated. The guard had changed the color of his hair, and grown a beard." Natan grew still, his breathing labored. "But, I can assure you, one never forgets the eyes.

"The guard was interrogated. He gave up the name of his direct superior officer at Auschwitz. The name he gave was Otto Milch."

"Are you telling us that my government knew about Otto Milch and still they allowed him to emigrate from Bolivia?" Aaron asked, his face tight lines of furry.

Natan nodded. "A few dollars put in the right hands, and anything is possible." He turned his eyes towards Saul. "That decision will now work in our favor."

"What do you have in mind?" Saul asked.

"We will insist the Americans turn Otto Milch over to the Israeli government to stand trial for war crimes," Natan said.

"And if the Americans refuse?" Aaron asked.

"Then we go public with what we have, copies of written testimony from survivors the man tortured, eyewitness accounts, everything we have that implicates Otto Milch as the sadist monster that he is."

"Jesus Christ," Aaron said, horrified at the thought of blackmailing America into deporting Otto Milch. The very idea sent shivers down his spine. "What about Jo? If this comes out it will destroy her."

"Believe me, I don't like the idea of hurting Jo any more than you do. So let's hope it doesn't come to that," Natan said. "However, we must exact justice for the six million who no longer have a voice. And we have to keep the Nazis out of the White House at all costs. Let's pray that bringing Milch to trial in Israel will be enough to scare them into hiding. We must try."

Aaron thought about his own parents—the sacrifice they made to keep him alive. No. He would not remain a bystander; the silence would cost him his soul. "I have a feeling my government will want Otto Milch's case handled with the utmost impunity. Let me make a call to a friend in the State Department and let's see if we can get Otto Milch detained quietly." Aaron stood.

The room grew silent.

"There's one more thing," Aaron said. "I know the timing stinks but while you're all still here, we have to go over Robert's Last Will and Testament."

"Today?" Rebecca asked.

"Today," Aaron replied. "As soon as Jo gets up."

* * *

Aaron opened the double doors to the library, switched on all the lights, and arranged four chairs in a semi-circle in front of the desk. He took Robert's will from his briefcase. He was flipping through pages and making notes when he heard footsteps in the hallway.

The door opened. Jo hesitated on the threshold. "Is it true? Are you going to read Robert's will today?"

"I'm sorry, Jo. I have no choice. As Robert's executor it is my duty to carry out his directives, and he stipulated that everyone be present when the will is read. Since I have to be back in Washington tomorrow morning, it has to be today."

Jo slipped out of her parka and draped it over the back of the sofa. She pulled off her gloves and yanked the scarf from her head. Her hair fell in ringlets around her flushed face. She rubbed her hands together and moved toward the fireplace.

"Are you okay?"

Jo scrunched her face. "Great! My best friend died. I just postponed my wedding, and now I have to listen to the reading of a will. How could I be better?"

"I didn't…"

Jo waved her hand. "That was snotty. I'm sorry. I'm just tired. The truth is, I am okay." Jo knew there was no denying her sadness, but making the decision about the wedding made her feel better.

"Do you want to talk about it?" Aaron asked, taking a bottle of Dom Perignon from the ice bucket on the bar and filling five Baccarat glasses, as he had been instructed to do by Robert.

"Not right now."

Rebecca, Saul and William entered.

"Good morning, sleepy head." Rebecca kissed Jo's cheek. "How did it go?"

"As planned. He was not a happy camper," Jo whispered.

"But you did it."

Jo smiled. "Yes, I did."

Aaron handed out the glasses.

"It's a bit early for me," William said.

"I know. And I'm sure when Robert requested that you all be sipping champagne when his will was read, he didn't envision it being this early in the day."

William, in a crumpled suit, with smudged glasses and hair falling into his eyes, pulled his slouched shoulders back and smiled. "What the heck." He lifted his glass. "Wherever you are, my friend, I hope the lights are bright, the stage is huge, and the audience appreciative."

They clinked glasses.

"If you'll allow me to begin?" Aaron said, moving behind the desk. "The Last Will and Testament is a legal document written to dispose of a person's property after their death. You will each receive a copy of Robert's will in its entirety. But, for our purposes today, I have taken the liberty of condensing it.

Aaron turned a few pages. "'To my lifelong friends, Rebecca and Saul,'" Aaron quoted from the document, "'I leave the enormous responsibility of overseeing the establishment, in the State of Israel, of an acting school—The Morgan and Robert Osborne Theatrical Institute—and a theatre—The Morgan Rabinowiszch Theatre of the Performing Arts.'

"Robert wanted to resurrect Morgan's familial name, Rabinowiszch, a name he said he'd tricked her into dropping when she came to Paris."

William thought back to the day he and Robert were walking along the Champs Elysees, trying to figure out how to protect Morgan from the Germans, a way to hide her Jewish identity. They had decided that dropping her last name was the only way. He smiled, knowing the wrong had finally been righted.

Aaron continued, "Robert envisioned the building of this project as his way of bringing Morgan back home to her people, and has bequeathed fifteen million dollars to this endeavor. The architectural plans are drawn and the land has been purchased.

"He stipulated that if either Saul or Rebecca were unable to oversee the project for any reason, then their son and daughter were to be designated. Of course, there are boards to be appointed and foundations to be established, but we'll discuss all of that at another time."

Rebecca took Saul's hand. The look that passed between them said it all; their lives were about to get a lot more complicated, and a lot busier.

"'To William,'" Aaron continued, "'the brother who stood by me, a silent force, and my strength. I leave you the sum of one million dollars. You kept me sane, and I loved you. Now go and have a good time.'"

William's face blotched red. Robert was his good time. Only the friendship mattered and now it was gone. He stood, muttered something unintelligible under his breath, and left the room.

Aaron waited a few moments, turning pages, giving everyone a moment to collect themselves.

"'To my Jo,'" Aaron continued. "'To the daughter I never had. I leave you my home in Sands Point, New York, all its possessions, and the balance of my estate.'

"A substantial amount of money has been earmarked for several charities," Aaron said, crossing his arms over his chest. "That still leaves you an heiress with a portfolio worth around six million dollars."

Jo was stunned. She knew Robert had a lot of money, but she had never contemplated that he was this rich or that he would be leaving it to her. "Six million dollars?"

"That much money can give you a lot of freedom," Rebecca said.

"Freedom?" Jo wondered if freedom was something to be bought. She was financially independent now, even without the subsidy her father deposited in her bank account each month. *I have always had money, and yet I've never been truly free. I'll think about this later.* Jo turned her attention back to Aaron. "Are you going to file a Petition for Probate and Letters Testamentary?"

Aaron smiled, enjoying the subtle way Jo reminded him she was an attorney. "Yes, Counselor," he said as William walked back into the room.

William picked up the bottle of Dom Perignon. "Robert wouldn't want us to be sad. He would want us to celebrate the life that he lived. The cook is making lunch, and in the meantime, let's drink."

* * *

After a long lunch, as they sat sipping coffee at the dining room table, Jo said, "I really have to get back to the City. Sweeny is going to Nepal in the morning, and I want to spend some time with her before she goes. I'll see you all tomorrow." She kissed Saul, shook Natan's hand, and hugged William and Rebecca.

Aaron walked with her to the door. He handed Jo the key to Robert's Bentley.

"You're kidding, right?"

"Nope."

Jo giggled. "I might get used to this heiress thing." She stood on tiptoes and kissed Aaron's cheek. "I'll be back early in the morning so I can see you before you go back to Washington."

29

Tuesday, December 12, 1972
New Brunswick, New Jersey

Kurt Blome and Alexander Lippisch met in Kurt's utilitarian office on the Rutgers campus at ten o'clock in the morning. The room
had a metal desk, a worn leather high-back chair, two metal folding chairs, and a half dozen green filing cabinets. A coat rack was
perched by the door.

Alex stood in front of the only window, his hands clasped behind
his back. "About an hour ago I got a call from a source inside the
State Department. The Israelis are demanding the deportation of
Otto Milch. They want him to stand trial in Israel."

"Son of a bitch," Kurt sneered. "I told Hans to keep Otto in Bolivia."

"Pointing fingers will not get us out of this," Lippisch snapped.
"I can't even say I'm that surprised. Think about it. The same night
the Israelis are seen going into Blumenthal's house, Robert Osborne
dies. It can lead us to only one conclusion: the information they
brought was bad enough to give the poor bastard a heart attack."

Kurt tapped the side of his head with his forefinger. "Excellent
deduction. Now, what do we do?"

Alex took a slip of paper from his pocket. "We came here by
invitation. The United States government will protect us to protect
themselves. That won't be the case with Milch. The Americans will
make a deal with the Israelis and give up Milch for a promise that
their government is not implicated in the process. I can assure you,
the Israelis want to see Milch hang, so they will agree."

"Then our problems are solved," Kurt said, a grin on his pudgy face.

Alex's face turned purple. "No, you fool! Otto Milch will squeal like a pig the moment he's caught. All of us will be implicated!"

"But you just said the Americans will protect us."

"When the Israelis have our names they will want us all." Alex picked up the phone on Kurt's desk and dialed the number on the sheet of paper. "We can't let that happen."

That evening
Miami, Florida

Calle Ocho, Eighth Street in Miami was Havana repositioned—a street created by the Cubans to mimic their homeland. Twenty-four hours a day, it beat to a rhythm of loud music, honking horns, and the smells of *café con leche, ropa vieja,* roasting chickens, and frying pork chunks.

Otto and Elaine Milch entered the Versailles restaurant. It was Otto Milch's favorite—an iconoclastic Cuban diner with wall-to-wall mirrors, chandeliers, murals and noisy patrons—a poignant, campy attempt at French opulence. The place and the people always energized Otto after the staid propriety of the Naples crowd.

Otto and his wife Elaine walked to their table, her bosoms bouncing, her tight dress hugging ample curves. There were low whistles, and clucking tongues of approval as they passed. Elaine flipped her died auburn hair from her face, and fluttered her false eyelashes.

The waiter pulled back Elaine's chair, his eyes dancing over her ample buttocks.

Over dinner Otto said, "I have great plans for us this evening. A new club just opened. You get to pick our guy." Otto licked his lips.

Elaine pasted a smile on her face. She had entered this marriage with her eyes wide open, determining that a life of luxury was worth certain compromises. She endured with stoic passivity Otto's perverted needs, regretting her decision only when Otto turned violent.

Elaine had more black eyes, broken fingers, and sprained wrists than she cared to think about. In the beginning of their marriage, she endured the sadistic, vicious attacks. Fearing that he might one day kill her, she turned to her brother-in-law. Hans stepped in and now the cruelty was only occasional. She was grateful for small favors.

* * *

Otto and Elaine came out of the restaurant. Their chauffer-driven Lincoln Towncar was sitting curbside. Peter, their chauffeur held open the door, and Elaine ducked inside. Peter then walked around to the driver's side and held the door for Otto. Neither one noticed the big rig eighteen-wheeler heading straight for them.

The truck veered right and sideswiped the car. The collision ripped the door off its hinges, and peeled steel off the Lincoln, tearing away half the car. Sparks flew and rubber burned as the chauffeur and Otto were crushed between the two vehicles. The truck teetered for a second before the driver shifted gears, hit the gas, and sped into the night.

Moments after the impact Elaine kicked open the door and fell to the pavement. She crawled to her fallen husband, her hands slipping on the pooling blood. Otto's face was obliterated, an eyeball hung from the socket, an ear was gone, his nose smashed like putty, his mouth open in a soundless scream.

"Help me! Help me!" Elaine shrieked.

Crowds gathered and the police and ambulance arrived amid explosive sirens and flashing lights.

Elaine sat on the curb with a blanket wrapped around her shoulders, watching in astonishment as Otto and Peter's bodies were covered with black tarps.

A paramedic with huge blue eyes asked if he could call someone. "Why?" she asked, vacant eyed. "Is there something wrong? Did something happen?"

"John, you better come over here. I think we have a problem."

* * *

Elaine's ambulance ride to Jackson Memorial Hospital was surreal; the wailing siren, the claustrophobic gurney, the weird lighting, the good looking guy checking her blood pressure. She was rolled into a curtained cubicle in the emergency room.

"My name is Doctor Colsky. I'm a psychiatrist, and I'm here to help you," a kindly faced man with transparent red-veined skin said. "I know you've been through a terrible shock. Can you tell me what happened?"

Elaine was lying on the gurney, her mouth pinched tight, her eyes suddenly wild. She sprang to a sitting position, swinging her feet to the ground. The doctor grabbed her arm. "Please, miss. We are only trying to help you."

"I have to get out of here!" Elaine howled, pulling her arm from the doctor's grasp.

"We need some help, please," Dr. Colsky yelled, losing his calm-er-than-thou demeanor.

Elaine kicked and scratched. It took two orderlies and the doctor to restrain her.

"I'm going to give you an injection to calm you down. In the morning, after you've had a good sleep, we will talk."

Three hours later, Elaine opened her eyes. Her mouth was dry as cotton and her head hurt. She looked around, bewildered. Then Otto's obliterated face, his bloodied body, and the black tarp flashed in her memory. A smile turned her lips. There was a million dollar life insurance policy in her name, part of the deal she had made when they married. *Double indemnity.* She started to laugh. *Two million dollars. I'm going to be rich!*

Elaine found her wrinkled, bloodstained clothes in a drawer next to the bed and dressed. She snuck down the stairway.

Otto was dead.

She was finally free.

Naples, Florida

Ilya Wells lay sprawled on the bed in her room. It was two in the morning, her special time, when she could wallow in her misery without interference from the servants, her husband, or her brother. She sipped vodka, watching a Johnny Carson rerun on the television.

The phone rang. *Han's will get it. Probably one of his whores!* She was too drunk to register that the hour was late and that there might be something wrong.

In his bedroom two doors away, Hans was awakened from a sound sleep by the ringing. He switched on the light, saw the time, and began to tremble as he reached for the telephone.

Ilya waited for the ringing to stop before she picked up the phone to listen.

"This is Sergeant Swanko from the City of Miami Police Department. I would like to speak with Doctor Hans Wells, please."

"This is Doctor Wells. How can I help you?"

"Otto Milch is your brother-in-law?"

"Yes, he is. Now, if you do not mind, I would like to know what this is about," Hans said, clenching his fists in fear.

"I'm sorry, sir. There's been an accident, a hit and run outside the Versailles restaurant." Sergeant Swanko hesitated.

"And?" Hans asked, his head pounding.

"Mr. Milch was pronounced dead at the scene."

"What are you talking about? There has to be a mistake."

"I am so sorry. But Mr. Milch has been identified by his wife."

"Was Elaine hurt?"

"No. She's fine."

At first, the words made no sense to Ilya. Then, like a burning fuse hits its charge, her brain exploded with the realization that there would never be enough alcohol or drugs to shield her from the pain of losing her twin, the only person who ever really loved her. She dropped the phone. The scream that followed was primal.

She crawled on all fours to the bathroom and pulled herself up, holding on to the sink for support. Vacant eyes stared back at her from the mirror. With determined hands, she opened the medicine cabinet.

Holding the blade between thumb and pointer, she pulled the razor across her wrist, and then watched like a fascinated observer as the arterial blood pulsated to the rhythm of her heartbeat. Within seconds, she began to feel lightheaded. She slipped to the floor, watching as her white gossamer Dior nightgown turned crimson.

Hans charged into the room moments after hearing Ilya's screams. He found her lying in an ever-expanding pool of blood.

"What the fuck have you done?" He howled, tearing a strip of fabric from her dressing gown. He made a tourniquet, lifted her arm above her heart, and applied pressure to the femoral artery to stop the bleeding.

"Leave me alone, you son of a bitch," Ilya snarled, sinking her teeth into Hans' arm.

He grabbed a handful of her hair and yanked hard. Ilya cried out. Her teeth disengaged and her eyes rolled back in her head.

"I really don't give a shit if you die, you sick, selfish bitch. But I have enough to deal with right now, and I'm not about to let you make things worse."

Hans retrieved the medical kit from his room, took out a vial of morphine, filled a syringe, and plunged the needle into Ilya's arm. Then he stitched her wrist and dressed the wound before carrying her to the bed. He had just finished changing her nightgown when Ilya's eyes flew open.

"No! No!" she howled, kicking her feet and scratching at his face.

"Enough!" Hans hissed, making a fist and applying pressure to Ilya's larynx.

She coughed and fought for breath.

"Are you going to stop?" he snarled, applying more pressure.

Ilya's eyes bulged. "Yes," she managed to say.

"We have a responsibility, you and I. That responsibility is to uphold the appearance of normalcy for Jotto's sake, and for the Reich. So make no mistake my dear, you are going to behave, because if you don't, you will spend the rest of your life tied to a bed, peeing in a bedpan. Do we understand each other?"

Ilya grunted her assent before losing consciousness.

Hans went into his bathroom, stripped off the pajamas and stepped into the shower. The blood from his arms and hands puddled at his feet, turning pink before disappearing down the drain. The water soothed him—made it easier to think.

He wasn't surprised that Otto was dead. He knew that was inevitable after speaking with his comrade Lippisch earlier in the day. After all, what choice did they have? The Israelis were demanding Otto's deportation.

"It's all your fault. You never should have brought him here," Lippisch had said, his anger, like a boa constrictor, wrapping itself around Hans.

Hans couldn't tell Lippisch the truth, that he needed Otto. That without him he couldn't control Jotto—that without Otto they might lose everything.

It happened so fast. Hans dried off, put on fresh pajamas, and slipped into bed. He looked at the clock. He would now have to do his own damage control.

He lifted the receiver off the phone beside his bed. As much as he hated doing this, Hans needed someone Jotto trusted to break the news to her, and he couldn't wait for Andy to get to New York.

He had spoken with Jotto earlier in the evening and knew she was back in the City and that Aaron Blumenthal was still staying at the Osborne home. He looked up the number in his address book and dialed.

On the first ring Aaron switched on the light, and reached for the telephone.

"This is Dr. Hans Wells. I am sorry to be calling so late but I must speak with Aaron Blumenthal."

Aaron was suddenly wide-awake. "Speaking."

Hans relayed the story of Otto Milch's death.

You lying son of a bitch! Aaron bit down hard on his lip. *I don't know how you found out what we were planning but I do know you had him killed.*

"I know it's an imposition," Hans said, interrupting Aaron's internal monologue. "But, I don't want my daughter alone when she learns about this. I was hoping you would break the news to her?"

Aaron's feet were already on the floor. "Certainly. I'm sorry for your loss," he said, hoping Hans would note the insincerity in his tone.

Aaron held the receiver in his hand, staring at it for a full minute before replacing it in the cradle. *First I had to tell Andy about his wife, and now I have to tell Jo about her uncle.*

* * *

Aaron looked at his watch as he moved down the stairs. It was only four o'clock in the morning in the States, but it was lunchtime in Israel, and as he expected, Saul and Natan were in the study.

"I just got off the phone with Jo's father," Aaron said.

"I thought I heard the phone ringing," Saul said, taking a sip of coffee.

"A strange hour to be calling, don't you think?" Natan added with a nasty sneer.

"Otto Milch was killed by a hit-and-run driver tonight in Miami," Aaron said. "Hans wants me to be the one to deliver the news to Jo."

"Shit!" Natan hissed, furry etching his face. "I need to verify this," he said, placing his coffee cup on the sideboard.

He dialed a Miami number, spoke in Hebrew for less than a minute, grunted, and hung up. Natan's shoulders sagged. "I wanted that bastard to stand trial." He looked at Saul. "The Nazis must have found out what we were planning, and decided to eliminate him." Natan took a deep breath as he assessed the variables, the choices, and the possible outcomes. "You do realize what this means. They are not going to let Jo go—no matter the cost!"

* * *

Prism-like snowflakes drifted into the headlights as Aaron drove into New York City. Because of the early hour, there was little traffic, and that alone was enough to make Aaron feel as if he were caught in some strange alternative universe. He turned up the radio, the blaring sound of a song he could not identify keeping him from nodding off.

Aaron thought about the call to his friend Abraham Friedman at the State Department. *Who had Abe talked to? Who betrayed him?* Aaron pounded the steering wheel. *How the hell am I going to protect Jo when the people surrounding her have tentacles that reach right into the very heart of government?*

It was five thirty in the morning when Aaron pulled into the no parking zone in front of Jo's townhouse. He knocked hard on the door, waited a few minutes and then pounded even harder. A few moments later, a shadowed eye looked through the peephole.

Jo yanked open the door wearing red flannel pajamas, her hair as wild as her eyes.

Aaron touched her arm.

"What's wrong? For God's sake, tell me what happened," Jo demanded, backing away as Aaron entered.

"Jo, you need to sit down."

"What I need is for you to tell me why you're here," Jo insisted.

Aaron had rehearsed what he would say. Now, he could not remember a word. "Your uncle Otto was leaving a restaurant in Miami last night when he was struck by truck. It was a hit and run. I'm so sorry, Jo. He's dead."

Jo tugged at her hair, and her mouth quivered. "How did it happen? Do they know why? Was the driver arrested? Where is my uncle? Can I go to him?" Jo put her hand over her mouth to stop herself from talking. A tear spilled down her face, and she wiped it away with her thumb. "This just can't be happening. Not again. Not so soon."

"What's going on?" Sweeny asked, running down the stairs. "Honey, what's the matter?"

Jo felt like a hot poker was sticking into her belly. While the pain was excruciating, it was not the same kind of pain she had felt when she learned of Robert's death. Maybe that kind of shock and agony happens only once in a person's life, and then the brain learns to protect and numb itself. She looked at Sweeny and said, "My uncle was killed in an accident."

Sweeny's hand flew to her mouth. "Oh, my God." She opened her arms to Jo.

"I'm okay," Jo said. "My parents are going to need me. Aaron, I have to get to Florida."

"I know. I'll take care of it. In the meantime, get dressed and I will take you back to Sands Point," Aaron said.

"Come on," Sweeny said. "I'll help you get your things together."

"I can do it myself. You have to get ready or you'll miss your flight to India."

"I'm not leaving you now," Sweeny said.

"Oh, yes you are! I need to know that one of us is having a good time."

30

Wednesday, December 13, 1972
Sands Point, New York

Rebecca pushed open the double doors to the library just as the grandfather clock in the hallway was striking eleven. She found Saul, Natan, William, and Aaron sitting on club chairs in front of the fireplace, smoking cigars and sipping brandy.

"Isn't it a bit early to be indulging?" Rebecca asked, admonishment in the tone of her voice.

"You forget, my beloved. We are still on Israeli time," Saul said.

"That's getting old," Rebecca replied, kissing Saul's cheek.

"How's Jo?" Aaron asked, stubbing out his cigar.

Rebecca shrugged. "She just spoke with her father. Because of the circumstances surrounding Otto's death, the body is not going to be released until tomorrow. Then it will be cremated in Miami and the ashes delivered back to Naples. The memorial is planned for Friday afternoon.

"She also spoke with Andy and convinced him to meet her in Naples, rather than here. He's going to fly into Ft. Myers on Friday morning. "

"At least that gives us some time to come up with a new plan," Natan said, crossing his legs, his face set in a worried scowl. "Is Jo willing to wait until Friday to go back?"

"She already told her father," Rebecca said.

"We have to get control of this situation," Natan said. "No matter what we have to do!"

* * *

Jo sat on the sofa in the study off Robert's bedroom. Alone for the first time since finding out about her uncle's death, Jo let the pain sift into her heart.

No tears came as she pictured her uncle, his sparkling eyes, mischievous grin, and the eccentric way he acted and dressed. Jo always believed that he was a little off, too feminine, too interested in girly things. It had never mattered. He had loved her absolutely, and for that reason alone, she would miss him terribly.

Jo's mind began to skim around the memories of the mind-control perpetrated by her uncle, but she could not hold on to the vision no matter how hard she tried. Her head began to pound, the beginnings of a fearsome migraine. *I am so tired. I have to rest.*

Jo flipped off the light in the study and headed down the hallway. She was about to push open the door to one of the empty guest rooms when the realization hit. *This is my house now. Robert's room is my room.* She turned around and headed back down the hallway.

Jo stood in the center of Robert's bedroom. She looked around, trying to absorb that his belongings, those things in his life that he had acquired, were now hers. She shivered, feeling his presence.

Jo knew how much he loved this room and how much time he had spent collecting each piece, traveling to auctions in London, Paris and all over America.

On the east wall of the room was a Chippendale secretary made by the Goddard-Townsend family of cabinet-makers. Only seven were ever made.

Standing beside it was a carved and inlaid Chippendale Longcase clock that stood just over nine feet high. The clock's mechanism boasted a mercurial pendulum, known for its accurate timekeeping. Robert had admitted to Jo, in a moment of confession, that he paid fifty thousand dollars for the clock.

A Sormani Partner's Desk and matching Cartonnier sat under the west window. Robert had said that this piece was his greatest find. French in design, it was crafted in the 18th century and had originally belonged to the Duc de Choiseul-Puaslin, Prime Minister for Louis XV.

Against the north wall stood a magnificent mahogany four-poster bed with carved posts decorated with ornate solid brass capitols. A round twelve-foot hand-knotted silk Persian carpet lay on the floor.

Jo's eyes turned to the bed. She was about to pull back the bedspread when she remembered the locked closet door. How many times had she teased Robert about that, accusing him of keeping a vault full of money? How many times had she begged him to let her see inside? Well, Robert was gone now. The house was hers.

Jo strode to the desk, pulled open the drawer, and held the key in her hand. Even now, she felt as if she were a naughty child that would soon be punished for her indiscretion. She walked to the door, her hand trembling as she inserted the key, turned the lock, and pushed open the door.

She flipped on the wall switch and moved into the eight foot by twelve foot walk-in closet. It took a moment for her eyes to get adjusted to the bright glare coming from the overhead fluorescent lights. She looked around. The far wall had ceiling-suspended pull-out panels, and the sidewalls consisted of a modular system with glass shelving.

The first shelf to her right held an actor's theatrical kit filled with powders, sealers, shadows, blushes, adhesives, removers, sponges, and brushes. Beside that was a rhinestone tiara and a jewel encrusted hand-held mirror enclosed in a glass box. Framed photographs lined every shelf. Jo laughed. *My modest Robert turned this entire room into a giant scrapbook. No wonder he didn't want me to see it. He was embarrassed.*

Jo walked to the end of the room and pulled out one of the suspended panels. It held a theatrical poster announcing the opening of Romeo and Juliet staring Robert Osborne and Morgan. Jo smiled, pulling out more panels, each one holding a poster of the plays Robert had starred in with Morgan.

Jo turned to her left. A photograph stared back. It was Robert as a young man. He had his arm around a woman. *Well, Miss Morgan, I finally get to meet you!* Jo picked it up for a closer look.

Oh, my God! Jo blinked several times. She reached for another picture. Everywhere she looked the face that stared back was a mirror image of her own face. *This is why Robert reacted the way he did that first time we met. I could be Morgan's twin.*

Jo moved from photograph to photograph. There was a framed article, circled in red: "October 28, 1939. Warsaw-Poland. It is with great sorrow that the Government of Poland announces the death of one of its most famous citizens..."

The truth was suddenly so obvious to Jo, like an arrow finding its bulls-eye. *She was my mother!*

* * *

Jo pushed open the door and stood on the threshold of the library clutching a picture to her chest. Saul, Natan, Aaron, William, and Rebecca were deep in conversation. Jo stared at Natan. She didn't want this stranger here. Not now!

Aaron was the first to sense a presence. He stood and moved toward Jo, seeing the agony in her eyes. "Jo. What is it? What's wrong?"

Jo raised her hand to keep him from touching her.

It took only seconds for the psychologist in Rebecca to see that Jo was disoriented and confused. She stood.

Jo shook her head. "Stay away from me."

"It's okay, sweetheart. Whatever it is, I can help you," Rebecca said taking a step.

"With more lies?" she hissed.

Rebecca moved closer. "I'll speak only the truth to you. You have my word."

"Then tell me who this woman is to me?" Jo said, holding up the photograph of Morgan.

"She's your mother," Rebecca said, her voice a gentle whisper.

"You knew. You all knew, and nobody told me!" Jo let her eyes linger on Aaron, William, and then Saul. "I trusted all of you. Thought you were my friends. You betrayed me." Jo felt as if she were standing in a hall of mirrors, every face distorted, nothing being as it should be.

"We wanted to protect you," Aaron said.

Jo raised her chin, determination coloring her features. "I want the truth."

William stood, capturing Jo with his eyes. "I will tell you," he said. "When Germany attacked Poland, Morgan was staying with friends at a villa on the French Riviera. Robert and I were in England, making arrangements for a command performance in front of the King." William swallowed hard. "When we went to England we had no idea Hitler was about to invade Poland. If we had known," he shook his head, "we never would have gone.

"Alone, obviously desperate to save her family, and unable to reach us, Morgan decided to take a train into occupied Poland. You can imagine how devastated Robert was when he found out she had gone. Then we made the biggest mistake of our lives." William paused, his face a death-like mask. "We held a press conference, hoping that world opinion would convince the Nazis to send Morgan back. All it did was bring her to their attention." A tear spilled from William's eye. "Saul, please, tell her the rest."

"Hold on, Saul," Rebecca ordered. "This is way too much information all at once."

"No it's not! I have a right to know," Jo said, turning toward Saul.

He patted the seat beside him. "Come and sit."

Jo stayed rooted in place.

"Please, child."

Jo looked at the photo of Morgan. *They think I can't handle the truth. Well, they're wrong!* She strode over to the sofa, sat with her back erect, her eyes riveted on Saul.

"Jo, are you sure you want to hear this now?" Saul asked.

"I've never been surer of anything in my life."

Saul glanced at Rebecca. The nod was slight.

"Your uncle," Saul began, "was with the SS during the war. He is the one that interrogated Morgan. Then he sent her to Dachau, the concentration camp, where Ilya Milch and your father were supposed to become her protectors."

"How could you possibly know all of this?" Jo asked, her face pinched, disbelief seeping from her expression.

"I helped Robert hire a man who has been tracking Nazis since the war." He looked over at Natan.

"So, you're not a friend of the family?" Jo said.

"I am now," Natan replied.

"Natan gave us his report right before Robert," Saul blinked several times, "had his heart attack. Ilya and your mother were pregnant at the same time. After you were born, Hans must have passed you off to Ilya as her child."

"Of course. That's why my mother never loved me. I wasn't her child and she knew it!" Jo felt as if someone had taken an ax and cut her in two.

"Look, what I'm about to tell you is going to be—"

"Just tell me."

Saul's mouth was suddenly so dry he could hardly swallow. "Your father and uncle were involved with experiments in mind control during the war. We think that is how they controlled Ilya and—"

"Me?" Jo's eyes were wild. "Is that what you're all thinking?" A steel door slammed shut in her brain. She could hear her father's voice, and knew that whatever memories were planted in her head would remain locked inside. Jo shook her head several times as tears streamed down her face.

Rebecca put her hand on Jo's arm. "It's going to be okay."

Jo stared at the fire as a log sizzled and died. *If only you knew.*

"I want you to listen to me carefully," Rebecca said. "I can help you with this. But you're going to have to be patient. Whatever they did to control your mind, it has happened over your lifetime. There is no quick fix. But there is a fix. I promise you, Jo."

Jo's shoulders sagged. Her life splintered into veritable moments of minute deceptions, each leading to the next. "My God." Her eyes blazed as yet another revelation hit. "I'm the child of a Nazi!"

Saul stood, his massive shoulders quivering, his eyes hooded in anger. "No more of this talk," he bellowed. "You are Morgan's daughter—her flesh and blood. That's who you are!"

"You don't know what they've buried in my brain," Jo countered. "I don't even know what I'm capable of. I could be some horrid creature that's been—"

"—able to resist their teachings," Rebecca said.

Natan slid his chair closer to Jo. "We are still not certain what they have on Taxton but we know that the Nazis are funneling enormous amounts of money into banks in this country. We have our theories why, we just don't have enough proof—yet.

"This much I can tell—this much I would stake my life on. If Anderson Taxton Junior is elected president of the United States, the Nazis will have gained access to the White House. If they intend to follow the Hitler doctrine, then Israel's very existence is at stake."

Jo locked eyes with Natan.

"There is one more thing I think you must know," Natan said. "We had begun proceedings to extradite your uncle to Israel. We thought having him stand trial for war crimes would dissuade the Nazis, and send them back into hiding. I'm afraid it has backfired."

Jo turned to Saul. "Is he trying to tell me that my uncle's death was not an accident?"

"We can't know for certain. But we think that your uncle was murdered to keep him from implicating his comrades," Saul said.

"We have to stop them!" Jo felt herself drowning in the horror.

Saul crossed his arms over his chest. "We will find a way to stop them."

"Of that you can be certain," Natan added. "If it is the last thing we do. We will stop them!"

31

5:00 a.m. Thursday morning
Sands Point, New York

Jo's eyes flew open. It was still dark. *Damn!* She wanted it to be morning. For a split second, she forgot where she was or why. Then reality struck like a bullet to the brain. *Please, God. Let me wake up from this nightmare.* She shook her head but the knowing was there. Her mind had been raped and manipulated by people she trusted and loved. Jo thought about Andy, how she had shared his bed, given up her career, believed him when he swore he would never hurt her again. *Did he even love me?* Suddenly Jo was enveloped in doubt, a wingless bird, stuck on the ground, disabled. *I'm not going there! I'm done being helpless and manipulated!*

She switched on the bedside lamp.

* * *

Aaron was sound asleep in the corner guest bedroom when the knock on the door awakened him. Jo entered, still in her pajamas, her hair in her eyes, looking so fragile Aaron thought his heart would break.

"I'm sorry to wake you. But I couldn't sleep and needed company. You got elected." Jo smiled.

"Give me a minute," Aaron reached for a robe.

He followed Jo down the hall and into Robert's study.

"God, I wish there was something I could say to make you feel better," Aaron said, as they entered the room.

238

Jo leaned in and kissed him softly on the cheek. "You always make me feel better." Jo tucked her feet under her as she sat on the sofa. "I don't remember if I told you that I leased the apartment in Albany."

"You didn't. That's great. What about closing down the office?"

"My staff is in the process of doing that now," Jo said.

"How do you feel about it?"

"After everything that's happened—I'm relieved," Jo said. "Now, tell me what the plan is for Naples."

"We leave at ten after three this afternoon. There's a Marriott right near the Miami airport. We'll stay there tonight and leave first thing in the morning for Naples," Aaron said, moving next to Jo on the sofa.

"This whole thing is going to get really ugly," Jo said, the very thought causing her heart to pound.

"We know that, and we don't want you to worry. We are going to protect you."

"Just how do you intend to do that?"

"By never letting you out of our sight."

Friday morning
Miami, Florida

Natan navigated the rented Cadillac through the early morning traffic that clogged the southbound lane on the Palmetto Expressway. Saul sat in the front passenger seat, a cup of McDonalds coffee in one hand, the Miami Herald newspaper in the other.

"Follow the signs to 8th Street and then go west," Jo said from the back seat. "Once you're on that road it will take you all the way to Naples."

Natan grunted an acknowledgement and turned up the radio.

Many miles later Jo asked, "Have you ever been to the Everglades?"

"I'm a city boy, remember?" Aaron said.

"It's one of my favorite places," Jo said. "I bet I've taken this ride over a hundred times." The vastness and the solitude of being in the middle of a place where nothing but God's creatures and a few Indians lived brought solace to Jo. She spotted a white ibis digging in the mud for food with its long, slender curved beak. "Did you see it?"

Aaron shook his head.

"Look. There's a great white heron perched in that tree. See the turkey vultures. Over there." She pointed off in the distance.

"They're circling for road-kill. Look at their bald red heads and silvery wings. When I was a kid I used to have nightmares about them."

Aaron pushed his nose to the window. "How the hell can you see anything when we're going sixty miles an hour?"

"You have to concentrate," Jo chided. "Look at the anhingas over there." Jo pointed to several large birds majestically drying their wings by the side of the road. "Alligators! Look, in the water."

Aaron craned his neck for a better look at the canal running beside the road. "I saw it! Look at that!" Aaron pointed toward the sky. "There are eagles nesting on top of the telephone poles."

"Did you see that giant turtle?" Jo perched on her knees and pointed.

Aaron opened the window and stuck out his head. "My God, it was huge."

"Someday I'll take you on an airboat ride," Jo said, talking above the whistling wind.

"I would like that." Aaron closed the window.

Jo glanced up at the sky. "When I was a young girl my uncle taught me to find images in the clouds—faces, angels, horses, mountain ranges."

Aaron reached for Jo's hand as she blinked back tears.

"One Christmas break, my uncle and father took me to Miami to meet Teresa, a famous Cuban dressmaker. I brought her a *Seventeen* magazine and she made me an entire wardrobe from the pictures in that book. I was the envy of every girl in my boarding school that term."

She tugged on her hair. "It seems so incongruous, me telling you about the good times. I guess that's why I'm having such a hard time integrating everything Natan said about my father and uncle."

Aaron squeezed her hand.

"All the lies. How am I ever going to trust anyone ever again?"

Aaron saw himself in that instant as the terrified little boy abandoned by his parents and left with strangers. "I know this is hard for you to believe right now, but not only will you trust again, but you will love again."

Jo needed to push the disappointment and anger aside. To distract herself, Jo did what she had always done as a child: she began counting the white lines on the black asphalt. When she got to five-hundred, she turned back to Aaron. "I'm scared, Aaron. Really scared."

"Please, don't be afraid. I'm going to take care of you."

The statement was a simple one. The implications were enormous and not lost on Jo. The kiss that followed was the culmination of a love that was birthed in the dawning hours of a Jerusalem morning.

In the front seat, Saul looked at Natan and smiled.

"*Af al pe chain*, in spite of it all," Saul said.

"*Baruch Ha'Shem*, thank God," Natan replied.

At that moment, they passed the turnoff for Marco Island. The next sign they saw announced they were entering the city. Naples was perched like a golden oasis between the Gulf of Mexico and the hundreds of palm-filled islands that surrounded her.

Jo went rigid at the thought of what lay ahead, the confrontations, the sadness. "Stay straight," she said, as they passed The Fish House restaurant on their left. Fifth Avenue was clogged with cars bearing license plates from every state east of the Mississippi. On Third Avenue, they headed south toward Port Royal, a neighborhood that sat between the Gulf and Naples Bay, its sprawling mansions hidden from view behind high walls.

"Turn left at Man-o-War Cove," Jo instructed. Automobiles were double parked on the swales. "It looks like the whole city is here. Turn right. We can park a block over and go in through the kitchen."

They got out of the car, cut across a neighbor's lawn, and maneuvered through a hedge opening Jo had used since childhood.

Jenny was standing in the kitchen when the four of them entered.

"My baby's home," she cried, opening her arms and pulling Jo to her enormous bosoms. "You okay, child?" she asked, her eyes assessing Aaron, Saul and Natan. "Who these men?"

"They're my friends. Say hello to Aaron, Saul, and Natan."

Jenny nodded a greeting and turned her attention back to Jo. "I'm real sorry about your uncle. He was a nice man. I know you gonna miss him." Jenny raised her arms above her head, as if at a revival. "The Lord, He has His reasons. It's not for us to question."

Jo smiled.

"That's my girl. You always had the prettiest smile I ever did see."

"Is Elaine here?"

"Honey child, no one's seen hide nor hair of your uncle's wife since the accident. Now, you better go pay your respects to your daddy. He's in the library. You go on now. I'll take care of your friends with some coffee and my special angel food cake."

"I would be honored to sit with you," Natan said.

"As would I," Saul added.

"Where you all from?" Jenny asked. "I never heard such an accent."

Aaron and Jo left the kitchen just as Natan began to embellish a story about being born on a remote island off the coast of Turkey.

Walking side by side down the hallway, Jo stopped at the ballroom doorway. Inside there were two hundred folding chairs, each one was covered in black satin. There were huge funeral wreaths adorning the east wall. A podium was in place, and an organ had been brought in for the occasion.

They kept walking, past a half dozen other rooms before Jo stopped. They were in front of an ornately carved door. She turned to Aaron, the terror etched on her face.

"Ready?" Aaron whispered.

"As ready as I'll ever be," Jo said, turning the knob.

Sunlight filtered through the open blinds of the library, and specks of dust drifted and bounced in the air. Framed maps of the world covered the fabric walls and ancient artifacts; Roman glass, shards from pottery, and carved marble statuettes sat on cherry wood shelves. Tapestry sofas and leather chairs were arranged in small groupings around the expansive room.

Sitting on three of those chairs, deep in conversation, were Jo's father, Andy, and the senior Taxton. Jo had not anticipated all of them being there, and her first instinct was to run. It was then that she felt Aaron's hand on the small of her back nudging her forward. It was all that she needed.

"Jo, darling," Andy said, rising. He tried to hug her. She pulled away. Embarrassed and confused, Andy stuck out his hand to Aaron. "It's good to see you."

Hans beckoned Jo with a slight nod of his head. Without thought, Jo walked over, kissed her father's cheek, and nodded to Anderson. Her coldness was not lost on any of them.

Aaron perched on the arm of a chair, every fiber of his being on high alert.

"How was your trip?" Andy asked, putting his arm around Jo.

She shrugged him off. "Sit down, Andy."

"I do not like the way you're behaving," Hans hissed.

I bet you don't! Jo's eyes blazed. "How could you do this to me?" The hateful accusation fell like a shroud over the room. Jo turned toward Andy. "Tell me something. Did you ever love me, or was I just a tool in your quest for power?"

"What are you talking about? You know I love you."

Jo swiveled her eyes towards Hans. "And you, Father? Was it always about the power? Did you ever love anyone?"

Hans crossed one leg over the other, a smug smile on his face. "I have no idea what you're talking about."

Jo pointed her finger and poked the air, condemnation coloring her face. "I know that Ilya is not my real mother."

Hans paled. Andy looked confused, and Anderson appeared shell-shocked.

"That's right, gentleman. My father is a Nazi, yet my mother was a Jew. How does that translate, Father? Do your comrades know about my true heritage? If not, I'm sure they would be very interested."

Jo turned to Andy. He looked so distraught, for a second Jo actually felt sorry for him. Then all the lies thundered down and she shuddered. "How could you let them manipulate you into turning on the country I know you love?"

Andy's face reddened, and hate seethed from his eyes. "You did this to me!" Andy sneered, stabbing a finger at his father. "You have ruined everything!" Andy stood, his entire body shaking. "Say whatever you will about all of this. But, I love you, Jo." His eyes filled with tears. "I always loved you."

"Then what happened? Why did you let them do this to you?" Jo asked.

Andy shook his head. As much as he hated his father at that moment, he knew that whatever he confessed would change nothing. His dreams of the presidency were dead, and Jo was lost to him forever because she would expose them. He collapsed into the chair.

Anderson turned to his son and spoke for the first time. "Do you think this is a game played by children? To reach the pinnacle of power one has to be willing to make adjustments and sacrifices. Eisenhower, Kennedy, Johnson, they all had their secrets. People do what they have to do. It's the way of the world. For Christ's sake, it's the way it has always been."

"Is that what you told yourself to justify your despicable actions?" Andy asked, disgust painting his face.

"I don't have to justify myself to you," Anderson growled. "It was a decision I made a long time ago. It is what it is!"

"You're right," Jo interjected. "Because whatever diabolical plan you all had is finished!" Jo let her words hang for a few seconds. "I will not be your pawn." She stared at her father. "Or your key into the White House. I will expose all of you if Andy continues his quest for the presidency."

"Don't be a fool," Hans said. "We are offering you the world."

"I don't want to be in your world, Father," Jo replied.

Hans stood. "This is your destiny, and there is nothing you can do to stop it."

"In case you didn't notice. I just did stop it!" Jo turned, took Aaron's arm, and walked from the room.

* * *

Jo walked to the kitchen in a daze. She was so distraught her lips quivered and she couldn't stop blinking.

"My Lord, child. What you gone and done to yourself?" Jenny cried, forcing a glass of water to Jo's lips.

Jo looked at Saul, Natan, and then Aaron. She couldn't focus. Suddenly there was a flash of light in the back of her eyes that momentarily blinded her. She began to sweat and her body shook as the pain took hold. Jo grabbed her head and cried out."

Aaron knelt on the floor in front of her. "What is it?"

"A migraine," Jo whispered. "I have to lie down."

"My room," Jenny ordered.

Aaron lifted Jo into his arms. She was crying softly.

Jenny's cubbyhole of a room was off the kitchen and next to the laundry room. She had a twin bed, a Lazyboy lounger, a television set, and a bookcase. Aaron laid Jo on the bed. Jenny covered her with a blanket and then closed the shade.

Aaron flapped his hand at Natan, Saul and Jenny. "I'll stay with her."

Jo put her arm across her eyes and moaned. It took several minutes but eventually she fell asleep.

Jo awakened confused and disorientated. How long have I been sleeping? She was afraid to move, afraid the headache would still be there. She waited. There was no blinding lights, no buzzing in her head. She moved her arm, then a leg. Nothing. The pain was gone.

Aaron had dozed off in the Lazyboy. He heard her moving. His eyes flew open. "Are you okay?"

"It's gone." Jo yanked her skirt down, kicked off the cover, and sat up. "I think we just had our first sleep over."

Aaron laughed. "Glad to see you haven't lost your sense of humor."

Jo looked at her watch. "I can't believe I slept this long. We better go. The service is going to start a few minutes."

32

The Memorial Service
Naples, Florida

Jo stood at the back of the ballroom. She was dressed in a black Ralph Lauren blazer, a grey cashmere scooped-neck sweater, a grey wool skirt, and pumps. She tucked a few strands of hair back into the tortoiseshell clip holding her blond curls at the base of her neck. As she moved into the aisle Saul and Natan moved to either side of the doorway, and Aaron took a seat near the back.

Jo scanned the crowded room for Andy and his father. Relief filled her when she realized that they were nowhere to be found. When she got to the front row, Jo stepped past her father. She deliberately avoided his eyes as she settled in the seat beside Ilya.

"Hello, Mother," she said, kissing the woman's over-rouged cheeks. "I'm so sorry. Are you okay?"

Ilya flinched. Her hand flew to her cheek, as if Jo's kiss had burned her. It was then that Jo saw the bandage wrapped around her wrist. Jo took Ilya's hand. "What happened?" she whispered. Ilya yanked her arm away and buried her chin in her chest.

"Please, tell me."

Ilya shook her head, refusing to look at Jo.

At that moment, Pastor Fred Pallano walked to the podium. He took the urn with Otto's ashes and placed it on the table beside him before welcoming everyone. He did a Doxology, and then read selections from Psalm 23, Isaiah, and Ecclesiastics. Then the choir from the First Presbyterian Church of Naples accompanied the organist. They sang *Amazing Grace, A Mighty Fortress is Our God*, and *Blest be the Tie*.

Ilya wept. It was the sound of a breaking heart, and it hurt Jo to see the agony, regardless of how angry Jo felt about this woman who had masqueraded as her mother.

The preacher gave a short, uninspired eulogy. Then he recited the Apostle's Creed, said a final prayer and it was over.

Everyone stood and began to file out of the room. Jo was offering her arm to help Ilya from the chair when a young, beady-eyed man stepped between them. "I will take Mrs. Wells back to her room."

Before Jo could react, Ilya was being led out.

Hans slid next to Jo. "You and I must talk."

"I have nothing to say to you! And you have nothing to say that I want to hear!"

"It can't end this way," Hans said, his voice dripping in desperation.

Jo turned her back on him and headed toward the exit. Natan, Saul, and Aaron moved beside her.

"Who was that with Ilya?" Natan asked.

"I've never seen him before. But, something is going on. Ilya's wrist is bandaged. It looks like she might have tried to kill herself."

"Take us to her room," Saul said. "It's time we had a talk with her."

* * *

Ilya's bedroom was on the southern side of the mansion overlooking the front lawn. The walls were covered in red silk from China, the room dominated by an Elmwood canopy bed and a 19th century Hualiwood cabinet from Zhejiang.

Ilya sat on a herringbone backed chair in front of a rare John Goddard mahogany dressing table. She stared into the mirror, pulling the pins from her hair. Her once glorious mane lay limp against her head, all yellow-grey and greasy. She dabbed at her eyes with a used tissue.

Dolf leaned against the wall, his hands stuffed in his pockets.

He had been hired by Hans to watch Ilya, and had arrived on the Wednesday morning after her attempted suicide. Now he was always there, hovering over her even when she went to the bathroom.

There was a knock on the door. Ilya turned back toward the mirror. She didn't care who it might be. She didn't care about anything anymore.

Dolf tensed. "Who is it?"

"We've come to see Ilya."

He opened the door a crack. It was all Natan needed. He leaned into it with his shoulder and pushed his way in.

Dolf blocked Natan with his tight-muscled body. His shaved head bobbed, his blue eyes threatened. Jo, Saul, and Aaron pushed passed both men.

"I'm sorry, but my orders are not to let anyone in."

"I'm sure those orders did not include Ilya's daughter." Jo shot him a furious look.

Ilya played with the button on the sleeve of her dress. She was mildly interested in Jo and the intruders but the tranquilizer Dolf had just given her was taking effect and she was having a difficult time concentrating.

Dolf looked at Ilya and then back at Jo. He shrugged. "You have five minutes."

Natan was beside Ilya before she could focus her eyes on him. He put his hand on her shoulder and leaned close to her ear. In German he said, "We must talk. I can help you."

Dolf's eyes flew open at the sound of his mother tongue. He leapt like a panther and caught Natan off guard, strangling him in a jujitsu choke that crushed Natan's trachea and cut the blood flow to his brain. "Whoever the fuck you are. You have made a very grave mistake." Dolf applied more pressure.

Natan knew if he didn't act quickly, he would be unconscious within seconds. Pushing past the agony, he plowed his elbow into his attacker's solar plexus just as Saul grabbed the man from behind. Dolf gasped and momentarily relaxed his grip. Natan used that second to slip from the chokehold, twist his spine and shoulders, and swing his left leg in a wide arc, smashing his foot into Dolf's chin.

The bone cracked. Dolf cried out in agony. As he slipped to the floor, he reached for the gun in his shoulder holster.

"I wouldn't do that." Natan put his foot on the bodyguard's chest. "Unless you want to die. Hold him down."

Aaron pinned the man's shoulders to the ground with his knees.

Natan pulled a syringe from his pocket. It was filled with diazepam, enough to neutralize but not kill. "Have a good sleep," Natan said, a smile frozen on his face as he drove the needle into Dolph's thigh. Natan stumbled back to Ilya's side. Jo joined him.

She looked at them both before picking up a brush and tearing at her tangled hair. "You know, I used to be beautiful, everyone said so," she slurred. She looked from Jo to Natan. "Who are you?"

"That's not important. All you need to know is that I'm here to help you."

She shook her head. "I don't want your help."

"Whoever killed your brother will come for you next," Natan said.

"You!" Ilya stared at Jo as if realizing for the first time that she was there. "What do you want?"

"Did you know I wasn't your daughter?"

Ilya hugged herself. "So, you finally found out what that bastard did to me!" She smirked. "Do you know what he planned for you? You were going to give him immortality." Ilya's eyes cleared, glazed over, and cleared again. "Only one little problem. You are the child of a Jewess." Ilya shrieked with laughter. "Herr fucking Hitler must be turning over in his grave. One Germany! Hah. So much for infiltrating governments from within—so much for their thousand year Reich."

Natan spun Ilya around on the chair and seized her shoulders. "What are you saying? Are there others?"

"What do you think?" she asked, her eyes those of a lunatic slipping toward the edge. She swung her hand across the dressing table. The bottles crashed to the floor.

Natan took her hands. "Who, Ilya? How many are there?"

She shuddered under his touch. "Hans knows. But he'll never tell you."

"What did you mean when you said one Germany?" Saul asked, moving to Ilya's left.

"Are you a Jew?" she asked.

Saul nodded.

Ilya smiled. "Perfect. Then you must listen very carefully. There is an East Germany and a West Germany."

"We didn't ask for a history lesson," Natan snapped.

"But, that's exactly what you need," Ilya snapped back. "You think you are safe now that Germany is divided. But, it's all a façade, a way to get the world to let down their guard. Germany will reunite and rise again under one flag. When they do, you will lose your precious Israel and the Jews will cry again."

Hate clawed at Natan. He pulled Ilya from the chair.

"Don't hurt her," Jo said. "She's been through enough."

Ilya shot Jo a grateful look.

"Why did you live the lie? Why didn't you say something?" Jo asked.

Ilya gulped back her tears. "If they found out the truth, that you, Hans's precious progeny had Jewish blood, they would have killed us all. That's why!"

Just then, the door to Ilya's room swung open. Hans was standing there, his eyes scanning the room. "What the hell are you doing here?" His eyes settled on Dolf lying on the floor.

"He's not dead," Ilya said. "Just sedated—compliments of the Jew." Ilya smiled at her husband as she slid the drawer open to her dressing table and pulled out the .22 Smith and Wesson revolver. She raised her hand and directed the gun at Hans's head.

"Don't be ridiculous." Hans took a step forward. "Give that to me."

"Back up," Ilya screamed. "Against the wall. Now! All of you!" She held the gun with both hands and waved it wildly.

"Put the gun down, Mother. We won't let him hurt you. I promise," Jo cried.

"You know what I'm going to do, Hans?" Ilya said, disregarding Jo. "I'm going to kill you. Just like you killed my brother."

"I didn't kill Otto." Hans's legs buckled. "You have to believe me. I loved him."

Ilya pulled back the hammer on the gun. "Next you'll be telling me Jotto is my child."

"I can explain. Our baby died and I—"

"Shut the fuck up."

Hans's eyes bulged.

"Are you afraid, Hans? I see your fear. I smell your fear." Ilya snarled, delighted by the control. "I'm going to do the world a favor."

"Ilya, I didn't kill Otto. For God's sake, I loved him like a brother."

"Liar…fucking liar!" She pulled the trigger.

"Don't!" Jo screamed as the bullet tore a hole in her father's chest.

Hans fell forward, clawing at his chest, sucking for breath.

Jo lunged for her father. "Get back," Ilya screamed, or I'll kill you too."

Aaron threw his arms around Jo and held her.

"Die, you bastard," Ilya howled as the blood spurted through Hans's fingers. She fired again.

Jo shrieked.

Natan went for his gun.

"Move and I'll kill the girl," Ilya howled, aiming for Jo's head. "You asked me why I never said anything?" She smiled at Jo. "I lived for only one thing." She shook the gun in Hans's direction. "That was to see him dead. Now it's over."

"Then give me the gun, Mother. We will help you."

"Don't you see? I can't do that. Not now." Ilya rubbed the shaft of the gun. Before any of them realized what was happening she placed the gun barrel between her teeth.

"No!" Jo howled.

Ilya pulled the trigger. Blood exploded from her head, bone matter and brains shooting out in all directions.

Saul yanked Jo's arm, turning her from the sight. "Look at me, Jo," he ordered. "My eyes. Watch my eyes. I'm going to take you out of here now." Walking backwards towards the door, he shouted, "Aaron, Let's go!"

Natan had taken out his handkerchief and was already wiping off any fingerprints that might implicate any of them.

Saul held Jo's arm tightly as they walked through the house. Jo's brain was on overload, playing tricks. She was flashing into the past, and then flashing into the future. The present remained elusive as her mind fought to shed the images of the horror she had just witnessed.

"My God, child." Jenny cried as they entered the kitchen. "What is wrong with you?"

"She's going to be okay," Saul said, patting Jenny's ample arm. "Take Jo to the car, Aaron. I'll wait here for Natan."

Jenny reached out and hugged Jo. "He's right. You best be going. This place is just making you sick." Jenny smoothed Jo's hair. "I love you, child. I hope you know that."

"I love you too. Take care of yourself," Jo said, her voice breaking with emotion.

Saul turned to Jenny as Natan walked into the kitchen. "We need your help, Miss Jenny."

She squinted her eyes and frowned. "What you need?"

"I want you to wait until we've been gone for fifteen minutes. Then you are going to dial 911 and tell the police that the door to Mrs. Milch's room is locked, and that you think something terrible may have happened."

Jenny's hand flew to her mouth. "What you talking about?"

"Ilya just shot Hans and then herself. They're upstairs in her bedroom."

"Oh, my dear sweet Jesus." She started to quake, her entire body bouncing

"Fifteen minutes," Natan repeated as the two men walked out of the house.

"What about the bodyguard?" Saul asked as they made their way back to the car.

"The syringe I used on him now has Hans's fingerprints on it."

Saul smiled. "You're good."

"I know. Isn't that sad?"

Driving on US 41 toward Miami, Florida

Natan drove east, back the way they had come only a few hours earlier. Everything had changed. They no longer had to worry about Hans's influence over Jo, and they no longer had to deal with Andy and his father. But they still had enormous problems—Jo and what would happen to her after such an ordeal, and figuring out what else the Nazis had planned.

Jo leaned against Aaron. The sun was setting and twilight turned the Tamiami trail into a blur of ghostly trees and darkening shadows.

No one spoke.

Aaron was lost in his own hell. He had always thought he was strong and resilient, but he was not feeling that way right now. He was perspiring, his mouth was dry, and more than anything, he wanted to vomit. He kept picturing Ilya's head exploding. He could only imagine what Jo was going through. He put his arm around Jo and pulled her closer.

Jo used every ounce of her will to force the images away, refusing to deal with what just happened. Instead, she thought about what had to happen next—what she was going to do with her life now. When they were forty miles into the Everglades Jo said, "Aaron, I need you to do some things for me."

"Anything," Aaron replied.

"I am going to give you general power of attorney. The first thing I want you to do is arrange for the funerals. Cremate them and then have the ashes buried. Then I want the house sold. I'm never going back there again."

"I'll take care of it," Aaron said, surprised at how clearly she seemed to be thinking.

"I want you to set up a trust fund for Jenny so she never has to worry about money ever again. Also, please tell William that I would like him to continue to live at the Sands Point house."

"Jo, you can tell him that yourself," Aaron offered.

"No, Aaron, I can't." She leaned forward and tapped Saul's shoulder.

Saul had been listening to their conversation. He had a pretty good idea what was coming next. He turned from the front seat, draping his arm over the back.

"I know you are flying from New York to Israel tomorrow."

"We are," Saul said.

Jo turned to Aaron. "I need you to get me a ticket on that flight."

Her request shattered Aaron's world. "Please, Jo. You don't have to go. You can stay with me. I'll take care of you."

Jo reached for his hand. "I can't stay here. You know that. I am going to need help. The kind of help only Rebecca can give me."

"There are good psychiatrists in Washington. You don't have to run away."

"I'm not running away. I'm running to. I don't know if I can explain this to you. But, I know I need to be in Israel if I am ever going to reclaim myself."

Aaron hated her words—hated the truth in them.

"Will you come and visit me?" Jo asked.

Tears filled his eyes. "Wild horses couldn't keep me away."

Jo smiled through her own tears. "It's not too late for us, is it, Aaron?" she whispered.

"You are the only woman I have ever loved. I will wait for you. No matter how long it takes."

Five Hours Later
New Brunswick, New Jersey

Kurt Blome and Alexander Lippisch sat side by side on a park bench in Boyd Park looking out at the Raritan River. Their impromptu meeting was inspired by phone calls they each received, first from Dolf and then from a comrade in Austria. The message had been clear—a new plan had to be set into motion.

Blome sucked in his lips and sighed. "A murder, a suicide. I just can't believe it. Hans knew Ilya was crazy. Why would he give her access to a gun?"

"That is beside the point," Lippisch said, scowling into the dark. "They are both dead. Otto's gone. It's finished."

"What about Jotto?" Blome said, scratching his face.

"We will keep an eye on her. If she causes any trouble. . ." Lippisch said, not finishing the sentence—he didn't have to—they eliminated their problems.

Lippisch smiled. "Our time frames may be extended but our goals are still the same!"

Both men stood, clicked their heels together, and raised their arms in the Nazi salute.

"To a thousand year Reich," they said in unison, setting their sights again on the Presidency of the United States.

33

The next day
On the way to Israel

The El Al flight to Israel left New York at eight in the evening. Aaron had secured two first class seats for Jo on the Boeing 707, hoping that she would sleep on the ten-hour non-stop trip. But, as the airplane reached its cruising altitude, and Jo was alone for the first time since the events in her mother's bedroom in Naples, the numbness lifted and her defenses came crashing down. Horrendous visions reared, strangling Jo in their grasp. The result was that she was afraid to sleep; terrified that she might dream about her father's murder and her mother's suicide.

Feeling as if she were smothering in her own skin, Jo got up and headed toward the main cabin of the airplane. The shades of the aircraft were drawn, and the lights were dimmed. She walked past where Rebecca and Saul were sitting. They were both asleep, as were most of the other passengers. In the very last row of the airplane, she found Natan wide-awake and smiling.

Jo leaned down so he would hear her above the din of the jet engines and asked, "Do you think we could talk?"

"I would like that," Natan replied. He moved over a seat and Jo moved in beside him.

"I have some questions I need answered and I think you are the one to answer them for me."

"I'll do my best."

"You all kept saying that if Andy got elected the Nazis would have access to the White House. That doesn't make any sense to me. First of all, Andy is not a bad person, and he would never allow a bunch of raving bullies to dictate the course of his presidency. And second, America has laws that govern and protect us. So even if he had been elected president, what could Andy have done? What could any of them have done?" Jo looked hard at Natan. "I want your take on all of this, and please don't try and soften it for me."

"Much of what I am about to say is hypothetical in nature," Natan replied. "Theories about what they had planned can only be conjecture. You may be right in thinking that Andy is not fully aligned with the Nazis but, I can assure you, when they were finished using the mind control techniques they perfected at Auschwitz and Dachau, he would have been."

"Even if they got Andy to do their bidding, what then?" Jo didn't want to appear stupid, but she had spent every ounce of her intellectual ability and lawyerly skills, and could not come up with answers that made any sense.

"Hitler's ideology included the eradication of the Jewish race. So let's assume that the first thing on the Nazi agenda would be the destruction of Israel. Let me give you an example of how they might have gone about that.

"The president has executive privilege to withhold information from the public and he has the power of presidential decree. In a top-secret memo that was leaked to the Israeli government, we learned that in May of 1970, Henry Kissinger, on a presidential directive, approved an arms package for Jordan. Those arms were sent with a codicil that Jordan would not accept arms from the Soviet Union, and that additional equipment would be sent to Israel. This was done without congressional approval.

"Now imagine, instead of that scenario the president decided to give arms to all of Israel's enemies, and give no aid to Israel? We are an emerging nation with an emerging economy. Without arms from the United States, Israel would be obliterated.

"When newly elected, the president of the United States appoints six thousand people to his government. Appoint, Jo. Without oversight. He also designates who will head the Central Intelligence Agency, NASA, and even the government owned Amtrak. Imagine the impact the directors of those three agencies could have on the safety and security of America?"

"Too simplistic, Natan. They would all be examined and their credentials would be assessed before the appointments were made," Jo said.

"Background information can be altered. But let's just move on. How about all the damage a president can do with the veto powers of his position—the rights that can be removed?"

"Americans would never sit back and let our freedoms be taken away," Jo insisted.

"I am sorry to say this, but hate is a powerful aphrodisiac. It turned all of Europe into a murdering machine. You don't think Americans would turn on her Jews? I can see the doubt in your eyes. Think about the way blacks have always been treated in your country. Now try to imagine a government that slowly took rights away from the Negro—took them back to slave status. It could happen. Take it from someone who lived through it!"

The lawyer in Jo wanted to dispute him point by point. She wanted to believe that Americans could not be manipulated into a frenzy of hate. But she had grown up with blacks being forced to sit in the back of buses, black water fountains and white water fountains, black bathrooms and bathrooms for whites only. She had seen and heard first hand about hate. She knew its power.

"What about all the things Ilya said about one Germany?" Worry etched Jo's face. "What if they are trying to put their people into power in other countries?"

Natan placed his hand on Jo's arm in a rare show of emotion. "Israel may be small but we are strong, a nation of warriors, born of the Holocaust. You can rest assured that no Jew will ever spend another night in a concentration camp, a ghetto or go to their death in a gas chamber or a work camp. Whoever is out there, we will hunt them down and stop them."

"And me? Will they just let me walk away?"

"They will see you as nothing more than a pawn in a chess game they lost. They will move on to their next move. All you need to do is keep a low profile and stay out of their way."

Jo stood. "Thank you. You've given me a lot to think about."

Natan shrugged. "Think about it later. Right now you need to get some sleep."

* * *

David stood curbside at the airport beside Saul's five-year-old Mercedes. He had been in Israel with Anna for less than six months but had fully embraced the casual lifestyle of the country. He was dressed in a white t-shirt that bulged at the sleeves where the Olympian's muscles pulled against his shirt. He wore khaki shorts, sandals and a huge smile. He kissed and hugged Rebecca.

"David Kandel, this is Jo Wells," Rebecca said.

"Fabulous to finally meet you. I have heard so many wonderful things about you," David said, hugging her.

There was something about David that Jo instantly liked. Perhaps it was his easy mannerisms, his open affection, or was it something else? Rebecca had told Jo about how David and Saul had met during the war and the God-driven miracle that had put them together again after so many years.

Saul stuck out his hand to David. "It's good to see you again, my friend. I missed you."

Jo wasn't certain, but she thought she saw a tear in Saul's eye as the two men embraced.

"Let me put your luggage in the trunk and let's get out of here," David said. He looked at Rebecca. "Your children are all waiting to see you. And Anna baked strudel."

Kibbutz Ayelet Haba-ah
Israel

Jo sat on a sofa in Rebecca's office, surrounded by dollhouses, toys, books, and clutter. She had only been in Israel for two days, and couldn't believe they were about to begin their first therapy session.

Rebecca took the chair from behind her desk and dragged it next to the sofa. She sat down and opened a notebook on her lap. "Are you ready to begin? she asked, a gentle smile on her face.

Jo nodded, even though she was terrified.

"It is my opinion that you were exposed to massive psychological indoctrination. The technique was elaborate, multifaceted, and multilayered. Your father wanted to control your personality. When his dominion over you failed, he brought in your uncle. Otto's power in fact did alter your emotional personality—thus the relationship with Andy," Rebecca said.

"We know my uncle influenced my relationship with Andy. But, there were other times, times when I would lose hours and remember nothing. After those sessions, nothing changed in my life. So, I have no idea what my uncle said, or what is sloshing around in my psyche."

Rebecca reached over and patted Jo's arm, a sad smile curved her lips. "That's why this journey you and I are about to take will be about deprogramming you. We have to start by slowly moving your mind into new directions. It will begin with challenging questions—many of them may be too painful to recall. You need to know that I am going to push you hard, and I will stay with the question until we find the answer.

"Nothing will be off limits and some of it is going to seem absurd. We are going to talk about God, the Devil—anything that I can think of to shake you loose from their lies. If we get stuck I will use hypnosis."

Jo panicked. "I don't know if I can allow you to do that to me."

"I am not going to do anything to you without your consent. So, let's cross that bridge when we come to it."

Jo shrugged.

"This is going to take time, hard work, and a willingness to face that which you may choose not to face. But, I believe with all my heart that you can do this. Now, it is your decision if you want to proceed.

Jo knew she had no choice. "I'm ready."

Rebecca began by asking Jo what bedtime stories her father read to her. Jo couldn't remember. Rebecca kept pushing, asking the same question over and over again. By the end of the session, Jo was quoting lines from Hitler's Mein Kampf. That revelation reaffirmed to both of them that their work had just begun.

March 1973
Three months later

Jo awakened early. She switched on the bedside lamp and climbed out of her lumpy single bed on to a bare wooden floor. On the way to the bathroom, she walked through her miniscule living room with its well-worn green plaid sofa, Formica table and two metal chairs that she used as a desk.

Standing in the tiny shower stall, Jo's elbows bumped the sides as she washed her hair. She dried off, pulled a cotton turtleneck over her head, and ran her fingers through her cut-to-the-chin hair. Dressed in jeans, sneakers, a scarf around her neck, she slipped into a wool parka and headed out the door.

It was windy and cold as she walked along the pebbled pathway toward the communal dining room. Snow-capped mountains served as the backdrop for Jo as she daydreamed about the routine her new life had taken.

She spent four hours a day, six days a week in ulpan classes learning conversational Hebrew. Jo understood much of what was said now, and she could converse when not struck dumb by fear that she would make a fool of herself.

What excited Jo most was that she was able to read the hieroglyphics that had seemed so foreign only a few short months ago. So now, when the instructor said they would be reading the newspaper by summer, Jo actually believed it was a possibility.

David and Anna were months ahead of Jo in progress but were in the same classroom and she had established a bond with them, although she found little time to cultivate the budding friendship. Once Hebrew class ended, Jo would first go to work.

Jo studied her chapped and calloused hands, hard won from working in various jobs on the kibbutz. In the huge communal kitchen, she scrubbed floors, rinsed dishes, washed and peeled vegetables. In the laundry, she sorted through heaps of dirty clothing. She had mucked out the barn and worked in the orchards. Jo thought about the babies and laughed aloud. That was her favorite job—the nursery, where she had changed so many diapers she could do it blindfolded.

The schedule was demanding, and the work ethic was unyielding. Yet, Jo enjoyed the no-frills lifestyle and the tight-knit camaraderie of the kibbutz environment. Her new friends were people that were unaffected, down to earth and honest in a way she had never known before.

There were times when Jo wished she could escape the insane routine, but she knew that keeping busy was what helped her survive the therapy sessions with Rebecca. They met from eight o'clock until ten o'clock, Monday through Thursday.

After each appointment, Jo walked back to the apartment, sat at the Formica table and wrote a letter to Aaron, telling him the details of her day. Then she would reread the letter that she received from him. It wasn't an idyllic situation, and it certainly didn't fulfill their needs but it helped them maintain the bond, and it reaffirmed their love in the only way available to them.

Jo would then fall into bed. There was no longer a question of nightmares versus sleep. She was exhausted and so, when the visions came she endured. She knew it was a scar that would never fade. She was learning to live with it.

* * *

It was a Sunday morning towards the end of March and Jo had the entire day off. Wearing two sweaters and her parka, Hebrew reader in hand, Jo headed for the park—an animal sanctuary situated a quarter of a mile from the front gate, on an isolated acre of land cultivated and cared for by the commune.

She followed the heavily foliated path, climbing over roots, ducking under low hanging branches, stopping every few minutes to listen to the sounds of the forest. The deeper she walked into the sanctuary the dimmer the light.

The path ended at a clearing. Jo spread the blanket she brought on a bed of dried pine needles in front of a huge fallen tree trunk. Unseen birds sang a symphony from the treetops.

She peered into the bushes. In the past, she had seen griffon vultures, short-toed eagles, deer, and rabbits. Nothing stirred.

Jo opened her Hebrew book and began to memorize phrases and idioms for a language she was determined to master.

"Hello, Jo."

Startled, she looked up. It was David.

"This is certainly a surprise. I thought all you did was work," David said in English.

"Even I take a break once in a while."

David nodded. "It's a good place to come for peace and quiet, and to study."

Jo laughed. She patted her blanket. "Care to join me?"

David sat with difficulty, his years of wrestling causing swollen knees and aching hips. "This is bashert, meant to be, us meeting like this. I have wanted to speak with you alone for a very long time."

"About what?" Jo asked.

"About the way you suffer."

Jo's back stiffened. "Is it really so obvious?"

David blinked several times. "To me, yes. Only because I know the signs. Only because I have been where you are." David touched Jo's cheek with the palm of his enormous hand. "I have a story I would like to share with you, if I may."

"Please," Jo responded.

"There was a time," David said, "when the sight of a dying man meant nothing to me. I could step over a dead body and not care. I could steal shoes off a corpse and only know joy." He painstakingly recounted the Nazi invasion of his homeland, the loss of his family, sailing on the ship to Palestine only to be turned away. He talked about his escape and the walk he took across Europe as he made his way toward Russia. He spoke of death and starvation. At times, he had to stop, to reclaim his voice, to wipe away the tears.

"I did so many things I am ashamed of." Looking off in the distance, David continued, "While living in Russia, I hid my Judaism—not just from the people I loved, but from myself." He let his words dangle for a moment. "And then I fell in love with my Anna, and we made the decision to leave Russia—to leave everything and everyone we cared about so that we could live our lives as Jews. Do you see the irony? What I hid from is what finally healed me."

"I have the blood of a Nazi running through my veins," Jo said, wanting David to know how she still saw herself, despite all the work she was doing with Rebecca to change that mindset.

David scowled. "From what I hear, you also have the blood of a very remarkable woman. Is she not who you are, who you choose to be?" Before Jo could reply, David continued, "If only you could see yourself the way I see you."

"I'm trying so hard."

"I know you are. But, you're like a dog chasing its tail. You stay so busy you have no time to be with yourself, to make peace with who you are, to accept those things about your life that you can not change." He reached out his hand.

Jo's eyes filled with tears as she placed her hand in his.

David smiled. "It is time to bring the magic back into your life. Can I tell you a secret?"

Jo laughed.

"My Anna is five months pregnant."

"David, that's fantastic." Jo hugged him.

"Miracles, my little one. Life is full of miracles. So, let us make a pact."

"What kind of pact?" Jo asked as the sun set on the Golan Heights.

"That for the rest of our lives, you and I will be friends."

Part 6

34

April 1973
Ben Gurion Airport, Tel Aviv

Jo stood amongst the crowd waiting for the passengers to clear customs. Aaron was coming for Passover and she had been there for an hour, waiting for him.

During the wait, Jo became enamored with one of the families. There were two little girls that appeared to be around three and six. The older child had blond hair with streaks of white and gold running through it. She had enormous blue eyes, a cleft chin and was dainty, even a little fragile. The younger child had dark hair and eyes, never stood still and was obviously mischievous as she poked her older sister and danced around in circles. The dad was solidly built, had a nice face, and wore the uniform of the Israeli Defense Forces. He had a gun on his hip, something Jo had grown accustomed to; soldiers in Israel were never without their guns. The mom was lean as a panther, with short hair and a gentle face.

Jo was watching the antics of the younger child when she glanced at the exit doorway of customs. Her heart leapt. Aaron smiled and waved as he helped a stooped-over, silver haired woman with swollen legs. In his right hand, Aaron held the woman's purse. Just as they cleared the doorway, the two little girls ran toward the old woman. She dropped to one knee, her eyes ignited with love, her aging body suddenly lithe. She opened her arms.

"*Savta, Savta,*" the girls shouted as they hugged their grandmother. The mom walked over, dropped to her knees, and kissed the woman's cheek. The soldier watched and waited. Then he moved in, reached out his hand to help the woman to her feet.

"*Ima,* mother," he said, making the word sound like a prayer.

She fell into the embrace of her soldier son. As he held her, he kept repeating the word, *Imi, Imi, Imi,* my mother, my mother, my mother.

The entire encounter had taken only a minute. Jo and Aaron watched—enchanted by the reunion. Ready for their own reunion, they embraced, kissed, and cried.

* * *

Driving Saul's Mercedes, Aaron navigated the scar-blistered highways, dodging motorcyclists that seemed intent on dying, beeping his horn at motorists going twenty miles an hour, and swerving out of the way of the crazies going ninety.

"Israelis have to be the worst drivers in the world," Aaron said, blasting his horn as another motorcycle veered into his lane.

"They're even worse than New York drivers, and that's saying a lot," Jo replied.

As they drove towards the Golan Heights Jo kept glancing at Aaron, still finding it hard to believe that he was actually here. And, weird as it seemed, they were both self-conscious, their conversation was stilted and their manner strained.

Fifteen minutes into the ride, Aaron asked, "Have you heard from Sweeny?"

A smile exploded across Jo's face. "Finally. William forwards my mail, and she finally wrote."

"And?"

"As of a month ago, she was in Katmandu. She's doing practice climbs and loves it. She met some trust-fund guy who according to Sweeny is way too handsome. She fully expects to have her heart broken. She sounds wildly happy. She didn't give me a post office box or anything. So, I can't write back. I suppose she figures if I needed to get in touch I would call her father."

"She's living her dream," Aaron said.

"That's my Sweeny. Have you seen William? There's something about his letters. He doesn't sound happy."

"I was going to speak with you about that," Aaron said, glancing at Jo before turning his attention back toward the road. "I don't like the way he looks. There's no spring to his step. It's like he's become an old man since Robert's death. I don't think looking after the house is enough of a challenge for him."

"They're breaking ground on the school and theater as we speak, and I know Saul could use help. Do you think he would come?"

"I think he would be on the next plane."

"Done. I'll call him."

They got stuck behind a truck spewing noxious fumes from its exhaust. Aaron tried to pass, cursed and hit the brakes. Jo patted his arm. "Relax."

"You're right. Sorry. What's happening with your friend David?" From Jo's letters, Aaron knew all about David and the special bond the two of them shared.

"He got an invitation from the Technion Institute of Technology. It's the MIT of Israel. They're doing some high-level, top-secret munitions testing and they want his expertise. That would mean he and Anna would have to move to Haifa for a while."

"Is he going to go?"

"According to Saul, he will."

"What do you think?"

"That David and Anna love this country and they'll do whatever is asked of them. Besides, Haifa's a big city and because Anna is over forty, her pregnancy is considered high-risk. Maybe it's for the best, her having the baby in a big hospital."

"Things happen for a reason. Tell me, Jo. Do you ever think about having children?"

"Wow! That sure came out of left field," Jo said, trying to sound nonchalant, when in fact she often thought about being thirty-two and not married.

"It kind of slipped out," Aaron said in way of a lame apology as he weaved around a stalled car. "I think about it a lot. I would like to have children some day."

Jo knew that Aaron wanted a commitment from her. She loved him and in some ways, she had hoped he would push her into making a decision. Jo put her hand on Aaron's arm. "I want children too."

She saw the soft smile touch his face and eyes, her reply dissipating the strain between them. The words were unspoken, but on some level, a pledge had been made and they both knew it. The conversation flowed easily after that, and they talked nonstop until pulling into the parking lot of the kibbutz.

It was past midnight when they unloaded Aaron's luggage. In the lobby, he signed the guest registration, and took the key to his room. They walked down a pebble path toward the two story building that served as the kibbutz hotel.

"This brings back some sad memories," Aaron said, recalling the night he had to tell Andy that his wife had died in a car accident.

"I figured you would feel that way. That's why you are not staying there." Jo bowed. "Follow me, kind sir."

They walked up an incline, skirted the main dining hall, and headed toward an opening amongst the trees, where a lovely cottage perched.

"This is saved for dignitaries. Golda has actually stayed here." Jo smiled as Aaron opened the door, and switched on the lights.

There was a queen-sized bed, covered in a green and pink plaid bedspread. On top of the five-drawer wooden dresser sat a vase filled with blue lupine and yellow corn marigolds. Beside it was a fruit bowl overflowing with dates, avocados, guavas, and mangos. Of course, no room on a kibbutz would be complete without its Formica table and metal chairs. The windows stood open and the cool mountain air blew in, encircling the gauzy drapery.

"Thank you for the kibbutz version of the Plaza Hotel," Aaron said, laughing. "It's fantastic." He dropped his suitcase. Aaron gazed at Jo. She met his eyes. Everything altered, their reality expanding as the floor evaporated, the walls disappeared, the light changed, and the night sounds softened. She moved into his outstretched arms.

Jo had imagined this moment—played it out in her head a thousand times; how she would look, how she would feel, what she would think. She had not even come close to being right. Their love, so long denied, was like a firestorm of sensuality and passion. Reason was put aside, the initiation of their intimacy the revelation of all God's mysteries. It surpassed physical joy as they surrendered themselves to the overwhelming and almost terrifying power of lovers gasping in ecstasy. It was a hunger she had never known. The first time was raw desire, the second and third, an intimacy that defied explanation.

* * *

The beeping of the alarm pulled them both awake. Jo mashed the button, disentangled herself from the sheets, and wiggled her way into Aaron's arms. "Good morning, sleepy head."

Aaron kissed her—the world was swept aside. An hour later, spent and giddy, Jo nuzzled his neck.

"I love you so much," Aaron said.

Jo kissed the tip of his nose. "I love you too."

Aaron got up, pulled off the bedspread, and wrapped it around his waist. He went to the suitcase and ravaged around for a few minutes. When he came back to the bed, he handed Jo an envelope. "I would like you to read this."

Jo pulled out the letter and carefully unfolded it.

> *Dear Aaron,*
>
> *It is with great sadness that I write this letter to you. I know you intended to come for a visit soon, and Adele spoke of little else. She wanted to meet Jo, to show her where you grew up and to share stories about you when you were a boy.*
>
> *My Adele is gone now. She died of influenza. Please know, my son, Adele may have only borrowed you, but she loved you as if you had been born of her body. Every letter you sent was cherished, and reread a dozen times.*
>
> *Before Adele passed, she made me promise that I would send you the enclosed ring. It belonged to your mother. She gave it to Adele the night you were put into our care. She asked that it be given to you when you married.*
>
> *May the next woman that wears this ring be as kind, and precious to you as my Adele was to me, and your mother was to your father.*
>
> *Until we meet again,*
> *Dad Grunwald*

Jo looked up when she was done reading. Aaron's eyes were filled with tears.

"I am so so sorry," Jo said, touching his face.

"She was a good woman," Aaron whispered. "I'm just sorry you will never get to meet her." Aaron leaned against the headboard. Jo nuzzled against him. He opened his hand to show Jo a gold band embedded with tiny diamond chips.

Jo took the ring. "Aaron, it is so beautiful."

"Will you marry me, Jo? Will you become my family?"

Jo looked at Aaron as she slipped the ring on her finger. It was a perfect fit.

"Is that a yes?" Aaron asked with a shaky smile.

Jo hugged him. "It's a great big humongous yes. It's the most positive yes ever said. Yes. Yes. Yes!" She kissed him as he slipped his arms around her. Jo started to cry then, tears of happiness. In the center of that joy something broke apart, as if a damn had burst and all the emotions she had held in check for so long surfaced. She was an orphan with no family to call with her good news. She sobbed.

"It's okay, sweetheart. Cry. You're not alone. I'm here with you. I'll be your family and you will be mine."

Jo couldn't believe that without saying a word Aaron knew how she felt. *This is what love is. It's caring so much for someone else that your thoughts intermingle, and emotions are shared without words.*

She put her hand to his heart. "I love you and I want to be with you for the rest of my life. If your parents were here I would tell them that I will take care of their son and, with God's blessings, we will bring forth a new generation—grandchildren who will speak their names and know of the great sacrifice they made to save their only child."

Aaron watched as Jo's shoulders slumped ever so slightly and she fixed her eyes on a spot a few feet over his head. "What is it?" he asked.

"I want to be with you more than anything in the world but I just can't leave Israel yet."

Aaron leaned into her shoulder. "I know. It's okay. There is no pressure, and no timetable. Whenever you're ready."

"Thank you, Aaron."

"Thank you. This is the happiest day of my life."

* * *

Twenty minutes later Jo and Aaron were walking hand in hand down the path towards the dining hall. It was a spectacular April morning. Birds called from the canopy of lush olive trees, flowers ached to bloom, tractors sputtered and sliced, children ran by giggling, and dozens of teenagers huddled in groups, their faces aglow.

David was on the same path, heading toward breakfast. When he saw them he quickened his pace to catch up with them.

"David, I want you to meet Aaron Blumenthal, my fiancé."

David's eyes grew huge and his smile dazzled. He gathered Jo in his enormous embrace, dangling her feet above ground. "*Mazal Tov!*"

Jo giggled as David placed her back down and threw his arm around Aaron, pulling him to his side. "She loves you, I love you."

Aaron knew in that instant that he too would be David's friend.

David used that same split second to do his own assessment. He could see a lifetime in Aaron's eyes, the hard-won self-confidence, and keen instincts, the intelligence.

"*Mazal Tov*," he repeated, pumping Aaron's hand. "You will take good care of my Jo."

Aaron laughed. "That's a promise."

"Fine. You should start by not starving her. If we don't hurry, we will miss breakfast."

* * *

The next two days passed as if God himself decided to put the world on fast forward. Rebecca and Saul were ecstatic and instantly organized an engagement party in the garden off Rebecca's office. Surrounded by Jo's new friends and all of Rebecca and Saul's children, they ate and danced to Yiddish music performed by the kibbutz Klezmer band.

The following morning Jo was in the kitchen at dawn, along with every female on the kibbutz. Passover would begin at sunset and preparations for the holiday had been taking place for days. Every inch of the kitchen, every pantry, corner, every nook and cranny had been inspected for any remnants of wheat. For the next seven days Jews did not eat anything leavened. This was done to commemorate that the Jews fleeing Egypt did not have time to let their bread rise.

The long tables in the dining hall were covered in tablecloths, and set with dishes used only during this particular holiday. As evening approached every member of the kibbutz gathered.

Jo sat beside Aaron as the candles were lit, signifying sunset, and the beginning of the Seder. It was then that the Haggadahs were read, books that retold the story of the Jews escape from Egypt, the Pharaoh and slavery.

There were blessings over the wine, ritual hand washing by the kibbutz Rabbi, dipping of parsley into salt water, the blessings over the matzo, the eating of bitter herbs to remind the Jews of the bitterness of slavery, the eating of charoset, a mixture of apples, nuts, cinnamon and wine, each ritual act representing a moment in the history of the Jewish people and their survival.

Jo couldn't help stealing looks at Aaron. He seemed so joyous in these surroundings, so content. *My first Passover.* Jo memorized every moment, intending to carry on every tradition in her own home one day. *My children will be nourished with these tenets, not the poison that was fed to me.*

As Jo was having those thoughts, Aaron leaned over and whispered, "We will do this in our home one day, surrounded, God willing, by our own children."

Just then, the rabbi announced that dinner could be served. Because the populace of the kibbutz was primarily Ashkenazi, European Jews, the food traditions of that community were followed. The meal began with deboned carp that was formed into fish balls known at gifilte fish. There was chicken soup with matzo balls, briskets, turkeys, potato kugels, apple fritters, and sweet matzo puddings.

At the conclusion of the meal, Jo turned to Aaron. "I can't believe we're really doing this whole thing again tomorrow night," Jo patted her stomach. "Thank God it's only for one night. I've never been so full in my entire life."

"I know. Isn't being a Jew wonderful?" Aaron said.

* * *

Two days later Jo stood at the airport departure gate, waving good-bye to Aaron. It had been difficult, this ride to the airport, knowing that they would not be seeing each other for a while. But, the parting was bittersweet. Aaron was going home to ready his home for its new resident, and Jo was going to begin closing the book on this chapter of her life. She felt empowered by his love, certain that whatever lay ahead, she was ready.

35

July 6, 1973
Haifa, Israel

The call came into the kibbutz office at three o'clock in the morning—Anna was in labor. The message from David to Jo was terse and to the point: come, I need you.

Jo commandeered the kibbutz's station wagon and drove the forty-five miles in an hour and a half. As she drove the winding roads, she thought about the miraculous past couple of months.

The day after Aaron went back to Washington Jo began studying Judaism with Seymour Shapiro, the somewhat eccentric and irreverent rabbi who had fled his congregation in Brooklyn, New York, to live on the kibbutz, his goal being to find himself. The rabbi was thirty-five years old, short, with a balding head, pock marked skin, a flat nose, bushy eyebrows, and thick lips. What he lacked in looks was set aside by his outrageous sense of humor.

Jo adored him.

They studied the Torah and Jo learned about *mitzvot*, doing good deeds, Shabbat, a commanded day of rest, *kashrut,* keeping kosher, and the commandments. The rabbi loved to argue and he would teach Jo a passage, then quarrel with her about what they read. He loved the minutia of the law, and tried to convince Jo that most of it was insidious, outdated, and outrageous. Jo disagreed, realizing only now that his cynicism had turned her into a devoted Jew who fell in love with the religion and its practical and didactic philosophy.

Jo smiled as she thought back to that Wednesday morning, July 4, when she and Rabbi Shapiro had a mock conversion, something Jo insisted upon, even though, as the child of a Jewish mother, she was already considered a Jew and had no need for a conversion.

She and the rabbi sat in the cinder block fallout shelter that served as his office. He asked questions about Jo's background and her motives for conversion. He had her state that she believed in the one God of Israel, His Torah, and that she had a genuine love for the Jewish people. Then Jo recited the Shema Yisrael—hear O Israel, the Lord our God, the Lord is One, and by doing so, she symbolically took her mother's religion as her own.

Jo knew it was an infinitesimal act—thunder did not roar and the seas did not part. But for Jotto Wells that small act of contrition changed her world. She was now ready to make decisions that would reflect her newfound commitment.

Jo was brought back to the present by a signpost for the Bnei Zion (Rothschild) hospital. She pulled into the parking lot and rushed to the information desk. They sent her to the third floor where she found David frantic and pacing the hallways.

"Thank God you're here," David said, squeezing Jo."

"What's going on? What did the doctor say?"

"Doctor? What doctor? They took her in hours ago and now nothing! I can't see her, they won't tell me anything. I'm going crazy!"

"If something was wrong they would tell you. First babies take a long time. You know that."

"Anna was in so much pain, Jo. She's not a kid. This could be too much for her."

"David Kandel, after everything that you and Anna have been through, after the courage she showed by defecting, you dare doubt her ability to birth a child?"

"See. That's exactly why I needed you here. Come. We will get coffee and then you can tell me everything you have been up to. That will help me pass the time."

Five hours later David and Jo were staring into the smiling face of an obviously exhausted doctor.

"*Mazal Tov.* You have a healthy son; seven pounds, six ounces."

David grabbed his arm. "And my wife?"

"The strongest forty-two-year-old I ever met. She's quite a woman. You can see her in a little while." The doctor shook David's hand. "May your son's years be blessed with health and peace."

David hugged Jo, his tears damp against her cheek. "A father at fifty-four years old. It is a miracle."

"A well-deserved miracle," Jo added.

David laughed. "Maybe so. Maybe so." He put his arm around her. "My son represents the future and the hope of our people. I am going to teach him to remember. I will tell him all about my parents, my grandparents, and the old rabbi whose clothing Saul buried on the grounds of Hebrew University. You see, my little dove, you and I have gone beyond the darkness—we have moved into the light."

The Brit Milah (circumcision)

On the eighth day of Moshe Kandel's life, David and Anna traveled from Haifa to Kibbutz Ayelet Haba-ah to bring their son into the covenant with the Jewish people. In celebration of the event, the dining hall was decorated with blue balloons and streamers. The children made a sign welcoming Anna, Saul, and Moshe.

Anna walked into the room carrying the infant. She had that new mother look—exhausted and bewildered, yet joyous. David strode beside her, head up, chest puffed out, looking as if he had just won another Olympic medal. Two hundred people applauded.

Jo and Saul peeked over Anna's shoulder for a better look at the baby.

"Say hello to your *kvatter* and your *kvatterin,* your godparents," David said to his sleeping son.

Rabbi Shapiro beckoned them into a corner.

"Where is the mohel?" Anna asked.

The rabbi bowed. "Trained and ready. You get two for one. Prayers and a mohel that has done hundreds of circumcisions." He winked at Anna. "It will be over before you know it. Come."

In the center of the room were two chairs. The rabbi took the child from Anna and handed him to Jo, honoring her as the *kvat-*

terin, the godmother. Jo placed the swaddled infant on the empty chair, her hands holding him in place.

The chair was set aside for the spirit of Elijah the Prophet, the Angel of the Covenant. According to Jewish tradition, Elijah attended every circumcision to testify before the Almighty to the commitment of the Jewish people. The rabbi recited a prayer asking for the spirit of Elijah to stand over him as he performed the Brit.

Saul sat in the second chair. He was chosen as Moshe's Sandek and he would hold the baby during the actual circumcision. According to Cabbalistic tradition, the lap of the Sandek is analogous to the altar of the Temple itself, and that by holding the child Saul's soul would be forever linked to Moshe.

The baby was placed on Saul's knees, his legs toward the rabbi. He was unwrapped and the diaper removed. The rabbi dipped surgical gauze in wine and placed the wet end in Moshe's mouth. He tickled under the infant's chin and Moshe began to suck.

"Hold Moshe's legs apart and down so they will be out of my way," Rabbi Shapiro said to Saul as he uncovered his instruments sitting on a table beside him.

Jo watched in awe at the speed in which the rabbi moved. It took half a minute for him to place two surgical clamps in place on either side of the foreskin. Then he took the Izmail knife in his hand, sharpened on both sides, stretched the foreskin over the glans and in one motion sliced away an inch of foreskin. The baby cried out once and then fell back to sleep.

There was very little blood as the rabbi covered the penis with gauze. He swaddled the sleeping baby, tucked him under his left arm, and lifted a silver chalice filled with wine in his right hand, reciting the blessing over the wine.

Then he held little Moshe above his head for the assembled to see.

"Our God and God of our fathers," the rabbi said, "preserve this child for his father and mother, and his name in Israel shall be called Moshe Kendal, son of David and Anna. May he be a blessing to his parents and to his people Israel."

* * *

The next afternoon Jo met Rebecca in the garden beside her cottage for their now once a week therapy session. Sitting on two plastic lawn chairs, Rebecca poured lemonade from a thermos and handed it to Jo.

"It's going to be hot today," Rebecca said.

Jo watched dreamily as a dove built its nest in the olive tree that shaded Rebecca's yard.

Rebecca knew all of Jo's moods and seeing her sitting so still was a definite signal. "Okay, young lady. What's going on with you?"

Jo wasn't sure where to begin. She thought back over the past seven months. Rebecca had taken her on a journey into the bowels of her own despair giving no ground, allowing no shortcuts. When they hit a roadblock and could move no further, Rebecca had convinced Jo to allow her to use hypnosis.

In those sessions, they discovered a vocabulary of hate planted inside of Jo's brain. It had not taken root because, as Rebecca pointed out, there was something bigger at play, something beyond explanation.

"Call it your soul, or genetic override, call it whatever you like. What's important is that the words did not stick and the hate is not there," Rebecca had said.

It took Jo a long time to accept that she was not damaged. When she finally did, her healing began and she was able to tackle a problem she had been unable to deal with before—facing the grief of losing her family.

With Rebecca's guidance, Jo came to understand that she had loved Otto, Hans, and Ilya, regardless of their behaviors. Acknowledging that was the first step in accepting the grief of their loss. There were still moments when the tears would come and the horror of their deaths would overwhelm her but she could now recognize those times, cry, and move forward.

She looked hard at Rebecca. "Have I come far enough? Am I well enough to stop our therapy?" Jo asked, tilting her chin. "Am I well enough to leave Israel?"

Rebecca knew this day was coming. She expected it and had tried to prepare herself, still, the thought of Jo leaving cut deep. "You are

more than ready. You're healthy, whole, and ready to move on."
Rebecca swallowed hard.

"I got this in the mail today," Jo said, handing an official-looking
piece of paper to Rebecca.

Rebecca's mouth dropped open as she read the document. "This
is a visa for Lithuania. You're going?"

Jo nodded. "Remember when you said to me that becoming
whole meant facing all the demons and embracing even those things
I might never understand?"

Rebecca nodded.

"I have done that and now I need to come full circle and see
where my birth mother lived. I want to touch something she may
have touched, to walk a street she traveled, to see things with my
own eyes that she saw with hers."

"Why didn't you tell me you were going to do this?" Rebecca
asked, the hurt visible in the way she crossed her arms over her
chest and pulled into herself.

"Because Aaron wasn't sure how long it would take to get a visa
originating from Israel. Communist-ruled Lithuania broke relations
with Israel after the Six-Day War and he knew it was going to mean
pulling in some favors, and I didn't want a prolonged good-bye. I
was afraid I couldn't handle it. I'm sorry if I hurt you. I certainly
didn't mean to."

Rebecca took Jo's hand. "I'm being silly. I only want your happiness. You have become a part of my family and I am going to miss
you so much." Rebecca said, the color rising in her face.

"And just like family, Aaron and I will come back and visit often. And you will come to us too." *Us. Just saying that makes me
feel whole again, a part of something real.* "Come. I have a call to
make, and I want you there with me when I make it."

* * *

In the lobby of the kibbutz hotel Jo entered the phone booth, deposited her coins, and listened as the international operator placed
the call. She glanced at her watch, realizing it was midnight in
Washington.

"It's me." Jo said.

"I can barely hear you. Wait a minute." Aaron swung his feet to the floor and switched on the light. He could see her face in front of him, the way her eyes caught the light and crinkled when she smiled.

"Can you hear me now?" Jo said, raising her voice.

"Yes. What's going on? Has something happened?"

Jo laughed. "Everything is perfect. I got the visa today. Did you get yours?"

Aaron's heart started to pound. "I'm picking it up tomorrow. Have you booked your flight?"

"I'm going to do it now."

"Give me the details when you have them. I've already arranged for a guide to meet you and be at your disposal until I arrive."

Jo smiled into the telephone. Even though he was thousands of miles away Aaron could still make her feel safe. "Thanks."

"Please deposit additional coins," the operator said in a static-drenched voice.

"I love you. I'll call tomorrow—at a more reasonable time. Shalom my beloved," Jo said.

"Shalom."

Aaron sat on the edge of his bed, his mind racing. He had waited so long, and prayed so hard for this moment. He would meet Jo in Vilnius and then she would come home with him. That was the vow she made to him—Vilnius and then home.

Aaron picked up the siddur, the prayer book he kept beside his bed. He turned to a passage he had always avoided until now.

I love that the Lord should hear my voice and my supplications. For thou hast delivered my soul from death, mine eyes from tears, and my feet from stumbling. I shall walk before the Lord in the land of the living.

Their time had come.

Tel Aviv, Israel

The following day Jo drove to the construction site where The Morgan and Robert Osborne Theatrical Institute and The Morgan Rabinowiszch Theatre of the Performing Arts were being built on a parcel of land abutting the grounds of the Tel Aviv University campus. Jo parked the station wagon and stood staring at the massive site. Three bulldozers were digging a giant crater into the earth and dozens of workmen moved about like ants in an anthill.

She spotted Saul standing beside the construction trailer; his shirt was stained with sweat, his face dirt-smudged. She waved and he waved back, all teeth and crinkling eyes as he reached for a thermos of cold water, splashed his face, took off the hard hat, and snaked through the footings towards her.

Jo opened her arms for a hug. Saul showed her his palms. "I'm all sweaty." He gave her a peck on the cheek. "A lot has happened since last you visited," Saul said.

Jo shielded her eyes from the sun and squinted. "It's really re-markable how quickly things are moving."

"There's something so noble about all this." Saul opened his arms in a wide arch. "This will outlive us all, and God willing tens of thousands of people will discover pleasure and knowledge inside these yet-to-be-built walls."

William waved to Jo from across the field, tucked the plans under his arm, and walked across the site. "What a marvelous surprise." He gathered her into his arms.

Jo laughed, delighted in William's tan, robust appearance. "You in shorts—who would have ever believed that could happen?"

"Thanks to you," William said. He pinched her cheek.

Taking William and Saul's hands, Jo led them to a grassy area not yet trampled by the construction workers. She sat and pulled them down beside her.

"We're having a picnic without a blanket or food…or ants. This isn't any fun," William said.

"You expect her to bring sandwiches? She hates the kitchen," Saul teased.

"I'm so glad you're both having such a good time at my expense. By the way, I don't hate the kitchen. I just hate the kitchen on the kibbutz." Jo pointed a finger at Saul. "I intend to become a very good cook one day. But you can take bets: I'll never peel another potato."

"Some Jewish wife you'll be!" Saul said, poking Jo's arm. "No

potato latkes, no kugels, no knishes, no brisket with browned potatoes simmering in broth...."

"Enough!" Jo scolded. "I have something serious I need to tell
you."

Saul had spent the previous night commiserating with his devastated wife, and had told William first thing this morning that Jo was
going to Vilnius. "You've come to say goodbye."

Jo tugged on her hair, nodding.

William put his arm around Jo. "This is a good thing. Your mother would have wanted you to see where she grew up."

"I'm going to miss you both so much."

"You're moving to Virginia, not Siberia," William said, pulling
her tighter.

"Just keep beds made up for all of us in that little mansion you
are going to call home," Saul said. "And fill the rest of the rooms
with little Aarons and Jos!"

* * *

Jo left Saul and William and drove to Haifa, a port city on the
Mediterranean Sea, at the foot of Mt. Carmel. Driving through the
narrow, twisting streets, she finally arrived in Romema, where David and Anna were renting a flat-roofed row house. It was dinner-
time and Jo knew that they would be home.

She knocked. The screen door banged open and David embraced
Jo. "Anna, we have company." David called, dragging Jo inside.

Jo took in her surroundings, a smile turning the corners of her
mouth. Meticulous Anna had obviously decided that being orderly
was no longer a priority. There was a pile of unfolded clothing sitting in a laundry basket; a stack of diapers lay on the dining room
table along with baby clothes, baby powder, teething rings, toys,
stuffed animals, and a soccer ball.

Jo spread her arms, wishing she could bundle it all up and take
it with her. She would keep this snapshot in her head: Anna sitting
on the couch, pillows stuffed behind her back as she nursed Moshe.
The absolute contentment on her face and the utter ecstasy on David's.

"Come and sit with me." Anna patted the sofa.

Jo moved next to Anna and kissed her cheek, peaking at her godson. "He's so cute."

"He is, isn't he?" Anna said, pride coloring her face.

David leaned against the wall. His eyes never left Jo's face. "I heard you're leaving."

"News sure travels fast," Jo said. "Who called you?"

"Saul, this morning. You are going to Vilnius."

"I wanted to tell you myself."

"And so, now you will," he said.

"I have been thinking about this a lot. It feels right to me. I want to try and make some sort of connection with my mother." Jo sighed and was silent.

Anna patted Jo's leg. "This is a good thing. And you are very brave to do it."

"What will you do once you're back in Washington?" David asked. "Will you practice law?"

"If it can help me achieve my goals, I will."

David put his hands on his hips, pointing at Jo with his chin. "That is not what I want to hear! Why can't you just settle down, get married, and have some babies?"

"That's part of the plan. Just not all the plan," Jo said. "Come on, David, you and I have had this conversation. There are people still out there, working to see Hitler's ideology perpetuated. It's my duty to try and stop them."

"Bullshit!" David hissed. His face draining of color. "You must let the Israelis take care of it. Your job is to fade into the woodwork and have a life."

"Calm down, my love," Anna said, flicking her eyes at David. "You already know that Jo is going to do what she must do. From you she needs encouragement and love. So stop being such a bully."

The baby pulled away from Anna's breast, letting out a gaseous wail. Anna put him over her shoulder. "David's just upset that you're leaving," Anna said, tapping Moshe's back.

"My son," David said, his eyes misting. "He must know you. And so, I insist that you make me a promise. You must swear that you will do nothing to put your life in danger. Swear that to me. Swear it!" he said, a hopeless, helpless look on his face.

Jo stood. "I will swear only one thing to you, and that is that I will never do anything that you, in the same position, would not do. Now, let's spend the rest of this evening together enjoying your son because tomorrow I leave."

36

July 1973

Jo flew on El Al from Tel Aviv to Heathrow airport in London. From there she took a bus to Gatwick airport where she boarded a Fokker F27 turboprop commuter airplane. Three hours later, she was circling the Oro Uostas airport over Vilnius, once known as the *Jerusalem of Lithuania*, where over one-hundred thousand Jews lived before the war.

Before leaving Israel Jo had spent countless hours in the kibbutz library studying the complicated history of Vilnius.

Soviet Russia had invaded Vilna, Poland in October of 1939, and turned the city over to the country of Lithuania, a semi-fascist state. The city was then renamed Vilnius and became the capital of Lithuania. Jewish refugees, fleeing from Polish cities occupied by the Germans, flooded into it. They found safety until July of 1940, when the Red Army invaded Lithuania and annexed the entire country, including Vilnius, to the USSR.

The Soviets—rabid anti-Semites—made life miserable for the Jews. They closed down all the Hebrew cultural institutions and banned all Zionist organizations. The Yiddish press, the voice of the Jewish people, was replaced by the communist party's propaganda newspapers, and many Jewish activists were sent into Siberian exile.

* * *

The flashing seatbelt sign and grinding sounds of the wheels locking in place for landing brought Jo into the present. As they

287

approached the runway, Jo peered out the window, watching as the city came into view, perched amongst a valley and rolling hills. The wheels touched down.

She was finally here.

Jo passed through customs without incident and then moved into the antiquated terminal that looked like it hadn't seen paint in decades. She ran her fingers through her hair, bleached to white gold by the Israeli sun and as unruly as always. Dressed in an eggshell linen skirt and turquoise long-sleeved blouse, and wearing make-up for the first time in months, she smoothed her blouse as she passed an old man wearing baggy pants and a stained shirt crying as he talked to a twenty-something man with long hair and black darting eyes.

A woman pushing a baby carriage approached a soldier with an empty left sleeve. Jo watched as the soldier kissed the top of the child's head before collapsing in tears into the arms of his wife. She swallowed the lump in her throat and quickened her steps.

A young man was holding a sign in front of his chest with her name on it. She waved. He was dressed in a white t-shirt, a jean jacket, khaki pants, sneakers, a full beard, and coffee-colored hair that had not seen a scissors in months. He stared at her with the greenest eyes she had ever seen.

"Larry Steinberg, linguist, anthropologist, and sociology doctoral student at your service." He stuck out his hand, winked, and bowed, relieving Jo of her luggage. "You certainly are beautiful. I am definitely going to enjoy this gig."

* * *

Larry's car was a dented rusty wreck parked with its backside sticking into the street. He yanked open the trunk, stuck her luggage on top of some fishing rods, and a pair of ratty old boots and then tied the trunk down with a rope. "That should hold it."

When he opened the passenger door with a tug, Jo moved in gingerly to avoid sitting on an exposed spring. The window on her side was missing, but Larry said nothing in way of an apology for his car's appearance as he pulled into the sporadic traffic and popped the clutch too quickly. It sent the car into jerking spasms. He laughed. "Welcome to Vilnius, hell hole of the earth."

"If you hate it so much, why are you here?"

"Great first question. I'm doing my dissertation on the German-Lithuanian collaboration of the *Final Solution*. Trying to figure out why the populace of Vilnius was so complicit in the eradication of their Jews. And, to answer what your second question would probably be—the Soviets have no idea what my dissertation is about. I am here because my family is loaded, and when enough palms are greased, rules get broken—especially in a communist block country."

Jo laughed. *This is going to be interesting.* "Where are you from?"

Larry took a hard right and said, "I was raised in Rochester, New York, went to Stanford for my undergraduate work and then moved to Boston where I attended graduate school at Harvard."

"Pretty impressive," Jo said.

"Compared to you, the first female senator from New York State, I am chicken feed. By the way, even though we're on the same time as Israel, aren't you wiped out? Would you like to go to your hotel now, and we can begin our tour in the morning?"

"If you wouldn't mind, I'd like to see a little bit of the city. Just so I can get my bearings."

"My pleasure. Right now, we are seven miles outside the city. There are two rivers," Larry said, one hand on the wheel, the other pointing in various directions at his whim. "The Wilejka enters the river Wilia in the valley. The town lies on a plain, tilting from the Pinsk Lowlands towards the Baltic Sea. To the east and west are the elevated upper layers of land on which the town stands."

Ten minutes later, they entered the city center. Jo peered out the window trying to comprehend that she was about see where her mother grew up. As they passed the three and four-story stone and brick apartment buildings, all in different stages of disrepair that bordered both sides of the street, she wondered if perhaps this was near the neighborhood where her mother might have lived.

"If you don't mind my asking?" Larry said, interrupting Jo's thoughts. "What are you doing here? It's not exactly on the list of the top ten cities to visit."

"It's where the maternal side of my mother's family is from. I wanted to see it," she said, deciding that was all Larry needed to know. "From what I was told they were fairly wealthy. Perhaps tomorrow you could show me where they might have lived?" Jo asked, tears stinging the back of her eyes.

"That's a tall order. In the good old days they lived all over the city." Larry downshifted, navigating the winding alleyways with little concern for the pedestrians and cyclists, blaring his horn and yelling obscenities. He hit the brakes and parked half on the street, half on the sidewalk.

"That's Jatkowa Street. It's the entrance to the Old Town Jewish quarter. Before the war, the courtyard of the Great City Synagogue of Vilnius was right over there." He pointed. "It was surrounded by prayer halls, communal offices, a rabbinical library, a ritual bath, and several smaller synagogues.

"Is there anything left to see?" Jo asked, her eyes searching the busy street.

Larry shook his head. "There were once a hundred places for a Jew to worship in this city, now there is only one synagogue left, the Choral Synagogue. The Nazis used it as an ammunition warehouse during the war. It's in a shambles, but at least it still stands.

Jo had seen pictures of Vilna in its heyday, before the Nazis, when Jews were linen weavers, bakers, cobblers, rope spinners, tailors, medicine men, tinsmiths, locksmiths, tavern keepers, fishmongers, carpenters, rug beaters, mechanics and umbrella makers.

Larry turned his green eyes toward Jo. "Many great Jewish scholars lived and worked here. But, for the most part the Jews that lived in this city were simple people. Religious people. Hard working people." Larry's eyes watered. "See that group of men standing on the corner?" he pointed. "There's a good chance you are looking at men that took part in the slaughter of Jews. They were called snatchers, and they were not innocent bystanders but willing participants."

His words exploded in Jo's head, catapulting her into the frozen waters of despair. *My father was one of those people. A Nazi. A man who tortured and killed Jews.* Tears streamed down her face. *How am I going to do this?*

"God, I am so sorry. I didn't mean to be so maudlin. Let me get you to your hotel."

Jo nodded. In corners of her mind, she had hoped, even expected to drive into the city and feel a sense of familiarity, a connection. Instead, she felt alienation, anger, and worst of all disappointment.

* * *

The hotel Lietuvana was a grubby three-story brick building with gray windows and chipped steps, located on Mickiewitz Street.

"Welcome to the best Vilnius has to offer," Larry said as they pulled into the driveway. He untied the trunk. A surly porter in a stained uniform took her luggage and grunted as he carried it inside.

"Get a good night's sleep. I'll pick you up at nine." Larry handed Jo a slip of paper. "That's the boarding house number where I stay. Call me if you need anything."

Fifteen minutes later, after showing her passport, and filling out the registration, Jo was handed a key to room 326. She followed the porter into a metal-gated, antique elevator that rumbled ominously and got stuck for a few seconds between the second and third floor.

Jo entered the hotel room, locked the door, and looked around. The place reeked of neglect from the threadbare carpet to the worn wood and tattered drapery. The twin beds were covered with faded moth-eaten coverlets, and the walls were painted an indiscernible color that might have once been white but was now blotched with brownish-yellow stains. The lamp had a cockeyed shade and it sat atop a night table whose drawer was stuck open like a toothless smile.

Jo opened the sliding glass door and ventured out to the tiny balcony where she was greeted by a rusted chair slimed with pigeon droppings. In the waning daylight, Jo scanned the rooftops dotted with TV antennas and laundry lines. *This is it! This is what I have fantasized about all these months.* She walked inside, pulling the glass door closed so hard it shook.

Jo dug into her purse for the peanuts she had taken from the airplane. She ate them, kicked off her shoes, and undressed. The mattress springs dug into her buttocks as she placed an overseas call to Aaron. Ten minutes later, the phone rang.

"We have your party on the line," the operator said.

"Aaron?"

"Jo, thank God. I was so worried. Was Larry there to meet you?"

"Right on time. How did you ever find him?"

"The Jewish agency made the connection for us. Seems he has been in contact with them, seeking information, asking for names, being relentless in his search to find collaborators, liberators, and survivors. I hear he's quite the character."

Jo was suddenly overwhelmed. "Aaron, when are you coming?"

"I'll be on a flight at eleven tomorrow morning. I should be in Vilnius sometime around four a.m. your time. I'll take a cab. Just leave a key for me at the front desk."

Jo's eyes filled with tears. "I wish you were already here."

"What's wrong, my love?"

"My mother." Her voice cracked. "I just can't visualize her here."

"Sweetheart, you're tired. Give yourself a chance to get acclimated."

"Aaron, I don't know what I was thinking when I came here. The people, so many of them took part in the massacre of Jews. I hate this place!" Jo felt as if she was on the verge of a tantrum.

"Jo, every day of their lives these people have to live with what they've done. We can never know how they suffer."

"Suffer? I don't think my father and uncle suffered! As a matter of fact, I don't think either one of them had one minute of remorse," she said, knowing her words were harsh and her tone harsher.

"Look, I don't know what they thought or felt. But, I do understand what you are feeling."

"Oh God, Aaron, I am so sorry. I didn't mean to take my frustration out on you."

"I know, and I only wish there was something I could do to make you feel better."

"It's just so hard," Jo said.

"I have a little prayer I say whenever things get too difficult. I ask God for the wisdom to live today and build a better tomorrow on the mistakes and experiences of yesterday."

"Live today and build a better tomorrow," she repeated. "That's what we are going to do. Isn't it?"

"Yes, my beloved. It's exactly what we are going to do. And Jo—"

"What?"

"Everything is going to be okay. I'm going to take care of you."

"I love you so much. Shalom, my beloved Aaron. Until tomorrow," Jo said, hanging up the phone.

* * *

Jo spent a restless night watching the clock beside her bed. At eight, she finally gave up, dressed, and went to the coffee shop in the lobby for breakfast.

Larry pulled up to the front of the hotel at one minute to nine.

"How'd you sleep?" he asked, yanking open the car door for her.

"Lumpy bed. Where are we going first?"

"The Vilnius Ghetto." He hit the gas and careened onto the busy street, avoiding a bicyclist by inches. He drove down Zawalna Street and stopped on the corner of Strashun.

"This is it," Larry said, again parking with two wheels on the sidewalk. He got out of the car and Jo joined him.

Larry stood with his hands on his hips, his eyes darting, his voice dark and angry. "When the Germans invaded the city they undertook the first mass execution of Jews on Soviet territory. Forty-thousand were slaughtered and another forty-thousand were then herded into the seven narrow streets just ahead of us. It was a slum before it became a ghetto in September of 1941."

Larry walked ahead, anger befalling every step. Jo followed behind, navigating the crooked narrow streets, moving past its dead walls. It was dirty and crowded, the smell of cabbage and sewage seeping into Jo's nostrils, making her feel nauseated. She gazed into the open windows as she walked and saw a man slap a woman, another man standing at a sink peeing. A woman was washing dishes and she could hear dogs barking, and people coughing and sneezing.

A man sneered at Larry and moved to the center of the sidewalk so that Larry had to step into the street. Larry raised his middle finger. Jo searched the eyes of the people that loitered in the doorways. She was overcome by hatred, an emotion she had never felt before towards total strangers.

Distracted, Jo took a right and walked down an alley with no exit. Frantic, she quickened her pace, and didn't see the garbage can lid on the ground. She tripped and fell. Sitting there on her rump with a skinned knee Jo could almost hear the children from the Ghetto begging their mothers for food. She could sense the vacant eyes of those mothers as they scrounged for a bit of bread, a rotten potato, a drink of water. She could conjure the old people, hunched over, helpless, staggering about, lethargic, and hopeless.

Jo could not justify any of this. If there was a God, she wanted no part of Him. She looked toward the heavens, knowing that only the sun, the moon, the sky, and the stars remained as witnesses to the suffering of an uncaring God.

After a time they ventured from the Ghetto to Niemiecka Street, the main artery of the Vilnius business district. Jo stopped and turned to Larry.

"Show me something that's left of the Jewish community. Show me anything!"

"Look, I know this is difficult. The city was once the capital of Yiddish culture, with the fabulous Strashun Library, schools and synagogues. On the eve of the war, some 240,000 Jews lived in the country of Lithuania-virtually all of whom were killed during the Nazi occupation. Today—what can I say?" He shrugged. "There are Hebrew letters on a gutted building near the train/bus station on Raugyklos. It's not worth the walk." He took Jo's hand. "Let's take a break. I'm starving."

Lunch was at Vienkiemis, a popular local restaurant where they ordered borscht, a cold beet soup, zeppelins, grated potato dumplings with meat filling and Lithuanian beer. They didn't talk much. When the check came and was paid, Jo said, "What's next?"

"That's up to you," Larry said with a smirk. "The city is famous for its beautiful churches."

"I wouldn't mind seeing something beautiful," Jo said, not bothering to tell Larry that she had grown up a Christian and had spent many an hour inside church walls.

For the next two hours, they visited the Church of the Holy Spirit, the 16th century Gothic church of St. Anne, and the Dominican Church. She found them lovely, but nothing exceptional. Then they drove to Vilnius University, and walked around the campus founded by Jesuits in 1579.

"There is one last place I want to take you today," Larry said, as they drove northeast from the old city. He pulled to a stop ten minutes later. "This is the Church of Saints Peter and Paul. It doesn't look like much from the outside," Larry said, leaning across Jo and shoving open the car door.

Jo was reeling from the number of churches she had already seen, structures built as a testament to faith, entrusted to patrons who stood witness to the annihilation of a people. She strode into the church with her arms crossed, and her mind closed. Her breath abated. The lantern-domed cathedral was washed in white light, and regardless of how Jo felt, she had to admit this was a Baroque masterpiece.

"They say two hundred artists worked here. The ornamentation was done by Pietro Peretti and the stucco moldings by Giovanni Maria Galli, both Italian masters. There are over two thousand figures painted here. No two are alike," Larry said.

Jo spent half an hour in the church, trying to see the place for its beauty, to absorb the great talent that it had taken to bring this building to such extraordinary heights. It was a useless attempt. She couldn't forgive a church that stood silent. They were all hypocrites, perhaps the guiltiest of all people: those priests that had done nothing to halt the carnage.

"I've had it," Jo said, tugging on Larry's arm. "Get me out of here."

On the way back to the hotel Jo told Larry about Aaron's imminent arrival.

Larry smiled. "He is one lucky guy. I look forward to meeting him."

As Jo was about to get out of the car at the hotel Larry put his hand on her arm. "I know you are hurting. This is a lot to take in at one time. But I promise, whatever you are seeking, you will find. Nathaniel Hawthorne said, 'happiness is a butterfly, which, when pursued, is always just beyond your grasp, but which, if you will sit down quietly, may alight upon you.' Rest, Jo. I know you'll find whatever it is you're looking for."

37

Ten O'clock that evening

Jo took a long shower, washed her hair, applied make-up, and put on the only silk nightgown that she owned. It was not as alluring as she would like, but it would have to do. She got into bed, propped herself on two pillows, picked up *Islands in the Stream* by Ernest Hemingway and began to read. Her intention was to stay awake—to wait for Aaron.

The next thing Jo knew she was floating above a huge field of golden wheat. The sky overhead was black, and the wind howled. A huge Swastika hovered horizontally a few feet above the field spinning like a centrifuge. The four right angles of its arms were spewing screaming bodies into the air toward huge smoldering fires, gigantic pits, and massive walls of stone. She was horror stricken and terrified.

Suddenly, like the onslaught of a violet storm, white bolts of lightning began shooting out from each body an instant before they were consumed by the fire, dropped into the pits, or smashed against the walls. The lightning flashed and then shimmered as the souls floated free, unharmed, and unafraid.

Jo hovered above it all, watching from her clouds in the sky, struck by the realization that regardless of how often human beings turned on one another, destroying and assaulting, causing untold anguish, there was more—there was perpetuity, time without end.

And then she was awake, staring into the now, afraid to blink, afraid the vision would fade and the knowing with it. She went over the dream again, every moment of it—the screams, the horror, and then the light, and the redemption. It was then that Jo knew she would take this knowledge forward. Peace enveloped her. It was the night she came to know God.

Just then, a key turned in the door. Jo jumped up and opened her arms to Aaron, kissing him before he could say a word. They made love then, as only those who are in love can do. It was a night Jo would never forget.

It was the beginning of their beginning.

* * *

The next morning Jo and Aaron walked from the hotel holding hands. The day was glorious, the sun shone, there was not a cloud in the sky, and the temperature was in the low seventies. Larry was waiting curbside, leaning against his car. He waved and came to meet them.

Jo made the introductions. Larry's demeanor changed, and he seemed reticent, maybe even a little shy. Jo thought that might be a good thing. The thought passed quickly as Larry put his arm around Aaron.

"Man, you must have done something really right in your life to wind up with Jo. What I wouldn't give to trade places with you."

Aaron laughed. Then he spotted the car. "Is that our mode of transportation?"

"Yes sir."

Aaron pointed to the almost nonexistent back seat and then at himself. "If I were a midget then perhaps…"

"Oops. Sorry. Jo didn't tell me you were so tall. There are no cars to rent and the taxis aren't much better than my car. I guess we could just walk."

And so they did. They walked for hours, up and down hills, meandering around dozens of streets, listening as Larry painted a history of the city for them. At two they stopped in a cafe for a leisurely lunch.

Late in the afternoon, they wandered into an antique shop where they were greeted by a dusty woman in drab clothing who followed too close to their heels, jabbering to Larry in Polish.

Jo moved through the crowded store, intending to do a walk-through and then leave. She loved antiques, but had never particularly liked antique stores—there was just too much stuff and within minutes, it all looked like junk to her. She was making a beeline toward the exit with Aaron close behind when she saw them—dozens of silver Kiddush cups, used for wine on the Sabbath, silver and brass menorahs, and Shabbat candle holders—mementos that should have been sitting on the dining tables of Jewish homes.

Jo began to shake. "Stolen. It's all stolen!" she hissed. "Tell her, Larry! Interpret what I just said," Jo demanded.

Aaron took Jo's arm. "This is a communist country. Insulting her will only bring trouble. Let's go." Aaron put his arm around Jo and led her into the street.

Jo took a deep breath and grimaced. She remembered the dream. "I guess I kind of lost it, huh?"

"Just a little."

Larry came out of the store scowling. "If you don't mind, I would prefer not winding up in the slammer." He looked at Aaron. "Your lady needs some down time."

Jo dropped her chin and mumbled an apology.

"There's a park on Gora Zomkova. It's only a fifteen minute walk from here," Larry said. "It's a pretty innocuous place, nothing there to upset you."

* * *

"Welcome to Bernadner Gargin," Larry said as they moved into the park.

Jo looked around. *This park could be in New York, Washington, Any Town USA.* There were apple, pear, fir, pine and birch trees, benches, a playground with swings, a slide, and a jungle gym. Young mothers stood in groups, their voices animated as they kept guard over their children. Dogs yelped as a game of kickball took place, a dozen boys running, laughing, and shouting. .

Aaron stuck out his hand to Larry. "Thanks for a great day. We'll take a cab back to the hotel. See you tomorrow. How is ten?"

"Perfect. Jo has my number if you need anything."

Jo kissed his cheek. "Thanks."

Larry held Jo's eyes. "It is my honor," he said, turning on his heals.

"You know, this is the first place I can actually visualize my mother." Jo's eyes caressed the scene. "She may have come here as a child. She may have played on those swings."

Aaron hung back as Jo walked toward the sandbox where a group of toddlers were playing. She kicked off her shoes, tucked her skirt around her bottom, and sat in the sand. A little boy with mischievous dancing eyes dumped a bucket of sand in Jo's lap. She laughed, dusting the sand from her skirt.

The child's mother rushed over. "*Zły Chłopak*, bad boy!" she scolded.

Jo shook her head and smiled. "Please, it's okay. I don't mind." Jo was met with a blank stare. Realizing that verbal communication was impossible, Jo patted the sand, refilled the bucket, and handed it to the little boy.

The mother shrugged her shoulders, looked at her friends, said something Jo didn't understand and went back to the bench to watch.

The boy looked at Jo with gentle trusting eyes, lost interest, and moved off to play with friends.

Jo found it impossible to assimilate what she was seeing— children playing in a park protected by caring mothers—children not dissimilar from the children of her Kibbutz. A reading she had memorized from Deuteronomy came to mind: *Fathers shall not be put to death for their sons, nor shall sons be put to death for their fathers; everyone shall be put to death for his own sin.* She sighed. *I do not want to be judged, and so I will not judge. That is God's job.*

Barefooted and suddenly exhausted, Jo dusted herself off. She took Aaron's hand and they ambled toward a giant birch rustling in the breeze. Aaron sat and leaned against the trunk of the tree. Jo put her head in his lap and closed her eyes.

* * *

The woman came to the park everyday and sat on the same bench. Her complexion was etched with the fine lines of age and her once lustrous blue-black hair was streaked with white. Her almond-shaped violet eyes were still bright, and there was an essence to her, the way she sat with her shoulders back, her head up, her posture perfect, her knees touching. Everything about her was elegant, regardless of the box-shaped dress, the clunky shoes, and the unstylish way she pulled her hair back into a bun.

From her bench she saw the crazy American, Larry, who had been hounding Jacob for another interview, bring two strangers into the park and then leave. It brought a smile to her eyes if not her mouth when the young woman kicked off her shoes and sat in the sandbox. The woman thought that in her youth she might have done the same. When the young woman and her companion, a tall, good-looking man with an air of confidence about him, moved to rest under the tree, she decided to meet these strangers.

She walked toward them. The young woman's face was in perfect profile and the older woman's heart began to pound furiously. She managed to get to a bench as her steps grew soggy, her vision blurred—her knees buckled. She gasped for breath, certain that her body was crossing over to the other side. She closed her eyes and waited for the angel of death to appear. When nothing happened, she opened her eyes and glanced again in Jo's direction.

The woman couldn't understand how it was possible that she was still here, and the girl still there! Daring to believe what she was seeing, daring to hope—she became a sentry, hoping against hope that she had not slid into the world of insanity yet again.

The couple eventually walked away.

The woman held back. She couldn't talk with them. They would think her insane. Her body trembled. Ten thousand nights she had prayed for this moment. Then it happened. She began to cry—the first tears she had shed in thirty years.

* * *

The woman was anxious to get home. She turned right on Gora Zomkova and two blocks later, she sprinted across the street. Her home, like all the others that lined the avenue, was a three-storied stone structure built in the 1920's. It sat on a plot of green grass dotted with birch trees and pines. She charged up the stone steps and pulled open the screen door.

"Jacob, Jacob, where are you?" she yelled, looking first in the library, then the den. She found him in the kitchen waiting for the teapot to boil.

"You're all flushed. Are you ill?" Jacob asked, placing his hand on her forehead.

"I'm fine." She began to shiver. Jacob put his arm around her. She leaned into his shoulder, her face stunned and ashen.

"What's the matter, darling?" Jacob asked.

"That boy, Larry, the one who came to your office to interview you—"

"I told him to stay away from you," Jacob said, his voice filled with furry. "If he has upset you I will—"

"Shh." She placed her finger to his lips. "You must listen. I need you to call him for me."

"Why would I do that?"

"I need you to ask him about the young woman he brought to the park today." She took a deep breath. "Sit down, Jacob."

"I don't want to sit. What's all this about?"

"I need to know who she is."

"What's going on?" Jacob asked.

"I think..." her voice caught as she searched for the courage to say the word. "My daughter...I saw her in the park today with Larry and another man."

Jacob's hands began to shake. He was horrified that she was might be having a psychotic break.

"Jacob Gold! Get that look off your face. I'm not crazy."

"Morgan. My precious Morgan. Do you realize how foolish this is? How could she be here? Why would she be here?" he asked, his face a desperate shade of fear.

"Just pick up the damn phone, and find out who she is," Morgan ordered.

Shaking his head, Jacob took the wallet from his pocket, and shuffled through cards until he found Larry's telephone number. "Are you sure?" he asked, reaching for the phone.

Morgan squinted, her shoulders moving imperceptibly. "Are you going to make that call or do you want me to do it?"

He dialed and waited. It was picked up on the fifth ring. "Larry, this is Doctor Gold."

"How nice to hear from you."

"I hope you'll beg my pardon for this intrusion into your privacy, but I understand you were with a young woman today. Can you tell me about her? Who she is, where she's from?"

"She's an American."

Jacob put his hand over the mouthpiece.

"She's an American," he repeated in Polish.

"And?" Morgan asked, shooting Jacob an angry look.

"Perhaps you would be kind enough to tell me why she's here?" Jacob asked.

"Why don't you meet us for lunch tomorrow, noon at the Lietu-vana, and you can ask her yourself?" Larry said. "I am certain she would love to meet you."

"One moment, please." He looked hard at Morgan and decided she must face whatever it was she thought she saw. Placing his hand over the phone again, he said, "They want to meet us at the Lietu-vana for lunch tomorrow."

"Invite them to come here," Morgan said.

"Darling, this might not be wise," Jacob whispered.

She took the phone from Jacob's hand. "Come for lunch at one. Please be prompt."

She placed the receiver on the hook.

Morgan turned to Jacob, her eyes moist, her lips quivering. "It has to be true. She has to be my daughter. Please, Jacob. Come and pray with me. Perhaps this time God will listen.

38

The next day

Larry borrowed a car from his landlady and picked Jo and Aaron up at six thirty in the morning. He then drove them to the Kernave Archeological Site, in eastern Lithuania about thirty five kilometers northwest of Vilnius, in the valley of the River Neris.

The day was balmy. Jo and Aaron were enthralled by the complex ensemble of the archaeological site, encompassing the town of Kernave, forts, some unfortified settlements, burial sites, and other monuments from the late Paleolithic period to the Middle Ages.

"I have a surprise for you," Larry said, as they were sitting on a blanket drinking coffee poured from a thermos, and nibbling on pączki, round donuts without a hole and filled with fruit. "We've been invited to have lunch with Doctor Gold and his wife. They are one of the few Jewish survivors still living in Vilnius."

"Why in God's name would a Jew want to live in this place?" Jo asked, gathering the coffee cups and napkins.

Larry rolled his eyes. "Got me. He's a Cambridge-educated physician and when I asked him that exact same question, he said it was a complicated issue—something about affairs of the heart, and putting others before yourself. He wouldn't elaborate. I thought I would find out more when I interviewed the wife but so far, I've been stonewalled. He won't let me near her. So, needless to say, I'm thrilled by their invitation." Larry looked at his watch. "I think we better get going."

* * *

Morgan peeked out the window, staring at her reflection. The glass softened the lines and hid the dark circles under her eyes, the result of a night without sleep. Her mind swirled around questions about her daughter, how she grew up, where she lived. Could she dare hope that her child had been raised with a loving family full of brothers and sisters, noise and laughter? But mostly Morgan prayed that her daughter knew about her and that was why she was here in Vilnius.

Morgan paced the rooms of her beloved childhood home. The house had been acquired by bribing a greedy Soviet official. It had cost Jacob his entire savings, leaving nothing for home repairs or furnishings. Morgan had never cared before, but suddenly all she could focus on were the marred wooden floors, the faded carpets and the stained, peeling walls.

She checked her watch for the hundredth time. Ten more minutes, if they're on time. The smell of brisket and potatoes, in the oven since dawn, reminded her that it was time to slice the meat.

Jacob sat at his desk in the study and pretended to read a medical journal. He had spent the night tossing and turning, petrified that a disappointment of this magnitude might precipitate another breakdown for Morgan.

"I'm going to the kitchen," Morgan said, standing in the doorway. "When they arrive you go and look. Then come and tell me if she's my daughter."

* * *

"This is the house," Larry said, reading the number on the post.

Aaron took Jo's hand. "This should be interesting," he said.

"Maybe they knew my mother."

"Wouldn't that be something?" Aaron squeezed her hand.

Larry knocked on the door.

Jacob stood on the threshold with his hand on the doorknob. His entire body was tense. He turned his eyes toward the heavens, said a silent prayer, and pulled open the door. What he saw standing there was beyond his comprehension, a collision of impossibility. He felt faint and had to support himself by leaning against the doorframe.

Larry reached to support him. "Doctor Gold, are you okay?"

"I just need a moment," he said in perfect English, shifting his eyes toward Jo. "Sorry, just a little dizzy." He righted himself, inhaled deeply, and said, "I'm Jacob Gold."

"Jo Wells. It's a pleasure to meet you. This is my fiancé, Aaron Blumenthal."

"A pleasure," Aaron said, reaching to shake hands.

"If you're ill we could come back another time," Jo offered.

"Don't be silly," Jacob said. "Come in." He pointed to the living room off to his right. "Please. Make yourselves comfortable. I'll go and get my wife."

Jacob moved down the hallway. Suddenly he couldn't get to Morgan fast enough. He charged into the kitchen. Morgan was cowering in the corner—begging with her eyes.

Jacob nodded. "It's her. It's your daughter."

With those words, the walls of ice encasing Morgan's shattered heart melted, and the years of isolation and hopelessness floated away, replaced by the greatest joy she had ever know. She reached out her hand. "Take me to her, Jacob. Take me to my child."

* * *

Jo, Aaron, and Larry found themselves in a parlor that reeked of a bygone pedigree. The walls were covered in faded silk, the curtains were threadbare, and the furniture tired. A vase of roses sat on an overly polished coffee table, a cool breeze from the open window caressed the room.

Jo was sitting next to Aaron on a three-cushioned sofa, her hand resting in his as they talked about the morning. Larry sat nearby, his lanky body slouching in the chair.

Jacob had his hand on Morgan's elbow as they entered the room. For a millisecond, she stood rooted in place, astounded by the similarity of their looks. She opened her arms and moved toward her daughter.

Jo stood, captured in the spider web of familiarity, the woman's saunter, the way she held her head, and the tilt of her eyes.

Morgan placed her hands on Jo's shoulder and kissed her cheek. "You are mine," she whispered, her voice encircling them in love.

Jo stared. "My God, it's really you!" She touched Morgan's cheek, her hair. "You're alive. My mother...my mother," Jo murmured, hugging her mother, the words muffled against the warmth of Morgan's face as they embraced and cried.

"Let me look at you," Morgan said, wiping the tears from Jo's eyes with her fingertips. "You are so beautiful." They hugged again.

Larry and Aaron watched, both openly crying.

"Come," Jacob said to the two men, wiping his own tears with a handkerchief. "Let's have a little whiskey and lunch." He kissed Morgan's cheek. "My angel," he whispered.

Aaron looked at Jo. I love you, he mouthed, putting his arm around Jacob's shoulder as they walked from the room.

It was just the two of them now—all else had disappeared. They sat on the sofa facing each other, their knees touching, their fingers intermingled.

"I don't even know your name," Morgan said, tears spilling over her face.

"Jo Wells."

"Hello, Jo Wells," Morgan said. "I've waited so long, and prayed so hard. I have so many things I want to tell you. So much to explain.

I never meant to leave you. I . . . ."

Jo patted Morgan's hand. "I know."

Morgan's violet eyes narrowed. "What do you know? How could you know?"

"I met Robert Osborne in New York while I was in law school...."

"Robert. My Robert?" Morgan was fi nding it impossible to comprehend what Jo was saying."

"We were friends."

Morgan began pulling out the pins holding her bun in place, wanting to look pretty when she talked about Robert. She shook her hair free. Ribbons of black and silver curls cascaded over her shoulders and around her face.

The transformation astounded Jo: the hard angles softened and the years melted away.

"You were friends?" She was silent for a moment. "Then he had to know that I had another man's child!" Morgan said, slashing at the unwanted tears running down her face.

Jo gave her a reassuring pat on the arm. "It didn't matter. He never stopped loving you."

Morgan shook her head. "Does he know you came here?"

Jo's mouth was suddenly dry as sand. "Robert's gone. He passed away in December of last year."

Morgan's hand flew to mouth. "It can't be true!" She hugged herself, rocking back and forth. She had never said the words aloud, but she had always held to the idea that one day she would see him again. Now it was too late. She buried her face in her hands and wept.

"I'm so sorry," Jo sobbed, rubbing Morgan's back. "So very, very sorry."

Morgan's chest heaved as she reached for a handkerchief stuffed in the pocket of her dress. "There was not a day that went by that I didn't think about him. Perhaps you will not understand this, but knowing that he was with you—it makes it better somehow."

"He loved me because he loved you so much," Jo said.

Morgan stood and walked toward the window. She pulled back the curtain and stared into the street. "I know you have to be wondering why I never tried to contact him."

"Please, I know how painful this has to be for you. You don't have to tell me anything. I just want to be with you." Jo went to her mother.

"I appreciate that," Morgan said, her fingers brushing Jo's arm. "But, I need you to know—to understand. Maybe I want your approval, or maybe I just want the opportunity to unburden myself. Whatever it is, I ask that you listen."

"I am here," Jo said.

The statement was a simple one, so raw and real that it brought them both to tears.

"So much happened during the war; the death, the horror. How do I explain this to you? It was as if the world had dimmed and there were clouds across the sun." Morgan made a fist with her right hand and rubbed it across her left wrist in a slicing motion, her eyes wild. "When they captured me I tried to kill myself."

Watching her mother imitating the act of cutting her wrists almost brought Jo to her knees. She grabbed for Morgan's hands and held them. "Don't do this to yourself."

"I was sent to Dachau," Morgan continued, disregarding Jo's words. "That's when I had some kind of mental fugue, rejecting what was real and creating my own fantasy world. Because I was given special privileges, it was easy to convince myself that the man coming to my bed was Robert." Morgan's mind flashed a memory, cold blue eyes, and a mustache. She shook the vision away.

"When I got pregnant and my belly began to grow, I fell so in love with you." Morgan blinked the wetness from her eyes.

Jo put her arm around Morgan.

"I will say this just once, and then it will be behind us forever," Morgan said, gathering her hair and twisting it back into a bun. "One day, right before my due date, I was taken to see Jacob at the camp hospital. We were friends from Vilna, but that day, as he examined me, we pretended to be strangers.

"Hans Wells, and by the way I didn't know his name then, insisted that you be born by cesarean section—with no drugs, so you would be perfect." Morgan's eyes were flat and unblinking, a woman speaking in a disassociated voice, a storyteller removed from the words she was reciting. "I passed out when Jacob was forced to slice my stomach open, and I don't remember anything after that, not until they lifted you from my belly, and I heard you cry." Tears stung Morgan's eyes as her expression changed, replaced by a ferocious and indignant anger. "And then he took you away from me."

She's talking about my father. Jo sucked in her breath.

"I wanted to die and would have if not for Jacob. He wouldn't let me go. He stood between me and the abyss, like a mother bear with her cub." Morgan rubbed her stomach with an open palm. "I just couldn't cope." She leaned her head back and dragged a dry tongue over her lips.

Jo stiffened, cold, and raw, enveloped in the winds of shame, asking herself again how she could have ever loved him? Aloud she said, "He was the only father I ever knew. I only found out recently about his past; what he did, who he was. But this…"

"I know it's a lot to take in," Morgan said, her face a valley of regret. "You are not to blame, my precious. You did nothing wrong. Come and sit with me."

"I need the bathroom first," Jo said.

"Of course. It's the first door on your left."

Jo moved into the tiny room with its pull-chain toilet and chipped porcelain sink. She sat on the toilet and buried her face in her hands, her body wracked in agony. She bit down to keep from crying out as she wept—tears of fury at the injustice and pain her mother had endured at the hands of her father.

It was ten minutes before Jo came back into the room.

"Are you okay?" Morgan asked her face racked with concern.

Jo pulled up a chair across from Morgan. "I'm fine."

The door opened. "Sorry to interrupt, but it's after two and we thought you might be hungry," Jacob said, carrying a tray of food; carved brisket, potatoes, and fresh green beans. Aaron was close behind holding a tray with a teapot and cups. They put them on the coffee table.

"It's chilly in here." Jacob placed a sweater around Morgan's shoulders. "Can I get you a wrap?" he asked Jo, moving to close the windows.

"Thanks, I'm fine," Jo said, glancing at Aaron.

"How are you doing?" Aaron asked. Jo patted her heart and smiled. Aaron smiled back.

"Are you taking care of our company?" Morgan asked.

"The reunion was a bit too much for Larry," Jacob said. "We had to send him home. He kept blabbering about miracles, and how he had stopped believing in them until today. As for Aaron and me, we're having a marvelous time getting to know each other."

Aaron leaned in and gave Jo a hug. "I love you," he whispered.

"Okay, we've intruded long enough. How about a game of gin?" Jacob said, taking Aaron's arm.

"Hope you have some money," Aaron said, laughing as they left the room.

Jo picked at her food, glancing every few minutes at her mother, enthralled by the way Morgan held her fork, balancing it between the third and forth finger, how she cut the food into tiny pieces, pushing everything into little piles before eating, all the same things Jo did.

Morgan took a few more bites and placed her dish on the tray. "It tastes like cardboard to me. I guess I'm just too pent-up to eat."

Jo put her plate on the tray as well.

"Can you tell me what happened after the war? Where did you go?" Jo had to know everything. There was no longer a choice. The crater of despair was open now, and it would only close with answers.

"After liberation from Dachau we were sent to a displaced persons camp in Cyprus. When they released us, Jacob took me back to Paris." Morgan rubbed her throbbing temples. "He got a job at a hospital. As for me, certifiable lunatic that I was, I took up residence at a psychiatric hospital. I was there for more than a year. It took that long for me to stop inventing stuff."

"Oh my God. That must have been so horrible."

"Horrible?" Morgan smiled. "Not really. In the beginning I was so drugged I didn't even know where I was. And then, when they reduced the dosages, and the memories began to surface," Morgan sucked in her cheeks, her face contorted. "I simply disappeared inside myself."

Jo could see her mother falling into the past in a way that frightened her. "Let me get you some water." She filled two glasses from the portable cart.

"Thank you." Morgan sipped. "I was always so sensitive. That's why I had such a hard time moving back into a world at peace. I was stuck—didn't want to move on—didn't want anyone else to either. Forgetting, it just didn't seem fair.

"Eventually, I did start to get well. That's when Jacob and my doctors tried to convince me to contact Robert." Morgan put the glass on the floor. "It was a ridiculous idea. I had been the concubine of a Nazi. How could Robert ever forgive me?"

"No!" Jo cried. "I won't let you say that. You had no choice."

"Shh, baby. Don't get upset. I have come to understand that it's not true. But, back then, well. . . I did believe it. So, when I read that Robert was returning from America and coming to Paris to appear in a play—I went crazy." The corners of her mouth curled, it was not quite a smile. "I couldn't face him. I only wanted to go home. Jacob understood. He brought me back here."

"Is that when you and Jacob married?"

"No, my darling. I couldn't do that," she said softly, avoiding Jo's eyes. "I was still married. For years, Jacob and I had a platonic relationship. We shared a home; we were best friends and confidants. He loved me, and I knew that but I had nothing to give in return. However, time dims memory and at some point, I don't even know when, I fell in love with him. Not with the same passion I had for Robert, but it is the kind of love that endures." She wiggled in the seat. "This old body needs to move. How about some fresh air?" She stood and stretched. "Let's take a walk."

At the front door, Morgan took a shabby sweater that hung from a hook on the wall and handed it to Jo. "It gets cold. Put this on while I go tell Jacob we're going out."

The sun sat low on the horizon as they entered the park. The treetops swayed in the breeze, and there was the din of twittering swallows, and chattering grasshoppers.

They sat on a bench near the playground. Morgan crossed one leg over the other and turned toward Jo, swallowing hard. "Was your father kind to you?"

"Always," Jo lied, not wanting her mother to have another moment of sorrow. She began to paint the portrait of an idyllic life—one of privilege and opportunity.

Morgan held up her palm five minutes into Jo's recitation. "Stop!" she demanded. "Look at me, child."

Jo slid her eyes toward her mother.

"God gave us a gift, the merging of kindred souls. We must honor that gift with truth, not lies."

"Please," Jo begged. "It's an ugly story. One you don't need to know. It's behind me now. They are all dead!"

Morgan scowled. "Remember what I said? Tell it once and then we will put it behind us."

An hour later, the truth was exhumed. Jo was depleted. She leaned forward on her elbows. "Until three days ago I was living on a Kibbutz in Israel." Jo slapped her forehead with the heal of her hand. "I can't believe we've been together all day and I haven't mentioned Rebecca and Saul."

Morgan squinted. "Rebecca? I don't know a Rebecca."

Jo beamed, her eyes dancing. "Let's see. I think you had a best friend in Paris. Her name was Claire and she moved to Israel with Saul. She goes by the name of Rebecca now."

Morgan pressed her hands together as if in prayer as she slipped into the vortex of youth, locking into her memory of Claire. "Tell me about her, please."

Jo retold with great joy the story of Rebecca and Saul. Morgan interrupted often, wanting more details, asking for descriptions, names, dates, times and places. Much later, when the narration was complete, she took Jo's hand in hers.

"There are some things in life that can never be replaced: the loss of a child, the loss of the man you love, the loss of your best friend. Today I have my child and my best friend back." Morgan tilted her eyes skyward. "Perhaps He," she pointed toward heaven, "and I can be friends again." Morgan took Jo into her arms.

A diamond sky and golden moon lit their way home.

* * *

Jo and Morgan entered the kitchen arm in arm. The room was warm and fragrant with the smell of brewing coffee.

"Welcome home, angels," Jacob said, bowing. He made a sweeping motion with his hand. "You will note the elegantly set table: fork on the left, knife, and spoon on the right." He winked. "Allow me," he pulled back a chair for Morgan and then a chair for Jo.

Aaron placed a platter of French toast on the table. "The chefs have been toiling for hours. We expect compensation commensurate with our toil." He pinched Jo's cheek and laughed.

They spent the next hour side by side at the kitchen table sharing moments from the day, and stories from their pasts—intimacies that serve to form the magical link that births a family.

"Will you stay here tonight?" Morgan asked as they cleared the table.

Jo smiled. "I would really like that."

Jacob pulled the car keys from his pocket. "Come, Aaron. I'll go with you to get your things from the hotel."

Morgan tipped her palm up and beckoned for the keys. "I've monopolized Jo all day. I'm sure they need some time together. You can stay here and help me clean up." She handed the keys to Aaron.

* * *

Morgan was washing the last dish when Jacob put his arms around her waist and kissed the back of her neck. She placed the dish on the drain board and turned. They held each other. It brought the world to a standstill. The seconds passed.

"Can you imagine? My child is going to sleep in our home tonight. My child." A tear spilled. "I haven't cried in years and now I can't stop."

"Tears of joy. That's God washing your soul," Jacob said.

Morgan laughed as she pulled the apron from around his waist. *Not bad for a sixty year old— He's still handsome— no bulging belly, a full head of hair, his face a kaleidoscope of gentle lines and creases.*

"Take your hair down for me," Jacob said.

She only did that when they made love. "They'll be back soon."

He reached over and gently slid the pins from her hair. "You've never been more beautiful." Jacob kissed her.

After so many years, Morgan could read the signals. This was not a kiss that would be a prelude to making love. She waited, unsure what it was that he wanted.

He pulled back and dropped to one knee.

Morgan's heart began to pound. "My darling, are you okay? What happened? Is it your heart? Here, let me help you up." She reached for his arm.

"Will you stop?" he said, swatting her hand away. "Nothing is wrong with me. I am simply trying to propose. Now that you are finally free, and while your daughter is here with us, I want you to marry me."

"The gesture is very sweet. You made your point. Now get up. I can't think with you on one knee." Morgan tugged him to his feet.

"I've waited so long. Please, say, yes."

Morgan placed her open palm on his face. "Sometimes I try and imagine my life without you in it. When I do that, I can't even catch my breath. You are everything to me. I would be honored to be your wife."

Jacob's face beamed. "Is tomorrow too soon?"

"Tomorrow is perfect."

The kiss that followed was the culmination of his dreams—a lifetime of waiting, hoping, and praying.

39

Vilnius, Lithuania

Jo and Aaron drove through the deserted streets, the wheels on Jacob's ancient Mercedes slapping against the asphalt. At the first red light, Aaron reached for Jo's hand. "How are you doing?"

"I never expected to find her. Not in my wildest dreams. I think I'm still in shock. And then, all the things she told me about what happened to her. And my father. . ."

Aaron looked at Jo in profile, his desire to shelter her becoming a living, breathing need that started at his toes. "Take it slow, darling," he said, accelerating as the light turned green.

"You got a different perspective. What did Jacob tell you about what happened in the camp after I was born?"

Aaron turned on the heater, buying time to put his thoughts in a logical order. "This has been a monumental day for you," he said, putting both hands on the wheel and staring into the night. "You have a lot to process. Maybe too much. Besides, I don't think I have the strength to tell you. Not tonight. I'm sorry."

Jo couldn't help feeling relieved. She too was spent. "Okay, just one more question."

Aaron nodded.

"Can we get them out? Can we bring them to the States?"

Aaron pulled the car to a stop in the portico of the hotel. "From what I know, applications for visas to visit family are fairly easy to obtain. The question is, will the Lithuanian government issue a travel visa to a physician?"

"Why wouldn't they?" Jo asked.

"Because he is needed here and once in America, most visitors from Communist bloc countries ask and receive political asylum."

"What can we do?" Jo bit at a fingernail.

Aaron stepped out of the car, and came around to open the door for Jo. He offered his hand. "We call everyone we know; we pull strings and make it happen."

"Thank you, Aaron." Jo smiled. "That's what I needed to hear. Now, let's go get our stuff, and check out of this horrible place."

The next morning

Jacob stood in front of the mirror in the bedroom he shared with Morgan. He looped his tie and snarled. "You'd think I could get this right the first time."

Morgan laughed, taking the tie into her hands. "Why are you so nervous?" Her eyes twinkled.

"Because I'm getting married today. That's why." He pulled Morgan into his arms. "And it's about time. Now, let me look at you."

Morgan made a slow circle. She was wearing a flowing lilac skirt that cascaded to her ankles, a white lace blouse with pearl buttons, and a lilac shawl. Her hair, still damp, fell in soft ringlets around her face.

"What do you think?" she asked.

"That you are the most beautiful woman in the entire world. That's what I think," Jacob said, kissing her softly.

* * *

Jo pulled the cream-colored cashmere scoop-necked sweater over her head and stepped into a chocolate silk skirt that skimmed just above her knees.

Aaron whistled. "Imagine, I get to look at this for the rest of my life. A luckier guy never lived." He slapped her bottom.

"And, if you want to continue to live you will get moving. It's after ten and God only knows what they must be thinking."

"I hope they're thinking we made love all morning." He beamed. "Cause it sure has been fantastic."

"Okay, Casanova." Jo handed him his sport coat. "Time to make an appearance."

She hooked her arm through his as they sauntered into the kitchen.

Morgan hugged Jo. "Did you sleep well?"

"Great."

"Have a seat while this is still hot," Jacob said, placing bowls of oatmeal on the table.

"This looks delicious," Jo said, adding blueberries, and a sprinkle of cinnamon.

When Morgan went to sit down Jacob pulled her chair closer to his. She giggled and kissed the tip of his nose. He whispered something and they both laughed.

Jo put down her spoon and pointed her eyes at Morgan and then Jacob. "Okay, what's going on?"

"Shall we tell them now?" Jacob asked, putting his arm around Morgan.

"Tell us what?" Jo asked.

"That this is the happiest day of my life," Jacob said.

"Don't make such a fuss," Morgan flipped her hand. "Just tell them."

Jacob stood. "This woman, who I've loved and adored for my entire life, has finally agreed to become my wife. We are going to get married today, and we would like you to be our witnesses."

Jo jumped up from the chair. "That's fantastic!" She kissed her mother and hugged Jacob.

"*Mazel Tov!*" Aaron pumped Jacob's hand and then he embraced Morgan.

* * *

The trees bent to the wind, and afternoon clouds hung in the sky—rain threatened. The car bounced over pitted pavement as they climbed the rolling hills toward the Ponary forest. Morgan sat in the front seat beside Jacob.

"This forest has a horrific history. Over one-hundred thousand Jews were slaughtered here. We would not have picked such a place to get married—if not for the rabbi, our only rabbi," Morgan said.

"He lives alone, with no phone, in a tiny house that sits beside a monument the Israelis built to honor the murdered Jews."

Aaron and Jo leaned forward from the backseat, not wanting to miss a word.

"The story goes that the rabbi was led into the forest one freezing winter day, along with hundreds of other Jews. They were all forced to stand at the mouth of an enormous ditch already piled high with rotting bodies. It was then that the shooters, people that the rabbi had lived beside and knew by name, took aim. The rabbi refused to turn his back. Supposedly, he was memorizing every face, vowing aloud to bring their names to God.

"Whoever took that shot missed, and although the rabbi lost an ear, he managed to climb from the tomb when night fell. He lived in the forest for the rest of the war, watching every execution, saying Kaddish every day for the murdered.

"They say the rabbi has never set foot outside Ponary since that fateful day. He prays morning and night—convinced that his supplications are cleansing the forest of its evil. Yet, he gladly accepts visitors, and some say he will even pray with the guilty survivors who frequent his home."

"What does he do for food?" Jo asked.

"Every day, regardless of the weather, people bring him cooked meals, homemade wine, breads, everything he needs. They leave it in a box under a tree at the end of the clearing. There is something else you need to know. He has the power to see into the future."

"You're kidding, right?" Aaron asked, surprised by the conviction in Morgan's voice.

Morgan shook her head. "Whenever someone dies in Vilna, he leaves a condolence note nailed to the tree. Sometimes, he leaves the note days before the death."

"How is that possible?" Jo asked.

"He has a very special gift. You will see for yourself."

The car pulled into a clearing surrounded by huge pines. A sea of dried brown needles crunched beneath their feet as they approached the house peeking from the trees, as if it were budding from the branches.

Jacob knocked. The heavy wooden door creaked open. The rabbi wore a long black coat, fur-trimmed hat, and coarse woolen trousers. His beard was pure white and long side curls dangled, half hiding the nonexistent ear.

"Doctor Gold and Morgan, how nice to see you." The rabbi turned his attention to Jo and Aaron. "Come in, come in. I'm Rabbi Berkowicz." He smiled—his eyes disappearing into a web of kindness and wrinkles.

Introductions were made.

"What a very special day this is going to be," the rabbi said.

They followed him inside, into a tiny sitting room. The chairs and table were honed from fallen branches, the couch covered in scraps of cloth stitched together and stuffed with goose feathers. Open books lay everywhere and feathers flew as the rabbi made room for them to sit.

Jacob took Morgan's hand. "We've come today, Rabbi . . . . "

Rabbi Berkowicz held up his hand. "I know why you're here. *Mazel Tov.*" He swiveled his wizened face toward Jo and Aaron. "For you, daughter of Morgan, it has been a long and difficult journey. But I knew one day you would come."

Jo felt as if she had fallen down the rabbit hole in Alice in Wonderland. She reached for Aaron's hand.

Rabbi Berkowicz smiled at Aaron. "Shall this union include you as well? Will I perform a double mitzvah?"

Aaron sucked in his breath, seeking out Jo's eyes. He stood. "Please, excuse us for a moment." He pulled Jo by the hand. "We need to talk."

"Before you go, Aaron," the rabbi said, holding his arm out like a stop sign. "What you are feeling is real. They are here. I just want you to know that."

* * *

Standing beside a tree twenty feet from the house, encased in the shadows of the forest, Aaron broke down and wept. Jo held him. When he regained his composure he began to pace in ever-growing concentric circles. Jo waited.

"I know this is going to sound ridiculous," Aaron said, hands on hips, eyes swollen, "and, maybe that man is crazy, but what he said—I believe with everything in my heart that my mother and father are here with us right now."

Jo opened her arms to Aaron, accepting without question his words.

"I know you wanted a big wedding—"

Jo pressed her lips against his cheek. "This is exactly what I want, Aaron."

They hurried back to the house.

"Let's make this a double wedding!" Aaron announced, kissing Jo.

It was a glorious moment to witness. They all hugged, dissolving in another round of joyous tears.

"It's time," the rabbi said softly. "Come with me. I want to take you for a walk."

They followed him into the forest, down a narrow winding path, over a stream, deeper and deeper into the woods. Birds sang from the canopy; it was cool and damp. Ten minutes later, they stopped in a scarred clearing full of excavated craters. The rabbi beckoned them to join him near one of the pits.

He opened his arms in an arch. "Death happened here. However, it was not the end. It was the beginning. The neshomeh, the soul, lives forever. Love is the only truth. Everything else is an illusion— even the ground beneath our feet. Listen," the rabbi said, his voice drifting with the wind. "They are all around you. Can you hear them?"

The wind ceased, the bird's call was silenced, wing vibrations from the mosquito and butterfly stopped, no incidental sounds, not a branch stirred, or an insect hummed. "In the silence they are calling to you. Hear with your hearts. They are sending you their love."

Jo looked at Aaron and squeezed his hand. Morgan moved closer to Jacob.

"In traditional marriage ceremonies we exchange rings. It is a symbol that represents the unbroken continuation of your love. To-day, instead of exchanging rings, I ask that you join hands and cre-ate a circle. It will represent the union and birth of a family—its past, its present and its future."

Jo reached for her mother's hand. It was soft, and comforting. Their eyes met, and in her mother's eyes Jo saw something she had never seen before—approval, love without rules, restrictions, or expectations. She brought her mother's hand to her lips and kissed it.

Then she looked toward Aaron, grasping his hand, feeling the protection and love in his touch—feeling completed. He was her everything. With his hand in hers, she understood what it was to love another, and to want to share your life.

Aaron took Jacob's hand. It was a gentle hand, the hand of a healer—caring and compassionate. The two men smiled at each other, their friendship sealed in a touch and a look.

Jacob placed the palm of his hand against Morgan's open hand and their fingers intertwined. Their touch merged the agony of the past with the glory of the present. Their touch closed the circle, uniting them all.

They were now a family.

The rabbi swayed and raised his eyes toward the heavens. "May the Lord bless you and keep you. May the Lord cause his countenance to shine upon you and be gracious unto you. May the Lord bestow his favor upon you and grant you peace, love, and happiness." Rabbi Berkowicz lowered his hands and his voice. "With the forest as your Chupah, your canopy, here, in front of these souls that have come to join us, and with their blessings and approval, I pronounce you, Morgan and Jacob Gold and you, Jo and Aaron Blumenthal, husband and wife.

"*Mazel Tov*. You may kiss your brides."

Kisses mixed with the forest orchestra; birds sang, trees bowed, and nature celebrated.

"You've made an old man very happy," the rabbi said. "If I were to follow tradition, our grooms would now break the wine glass, reminding us that even at the height of one's personal joy, we must remember the destruction of the Temple in Jerusalem. But, I will allow nothing to be shattered on this sacred ground—it is a vow I made to Ha-Shem, our God." Rabbi Berkowicz looked at them. His ancient eyes filled with tears. "Today you have been given a gift that will forever remain wrapped in a golden light. A vision has been shared, individually and collectively. You are now one. I'll pray for all of you. Go in peace."

"Thank you, Rabbi. We'll never forget you." Morgan moved to kiss him. He backed away.

"Some traditions I can break, others I should not." His eyes twinkled.

"Thank you, Rabbi," Jo said.

The rabbi leaned toward her. "Hear me, child. Hear me and re-member what I am about to tell you. Your mother was an illusionist, using the stage to create an alternative reality. You want to be heard, create fantasy. This is your destiny."

"I don't understand what you're telling me," Jo said, desperate to know the meaning of his words.

"Have faith. Trust. In time it will be revealed," the rabbi said, turning back toward his house.

The four of them followed, walking two by two, surrounded by the unseen, feeling that presence, silent in their wonder and joy.

* * *

As Jacob pulled on to the main highway, thunder sounded, and the rain crashed against the front window of his car. The wipers squealed against the glass and stopped. "We'll have to wait for the weather to clear," he said, pulling to the shoulder of the road, and opening the window a crack.

Morgan peered into the backseat. "What a week! I have my daughter back, and now I also have a son—my kinder, my chil-dren," she said, using the Yiddish of her youth, her voice cracked.

"Yeah, well don't forget, as of today, you also have a husband." Jacob leaned over and kissed her cheek.

"Mother, can you tell me what happened back there?" Jo asked, her voice loud to fight the sound of rain splattering on the roof. "The silence. It was as if the world stood still."

To see better, Morgan shifted in her seat. "I choose to believe that God came to visit, and that all the creatures of the universe held their breath in His presence."

"And what about what the rabbi said to me? What do you think he meant?"

"I don't know. But, I believe you will know one day." In Morgan's great joy, she also knew that her daughter would be leaving soon. The tears welled in her eyes. "I wish we could be together forever."

"Mother, we can be," Jo said. "You could come and live in America."

Jo looked at Jacob with pleading eyes.

"I could teach. I always wanted to do that," Jacob said, turning toward Jo and Aaron for the first time. His eyes were wet. "Families stay together. That's what families do. We will come."

Two Days Later

The sun was at its zenith. The asphalt shimmered as Jo, and Aaron walked from the tarmac to the waiting airplane.

"Please hurry," the flight attendant said, anxious to board her passengers.

Jo began to walk up the stairs. The days had slipped by too quickly. She looked back at her mother. Morgan stood in the sunlight, hugging herself, tears streaming down her face. *I'm not ready. I can't leave her. One more kiss. One more embrace. Did I tell her I love her? Did I tell her I would be back? What if we can't get them out!* She fought her way down the stairs. Crying, she ran into her mother's arms.

"It's going to be all right, my darling. I know what you're thinking. I know you love me, and I know we'll be together one day very soon," Morgan whispered, kissing the tears from Jo's cheek. "Go, child. Your husband and your life are waiting."

40

Two weeks later
McLean, Virginia

The evening temperature hovered near eighty as Jo collapsed on the lounge chair, pulled up the strap on her sundress, and kicked off her shoes. Aaron handed her a martini and slid his chair next to the lounger. A crescent moon hung in the star-filled sky, and insects hummed.

"I spent half a day at the Department of Immigration and Naturalization." A mosquito buzzed Jo's ear. She swatted it away and swore under her breath. "They gave me the runaround—said a B2 visa could take months." Jo balled her fists. "I should be able to make things happen. I'm so frustrated I could scream."

"I made a half dozen calls today as well," Aaron said. "But, the truth is, it's only been a couple of weeks."

"Every day feels like an eternity." Jo tilted her head to one side and a tear slipped down her face. "I miss her so much."

Aaron stroked Jo's hand. "I know. And I promise you that we'll get them out. It's just going to take some patience."

A name popped into Jo's head. "Steven Stein! I forgot all about him. We were friends in law school. He spent five years with the State Department before joining McCarthy, Clemmins, and Hall."

"That's one of the best law firms in Washington," Aaron said.

Jo smiled. "And he had a crush on me all through school."

"Should I be jealous?" Aaron pulled Jo to her feet.

"Absolutely," Jo said, losing herself in his kiss.

McCarthy, Clemmins, and Hall.
McLean, Virginia

The black Cadillac limousine slid to the curb in front of the prestigious Farm Credit Drive address. When she arrived at the twenty-second floor, the receptionist's eyes flashed recognition. "Mr. Stein will be right with you, Miss Wells."

"Excuse me, Sara," Steven said, striding into the reception area, a huge smile pasted on his face. "It's no longer Miss Wells—she's Mrs. Blumenthal now. And still absolutely gorgeous."

The vivacity of his energy was invigorating to Jo. She accepted his kiss with one of her own.

He took her arm. "I hope you don't mind if we eat in the firm's dining room?"

Jo smiled as she appraised Steven. Prosperity and too many hours of work had taken its toll. His hair was in need of a trim, and his body carried an extra twenty-five pounds.

"Oh, I know that look," Steven said. "You're dying to tell me I need to exercise and take better care of myself. And, all of those thoughts in the first two minutes. God help me, what you'll be thinking in an hour."

Jo laughed.

Entering the dining room, all eyes turned toward Jo.

"You're quite the celebrity, Mrs. Blumenthal," Steven teased.

"And this is quite the room, Mr. Stein," Jo countered, noting the plush leather upholstered chairs, heavy mahogany dining tables, and lavish brocade draperies. "This sure feels like a good-old-boys club to me."

"Don't even think of going there with me. We have ten female attorneys in our practice."

The waiter pulled back a chair for Jo. She looked around. A female face was not to be seen. "Do they have their own dining room?"

"And here I was worrying that you might have changed." Steven smiled. "This is the executive dining room. We don't have a female partner yet. But we will!"

Lunch was served on hand-painted Limoges chinaware, and Chateaux Lafite-Rothschild was poured into magnificent cut crystal glasses.

"I can remember when Heinz vegetarian baked beans out of a can were the best meal of the day for you." Jo giggled. The years melted away.

"Yes, and I can remember when living like a pauper was a socio-economic experiment for you," he responded slyly.

"Having a lot of money is not always what it's cracked up to be."

"Neither is living on baked beans."

Jo chuckled. "It's really so good to see you again."

"You too." Steven's eyes lingered on Jo. "What's going on?"

"So much I don't even know where to begin. Did you see the story in *Life* magazine?"

"I did. And I'm so sorry."

"I just don't understand why anyone cares so much about what I do. My uncle was murdered years ago. Robert's been gone…for too long. Andy and I are old news. For God's sake, I have a husband now. Why can't they just leave me alone?"

"Because the country was in love with you. They wanted you to be their First Lady."

"I don't want to be fodder for the tabloids." Jo felt herself begin to perspire. *How much do I tell him? What does he need to know to help me get a visa for my mother and Jacob? Nothing.* Still, she found herself hungry with the need to talk. She pulled a dollar bill from her purse and handed it to Steven. "Consider yourself hired. Everything you hear from this moment on falls under attorney-client privilege."

Jo began. Once she started, she couldn't stop. She named names, shared every detail. "I was born in hell, Steven, on a day when the sky was filled with the ashes of human flesh. All I have left is my mother." Her eyes filled with tears, she wiped them away self-consciously. "I need to get her out of Lithuania. I need to expose the people who helped my father, a known Nazi, get into the United States."

Steven's own demons reared. As a Jew, and the child of survivors, the Holocaust had shaped his life, too.

"Jo, you know I'll do whatever I can to help with your mother. I still have some pull at the State Department. But…" Steven poured

Jo another glass of wine. "As your attorney, it's my job to be honest with you. No one is going to believe Nazis are infiltrating the government of the United States."

"I know. They'll say I'm a lunatic." Jo sipped the wine.

"It's not just that. It could be very dangerous."

Jo placed her glass on the table and aimed her eyes towards Steven. "Will you help me?"

Steven grunted. "Damn. I know this is a mistake." He reached for a cigarette. "There is a man, his name is John Lofts, a lawyer with the Justice Department. He's been digging into newly declassified CIA and NATO files. He's not Jewish, but if anyone is going to believe you, he will. But I am warning you, be careful. These people have already shown you that they play for keeps."

"Please, just make the introduction. And find out who we need to see in order to expedite the visa."

"Done. Now tell me, have you considered going back to work? I might be able to wrangle you a partnership. As you pointed out, it is high-time we had a female on our letterhead."

"I'm flattered. Really. But, I don't think so."

"If you change your mind, the offer stands."

"I'll think about it."

March 1974
McLean, Virginia

Eight months after arriving, Jo's life had settled into a routine that was arduous on its calmest day. She was out of the house by seven, took the train into Washington, and spent the next half day digging into files with John Lofts, a thin, studious man of forty with a long spindly neck, thick glasses and a look of expectation that never wavered, reminding Jo of the treasure hunters she had seen interviewed on television.

After taking notes on their discoveries, Jo would trek back to McLean, gobble down a quick lunch prepared by the cook, and then ascend the stairs, close the door, and spend the rest of the day transcribing the days findings in an office she had set up in the west wing of the house.

The converted guestroom had beige wool carpeting, flowered

wallpaper, a huge Duncan Fife drop-leaf table that served as her desk, a half dozen filing cabinets, a leather sofa, and two leather chairs.

Most nights, as with this one, Aaron would come home from work and bribe Jo from her work with a glass of wine and a description of what the cook had prepared for dinner.

Aaron pecked Jo's cheek. "Sirloin on the grill. Potatoes Anna. Fresh asparagus."

"In a minute." Jo pulled out a file and handed it to him. "We found this today," she said, her voice a fevered pitch.

Aaron stared at the file—the hundredth he'd read since Jo began her odyssey with Lofts. "Come on. Let's do this after dinner."

"Please, just read it."

Aaron sighed. He sat on the sofa, put on his reading glasses, and opened the file. "When I finish this, you and I are going to have a very long talk."

"Just read it."

Within seconds, Aaron was lost inside the horror of an alternative universe where every word was sharp and painful.

"Holy shit!" He said, ten minutes later. "This is the most damning one yet. The deception...it's beyond comprehension."

Jo began to pace. "The French Curie Clinic, the Rockefeller Foundation, the Carnegie Fund, Dow Chemical, W.R. Grace, and Imperial Chemical—they all employed Nazi scientists—the same scientists responsible for advanced research into biological and chemical warfare during the war. These are the very same scientists who used women and children for their experiments."

Aaron waved the papers at her. "This implicates the man who was vice chairman of the Swedish Red Cross, Count Folke Bernadotte. I always thought he was one of the good guys!"

Jo smirked, attacked by rage. "We have proof that the bastard permitted the Red Cross to be used as a vehicle for Nazi intelligence during the war. After the war, he used the Red Cross to arrange passports for fugitive Nazis." She grinned defiantly. "The Israelis know that. That's why there's no Red Cross in Israel."

Aaron stared at Jo, saying a silent prayer that Morgan would get here soon so that Jo would focus on something beside the dusty documents that had taken her away from him. He laid the document on the desk and leaned on his palms, eyes drilling Jo. "You signed an agreement with Lofts. You can't go public, so what are you going to do with all this information?"

Jo leaned over and yanked open the drawer of a filing cabinet. She pulled out a thick folder. "I want you to read…."

Aaron held up his hand. "I'm done! This has to stop."

She took his hand. "This is different. It's something I've written."

"What are you talking about?"

Jo handed the folder to Aaron. "Please. Just read this for me."

Aaron loosened his tie, and threw his jacket over the sofa arm. He read a page, looked up, as if he were going to say something, and then went back to reading. He recognized the storyline at once: a young girl is raised in Vilna, Poland, the product of a physician father and a devoted mother. A well-rounded education is the stalwart goal of the parents—that and arranging a proper marriage for their daughter. Yet, this young girl aspires to only one dream, becoming an actress.

Aaron looked at Jo. "When did you do this?"

"Please, just keep reading."

Twenty pages into the manuscript, a famous French actor comes to Vilna. What followed were details steeped in fact and sprinkled with fiction. Aaron recognized Morgan, Robert, Claire, and Saul— they were all there in the story, shrouded in other names.

Jo sat close, reading over his shoulder, feeling as if her very existence depended on what Aaron would say when he finished. At one point, she went to the kitchen, made peanut butter and jelly sandwiches, and brought them back with a thermos of coffee and cups. Aaron ate and drank, but never took his eyes from the page.

He read into the night. Jo watched, trembling at the realization of what she had done—using her voice for fiction. *I write briefs, deal in fact, and yet here I sit, the creator of what?*

Jo thought about how badly she wanted to reveal what she knew, to scream, pontificate, and warn. *What would I say? Who would believe me? I have no proof!*

She hugged herself, accepting what she knew as truth: the writing had created a stopgap, a way to unleash the frustration and rage that had taken over her life. The process was cathartic.

The manuscript was only half finished, the challenge of the blank pages calling out to her. *Sure, I make stuff up, fill in the blanks, get a little theatrical at times, but the message is still there.* Jo never made light of the events! *One day the truth will be known. Until then, this story will serve a purpose.*

Just as the sun was beginning its watch on a new day, Aaron read the last page. He placed the manuscript on his lap. He smiled and kept nodding, like a turtle poking his head from its shell.

"Why didn't you tell me?"

"I wasn't sure I would keep going. What do you think?"

"You don't know, do you?" Aaron asked, his eyes alight with the question.

"What are you talking about?"

"The rabbi, what he said to you—'You want to be heard, create fantasy. This is your destiny.'"

Palm pressed to her mouth, Jo sobbed. "My God! That's what he meant."

"Yes, my beloved. And, he was right. This is your destiny."

* * *

From that evening forward, the focus of Jo's days changed—she didn't go into Washington anymore, she just wrote. At first, she was protective of the new words, trembling and fearful of Aaron's critique. But, as the days passed, she began trusting his instincts, and stopped brooding every time he suggested a change.

The pages filled, the book birthing itself, until the day Jo had to write herself into the story.

They were sitting in the drawing room off the grand parlor, nibbling crudités; Mozart was playing in the background, as Aaron read the day's work.

"I don't get it, Jo. There's no feeling."

"What are you talking about?" Her hands grew cold, and her neck tensed.

"It's just words. You're not telling me how you feel."

Jo pulled the paper from Aaron's hand. "I'm doing the best I can."

"Listen to me, darling. This is about you. No speculation, no innuendo, just the truth."

Jo reread the pages, pulling at her hair and fidgeting the entire time. "This took me all day. I really thought that it was good. But, it's not! It stinks!" Her face turned red. "I don't want to talk about this any more tonight," she said. "I am going to take a shower."

* * *

Jo awoke the following day feeling really sick. She vomited all morning.

"I'm taking you to the doctor," Aaron insisted.

"I'm sure I just ate something that didn't agree with me."

"I don't like the way you look. We're going!"

It was an examination that changed their world. On June 1, 1974, they found out that Jo was three months pregnant.

"I'm going to be a father," Aaron beamed, tasting the word. They were standing in the street as their limousine pulled to the curb. He opened the door. "Be careful," he said.

Jo shot him a look as she ducked into the car.

"It's important that you rest. I'll come home early every day and…."

"Aaron Blumenthal!" Jo's eyes burned. "You will do no such thing. I have a book to finish."

"But—"

"But nothing." Jo took his hand and placed it on her belly. "I'll gestate our child, Aaron. All I need you to do is love us."

* * *

It took two more months for Jo to finish her manuscript. During that time, her only diversions were the phone calls to her mother, and the letters they exchanged. She didn't entertain, didn't cook a meal, or even go for a haircut. She just wrote, rewrote, and vomited morning, noon and night.

She was five months pregnant when she sent a finished copy of her manuscript to Steven Stein. Three days later, the phone rang at seven o'clock in the morning.

"Who the heck is calling this early?" she snarled, reaching to answer.

"Sorry to call at such an absurd hour."

"Steven. What's wrong?"

"Wrong? Are you kidding? I just spent the entire night reading your manuscript! I am going to hold myself in abeyance and simply say," he waited several seconds, "Wow!"

Jo swung her legs to the side of the bed and sat. "You liked it?"

"I loved it. I intend to make a call when I hang up from you, and wake someone else up. Her name is Joyce Nesbit, and she is considered by many to be the top agent in New York. I can't promise you she will read it as quickly as I did but, I feel certain she will be interested. Great job."

Six weeks later

Jo was arranging the layette in the nursery when the call came from Joyce Nesbit. She sat in the rocker, the receiver on her expanding lap, the phone in her hand.

"Mrs. Blumenthal, I am sorry it took me so long to get back to you. I receive about a hundred manuscripts a week, and I swear, yours was put near the top."

Jo felt like a thousand butterflies had taken wing in her stomach. "I certainly understand. And, please call me Jo." *Just tell me if you liked it!*

"I think the book is marvelous."

Yippee! She pounded her fist in the air. "Does that mean you want to represent me?"

"That's why I'm calling."

"Thank you, so much," Jo said, giggling into her hand as the baby kicked. "What happens now?"

"I will send you a contract. I know you're a lawyer, but I suggest that you have it looked over by an entertainment attorney. When you sign it and send it back, I will then begin contacting publishing houses. I would like you to know that I intend to put it out for auction," Joyce said.

"Explain what that entails, please."

"I will contact the editors that I respect at the publishing houses, and inform them that I am going to hold a best bids auction for your book. I will give them a date and time for them to submit their best offer."

"And once you have an offer. What happens then?" Jo asked, rubbing her stomach.

"They will assign you an editor, and you will begin to rewrite and polish the manuscript. From this phone call to publication will probably take a year."

"That's good because I'm going to have a baby in a few months."

"I know. Congratulations. I hope you understand that you will have to go on the road. Anyone who publishes the book will want that. But because of the public fascination with you, I am sure we can get you on the talk-show circuit, and keep the travel to a minimum."

"Just make sure they know in advance that I will be taking my baby with me."

"Not a problem. I'll send out the contract by UPS. I look forward to representing you. Good day."

December 4, 1974
Random House East 50ᵗʰ Street
New York City

Kurt Blome sat behind the wheel of the Mercedes, Alexander Lippisch sat beside him.

"I just don't understand why we haven't been able to get our hands on the fucking manuscript?"

A man without a topcoat tapped on the window. Lippisch lowered it.

"She just signed the contract. It's a work of fiction," he said, his teeth chattering.

"Well done," Lippisch said, offering an envelope through the window. "There's more when I get a copy of the galley proof." He pressed the window button, dismissing the messenger.

"You see. I told you there was nothing to worry about," Blome said, his eyes darting toward Lippisch. "This is the best thing that could have happened. It's a novel. That will trivialize her."

"When Lofts goes public with his findings, the public will want its pound of flesh. Especially with Nixon's impending impeachment. We have to be certain that no one, and I mean no one, can point a finger at us!"

"Jotto Wells doesn't even know we exist," Bloom said, "even though we've been watching her every move."

"She's been digging in those files with Lofts. Who knows what connections she may have found? I'm tired of worrying."

"Relax. Everyone who could ever implicate us is dead. Forget about her. Focus on your son, as I am going to do with mine. They are the future. She is nothing more than a distraction."

Lippisch bared his teeth. "If the day comes that I think she poses any kind of threat to us—she's dead!"

41

December 30, 1974
Mclean, Virginia

Jo was fast asleep on the king-sized bed, wrapped in a goose down comforter, a pillow over her head, when the alarm clock buzzed. She mashed the button and turned too quickly.

"Damn!" She grabbed her stomach, and took deep breaths. The stitches pulled, the result of the Caesarian—an operation that became necessary when the baby decided to present herself to the world tushy first.

Jo slid off the bed and took careful steps. At the full-length mirror in the dressing room, Jo let the nightgown slip to the floor. She frowned at the reddish purple stitches folded into her distended belly. With gentle fingers, she prodded, curious at the heat being generated at the site of the incision and the numbness that surrounded it. She snarled at the tiny stretch marks that circled her navel like a Ferris wheel without riders, and turned to the side. She sucked in her belly. The muscles were too sore, nothing moved.

Jo poked at the bags under her eyes.

I look like shit! I need a shower.

The bathroom had marble floors, a bidet, double toilets, and sinks. The warm stream of water soothed and relaxed her. She took the soap and gently washed her bruised, achy body as her thoughts wondered back over the past three weeks.

As a surprise, Rebecca had come for an extended visit, all smiles, suitcase in hand, announcing that she was needed and taking no chances at missing the birth of her godchild.

What a dangerous pair they had been, spending their way through every store within a ten mile radius. And they didn't just buy baby clothes, they bought everything and anything that tickled Jo's fancy from negligee, that didn't fit, to shoes that bit into her puffy feet.

When they weren't shopping, they were eating—three huge meals a day, and that was before dinner. Throw in pastry shops and ice cream parlors, and it was now clear to Jo that she had eaten her way through the final weeks of pregnancy.

I was a little piglet and now I have to pay the price!

Jo stepped from the shower, dried off, and wrapped herself in an over-sized terry bathrobe. Making faces in the mirror, Jo attacked the snarls in her hair, tugging and patting the curls into place.

Jo moved to the walk-in closet, and flipped on the light switch. The room smelled of Chanel N°5 parfum. She let her eyes linger on the left-hand side of the closet where tailored-to-perfection cashmere suits hung, and lovely silk dresses in creamy tans, sugar whites, pale blues, and lemon greens dangled undisturbed. She nuzzled a fitted-suede jacket, and hugged her favorite pair of jeans—positive that they would never fit again.

She turned and glared at the right hand side of the closet where the maternity clothes hung, tugging a black silk top from the hanger, and yanking the matching pants out of their clips. The elastic banded pants, with fabric sewed to make more room for the belly, made her furious. *Ugly. God-awful ugly.* She sat in the chair in the closet, wiggled into the pants, and pulled the top over her head, swallowing tears.

In the bedroom, the fireplace was lit, and winter light poured through the open shutters. Trees scraped against the window, cars crunched up the driveway and doors slammed deep within the mansion. *Okay. Enough!* Jo sat on the lounger and closed her eyes. *Think about the reason you look like this.*

Still breathless by the magnitude of the event, Jo caressed the memory of when she first held her daughter. She loved Aaron, loved her mother, and loved the missing-in-action Sweeny. But this was something different. This was the kind of love that transcended well beyond reason and made everything else shrink in its presence. This tiny helpless bundle was her world.

The emotions might have overwhelmed Jo, if not for the words Aaron spoke the first time he held his child.

"I always thought I understood how my parents must have felt when they gave me away to the Grunwalds." He shook his head, tears running down his face. "Now I know I never understood! Not until now."

Jo had begun to cry then, hysterical within moments. "I want my mother!" she had sputtered, angry and bitter.

"I'm so sorry, darling. I tried so hard. But, I swear to you, she will come."

"Not in time, Aaron. Not in time!"

Jo knew she had crushed the man she loved with her selfish words, and if not for the raging hormones, she would have never fired the accusation his way. *I'll make it up to him.* She dabbed concealer on the dark circles under her eyes.

"I see my sleepyhead is finally awake," Aaron said, strolling into the bedroom.

"You startled me!"

"Sorry." He leaned down and kissed the top of her head. "Feeling any better?"

"Don't I look better?" Jo asked, sarcasm dripping.

"You look wonderful."

"Oh, the lies men tell."

"Not this man!" Aaron said, pinching her cheek.

"What time did William, Saul, and David get in?"

"Around three this morning."

"They must be exhausted," Jo said.

"That might be true, but for the last two hours they have been standing in the nursery watching our baby sleep. I finally booted them out. Now they're in the kitchen having breakfast."

Jo gave Aaron a sideways glance. "See this mess?" She pointed to herself. "I've got work to do, and you are distracting me."

"You're gorgeous just the way you are."

"Aaron, if you value your life you will get out!"

"Pure perfection," he insisted.

Jo picked up the hairbrush as if to throw it.

He held up his palms. "I'm going. I'm going."

* * *

Jo stood in the doorway of her daughter's nursery. The sun's rays sifted through the gossamer drapery like golden slivers dancing—a pool of light reflecting off the lilac walls. It smelled of powder and baby, reminding Jo of the children's house on the kibbutz—only now, it was her house, and her baby.

The nurse backed out the door as Jo moved to the crib and lifted her daughter. She sat in the rocker, holding her ten day-old baby, lost in the perfection of the tiny face. Jo could see herself in the almond-shaped eyes and Aaron in the shape of the mouth. She clutched the infant to her heart.

"Today, my little princess, is a very special day. You are going to the synagogue to be named. You will enter into a covenant with your people. Daddy and I will teach you to stand tall and be proud of who you are and where you come from. You will be loved, my precious, and we will keep you safe."

Jo heard a sniffle. She swiveled the rocker and gasped. It was Sweeny, in all her redheaded, freckled splendor, wearing goatskin boots, a brown leather skirt that hit four inches above her knees, and an alpaca electric green boat-neck sweater.

"Did you miss me?" Sweeny said, striding across the nursery, kneeling on the floor beside the rocker, her face inches from the baby. "Look at this fabulous little creature! You did good, honey."

"Oh, Sweeny. How did you know how much I needed you?" Jo cried.

"I always know, honey. And I would have been here sooner but…" she flipped her hand at Jo. A huge diamond taking up half her finger sparkled back.

"The trust-fund baby?" Jo asked. "The one who was going to break your heart?"

Sweeny nodded. "We were about to explore the Amazon when I called Daddy. He told me that the baby was due any day. That's when I told James McKnight the fourth that I was going to Washington to be with my best friend. I also hinted that I might not come back. That's when he fooled me and proposed.

"So, instead of coming here I found myself in an audience with his family in London. I'll save that story for another time." She winked. "I guess I passed muster 'cause my mother-in-law to-be slipped this baby on my finger. But, I'm here now. That's all that matters! Give that little creature to me." Sweeny took the baby. "I have a lot to tell her."

* * *

Jo's hand slid over the banister. Sweeny held her arm as they walked down the circular staircase that was the centerpiece of the house. Aaron followed close behind, the baby in his arms.

They moved into the living room with its skylight, walls of glass, and old photographs. David opened his arms, and Jo moved into his embrace. He held her, his tears wetting her face. "I've missed you so much." He kissed one cheek and then the other. "Anna sends you her blessings."

Saul pecked Jo's cheek and kissed her hand. "I can see that motherhood agrees with you. Having three or four more children should do the trick."

Rebecca shot him a look. "Men! God forbid they were to carry even one child. The population would be zero."

William hugged Jo, his eyes riveted on the baby.

"Would you like to hold her?" Aaron asked, placing the baby in William's arms.

The baby was passed from one loving set of arms to another; all the while being cooed, kissed, and promised everything from a car the moment she was old enough to drive, to a lavish wedding.

Aaron glanced at his watch. "I think we better get going."

"You go ahead," Saul said. "I'm expecting an important call from Israel in the next few minutes about a construction problem. William and I will follow."

Temple Beth Shalom

Aaron cradled his daughter. Jo was flanked by David and Rebecca, Sweeny followed. They entered the synagogue, their shoes echoing on the Jerusalem stone floor as they moved from the foyer into the domed one-thousand-seat sanctuary. Stained glass windows blinked light into the room and the cantor's melodious voice danced around them, the sweet tune a memory that reached into the past while gathering the future.

Jo looked at Aaron, determined to memorize this moment of her life. His eyes smiled back.

The rabbi recited a prayer in Hebrew and then smiled. "Come, come," he said, waving his arms. Three hundred eyes turned. "Bring the baby to the front row. She must feel the nearness of Torah in her life."

William and Saul slipped into the pew twenty minutes later, as the Sabbath service continued, a blur of prayers and song.

"Time to name this little princess," Rabbi Pomerantz said, once the Torah, the Five Books of Moses, was rolled open on the podium.

The entourage—Jo holding the baby, Aaron, Rebecca, Saul, David, and William—made their way up the three steps to the bimah.

"In naming your baby we are celebrating Jewish survival, Jewish values, and Jewish destiny—for that is what a Jewish woman represents to our people," the rabbi said, his prominent chin pointing at the congregation, his ebony eyes solemn. "This is a most profound spiritual moment. The Talmud tells us that an angel appears to new parents and whispers the Jewish name that their daughter will embody."

Jo shivered, feeling the presence.

"Your baby is being named for her father's mother, and her mother's grandmother," the rabbi said. "In this act, you acknowledge the roots that produce the tree of life for the Jewish people—a bond from this new soul to the souls that have passed. It is a continuation, its magnificence heralded in heaven," the Rabbi said, his voice rolling over the congregation.

The baby gurgled, squirmed, and kicked her satin-slippered feet, her pink lace dress bunching up around her face. Jo slipped a pacifier it into her daughter's mouth.

"Who are the *kvaterin*, the godmother, and the *kvater,* the godfather?"

Rebecca and David moved forward.

The Rabbi took the baby from Jo's arms and handed her to Rebecca. "Would either of you care to say something before I begin?"

Rebecca nodded to David. He took a deep breath. Looking from Jo to Aaron. His eyes settled on his godchild.

"As a young man, I wandered in the forests of Russia, lost, disheartened and embittered. For many years, I remained embittered. Then in the Judean hills of Israel, I found my God, married my wife, and was blessed with a healthy son. For a man like me, this was enough. This was everything.

"And yet," he said, turning to Jo and Aaron, "I have been given another mitzvah—to become the godfather of your daughter. I don't have the words to tell you what this means to me. But, I can tell you that I will love and protect your daughter all the days of my life. And if, God forbid, she ever comes to me in anguish, I will put aside my life to help her."

An eerie silence filled the sanctuary—a quiet as mysterious as the quiet experienced in the Ponary forest. Time suspended for seconds, time enough for Jo to know. She turned toward the congregation. Her body trembled in disbelief.

Aaron put his arm around Jo. "I knew you needed her," he whispered.

Morgan glided down the isle, Jacob by her side, her eyes finding Jo's. In that moment—for that instant in time—all was right with the world.

Morgan climbed the steps to the bimah. She opened her arms. Jo sobbed as Morgan held her. "Shh, baby. It's all right. I'm here now," Morgan said, weeping despite her resolve not to.

Morgan felt a hand on her arm. She turned. It was Rebecca, the same smile, the same eyes—forty-years of separation vanished. "Take your granddaughter," Rebecca said softly. "She's been waiting for you."

Morgan held Esther Sara in her arms as the Rabbi placed his hands in blessing over the infant's head.

"O my God, the soul which you gave us is pure. You created it.

You fashioned it. You breathed life into it. Blessed shall you be in your coming.

"May the Lord bless you and protect you, *Esther Sara Bat Yosefa V'Aharon*. May the Lord cause His countenance to shine upon you and be gracious unto you. May the Lord bestow His favor upon you and grant you peace."

The End

Acknowledgments

This book was inspired by my beloved friend, Menachem Perlmutter, architect of the Negev, humanitarian, and survivor of the Holocaust, who touched my heart with his undying love and belief in the goodness of humanity. Writing is a lonely endeavor and friends and family are my lifeline. I found direction and encouragement from the incredible people in my writing group, Deborah Weed, she is the magic under my wings, and Lily Prellezo, and Orlando Rodriguez. I want to thank the following people for reading and always believing in me: Judi Wolowitz, Michele Kabat, Alan and Marjorie Goldberg, Barbara Glicken, and Irving Glicken, Irwin Hyman, and my beloved teacher, Leejay Kline, and Dr. Susan Baker-Weiner. Above all else is my family, they are the air that I breathe, the reason that I live. Todd, Jordyn, and Emma Brazer, Carrie and Maxwell Brazer, Judd, Ayda, Tiffany and Julia Brazer, Barry, Ellen, Heidi, and Samantha Brazer, Mitchell, Becky, Mathew and Megan Brazer, Bonnie, Joseph, Rachel, Alexandria, and Ryan Grote.

And So It Was Written

A New Novel by Ellen Brazer to be Released in 2010

I see him, but not now;

I behold him, but not nigh.

There shall step forth a star out of Jacob;

and a scepter shall rise out of Israel,

and shall smite through the corners of Moab,

and break down all the sons of Seth.

The Star Prophecy of Numbers 24:17

Chapter 1

En-Gedi-Judea in the year 125 CE

The clouds shifted away as the blazing sun streamed over the enclave of En-Gedi, an oasis in the Judean desert thirty miles from the holy city of Jerusalem. The region is a rugged no-man's land made up of deep gorges that fall towards the Dead Sea from the eastern slopes of the Judean mountains. A waterfall spilled from the bluff into the brook below. The precious water languished in pools before spilling into the riverbed that led to its home in the Dead Sea.

Livel Cohen and his brother Masabala were playing in the palm grove that sat on the northern edge of the oasis, their antics watched by a herd of wild ibex, mountain goats with great curved horns that grazed on the steep cliffs overlooking the village. The boys darted from tree to tree, laughing, calling out to one another as they pretended to be Jewish zealots in search of Roman soldiers.

Livel was sixteen, with huge liquid eyes the color of coal and a bulbous nose that perched on the end of his angular face. He had narrow shoulders and a narrow body. Livel was rather homely until he smiled or laughed; then his features ignited and his face was magnificent. He smiled a lot.

In contrast, his younger brother Masabala was a handsome child with thick ebony hair and enormous sable eyes that reflected a maturity beyond his years. He had long legs, a sleek body, and at fifteen, he was already two inches taller than Livel.

"Take that, you Roman swine!" Masabala held a stick in his hand, wielding it like a sword. He came toward his brother, his stance threatening. He sneered and pretended to stab Livel.

"No, no! Have mercy, I beg of you!" Livel cried, grabbing his chest and falling to the ground.

"Mercy? Never!" Masabala howled, motioning as if to stab his Roman victim yet again.

Livel pulled Masabala to the ground and began to tickle him until they were laughing so hard they couldn't catch their breath.

"Enough!" Masabala screamed.

The boys turned on their backs panting.

"Let's go explore," Masabala said a few minutes later.

"That's not a good idea. You know the Roman garrison is camped nearby and Father says they kidnap Jewish children and make them slaves."

Masabala swatted the air with his hand. "You know he says that just to scare us." He sat up, his eyes mischievous. "I saw a cave the other day that we've never been in. Come on. I want to go!"

Livel stood. "Okay," he said. Livel adored his brother and could never deny him. "But it will be dark soon so we have to hurry."

"I can't wait until I'm older," Masabala said as they walked in the desert, the white clouds dusting against an azure sky, the sun singeing the air, their sandals little protection from the burning sand as they headed toward a ridge of low cliffs. "I'm going to be a soldier. It's too bad you won't be by my side," he teased, knowing that his comment would irk his brother.

"Don't be so sure of that," Livel said, scratching his leg where a mosquito had stung him.

The boys broke into a run. Masabala was swift as a gazelle, his stride long and elegant. Livel spurted beside him, his gate awkward, and his steps uncertain.

"Father will never allow you to be a soldier," Masabala said, breathing hard.

Livel stopped dead in his tracks. "You don't know that!"

Masabala slid in the sand, turned, and placed his hands on his hips. "Yes, I do. Everybody is talking about you. Mother says even the rabbis in Jerusalem speak your name in whispers. You are going to be a great rabbi someday."

Livel knew that his brother's words were true. He could recite more commandments by heart that anyone in the entire village; he could speak Hebrew, Aramaic, and had learned to speak Latin after spending just a week with a Roman merchant that had come to the village selling seeds.

"I am going to be a great commander and lead our people to victory!"

Livel laughed and punched Masabala's arm. "I'm sure the entire Roman garrison will one day know your name, oh great Masabala, and they will tremble in your presence." His words were light, but Livel did believe that one day his brother would become a great soldier and able leader.

Livel kicked at a rock and began a silent game of chasing

and kicking, lost in thought. He knew he had a unique gift—information stayed in his head, stored in compartments, available verbatim as needed. His reputation as a prodigy would mean that soon he would be sent to study under the tutelage of the great rabbis in Jerusalem.

Masabala kicked the rock away from his brother and ran backwards. "Come on genius, I'll race you!"

The boys sprinted toward the ridge that led to the cave Masabala wanted to explore. It was then that they heard the thundering sound of horses' hooves and the unmistakable clanging of armor. Horrified, the boys froze. The Romans were unmerciful adversaries. If they didn't kill them they knew they would taken into slavery.

"Listen to me," Livel said, grabbing his brother by the shoulders. "You were right. You are the soldier and now you must do what a soldier would do. Run like the wind and warn Father!"

"And leave you behind?" Masabala's eyes filled with tears. "I won't do that! We can hide."

"Where? They will be here before we reach the cave! You go. I will distract them and then follow." He gave Masabala a shove. "Keep low and run. Go now!"

Livel watched his brother head toward home. Then he crouched and began to run himself, not from the soldiers but towards them, intent on putting as much distance between himself and his brother as he could. Once the soldiers were in clear sight Livel turned back towards his village, running slowly, waiting to be caught.

Within moments ten fully armed Romans who were on patrol searching for the Jews that had attacked their camp earlier in the day were upon him. A soldier dismounted and unsheathed his sword. Livel stood paralyzed, his body convulsing in spasms of terror.

"Looks like this one is a real hero," the soldier said in Aramaic, poking Livel with the tip of his sword. With squinted eyes he peered into the distance.

Terrified that the soldier might spot Masabala, Livel drew back his foot and kicked the man in the shin.

The soldier howled and grabbed Livel by the scruff of the neck. "What are you doing out here alone?"

"I like solitude. Now, let go of me!" he replied in Aramaic, wiggling free.

The soldier smiled at his friends, menace turning his eyes to fire. "My, my, my, a well-educated young Jew. Put him on a mount."

Tears streamed down Livel's face. He tried to run but was grabbed around the waist.

"Do you want me to tie you onto the horse, boy? Or perhaps

you'd like to be dragged behind," the soldier yelled, dangling Livel from the ground, his breath hot on the boy's neck. Livel was tossed on to the horse and strapped to the saddle.

As they rode away the boy looked toward the heavens and began praying aloud to the God of Abraham.

"Shut up," one of the soldiers yelled in Latin.

"Leave the boy alone," came another voice. "He's not bothering anyone."

"He's bothering me."

Then another voice intervened, softer and filled with authority. "He's frightened. Let him be."

They traveled throughout the night, moving rapidly whenever the rugged terrain allowed them to do so. Livel prayed until he no longer had a voice and when exhaustion overcame him, he fell asleep leaning on the soft mane of the horse, dreaming of home, his parents, and his little brother.

At dawn, the troop halted and Livel awakened with a start. Torrents of anguish washed over him as the sleep world dissolved. Recalling his mother's eyes and his father's voice he began to cry. I want to go home. Mother, Father, save me. Help me! He was not a man-child now, but a young boy. He longed for the safety of his parents' arms.

CPSIA information can be obtained at www.ICGtesting.com
Printed in the USA
LVOW080720140313

324227LV00002B/255/P